PAY THE PIPER

ALSO BY JOAN WILLIAMS

The Morning and the Evening
Old Powder Man
The Wintering
County Woman
Pariah and Other Stories

PAY THE PIPER

JOAN WILLIAMS

E. P. DUTTON  NEW YORK

Copyright © 1988 by Joan Williams
All rights reserved. Printed in the U.S.A.

Publisher's Note: This novel is a work of fiction. Names, characters, places, and incidents either are the product of the author's imagination or are used fictitiously, and any resemblance to actual persons, living or dead, events, or locales is entirely coincidental.

No part of this publication may be reproduced or transmitted in any form or by any means, electronic or mechanical, including photocopy, recording, or any information storage and retrieval system now known or to be invented, without permission in writing from the publisher, except by a reviewer who wishes to quote brief passages in connection with a review written for inclusion in a magazine, newspaper, or broadcast.

Published in the United States by E. P. Dutton,
a division of NAL Penguin Inc.,
2 Park Avenue, New York, N.Y. 10016.

Published simultaneously in Canada by
Fitzhenry and Whiteside, Limited, Toronto.

Library of Congress Cataloging-in-Publication Data

Williams, Joan, 1928–
Pay the piper / by Joan Williams. — 1st ed.
p. cm.
ISBN 0-525-24543-X
I. Title.
PS3573.I4494P34 1988
813'.54—dc19   87-30688
CIP

DESIGNED BY EARL TIDWELL

1 3 5 7 9 10 8 6 4 2

First Edition

FOR LESLIE WELLS AND E. F.

The author would like to thank
the John Simon Guggenheim Foundation for its support
during the writing of this novel.

PAY THE PIPER

I always liked this bathroom wallpaper, though I never expected to lie here staring up at it. The background color is beige, soft, warm, caramel-colored; before, the color meant serenity to me. There is a somewhat indistinguishable design of pale tangerine and blue that reminds me of morning glories; perhaps this comes to mind because those flowers make me remember summertime and the South when I was young. My childhood, however, never seemed innocent.

The hour is late. There is enough light from the bedroom beyond and from a streetlight on the suburban road to allow me to see Hal's face clearly, as he could see mine if he looked at it. He keeps staring past me at nothing, I suppose, because there is only the darker corner of the room beyond the toilet, where he holds me.

The wallpaper and the rug of a slightly darker beige I chose with care; I've been proud of the result. Being of a literary nature, I have not spent much time thinking about decorating houses. My mother used to say with disdain that all I did was keep my nose in a book. As far as she is concerned, this never paid off, though I have written three novels.

I wonder if he is thinking anything. I don't believe he is deciding whether or not to kill me.

The pressure of his hands around my throat, his thumbs to my windpipe, has neither increased nor lessened in the time he has held me on the floor with the back of my neck in the niche of the toilet where the seat divides; the porcelain grows so hard.

"Laurel," he said, coming into the bedroom. My heart stood still: only the one word, my name Laurel.

I had locked the back door, not knowing he had a key. Six years we have lived in this house, yet I did not know there was a back door key. Always, I have been passive and not demanding enough. My not having a key was no oversight. It was Hal's animal-like nature to love secretiveness. He skulks about, like a fox or hound in a chicken yard. Married three times, Hal has not yet learned to be head of a household or that the act of cohabitation is supposed to mean sharing.

I bolted other doors. Our habit was to lock the garage, which opened on an electric buzzer. From the garage we entered the house, so I had never thought about a key till the moment I heard him fit the lock and then heard his steps across the kitchen floor, and his presence coming up the carpeted stairs. Where was I to go?

"Laurel," he said, coming into the room.

"Hal," I said. "Don't."

Why did I not jump onto the big bed and scramble across? I suppose because I thought he could beat me to the door. I should have tried that escape route, though. Perhaps foolishly, as I had thought for years, I thought Hal would come to his senses. I had begun to shiver.

I knew in the beginning something was attractive to me about his making me terrified, something uncivilized out of my past for which I longed again: something bound up with fright in childhood and with a sensuality I had not understood. Having wanted to escape mine, maybe in the end we all do want to marry our fathers. But with Hal by now I've had all the blows to my head and face I can stand.

After saying "Laurel," he walked me backward into the bathroom and shoved me down. Now I lie with my back aching and the thought that at any minute he may flip me forward and put my face into the water as he threatened. "Laurel, I'm going to drown you in the toilet. It's what you deserve."

I am powerless. There will be a brief last minute when I will not want to die while I picture the degrading manner of my death. How hard to believe this is me, here, and that Hal is my husband. When I once had everything, how have I let this come to be my life? What mysterious thing haunted me from the past, the South, that forced me to go back? Imagine that a shot fired nearly two thousand miles from where I lived, about which I knew nothing at the time, has come to wreck my life.

I'm afraid to plead. One word might topple him over the edge of sanity to a place where he has been before. If I say, "Darling, this isn't you. Let's go to bed," the words may enrage him more because he'll know the man here *is* him; or if I threaten, "You'll go to prison for the rest of your life this time," he may be only angrier.

Time passes so slowly. I have been lying here a long while. I feel I'm in a frame from a movie. Always I will be here. Sometimes I say, "Hal."

Then he says again, "Laurel," mocking and menacing. "Laurel."

Beyond him I can see family pictures on the wall. Black and white, they are partially lit from the streetlight and from the moon and the bedroom. I see my son, Rick, with an old black man on Hal's plantation, skinning a rabbit. I picture my son with agony and longing. The photograph was taken when he was fourteen; hard to believe ten years have passed. Hal, if you are going to kill me, let me apologize to my son first for bringing you into his life.

I wonder if my son will mourn me. In the half-light, I see how much Rick looks like his dad. If only I could talk to William again, this time we might say what we think. I see my mother, trying to smile head-on at the camera, and realize what a fearful lady she really is. Who'll see about her growing old, since Rick deserves to be free? How much grief I've caused the only people I had really to love.

I see pictures of Hal's children by his other wives. "Hal, your children can't stand—"

His pressure tightens on my Adam's apple, and I'm not so dumb as to keep running my mouth, as he would call it.

Don't I feel attraction still? I wonder why Hal does not honor honor. It's strange that I have to suffer for his inability to pay back a society to which he doesn't even consider he owes anything.

All night I was depressed, finding myself at a roadhouse where no one I used to know would go. I have been drowning already a long time before tonight.

Hal is wearing his kilt and the cropped black jacket that goes with it for formal wear. His knees seem so pale. He lost his bonny cap when I whacked him across the face in the garage, and my bracelet caught his face. He was cut above one eye and across the bridge of his nose. All this while blood has been pouring and is even on the walls. I cannot understand how there can be so much blood. Sticking from one of his long socks is a skean dhu—a dagger—as true Scots wore them. Lying still so long, I've been thinking about grabbing this little knife and stabbing him, knowing no jury would convict me. But I'm afraid, in grabbing, I'll miss and that, kneeling over me already, he will take it and stab me instead. Finally my rational sense convinces me the risk is too great. I go on waiting for the moment when the balance may tip and Hal lose his reasoning.

I go on staring at his small face, thinking how the predicament I'm in is not funny. Because Hal has killed one person, and there is every reason to believe that in his drunkenness my husband may kill me too.

1

She felt strange having hidden something in the house. She did not even know why she hid the letter, a perfectly innocuous one from someone she did not know. But that was the whole point, Laurel thought; she had the sensation the man was going to become important to her. Yesterday when she read the letter for the first time, a voice announced to her quite calmly, You're going to marry Hal MacDonald.

That thought made the idea of leaving William—one she had toyed with so long—so much easier, because having something happen that seemed fated, having the letter arrive just now and the possibility arise of meeting someone else, seemed to be what the gods intended—that she leave William and marry Hal. Already she felt that was what she was meant to do, to live back in the region where she was born and to belong to a man close to the soil, and she gazed out at the cold New England spring from her suburban window, thinking how this landscape had never become part of her. Laurel laughed to think she had been around what seemed a whole world, only to return, perhaps, where she had started.

"What's up?" said Rick, coming in, the product of her and William's disparate backgrounds. She turned guiltily. He seemed a young seal, his hair slick and shining from his shower, still wet, and she found herself giving advice that would bore him: "Don't go out in this weather with your head wet." Hearing her mother's caution, which once irritated her, Laurel thought how unintentionally you relived your past. "You'll catch cold," she said.

"Yeah. Yeah." He dabbed at his head with a paper napkin to satisfy her.

His question had meant, what was she doing with all the fancy dishes out, and she told him, "My book group's coming."

"Your bourbon and lettuce leaf club."

He grinned impishly, and so perfect was his mimicry that Laurel was astonished by his perspicuity at thirteen and that he was her own. "Gran's certainly the pot calling the kettle—"

"Mom. I don't want to hear about all that past time. Gran drinking is not the grandmother I've ever known."

"You're right. I'm sorry."

She dished up oatmeal and avoided his face, which the moment he spoke had been clouded. How could she stand here on this April morning, in her large kitchen, in a house in a good neighborhood, and think of breaking up this household and causing this boy so much unhappiness? She had felt queasy waking up and held her breath against the oatmeal's smell while carrying the bowl to Rick. It was sad she could know so positively she was not pregnant. When had she last slept with anybody? That, of course, was her main reason for wanting to leave William—his refusal to have sex; he had gotten it elsewhere until recently, when after a night of confessing transgressions they promised to have no more affairs and to start over with a clean slate. She had tried much harder since then, but when she made a move toward him in bed, he remained far over on his side and with his back toward her. Maybe it was going to take a while to learn a new pattern. She had given up Edward without any effort, except that she really liked him and he helped her enormously with her writing, but nothing was ever going to become of the affair beyond a few afternoons at the New Weston when he came into the city from Princeton.

"Thanks," Rick had said.

"What else am I here for but to wait on men?" Looking at the floor, she added, "And dogs," speaking to the two sitting there and watching for food so hopefully.

"I hope we're not becoming a typical slovenly housewife though, Laurel," Rick said, deepening his voice and drawing down his chin into a face of disapproval.

She laughed and touched the neck of her old robe, drawing it more closely together, though there was not much cleavage to show, sadly. "Listen, brat. A lot of women not only don't get dressed first thing in the morning, they don't get up and fix breakfast, much less real, long-cooking oatmeal."

"I know it. A lot of my friends and their dads eat Cheerios. How come they let their wives get away with that stuff?"

She said in her subdued way, "I suppose other women know how to rule the roost better than I. I'm a patsy. A sucker. And I like being dominated to death." She put one hand atop his head, smiling. "Oh, mutt. Pretty soon we'll be in Mississippi again."

"Yay. I can't wait."

"I feel I owe Dad getting up. He works his tail off to make us a living," she said.

"Did Gran always get up?"

"Yes," Laurel said, which was not a lie: there was only one different quality to her doing it, which Rick need not know. She thought particularly of those times her father set out, a traveling salesman, into dawn, with his breakfast churning in his stomach. She could remember her sense of guilt about being in bed herself, and could see him again in his wool shirt, cord breeches, and high-laced boots and hear his harsh crying across the hallway separating the bedrooms where her parents slept—Kate, are you going to get up and fix my breakfast?—and even so young, she had understood her mother's deliberate delaying to antagonize him, until fear drove her up to slam-bang in the kitchen. His car would roar off with a sound equal to his fury and diminish down city blocks, while she lay buried in her pillow believing she heard it on and on. She was always trying to decide which of them was wrong, with a loneliness she remembered too well.

"Mom, I'm not really hungry. When Dad's not here, I wouldn't mind having cold cereal."

"OK. Eat what you can. I wish you'd told me."

"He's coming back tonight?"

"Yup."

Rick glanced at a paper magnetized to the refrigerator. "I haven't done the list of things he left for me."

Her gaze went there too. "I haven't done all of mine either. But I swept the basement."

"Great. Thanks."

"I was down there doing laundry, so why not. Just don't tell."

"Sorry, Mom," he said, setting his bowl on the floor and apologizing about her wasted time cooking—William would have taught him that, and what would she have become if she hadn't known William?

The older dog, Buff, licked daintily, while a recent acquisition, a bloodhound named Jubal, sat back with reddened eyes waiting his turn. Buff, the matriarch, had let him know this was her territory long before he ever showed up here. Good for you, Buff, Laurel told her silently. "Jubal, you smell terrible."

"The bus!" Rick cried. His chair's legs scraped backward, and the alerted dogs rushed for the door. In the distance air brakes soughed and groaned, though otherwise in the upper-class neighborhood there was no noise for miles, only silence. The yellow school bus had readied itself to climb a hill down the road, and Rick knew how many minutes before it would pass apple trees and arrive almost at his front door. He rushed upstairs to brush his teeth.

Laurel had his jacket, books, and homework, neatly laid out the night before, and handed them over after he clobbered downstairs.

"Thanks."

"That's what mothers are for," she said.

"There's a pickup ball game this afternoon."

"You've got to go." Leaning into a cotton picker's basket she'd brought back from Mississippi one summer, she extracted his catcher's mitt.

"I won't get everything on the list done."

Not wishing to be disloyal to William, but thinking there were limits to things, she said, "We'll just have to do our best."

He reached out and lightly flicked her on the arm. "Touch last!" he cried, and bounded into the driveway, laughing back. She shooed him off with a wave that recognized his child's game from the past, when she and William were going out, and Rick dashed about the car windows to see who could touch each other last. As if he never wanted to part, Laurel thought suddenly, near tears. From behind the door's glass panes, she watched till Rick's light jacket bobbed aboard the bus and then, obedient to their day's ritual, Jubal and Buff returned home, having accompanied him.

She looked at the refrigerator and clicked off mentally what she'd accomplished since William left on his business trip to Washington. She'd taken her new skirt to be shortened to the length he'd suggested, and she'd called the fuel company about a leak in the basement and bought an extension cord. But she had not followed his regimen for working out. He had posted how many sit-ups to do daily, keeping her toes attached to something, and a schedule with barbells, their weights increasingly difficult as time went by. She would tell him, for once, she was not going to do what he said; and that's that, she added to herself in her mother's definitive phrase. Jogging was enough for her.

You, William once said, did all right for a little girl from Delton. Marrying into his prestigious family, he had meant, more or less kindly. She certainly agreed, after the background she came from. She carried about her own epithet: the little girl from Tennessee. Yet she had stacked up a few Brownie points before meeting him and was neither a country tack nor stupid. She'd published two short stories in reputable literary quarterlies; this fact kept William's patrician, stalwart, and productive Bostonian female relatives from relegating her to the dust pile where they cast most Southern women, among the flirty, flighty, and mundane.

She considered her middle-class Southern background, where materialism was success. If only she'd had the nerve, at some point, to tell William's relatives she could at least cook. They pridefully announced they could not boil water for tea. There was fine art on the walls of William's relatives' houses, and fine furniture in them, but still their houses had a sparer, plainer, and more austere look than comparable Southern houses she had known. When his relatives' rugs and upholstering wore out, these things were often left that way, as if from respect; books sat on shelves, with tattered jackets, because someone was always pulling them out to read them. In Delton, one of her friends had her Book-of-the-Month Club books covered in forest-green felt to match the color of her slipcovers; another old friend as he grew successful bought the whole of the Modern Library, though as she gazed at his lined wall, he confessed the only novel he'd read since college was "The Man in the Long Gray Underwear." "Gray Flannel Suit"? she timidly suggested. William's mother and the aunt who helped raise him wore conservative clothes whose hemlines stayed mid-calf no matter what fashion predicted. When Aunt

Grace once looked surprised, saying, "You don't speak French?" Laurel replied, "La plume de ma tante," and cringed. For years, she longed for some snappy or devastating reply, but none had yet come. William, when they married, pointed out the difference between baking powder and baking soda, because, coming from the South, she not only had never cooked but had never washed out a pair of underpants for herself until she went to college.

Jubal and Buff could not understand this morning why there were no egg, toast, or bacon scraps. Laurel opened the dishwasher to put in Rick's dish, seeing there dishes from William's last meal, and thought how she had said, "I don't mind cooking your breakfast every morning, but it seems silly since you throw it up."

He had stood there with his briefcase, broad-shouldered in the old tweed jacket he went on wearing generously year after year and watery-eyed from tossing his cookies. "Maybe it's the grease," he had said.

"You're the one who wants your eggs fried in bacon grease," she had reminded him. "But you threw them up scrambled and soft-boiled, too."

Then William had left, and there had seemed some incongruity in a man's going to Washington, D.C., on a business trip for his high-powered company and yet throwing up his breakfast first, day after day, because his new job and his new boss made him nervous. While knowing how dependent she was on William, she believed she had a different strength; she knew she had more guts, because she'd hardly ever thrown up in her life, and then usually for the reason her mother taught her, which was when she'd drunk too much alcohol. Stick your finger down your throat, her mother advised. Recently, William had thrown up one night more terribly than anyone she had ever heard, after being invited by a stepmother he'd never seen to come for dinner in New York and collect some personal effects of his late father's. These things turned out to be quite useless—an engraved, flat, silver cigarette case and diamond cuff links—causing Laurel to wonder at her austere mother-in-law once married to someone as debonair as William Powell. They came home, and William shut himself in the bathroom.

All the time he was being sick, she prayed he might also vomit up all the mystery, pain, and loss, all the guilt, about never seeing again the father who left when William was four. She had determined, early on, she'd never take Rick away when he was small. How could she do it, even now, when William cared almost inordinately about his son? Whenever she thought how awful her parents had been, she was glad at least to have known where she came from.

William had a last faceless memory of his father. Awakened in dampish Dr. Denton's and brought into a room with subdued lamplight, he stood rubbing his eyes, with the rear flap of his sleepers hanging open. Privately, Laurel thought William had projected himself into a Norman Rockwell cover for *The Saturday Evening Post,* but she had never said so and went on sharing with him that image of himself. William had been taught to say Ma-*Ma* and Pa-*Pa* in the French manner, with accent on the final *a*. She never mentioned that was a long way from Southern pronunciation: which was Momma and Poppa even when similarly spelled; most commonly people said Daddy, even into adulthood. She did not know any Southerners who called their parents Mom and Dad.

"Dear," his mother had said that evening, "your father and I are divorcing. That means we're not going to live in the same house any longer. Please tell me now which of us you'd rather live with."

Understanding only that he wanted to go back to bed, he put his head into his mother's lap, and the die was cast. For a child that age, it was a strange question. But Mrs. Perry was an artist in the grand sense of the word. "My mother the painting machine," William called her. "It's only by accident that she's a person." She was the only woman Laurel had ever known whose career was more important than anything else. But then, she had known few women who did anything besides keep house.

His paternal grandmother had wanted William, and urgently, eagerly, Mrs. Perry would have turned him over at any time. But his father, having lost, refused ever to see William again. "What kind of man could he have been," Laurel said once, "not to see his son. He must have been crazy." Though he tried to agree, William was convinced there had been something wrong with him to have been so abandoned. As a father he invented the relationship between himself and Rick he'd dreamed of as a fatherless child. It was sometimes a little hard on Rick. Once Mrs. Perry confided to Laurel that after divorcing she realized she should never have married at all, and for a moment put her hands over her face. Laurel had wondered what she was thinking. She had been surprised to realize just how locked into convention and its pressures women always had been, for no one could be more intelligent, motivated, strong-willed than Mrs. Perry. Yet she had felt she had to marry and have a child.

They had lived with his Aunt Grace, who spoke fluent French, and always, too, William had the feeling of living in someone else's house, not his own. When she and William bought this second, larger house in the suburbs, where they planned to stay forever, he walked about, a little teary, saying at last he was home. Laurel's eyes had prickled in sympathy, though his insecurity was essentially foreign to her, as she had always lived in her own true house. To think of an emotional man as a sissy was a stereotyped idea, she kept telling herself. But she had to go on fighting her feeling that most highly educated Eastern men she knew were somehow effeminate.

That evening as William came from the bathroom, he blamed his being sick on his stepmother's dinner. She said flatly, "Roast beef, boiled potatoes, and string beans? It wasn't the dinner, it was seeing somebody connected to your father." Then she added, "I'm not sick," which meant nothing since her emotions did not affect her stomach but made her face break out. Once, after Rick's birth, William confided he'd always been sorry she never had morning sickness. She asked, "Why, so you could have it vicariously?" and all he did was nod without shame.

Last night she had made a gelatin salad and this morning, lifting waxed paper, she shook the mold tentatively. The salad seemed jelled, a success; she had only to dread the moment of turning it out onto a platter, praying it stayed whole. She had started the dishwasher, and its sounds made her temples ache. When she asked herself, What is wrong with me, a sinus headache? she knew she was lying. She had a hangover.

Years ago, at the height of her own alcoholism, newly widowed, her mother had said, "If you get past the first drink in the morning, you're all right for the day." But Laurel never got up thinking of a hair of the dog. She had heard secondhand about things that happened in those years her mother lived as a widow in Delton, drinking, before she moved east. She knew how fractured her life had been because of her parents' behavior, the years when so little attention was paid to children growing up.

Laurel considered what she had read on the subject. Was alcoholism inherited? Or had her own liking to drink come from her initiation in Delton—in the days of brown bagging? Confronting her own tendency, Laurel gave her mother credit. She came once to babysit with Rick when she had been drinking, and William announced, "Kate, we love you. But if you come around Rick anymore when you've been drinking, you'll never see your grandson again." She admired William, but admired her mother more. Hers was the harder part. Her mother quit drinking cold turkey, those years ago.

Married to William, Laurel felt that her hardest times were living in a New York brownstone until Rick was two years old. Nothing in her life as a Southerner had prepared her for such an existence. All day, she was alone with a baby in a fourth-floor walk-up; she looked from a bay window to a sliver of Hudson River, her one contact with nature except for treks to the park along Riverside Drive, where she sat among strangers. Mostly, these other mothers were native New Yorkers with whom she had nothing in common, whom she understood no better than shopkeepers on upper Broadway, rude in a way no one in the South was ever rude. She began realizing what she had left behind, a circle of girlfriends having their babies together and ever-present black help even on a young married's low income. She had well understood ghetto mothers throwing their babies off rooftops and down air shafts. Despairing, she once dosed Rick with paregoric to make him sleep, needing respite. Then, panicked, she threw the bottle away, not to be tempted again.

It was back then she began talking so affectionately about the South, this place she eagerly left, until William was forced to say, "I didn't bring you east, Sister. I found you here." She could only accept his words in silence while considering two things—that "Sister" was not a particularly endearing way to address one's wife, and couldn't he have said, instead, Here is where I fell in love with you? All right, Buster, she had always wanted to reply. But she did not want Rick to hear the anger and arguments she grew up knowing, so Laurel was silent.

In their dating days, back in Greenwich Village, William commented then that she could drink him under the table—all that bourbon and branch water she'd taken for granted. She had explained people she knew drank like that in the South; there wasn't much else to do in her part of the country. She had added, "I had an Irishman to teach me," and told him about Kevin Shea—a boy William would thereafter refer to as the double Irishman and sometimes, rather piercingly, as her first husband. "My parents had it annulled," she would say. "It doesn't really count." Several teenage couples that summer, after graduating from high school, went to a justice of the peace in Mississippi, beyond

Delton's city limits. It was something to do, I suppose; she had shrugged, telling the story. Nobody had expected to settle down in a vine-covered cottage, or at least she hadn't. She never knew what Kevin had in mind, for by the time she went off and got married to him, she half perceived that he was stupid as hell. "Why would you go through with it then?" William asked, who that summer had been a virgin camp counselor in Maine lusting after the somehow nubile mothers of his campers. Now at her New England window, Laurel remembered touching Kevin's high school fraternity pin dangling over her bosom—they'd been going steady for two years—and telling him she wanted to change her mind. Wildly, in his manner, he drove into a weedy ditch bank and told her he'd leave her. The thought had been so terrifying she'd gone ahead down the highway and faced the old man with tobacco juice on his galluses. Since she cried during the ceremony, the justice thought she was a trembling, happy bride, but she knew better.

William, on that date in the village, had said his mother strongly disapproved of alcohol. She would not let him drink a soda after dinner, afraid he'd get used to something fizzy at night. Then he told her about his mother's accomplishments and about his Aunt Grace, who was a landscape architect ahead of her time. He told of an uncle who wrote tomes about naval history and of one who died an untimely death just after being appointed to the Supreme Court. She listened to him mention lawn bowling at the family seaside summer place—lawn bowling? Without asking, she quickly imagined what it must be. And there was Roque, a complicated croquet, William added. Oh, yes; she nodded affably. Every evening at bedtime, his mother read him Dickens. . . . Laurel lost track of his words, wondering where she might have been if she'd had parents who had heard of Dickens. She only told William she spent childhood summers at her maternal grandmother's in Mississippi, forty-five miles from Delton, and had loved it there, without saying her grandmother kept a cache of Garrett snuff in her closet, or that she had uncles who were what her father called dirt farmers; William got a kick, like everyone else, out of the fact her father sold dynamite—that's a blast, Rick had said.

The enormous differences in their backgrounds had not been insurmountable, and the problems she and William had they would have brought to any marriage. What seemed important was how they reacted to each other's insecurities.

In this different milieu to which she'd brought herself, unlike her original one, she'd learned iceberg lettuce was considered fit only for rabbits, and despondently she washed the head bought yesterday. Ennui filled her at the idea of having to pat dry all those cupped leaves on the counter. There were patches of snow, still, under forsythia bushes only beginning to flower, while in Delton spring's full flowering was almost over and summer nearly begun. When she thought of the place, she smelled sweet scents, warm earth, as if April were there perpetually.

Usually, she did not telephone anyone in the morning because of her working schedule, but this morning was different: the book group was coming, and with an incipient hangover she could not think. She decided to phone her mother, to break up her mother's routine of silence in the morning. Laurel pictured her watering the geranium in the kitchen while her solitary egg boiled. The radio would be on for company. A puff of breath sounded against the mouthpiece when her mother answered, and then she coughed several times. A smoke ring would be in the air, Laurel thought. Living alone, her mother said her voice grew husky from not being used. Sometimes she phoned Information, making up a name, just to use her vocal cords. Laurel hoped without hope her mother would ask her something important, like, How's your novel coming? rather than always asking what she was having for dinner, what train William was taking, or what she was going to do with a bloodhound. Too frequently, her mother's conversation held dire hints that things would go wrong. In turn, Laurel wished she might confide something close to her heart or on her mind.

I'm dying for a cock between my legs.

Suppose she just blurted that out, she thought; though since she was forty-one and married, she guessed her mother assumed a cock was available. However, she was certain that if she mentioned sex, her mother would reply, "Ugh."

"Mother, what's a surefire way of turning out an aspic ring?" She spoke with a happy, ringing voice to indicate her mother was a necessity in her life.

"Don't talk so loud, I'm not deaf," Mrs. Wynn said. Then she said, "There's not any way."

"Mother, I remember something you used to do."

"Nope. Put a hot dishtowel over the bottom."

Laurel closed her eyes, telling herself she ought to be used to these non sequiturs.

"William take his umbrella? It's raining in Washington."

"Yes," Laurel lied, to spare herself conversation about how she and William ought to look at television more so they'd know the weather.

"At least, with him gone, you get a rest from cooking those two damn dinners every night, Rick's and then yours. I don't know how you've stood it. You've cooked more than I ever did in my entire life."

She wished to say, You didn't do any housework, Mother, because you lived in the South, but that would leave her open to the remark that she hadn't had to leave home.

"Your bourbon and lettuce leaf club coming?"

Laurel thought she answered in a level voice, but Buff flickered pretty eyelashes her way. "My book group," she said between her teeth, though what right had she to feel this way? Because wasn't her mother maddeningly right, as usual? She had an uncanny habit of speaking to the truth of matters she knew little about, and this month Laurel had not even bothered to get the selected book.

William, in his infectious jovial manner, laughed about Mrs. Wynn's common sense, and she would say, "You mean I'm country." "Not at all," he would cry truthfully, and jolly her back to a good humor; he and her mother were uncommonly close. Mrs. Wynn had been moved to remark, "I feel sorry for William. I feel I'm the only mother he's ever had," and he would tell anybody, "What do you think of a guy having a mother-in-law who gets up and gives him the most comfortable chair when he walks into a room?"

"He get his briefcase fixed?" Mrs. Wynn asked.

"It's not fixable. He just carries it anyway."

"That banged-in case? To New York? To Washington?"

"You know what aplomb William has," Laurel said.

"I swear," said Mrs. Wynn.

Not wishing to be disloyal to William, Laurel thought his behavior had been silly when he bashed his briefcase on the hood of a cab on Sixth Avenue because the driver started up too fast while William was still crossing with the light; the case was an expensive ostrich-skin one she had given him, and she hated its demise. William carried it on into the city, and now to Washington, where in his raconteur's way he'd regale everybody with the story, turning it into a fable about how the tables were turned on him, imitating perfectly the cab driver's New York accent when he cried, "I don't want no altercation with no individual!" Rick, laughing when he heard the story, had said, "Dad," meaning inimitable Dad. Was she the only one who thought William's behavior a bit cuckoo?

However, she thought about a man earning money and having to share so much of it with his family, and how William put suede patches on the elbows of his jackets, and had the lapels of his overcoat covered with velvet when the edges wore out, starting a fashion trend in his office. "Why don't we go in together and get him another case?" she asked.

"Why should I?" said Mrs. Wynn. "I didn't ruin that one."

"Never mind." Laurel had another inspiration. "Mother, why don't you get a kitten?"

"I don't want a goddamned cat in this apartment. A cat box! Are you crazy?"

"Yes," said Laurel.

"What?"

"Nothing. I have to go. The fuel guy's here."

"Go on. I'm not stopping you. Don't make the towel too hot."

Wait! How hot's too hot? She held the dead connection, feeling, as she often did, that she wanted to call right back and tell her mother something, or ask her a question. Something was unfinished, something languished that needed saying; all their conversations about nothing were wasted moments, when something important should have been accomplished.

She went toward the door. A young man stared through the glass panels, and she saw herself as an idle rich housewife still in her nightclothes. "I've got a cold," she told him, opening the door and standing back. He came in and stood so close she read tiny yellow stitching on the pocket of his brown uniform: *Earl*. What's up, Earl? she thought, flooded by memory of a plumber telling her and William the suburbs were a field day for service people while "you gray flannel types," he'd said, eyeing William, "are in the city." Nobody could know how many times he answered a call to find a housewife in a revealing negligee, he'd said.

Having told Earl the problem, she led him to the basement, feeling his breath at her back and aware of the rising and falling movements of her behind under the robe; it caught in her crack and mercifully released itself, for she'd never have had the nerve to reach around and pull it out.

The house suddenly seemed too large for three people, and she was embarrassed, though Earl had no idea who lived here. There was a difference in a house when a man was in it. It seemed more solid. Laurel wanted to turn and cry out to Earl her troubles since William had been gone, ask him to solve her pencil sharpener's falling off the wall and scattering incomprehensible screws, have him change the burned-out bulb that wouldn't come unscrewed and figure out if the iron's cord was dangerous now that Jubal had chewed it.

When he knelt her robe brushed softly across one of his boots. They were both acutely aware of each other. Quickly she moved to the staircase. But had he lifted his bent head, his face would have met her crotch. Her pubic hair tingled. He busied himself inspecting the leak and announced they needed fiberglassing. Were they on a maintenance plan? She had no idea and bit back saying she'd phone her husband, but he was out of town. Earl said he would phone the main office in Bridgeport and followed her back to the kitchen.

He hung up, stuck a pencil into his pocket, and looked directly at her. Laurel moved toward the door, yanking and tugging at Jubal's collar as if he were as dangerous as a tiger. He'd do the work in a few days, Earl said, and don't worry in the meantime. "Thanks a lot," she said, and watched him back from the driveway with his truck ringing its shrill warning to the unwary. If she had wanted a quickie, what move should she have made? Laurel had no idea.

The tap water ran warm. Ought she to boil water for the towel? On the fingers of one hand, she could count things her mother had mentioned to fit her daughter for life: eggs stayed fresher in their own carton in the refrigerator; glasses that held milk washed out more easily if you ran cold water in them as soon as they were empty; oranges squeezed better if you rolled them under your hand; a finger down the throat for too much alcohol. By herself, she had assimilated her mother's method of cooking leg of lamb. "That's all, folks," she told her canine audience, who said nothing. When the phone rang, the two dogs looked at her questioningly, and she said, "You know who."

"Did your mold come out all right?"
"I didn't know how hot's too hot."
"What?"

"Nothing."

Another smoke ring must have appeared; her mother puffed against the speaker. She would have pulled her dainty lady's chair close to the phone, her television turned to a soft pitch, her cigarettes and lighter handily nearby. Laurel said, "Mother, I've got to go. They'll be here soon, and I'm not dressed."

"Go on. I'm not stopping you." She hung up.

How did she always leave herself open to this? Laurel thought. Her telephone pad caught her eye. The message scrawled across a page looked as if some half-literate had written it. Only now the memory came back of a man phoning William. She had stood here last night trying to keep her voice on an even keel and trying to understand his words, though he seemed at the end of a long yellow funnel. She had been sober enough to realize she was crocked, and wondered if he could tell. She wrote the message over, hoping his telephone number was right. What scared her, though, was to think the whole incident had erased itself from her memory.

Sunday nights after Rick was asleep it was her habit to grow maudlin before TV, drinking Scotch and watching the Judy Garland show. She liked growing weepy and shedding tears. Judy, aging, was still her idol, the way she had been when Laurel was growing up star-struck in Tennessee and herself unable to carry a tune. Over the years, she and Rick always watched any rerun of *The Wizard of Oz,* and Laurel cried when Dorothy clicked her red heels and said twice, "There's no place like home." After a while Rick began to wait for that moment, already turning to watch her, laughing at her as she laughed at herself, but always a little puzzled as to what caused those tears to course down his mother's cheeks. She knew she thought of the South as a home she had left. But wasn't there something else too?

This year Rick asked, "Am I too old to watch this show?" She knew he meant watch it with his mother, so she cried, "Of course not! It's a classic."

"OK, munchkin, keep cool," he had said.

In the dining room she squinted against sunlight bounding off old snow and had entered thinking her table was set. She knew she had been in here last night dancing and singing around the table to her heart's content, "I'm a one-man wo-man looking for the man that got a-way," and stomping her feet also, in Judy's manner. Not once would she have been on key.

She saw now there was no water in the centerpiece, and the flowers drooped shamed heads. There were no napkins, teaspoons, or water glasses in sight. What happened to the remainder of last evening? she wondered in quick misery.

The phone rang, but she could not believe the caller would be her mother.

An efficient-sounding woman on the other end said she was somebody's secretary, and this somebody was trying to reach William.

"I'm sorry," Laurel said. "He's in Washington. You can reach him at the Mayflower."

There was a moment's hesitation before the woman gave a short, throaty laugh. "I'm in Washington," she said. "Mr. Perry's been working in our office. I called the Mayflower. He checked out yesterday."

"Then I have no idea where he is."

Always she would remember that laugh. It had been all-encompassing and all-knowing, as though the woman had seen and heard everything and knew it all. Laurel knew what she saw: the dumb little broad in the suburbs with the station wagon, and the bright busy executive husband out conquering the world.

2

If only you weren't so scatterbrained! The judgmental voice in her head spoke, and she was ready for it. She was lost, but maybe she did not really want to find the address. She turned along silent winding roads with stone walls, thinking how odd that she knew so little about Soundport, Connecticut, when she had lived here nearly ten years. Being lost in the town, she reacted in a way she knew to be typical by blaming her current difficulties on the whole of the Northeast. *You couldn't wait to get away from home. Now you've got to run back there every summer.* Whenever her mother spoke like that in person, her eyes seemed as viscous as the insides of smashed green grapes. Just then, on what seemed an alien street, where forsythia only budded, Laurel had an insight: I never meant to leave home forever.

For years after college she moved back and forth between East and South like a piece on a Monopoly board. Then she'd met William and married. She had been grateful, for by the standards of Delton she was already an old maid. She got down on her knees in her one-room hole-in-the-wall apartment in Greenwich Village and thanked God for William's proposal—not knowing he would soon say he'd changed his mind. She was not certain how they happened to keep dating, though she was not the kind of person to let go first. Now it seemed ridiculous that she had stopped by a dime store to buy a wedding band before seeing a gynecologist who had never heard of her. She had been ecstatic about getting married, though terrified about carrying off a seven-month baby under the collective eyes of Delton, eyes she felt followed her everywhere. One night in their apartment, William mentioned having paid for an abortion before he knew Laurel, when he was uncertain the baby had been his. Sitting up, she said flatly, "You married me because I was pregnant." She expected him to deny the statement.

"I couldn't keep going around New York knocking up girls and getting abortions," he said.

She told herself William did not marry her only for that reason, even if he thought so. Remembering her loneliness back then, she knew if William had disappeared there was no one with whom she could have shared her pregnancy. Might she have killed herself? Nevertheless, what William had said hurt her feelings and the hurt lasted. She was hurt now. She had mentioned the call from Washington, and William said, "That woman's crazy. Of course I was still there," and she let pass the fact that she did not believe him.

Rounding a corner, she stared in surprise at the panorama of Long Island Sound spread out before her; there were wrinkles of sunlight on the water, and a rocky jetty and willowy grass. People stood on the beach bundled up to paint this landscape which refused to belong to her; in her mind's eye she focused on opaque muddy pools with inquisitive cows huddled nearby and imagined the smell of summer-dried pasture grass: *TK*, Laurel thought in William's company's editorial jargon; more to come, that meant, when set into incomplete copy. Her life was different from the lives of her girlfriends in Delton, who did not sit around their bridge tables discussing writing and editing. She could envy their talk about black maids who took care of their children, cleaned their houses, and were their best friends. She thought her life more interesting than if she'd been a Delton matron. Back in that city there was no family of the caliber of William's, despite the upper-crust society to which Hal MacDonald belonged. The South's old class and caste system bothered her still.

Laurel thought that the reason she kept going back south was that she was trying to reshape the past. For instance, her parents could never have gotten into the Delton Country Club. She was long past that kind of thing now as William's wife, and yet in Delton people did not matter unless they belonged there. Married to someone like Hal, she could have made it. But in those days someone like him seemed beyond the pale. . . .

Stop biting your fingernails! Laurel put her hand back on the steering wheel. Having been lost so long, she was going to be late. Maybe she should not go at all. The seedy office she was looking for would not be in this rich neighborhood near the Sound, not that anything in Soundport was very seedy, God forbid. She missed tacky things in the South, old and dilapidated things, clay hills and bar-b-que stands with smoky smells and poor people, blacks and whites.

In Soundport there was one black man, a Ph.D. who taught Chaucer at Columbia. In the dashiki he lately had begun to wear, and talking about "helping my people," he sat recently at her candlelit dining room table, and she had longed for people in Delton to know she had a black man to dinner. These days, he proudly got off the train at 125th Street to head toward Columbia. She took Rick south so he'd know black people, and they moved to liberal Soundport so he'd grow up with Jews and Catholics. Then, on his first day of school ever, he came home miserable because his desk was next to that of a Chinese.

They had avoided moving to what William called the apartheid towns, New Canaan, Darien, Greenwich, not wanting Rick to grow up where prejudice was so obvious; thinking they'd be bored, too, by husbands in lime-green golfing slacks and wives in Papagallos, wraparound skirts, and round-collared blouses.

Catholics, she learned, moved to Soundport for the same reason Jews did; she and William realized there was suspicion about them in those other towns—where they'd gone comparison shopping while house hunting. They passed the Anglo-Saxon test obviously but realtors always casually inquired, "Are you interested in the parochial school?" She often wondered if Catholics were shown houses in some ghetto she and William never saw.

Once in the suburbs, what man wouldn't fall into the habit of infidelity, able to spend the night fifty miles from home in a hotel room paid for by his company. On late evenings, she had to be agreeable about William's excuses because always they were partly valid. William did not drink midday but had to attend three-martini lunches. Afterward, editors were lax about editing, writers were slow with copy, and everyone's schedule was affected. She thought it amazing the company's magazines got to the stands on time or at all. Some nights William had to wait for a story from a stringer in some far-flung place. Naturally, it would be ridiculous to take a midnight train home and get up to catch the 8:02 back to the city. She might be stupid to suppose William alone those nights. Commuting made affairs too damn easy, for men. In the suburbs, women were limited. Men around in the daytime were not so interesting, and you were home with the kids. She was often glad William was not coming home, and she could spend less time in the kitchen. She could drink as much Scotch as she liked. On regular evenings, she had Rick's dinner ready at six, and she and William might eat an hour after he came home, by eight thirty, after the one predinner drink he allowed himself. She was never able to start the dishwasher before 10 P.M., when William was already in bed. She came upstairs carrying a nightcap of brandy and soda until the night William said, "I'm tired of listening to that ice go tinkle, tinkle, tinkle, upstairs every night."

On the night of their mutual confessions, William mentioned his longtime girlfriend was Jewish. He might have married her, he said, only his family would never have approved. All the years they lived together and William was having affairs she never suspected, till the night he told her about them, had he been thinking about divorce? Maybe he had exactly the idea he told her several of his friends at work had in mind. These men were silently waiting till their last child went to college and then planned on leaving the empty nest emptier.

She saw them again that night, lying companionably across their bed, side by side on their stomachs, waving their legs in the air like teenagers confiding secrets. The first night he spent with this younger woman, he said her mother phoned the hotel room thirteen times about her daughter being there with a married man. William looked so proud, she was irked. She considered herself long past enjoying being in a situation so childish.

That night William said something that made other things click into place. She sat up, saying, "Is she the girl who came to watch me have my picture taken for *Events* when they were going to review my book?"

"Yeah. She wanted to get a gander at you. I didn't know she was going to do that."

"Well, weren't you furious?"

"I was flattered she cared so much."

"Flattered! I think it showed incredible nerve," she had said.

She thought the incident gave even a tawdry touch to her book. She had suspected nothing when the photographer said a researcher on the magazine liked *Rainbow's End* so much she wanted to meet Laurel. She smiled when the girl came in and said, "Hello." The girl never replied and walked out in the middle of the sitting.

"She didn't like you for sour apples," William said, stretched out across their bed.

"William," she had said, "do you think your girlfriend's going to tell you how great your wife is?"

"I guess not."

"I know not."

He had referred to the girl as his mistress, a term Laurel hated. It had an old-fashioned formality that suited William. To her it implied being kept, which made her shudder. How did William reconcile that side of his life with his avid presentation of himself in the suburbs as a Little League coach, a Cub Scout den father, a member of the PTA and organizer of the kids' ball teams marching in the Memorial Day parade?

She could not keep from asking, "Did she like my book?"

"Yeah."

"She'd better have," she muttered. She saw that girl still, so thin she moved loosely in a black sheath.

William said he had stopped keeping the affair a secret; the photographer would have known why the girl wanted to meet her. She hated other people knowing something going on behind her back. Strangely, she had not been jealous. She had no visions of butts in the air or arms and legs entwined. She did not express to William sorrow over his dalliances and all the years she had been fooled, but let Edward wipe the slate clean.

She supposed there was no way to go back to Edward. His masculine pride was hurt when she broke off, at William's request. To drop Edward a cheery note suggesting lunch the next time he was in town from Princeton would be too obvious. Lunch was a euphemism for an affair, and understood as that in a case like hers.

She wondered if she was too low key to feel jealousy. William and his mother often tired her with their Yankee spirits and Yankee energy. She thought the briskness of their lives matched weather they had always known: winter snows and sea spray on their faces in the summers. When

Mrs. Perry visited, she suggested Frisbee, a game Laurel thought them too old to be playing. To William and his mother, games were fun only if you made up rules more difficult than the original ones. She saw herself rooted to one spot, as Mrs. Perry and William leaped midair, shouting out new rules as they went. Mrs. Perry had said, "Laurel, you only stand about. Have you no competitive sense?" She remembered feeling tongue-tied and ashamed.

Now, at last, she saw something recognizable in Soundport, a school where they watched Rick play basketball one Saturday morning. He scored no points and missed the basket at the game's most crucial moment and came off the court tight-lipped.

While William pushed Rick into sports, he knew when to back off. "Old man, basketball's not your forte." He clapped Rick on the back. "So what!" William laughed so hard, Rick could laugh at himself. She was always proud of William as a father and the way he instructed their son. When Rick was still very young, William had knelt down, saying, "Now when you are introduced, you put out your hand to shake and look the other man straight in the eye." She tried to imagine having parents who used words like "forte" to her, or used them at all.

Now that William had the same weekend off as Rick, the two of them shared a lot of strictly male activities. Yet she would not complain. Not after those ten years William worked in New York on Saturdays and Sundays and was home two days midweek, the dire editorial weekend. It was death on marriages and on women home those long two days with children. William always spent Sunday nights in town because of late closers. Ultimately, William felt shortchanged about not seeing Rick on his weekends and changed jobs within the company. It was then he began to throw up his eggs every morning.

She went back to thinking how little advice she'd received in her life. One time her mother's arrived after the fact. When she was back in Delton to be married, her mother said, "Here's a little present" and handed her a white satin-covered douche bag. If only, Laurel thought, she'd had the presence to say, "What's that, Mother?" Or if only she had had the courage to tell her, "It's too late. I've got one in the oven."

In Delton to get married, William talked about how much people drank. She had had thoughts about men who didn't drink in the crazy kind of manner they drank in the South; William would be better off, and their sex life might improve, if he could let his hair down. For her, alcohol was sexually stimulating. When they married she had to cut down her consumption. She was less free, though glad he kept her in check. Once, in college, William got drunk and came to himself digging a hole. He feared losing control again, coming to from a blackness to find himself doing something for which he had no explanation. Some clue to William lay in his behavior, as he suspected, though she'd kindly said, "Maybe you were digging a hole to China." Actually she considered the action odd.

She refrained from asking if that was the same night he woke up, after a lot of beer, to find a frat brother blowing him. William was still bothered by that too. Knowing he ought to make the boy stop, he'd let the act conclude. Was that natural? she wondered, suspecting if she asked another male, he'd cry, "I'd have beat the shit out of the bastard." Which might not be true. If she had a daughter, one of her first pieces of advice would have been to explain how men liked blow jobs; it was the kind of blunt, motherly advice girls ought to be given.

William had squelched her own passion; she could see in vivid intensity the garden where it had happened, at their first little house in the suburbs. Those days had been her first attempts at gardening in a Connecticut soil which grew rocks better than plants, astounding her; in her past, if you stuck a seed in the ground, it multiplied. She had planted tuberous begonias, which bloomed with showy effects, as the catalog promised, but instantly shed their flowers. How William laughed!

On lawn chairs near her garden, one evening after

Rick was asleep, while they had the one predinner drink William allowed them, though she doctored hers in the kitchen when she checked on dinner, she was moved to climb atop him, her mouth wet and agape. He shoved her aside. "I've never seen such a selfish exhibition in my life. I'm astonished at your selfishness," he'd said angrily.

Climbing off meekly, she'd blamed her crudeness on her middle-class background and the lush, nearly tropical vegetation of her youth. Upper-class Easterners, she thought, had been refined so long they'd had the passion refined out of them. She used to long for it to rain in the East as it rained in the South, tumultuous storms that beat the earth, while thunder and lightning crashed overhead, until the rain was spent as quickly as it started, and the sun came out as hot as if rain had never been; the whole earth steamed and smelled as rank as sex.

She paid no attention to her mother's warnings about going south in the summer with Rick and leaving William for a month; her mother reinforced the advice by saying Mrs. Perry thought Laurel was asking for trouble. She was only surprised the idea of sex rose to Mrs. Perry's mind. Since her own career was uppermost, why didn't she understand her daughter-in-law went south searching material to write about? Because of Soundport's proximity to the city, they easily rented the house to New Yorkers who, like realtors, referred to suburbia as "the country." She always laughed, wishing they could see the countryside where she and Rick went, and know its people. If William screwed around while she was at home, why not do what she wanted to?

Her mother had had some indication of unrest, but Laurel had not told her about the night of confession, not wishing to mention Edward. She had not revealed William's stunning remark, "I'm known as the biggest asshound at *Events* magazine." When he said that with pride, rather than being angry, she'd felt a little sorry for him.

This could not be the right street, this cul-de-sac of

ranch houses. She wanted to back down, for the atmosphere was wrong for the business she had to conduct. When a boy answered the door, she turned to go away. "I was looking for a Mr. Woodsum."

He was tall and thin and could be Rick in a few years; he wore the same L. L. Bean chamois shirt and khaki trousers that both William and Rick wore, and he had on a new kind of loafer, with tassels, which Rick had coveted and which she and William denied him.

"This is right," the boy said, opening the door wider.

She had to step into a small foyer, and kept her eyes on the boy's shoes; she saw, as Rick had said, this was the kind of loafers all the kids were going to have; she and William called them tacky.

"Dad's down in his office."

The boy opened another door toward a basement. She went down and saw at the room's far end a silver-haired man behind a desk. A green glass-shaded lamp on it cast eerie shadows. Summoning courage, she started across, calling out in William's hearty manner, "Hello! I'm Mrs. Perry," and she put out her hand, while not quite meeting his eyes.

She was astonished that he stood up; she was astonished there were tall cases full of books. He had manners. He read. She had expected a squat, tough man with a fat black cigar and a thin, profane vocabulary. He said, "Won't you have a chair?"

He waited till she was seated. His eyes were quite blue and seemed to stare through her. She had the feeling he had inspected her elsewhere.

Laurel said, "I told you on the phone, I'm thinking about getting a divorce. I hate to do this, but my husband—"

"I understand."

"A private detective's evidence helps?"

"Sometimes. Usually in most cases." She looked at him so closely, he put down his pencil and smiled. "You have children at Elmwood Elementary?"

"My son went there."

Mr. Woodsum reached to the floor and brought up a black hat with a silvery badge.

"I thought I recognized you," she said. "I saw your picture in the paper recently, too."

He was the school guard at that crossing, and a famous one. When cars with children inside drew up, he stepped off the curb and tossed a handful of candies through a window. She drove Rick to school sometimes, and he had said, "What a great guy," reaching around to pick up scattered peppermints. Which of Mr. Woodsum's jobs was his real one, and which job was moonlighting?

She gave him the information he asked for: when she was leaving town and where William worked. His eyebrows rose. "A difficult building to find anybody in," he said.

When he asked for a description of William, she closed her eyes; she gave his height and weight, but a distinguishing characteristic he could see? He laughs a lot, she thought. The mole beside his eyebrow was too small. She did not want to think of Mr. Woodsum in a Sherlock Holmes cap, tiptoeing up to William with a reading glass. She shrugged, whispered, "I don't know."

She wanted to lean on Mr. Woodsum and say there were hurts she couldn't reconcile herself to, and she wanted to ask his advice about things that had happened and see what his opinion of them was. She could tell, however, that Mr. Woodsum was like a doctor. He would do the best for you he could without really wanting to hear everything that had caused your pain.

"You brought a picture?"

Laurel had a candid shot in her purse but did not want to open it. "Only an old one." In her study she had gone through shoeboxes full of snapshots; these were a record of her fifteen years with William and of Rick's whole life. She had meant many times to paste the pictures in some orderly fashion into an album, and how like her that she never had.

"I believe I'd better see it, Mrs. Perry."

When she handed over the picture she saw to her horror that on the back Rick had printed in his childish scrawl of some years ago two words: *My Daddy.*

William had been snapped by a friend at the beach without his knowledge, while reading *The New York Times.* "I'm glad I wasn't picking my nose, old buddy," he had said. For him to be viewed the same way a second time seemed unfair. What kind of person was she? As Mr. Woodsum looked at the picture, she longed to be home. She did not mind cooking those two damn dinners every night as much as her mother thought. Mr. Woodsum slipped the picture into a manila folder, and with a hollow feeling she thought, My file; I don't want one.

"I think I'd better see Mr. Perry in person. This picture's not too good."

"See him how?"

"Does he go grocery shopping with you, perhaps on Saturday?"

"William? No." She'd have hated William to be one of those pussy-footed husbands who follow wives around grocery stores as if they had nothing else better to do. "He never goes grocery shopping."

"Mrs. Perry, it's your money. I can't assure you of anything with this picture to go on."

"Well, this Saturday," she said reluctantly, "we're going to look at a new car at the Chevrolet place."

She wanted to tell him how they never bought anything on credit, how buying a new car was a large event in their lives, how conscientiously William had pored over *Consumer Reports;* she wanted to say how she felt disloyal replacing faithful products with newer ones.

"Fine," he said. "Call me just as you're leaving home."

How could she call? she wanted to ask. And she knew right off, she'd find a way. She could see herself already running back indoors to the bathroom while William sat impatiently at the wheel of the old car. Why was she apt and capable? Why did people know innately how to be sly? She longed to ask Mr. Woodsum if everybody had the same ability to learn so quickly to deceive.

"I'm afraid I'll have to ask you for a retainer's fee." He seemed truly apologetic. She wrote out a check, wishing her father had not died and left her money.

"Don't forget the viewing," he called after her.

She said, without looking back, "I won't." William laid out waxen in a coffin rose to mind, and he would hate that idea since his family believed only in cremation. At her father's funeral he had made fun of people coming up to the casket and saying things like, "Look at that rascal, doesn't he look peaceful?" "Wasn't he handsome?" "God broke the mold after he made old Frank."

"This is barbaric," William had said. "Primitive. I've never seen anything so disgusting."

"It's Southern," she had said, shrugging.

She found her way back to town where gulls were wheeling and dealing over the saltwater inlet that ran in from Long Island Sound. In a bank, she transferred money from her savings account into the checking account to cover Mr. Woodsum's check, thinking how she'd always been aghast at the idea of being a woman who had to ask her husband for every penny. Had she been in that position, she could not have seen Mr. Woodsum. She might have been better off. Across from the bank, she looked at the marquee of a movie she wanted to see. William said they had seen it. Then he clapped an obvious hand to his mouth saying, "Oops. I must have read a review in *Time*."

How many movies had he seen twice? she wondered. William's wanting her to know the truth was curious. Laurel shopped carefully, having never been a piker about cooking, though she hated time spent in grocery stores. She bought bubble gum, hoping Rick did not already have the baseball cards inside. She spied Almond-Mocha ice cream and was thrilled. She bought a lot. It was William's favorite flavor and hard to come by. She rummaged around in a bin of odds and ends, hoping to come up with a device she once bought William, which he was crazy about but lost. His habit on the train was to cut out newspaper items of interest for his work; the little cutter slit them out without raggedy edges and had its own case. Alas, there was not another one. She thought the marriage revolved around William and his likes and dislikes.

She came from the store thinking of her habit of silence. Too often in childhood to speak out had had disastrous results. Long ago, she told herself about her parents, "They'll never make me cry again. I won't feel anything." Perhaps she had learned her lesson too well. A time came when her father threw up after a week-long binge, her mother frantically spreading newspapers around the floor, and she had been unmoved that her father thought he was throwing up blood. She had stated, "It's the tomato soup he had for lunch."

"What does she think it is?" He used her mother as intermediary too.

"She says it's tomato soup," her mother had said.

She remembered a sad sense of fury that she, so young, was the one to decide if her father was dying of a hemorrhage or losing his lunch. She wanted then to be where people loved her better, and where such scenes did not take place.

Laurel went from the store to a cleaner's and picked up William's shirts. Then she stopped at the end of her driveway to collect the mail. There was nothing interesting today. But there would not be anything as interesting as the correspondence her friend in Delton inadvertently had started.

She had been surprised to hear from Catherine a few weeks ago. Enclosed in her letter was an article from the *Delton Advocate* written by Hal MacDonald about his incarceration. She could not believe he was in prison in Mississippi. How could a man from his background survive such a place, even its ignorance? Her heart went out to him with more sympathy than she'd ever had to feel for a contem-

37

porary. The article was not only moving but beautifully written. Laurel had had to write him in return; she sent her first novel as an introduction.

Even now, the awe with which she used to think of the MacDonalds in her growing-up days in Delton could come back in memory. She wondered if she could go to that prison and meet him. She had seen him once in that long-ago time, and she could remember everything about it vividly. She knew so much about him, having never met. She knew his whole life-style, so different from her own back then—the country club set, a great plantation down in Mississippi. She may have been there once.

In high school she knew both his sister and his wife. In public school, Catherine had insisted before ninth grade that they transfer to Miss Poindexter's School for Girls, a move that changed her life's direction, Laurel thought. "In time to join a sorority," Catherine had reasoned. So Laurel set out into as much of Delton society as she knew. That remembered past came back when, in her house alone, she could real Hal MacDonald's letter again.

April 11

Dear Laurel:

I have reread your lovely letter and hardly know how to answer. I was surprised to find it and your novel. I don't know why I can't remember you as a child but do remember reading an interview about you some time ago in the *Mid-South Review*. I didn't connect you at the time with someone I should know. Being editor of the prison newspaper, for which I originally wrote my article, which was picked up by the *Delton Advocate,* is different work from any I've known—cotton farming's been my life. But I enjoy what I'm doing. It gives me the opportunity to use my mind some, for which I'm grateful. And the work is a lot more pleasant than being in the line camps and working in the fields all day. Actually, Laurel, I'm somewhat unique here because convicts with a university degree are rare indeed, whereas on the outside I would be, as I've always been, just one of the crowd. I've been well treated since coming here and I'm not blind as to why—I had help from friends on the outside. I came here determined to get along. I made up my mind to make the best of an unbelievable situation. I've been made full trusty, which means more privileges than a regular convict.

I have periods of such wrenching, absolute, exquisite misery, though, as I've never known in my wildest dreams. It doesn't last and is usually brought on by worrying over the complete destruction of my family, Sallie and our little girl, Tina, and the fact I'm helpless to do anything about anything. The situation I'm trying to describe would be true in any kind of confinement. Here we live in "camps" and each camp has "cages" where the prisoners live. At first I didn't think I could live like this and keep my sanity. I mean, I really doubted my ability to stay sane. And that scared me. This prison isn't perfect but it's a vast improvement over a few years ago. There is conjugal visiting, though most men in prison no longer have wives, or have them in name only. On visiting days we can be outside with our families. I usually arrange a picnic under a mimosa I like. But I'm always too excited to eat. Thank you again for caring enough to write me. I will write again when I've had time to read your book.

Hal MacDonald

Exquisite misery, Laurel thought. How could she not be moved by a man sensitive enough to write those words. Of course he didn't remember her as a child—she was living on the wrong side of the tracks from the people and places he had known. Hurriedly, Laurel put away the letter. The punctual yellow school bus had lumbered up the hill down the road and passed apple trees next door to stop at the nearby corner, where Rick stepped off in his penny loafers.

3

She might well be going to Timbuktu, Siberia, or Mars as far as her Soundport friends were concerned: Mississippi? They went on questioning year after year: Why? What's there? "Nothing," Laurel would answer, knowing they would not understand if she told them. She would smile, realizing they did not see the smile's mysterious quality, either. In their ignorance, they did not question the trip's real oddity: Going to Mississippi in July! they ought to be shouting. You are crazy!

Highways were less traveled on Sundays, and she always started the trip early that day. Rick was beside her as she pulled from the driveway, with its abutments of stone walls. Buff stood innocently on the back seat, having no idea how long her ride was about to be. Jubal had been shipped off to "camp," as William called it, and, no matter how good the kennel, would return hangdog and medicinal-smelling. After so many years, their departures were heavy with ritual.

If only the stage setting with Mr. Woodsum had not taken place. While she could stop at a phone booth on the way, it seemed too late to call things off, and there was the deposit, spent. She must not calculate what she was doing in terms of money, Laurel said to herself, at the steering wheel. She backed slowly, fixing things in her mind's eye. William stood on the porch in his paisley bathrobe, which was old. Something happening at the school bus corner caught her eye. A car came around it, an old gray derelict car with rusty spots. "There's Gran," said Rick, his young voice husky with its early morning usage. His eyes were not fully open. "Doesn't she know we're leaving?"

"Of course." How many times had they talked about the exact hour? And she told her mother she was not the only wife who left her husband to his own devices in the summer. Other wives settled in the Hamptons or on the Vineyard or the Cape and husbands came on weekends; they had many nights alone in the city. Once they went to Fire Island and William laughed that on Friday evenings wives and children went to meet what was called "the daddy boat."

On the porch, William had not shaved; there was his faint darkened stubble, his familiarity as Dad and husband. She had smelled coffee on his breath when she stood on tiptoe reaching beyond his chin, where the top of her head came, and their mouths brushed in goodbye. He had grabbed Rick in a crunch that made the boy cry out and look sheepish. Somewhere in the distance an inconsiderate lawn mower began; the smell of grass would reach them if they stayed long enough. When would they get off with her mother here? Mrs. Wynn parked and came along the roadside, her eyes downcast, embarrassed by her arrival. Bile rose to Laurel's throat. She wanted to drive away, saying, If I wait another minute, I won't make it with just one night on the road. "I'm not going to keep you," her mother called, stepping along carefully through damp grass. "I couldn't sleep." Her long nails grasping the rolled-down window seemed those of a swimmer holding on to something for dear life. Her eyes briefly met Laurel's. Her sleeplessness was because of Mr. Woodsum, she meant. Laurel looked away.

William called, "Hello, old dear. I'll be right back. Got to go indoors and poo."

"Dad." Rick laughed. "Tell the neighborhood."

"Here's a little money, Rick."

"Gran, thanks." He reached across the front seat. "It'll help with my twenty-two."

"Bah. You don't need another gun."

"He only has a BB gun, Mother."

"Bah. He doesn't need that. He's not supposed to shoot it in Soundport. That's why he's always in trouble with the police."

"That's why he likes Mississippi," Laurel said. "To be able to use the gun."

If she says Bah again, I'll kill her, she thought. "Bah, he doesn't need to shoot anything," Mrs. Wynn said. She meant to remind them she grew up in Mississippi with a passel of brothers clomping mud into the house and bringing in bloody, stinky birds and animals she had to see plucked and gutted and had to smell cooking and finally had to eat. "I brought William my little extra fan. He says the apartment he subleases is so hot every summer."

"He's taking the air conditioner out of my office," Laurel said.

"Going to be comfortable." Mrs. Wynn tried to smile and make eye contact again, but Laurel refused. If her mother attempted to malign William, she would champion him, because it had always been her nature to take up for any underdog.

Mrs. Wynn looked away toward the neighborhood. "A lot of long days while you're gone. Sundays are the worst."

"Why don't you start going to church, Mother?"

"Why? What for?" Her eyes lost their sadness.

Where had her mother's feisty nature come from, so unlike her own? Laurel wondered. From having so many siblings? She could remind her mother she could wear her new clothes: people did not particularly go to church for Christian reasons. Between piousness and Christianity there is a fine line, it's been said.

"If I go to church, all they'd do would be to start asking me for money, or to be on some committee. They're always building something." Her mother's voice wavered. "Maybe you won't stay so long."

"How can I not stay, Mother? The house is rented."

"Do you have Jewish tenants again?"

"Yes."

"That's good. They're the best. Always leave the house better-looking than the way you left it."

"Thanks," Laurel said.

"I'm not going to any church. When I was little, I had to go to church twice every Sunday and to prayer meeting on Wednesday nights. And then every night for two weeks during protracted meeting."

"You mean revival?"

"Whatever they call it now."

Amused, Laurel would not laugh. But she watched her mother walk away with a different sense, noting her short legs, her round ankles, which gave her a peasant girl's look despite her fashionable clothes.

"The house looks fine, Mom."

Laurel smiled, but the little barb had hurt, with a familiar feeling. As she edged the car slowly backward, fir trees beyond the house receded and grew more slim. Well, it was her fault all that work had to be done, cleaning out drawers and closets for other people to use, fluffing down cobwebs she had paid no attention to before. The slim New Yorker who came to rent the house had brought a child who seemed a minor appendage to her life as an executive. How did women acquire such acumen? How did they know how to command offices and make important decisions? Being a writer and staying at home, she was considered by other mothers not to be doing anything. They were running around Soundport on committees. It was therefore logical that she should chauffeur the neighborhood kids. But she would like to be out in the world, jumping into cabs, calling out directions, having a limousine wait for her outside Four Seasons, be recognized in Bendel's and have little time to shop. She longed to have an engagement calendar scribbled over with appointments and to have to make a lunch date three months in advance. As the tenant inspected the house, Buff came up cordially to sniff the skirt of her daughter, who shrieked in terror. "Don't touch the doggie," the mother cried. "The doggie has germs." "Oh, get away," Laurel told Buff, meaning the opposite might be true. The poor city child would never love a dog or have the love of one in return. Once again, she had felt how out of her element she had always been in her exposure to New York.

Mrs. Wynn looked back. "Poor Buff," she said. She got in a parting shot in a warring game Laurel never played. Just when she could feel sympathy for her mother, Mrs. Wynn ruined the moment; often that was the case.

"Does Buff mind being in the car two days?" Rick said.

"No."

William on the porch again drew his chin into a long face and wiped at an imaginary tear. "See you soon, pal."

" 'Bye, Dad." Rick hung out the window.

Laurel, smiling through the windshield, thought, No sad face for me and no long goodbye.

Rick shouted, "Gran, fly down and drive back home with Mom."

"I'm not going to Mississippi in August! I lived to get out of that heat, period. Send me a postcard from wherever you're going out west."

"Thanks a lot," Laurel said.

Rick settled inside. "I knew she wouldn't come," he said.

He rose onto his knees and looked back until the house no longer filled the rearview mirror and they were around the corner from two familiar people, her mother and her husband. And suddenly, it seemed odd to Laurel that they were there together while she drove away leaving them.

On the front seat lay a piece of paper covered with what she called William's "squinchy" writing; it was hardly decipherable. His listing exit numbers and highways for her was the only way she got through New Jersey and Pennsylvania each year. She could not understand maps. In her worse times, she thought his handwriting showed a mean, suspicious, small nature, but Rick's handwriting had turned into a carbon copy. So she changed her mind, deciding that in handwriting analysis probably opposites were true: small writing meant largesse of mind, a warm, loving, and sympathetic nature. She smiled at Rick, playing with a Slinky train at his age, folding the wire in and out like an accordion.

Later, as they traveled into New Jersey and passed green exit signs for Princeton, she wondered about Edward and if he still lived there. She fumbled for William's paper because soon she needed the exit for Pennsylvania. "Mom, why can't you remember how to go year after year?"

"I'm stupid. Once we get to Virginia I'm OK. It's the same highway nearly all the way after that." All the way *home*, she thought, home free. In Virginia, the countryside began to feel, look, and smell Southern. She slowed again for a toll. "Do you realize it costs almost eight dollars to get from Soundport to Philadelphia? In the South there are no toll roads."

"What am I supposed to say about that this year?"

"Jesus, God!"

"What, Mom?" The Slinky train fell from Rick's hands.

"I missed the basket. Help me. Help me find the right change."

"I thought you'd had a heart attack. Get out and get that money." But Rick grabbed the purse she held out and found coins.

"I couldn't get out." Laurel breathed slowly again, driving on. "The sign says not to."

He repeated, "I thought you'd had a heart attack." The Slinky train lay in his hands. "Dad says your whole generation grew up afraid of authority."

"Oh, be quiet till I get out of this traffic." She rose in the seat while cars flowed around her, gaining in speed and spreading in all directions; if she was not in the far lane in time for the next exit, she'd wind up in Atlantic City or someplace worse. The sound of a car horn bleating like a lamb in the line of cars that waited while she fumbled at the toll booth came back: another dumb female, William would have said.

"They're all out to get you, Mom," Rick said.

"All right, Dad." She smiled again at his mimicry. Not until they flew down a ramp like a roller-coaster ride did she stop praying: God, William, somebody help me.

Rick looked at her curiously. "Why are you always so afraid?"

"I held everybody up. They won't love me."

"So afraid," he said, like a whisper. "Dad says you do so many things great. Why don't you have any confidence?"

"Because of the past Dad spoke about."

"Dad saves every rubber band off the Sunday paper, and you have a drawer full of candle stubs. You both save every teensy bit of aluminum foil. He says that's because you both grew up during the Depression."

"It marked our lives. My father yelled so about bills, I dreaded having new clothes. If we weren't already poor, I thought we were going to get poor. Gran shopped for dresses in bargain basements when she could afford not to. But my father never let up about money." Gran, Laurel thought: everything was not easy.

"You and Dad are the best parents of anybody I know. I'm glad I didn't grow up like either one of you. I wish I could have known my grandfather, Pappy."

"I wish so too. It was unfair he died when you were four months old. I'd always wanted to have a boy for him. What he had craved was 'a tough little nut.' It was a terrible disappointment when I was a girl."

"How do you know?"

"Because a black woman who was Gran's best friend's

46

maid told me. She was there when I was born: Sudie. If I knew where to find her, I'd peel me a niggerhead."

"Mom?"

"You know I'm kidding. That's the kind of thing I grew up hearing: Ah'm goin' peel me a niggerhead: phonetic. Boys used to go coon-conking, or said they did. I don't believe any of them really drove around Delton throwing eggs at Negroes. Back then, blacks couldn't have done anything about it. What a turnaround. They used to be terrified of us, and now we're scared of them." Justice was a word she believed in.

"Why'd that maid tell you?"

"I guess she didn't assume it would always hurt. I wanted to have a boy for Dad too. Men want sons."

What was she to say if Rick ever asked why he was an only child? She wasn't certain why; after a time, another baby just never came. Perhaps he thought he already knew enough. When William brought home flowers for their tenth anniversary, Rick said, "If you've been married ten years today, how come I'm—?" And then he hushed; his eyes had a light that lasted, closed. Later, she and William dissolved into one another's arms. "Whew," he had said. "Well, that's over, and a lot sooner than I'd have expected." They had both been impressed at how quickly things had dawned on Rick. But what had it meant to him to know his mother was knocked up when his parents married?

Laurel said, "What are you smiling about?"

"I was thinking of Dad at home in Pappy's old robe."

"You can inherit it."

"That robe sucks. And it's all worn."

"Apparently, Pappy thought it was too fancy. Dad and I gave it to him. After he died, my mother said he never took it out of the box." Why be told that? Why were people so unsparing?

"I'd chuck it out."

"You're a spoiled Soundport kid."

"Am I?"

"No. Don't worry. And your parents aren't rich."

"I'm glad," Rick said. "I know kids who're already talking about what kind of car they want in high school."

"You can use mine. I'm always home."

Rick gave her a loving pinch without hurting. "You're a good mother. You're always under my thumb."

"I know it. How come I do everything my squirt of a kid tells me?"

"And the most famous mother in the neighborhood. How old was I then?"

"Seven."

She had to repeat the story exactly: how when she won a large monetary award for her first novel, she was written up in the Soundport paper. One day Rick said, "You're famous in our neighborhood. Did you know that?"

Thinking he had overheard parents talking of her literary achievement, she'd said modestly, "No. Why?"

"When we play touch football in the backyard you bring out lemonade," Rick said.

Pretending now to be an interviewer, using her writing name, he asked, "Which way had you rather be famous, Miss Wynn?"

"For writing or for lemonade? I'll choose lemonade. I think that's what life's really about."

On the next morning, they passed Knoxville and wound through gray morning haze in the Smokies over a circuitous two-lane mountain highway. Truck drivers suggestively tooted diesel horns if she passed them—they somehow felt that seeing a single female on the road gave them the right. Then she was saying, "I can't believe you've done this, Rick." He had held his Slinky train out the window, it unwound, and now it was wrapped somewhere underneath the car. "You're too old to be playing with a Slinky train."

He was frightened; something serious might be wrong with the car. Laurel controlled her temper; she had always thought herself too irritable and as a mother wanted to change her ways, though to change her spots seemed impossible. Her parents always made such large issues out of the smallest happenings, and she did not want Rick to have that past. Whatever she had done wrong seemed to them beyond belief. "I swear," they would say in turn, with a finality that included the past, the present, and the future.

"I just don't know what to do about the car," Laurel said.

"Well, Laurel." Rick drew down his chin and deepened his voice into his father's. "I'd back carefully. If there's a problem, I'm sure Rick will run to that garage and see about a tow truck." Distantly, they saw a dilapidated cedar structure and a typical country store with two gas pumps in front.

"Good thinking." Backing along the shoulder of the road, Laurel was proud of being able to go in a straight line. She equated this ability to being her father's daughter, as she equated her tenacity on the road to him and her ability to make the long trip alone, too. Sometimes she worried about having what seemed too much male strength; for instance, she had never shed a tear in front of William.

Laurel parked in cinders before the grocery. The landscape beyond it seemed to beat and pulsate with a lonely silence. There was nothing but emptiness and yellow spurts of stinkweed sticking up for miles. Buff waited on the porch, looking through a screen door with cotton wads stuck to it, hopefully warding off flies.

She nudged Rick. "You ask."

He held up Buff's plastic dish. "Is there a place I can get my dog some water?"

A woman sat on a stool, her hair skinned back so tightly, her eyes looked Chinese. She had the vacuous, blue-eyed look of country people who seldom see anyone and have no news. Nearby an old man sat in a rocker spitting tobacco juice into a can labeled Bartlett Pears, which brimmed full. Yuck, Laurel thought. "There's a bathroom back yonder I hate for you to see." Rick followed the woman's directions, carrying the bowl ahead as if soliciting.

This was not really her countryside here, and yet she felt a sense of coming close to it; here it was possible to stand without air-conditioning and not be soaked in perspiration, the air was not so heavy. In the rackety cedar building beyond, a man stood humped over welding, sending blue and green sparks into the air. Laurel explained about the car. "Bubba could he'p you if he has a mind to," the old man said, spitting.

Rick came back, the bowl slurping water to the floor. "Hey, Mom," he said. "Fireworks. Can I get some?"

"You've got money."

"That boy don't want to use his'n." The woman laughed.

Laurel tried to whisper. "Get them at Loma's. I like to buy as much as possible from her."

"Last year she didn't have anything good. They're getting stricter in Mississippi. How about at least five bucks' worth? Remember last year I doubled my money selling firecrackers back in Soundport?"

"I'm not bailing you out of jail for selling illegal contraband. Five bucks? Use your money."

"It's for the gun." He adopted a younger kid's whining: "Pleee-se, Mom."

"Oh, here," she said.

"I'll use my own quarter for this paper."

"What do you want a newspaper for?"

"It's got an article about Mickey Mantle."

"Mickey Man-till. Where'd you get that accent?" She wondered what his accent was. He'd grown up hearing southwest Tennessee mixed with Beacon Hill Boston and Connecticut suburbia. And what was that? "We have to ask that man if he'll help us."

"I'll be picking out fireworks."

"You don't want to go?"

"You can go alone, Mom."

She gave him a half-pleading look and went onto the porch, telling Buff to stay where she was. Why must she be worried about going to ask a garage man to fix her car? Laurel knew as she walked his way it was because any

50

refusal or hesitancy on his part she would take as personal rejection. And she stood right beside Bubba's elbow but he did not look up. She adopted William's hearty, winning, breezy manner and said, "Hello. Hello."

"What can I do for you?" he said, with a suspicious mountainside manner.

She said, "I know it sounds ridiculous." Then she explained to him what had happened.

"Kids'll be kids," Bubba said. "Bring the car on over here."

Laurel went back for it, wondering if to drive it further might not be bad for the car. But she would not protest. Why, she questioned herself, because Bubba might not like you?

"You a long way from home," he said, looking at her license plate; then Laurel thought, Lord, she was home. Because all summer long, country people said the same thing to her, with the slight idea that something must be wrong. Did they never go anywhere? she wondered. She felt a great need to explain to Bubba she was not some agitator from the East—though the time was late for that—but that she belonged, and anyway she was more apt to get good service, being part of where they were. "I came from Delton. And I have people in Mississippi. I go back every summer to visit them." She had purposely used the word "people" as a Southernism.

"Making this long trip by yourself?" Bubba chose among tools.

"Yup. Except for my son."

"Wire's caught up in the rear axle. Got to run her up on the lift." He began to snip with wire clippers, giving her a sideways glance. "If you come up down in this part of the world, how'd you get so far up the country?"

"Oh." She shifted her feet about in his sawdust, wondering herself; then she said, "I married a man up there. It just happened." That was the whole truth.

"You still married?"

"Yes."

He gave her another sharply angled look. "If I was married to a good-looking woman, I wouldn't let her be running around the countryside loose."

She was not running around loose, she thought angrily. She had given him a viable, justifiable reason about why she was on her way south; why was she made to feel odd making this trip?

"Done. You ain't got much toy left."

"The car's still all right?"

"Good as new. It *is* new, ain't it?"

She nodded. She hated again those moments in the showroom when William moved about turning steering wheels, grinning like a small boy: his conservative family seldom bought new cars: her salesman father, except during the war, had a new one every year. In her mind's eye, Mr. Woodsum remained stationary in a yellow convertible, asking questions of a salesman. It was tawdry, Laurel thought, a scene that should have been far removed from their lives, and William, despite moralistic attitudes, had brought them to it.

"You going on down the road, or staying round here?"

"Going on down the road."

"If you was to stay here, I'd carry you on over yonder to that store for a Coke," Bubba said.

Laurel smiled. "That would be nice." What made such men assume you would like to go? "How much for the work?"

"Not something I've priced. Gimme a couple of bucks."

She opened the car door. "If you was to come on back this way, I'd carry you on over yonder yet," Bubba said.

"I go home a different way. Through St. Louis." She fended off such suggestions all summer from the most outlandish men, being alone. Always she felt the safety and security of being married; nothing could harm her, really, while there was William.

"Mom. Buff's gone."

"She couldn't be gone. She never goes anywhere." Laurel got out of the car.

"I've called and called."

She looked toward the highway where another diesel truck passed; the silhouette of its driver inside looked like a paper doll. "She wouldn't go to the road." They looked out over the scraggly land with its yellow weeds; after following footpaths through it, their shoes seemed to have been dusted by dry mustard. They picked cockleburs from their clothes and went on calling, "Buff, Buff," her name echoing back to them from hidden hollows.

"We can't leave her," Rick said.

"I know." But how long could they wait? One time Rick had said that when Buff died that would be the end of his childhood; they had had the dog so long, he did not remember a time without her. But that's not now, God. Laurel's lower lip trembled. It's too soon. Yet that's what she was thinking of doing to Rick's childhood; to divorce his father would end it. He'd never have again the innocence he now had. And what about herself? She was walking along thinking she must call William and ask him what to do next.

Then the miracle happened; the little body came running toward them. Rick fell on his knees and instantly got up holding his nose. "Whew!"

"She's been rolling in cow plops," Laurel said. "Buff, how could you?"

She was embarrassed by the iridescent greenness in the dog's coat, explaining the situation to the store's owner and buying paper towels. They scrubbed Buff down the best they could. The woman stood at her screened door laughing. "Got your chance, didn't you, girl. A dog will do it every time it can."

"So what else is going on we don't know about behind that ladylike façade?" Laurel held the graying muzzle between both hands.

Within miles of Delton, the land turned totally flat. She switched on a local black radio station, liking to hear the caterwauling jive talk, the soul music. *Almost there.* Rick stirred from sleep. He knew exactly on the trip where they were; his fingers beat time to the music. The sun stood low in the direction of the Mississippi River; and now the sky had a great, wide, open look and alongside the road there were virgin trees; there was a lonesome sense to the emptiness and raw beauty. Laurel remembered in her past standing alone in her Delton house one night and looking out while on a record player behind her Judy Garland sang "Blues in the Night": *a whoo-ee da whooo-ee*. And she had told herself then, I'm going away from this place some day.

She had promised Rick never to say again: It takes as long to get across the state of Tennessee as to get to it from Connecticut. As they rounded Delton on curlicues of concrete that were new since her time, she thought about how many people she knew in the city she was passing, all of them unaware she went by, and she wondered how many of them would have cared; people were so involved with their own lives. They knew little about her life, but she knew their habits. Now, shortly after five o'clock, Delton husbands would be heading home from work. She'd often wondered what couples did with such long evenings; night was well into itself by the time William got home on normal evenings.

In Mississippi, she had to tell Rick again about the entire town of Whitehill being moved back in the forties because of a federal dam being built nearby. This year he thought to ask, "I wonder if they took the water out of the water tower before they moved it?"

That tower was a landmark back in the days she drove down to her grandmother's with her mother, from Delton. Soon, then, they turned off blacktop onto gravel. She longed for those old days, olden days now, when there had not been electricity or running water for years she could remember; what a shadowy, exciting existence it had been, moving from room to room by the light of kerosene lamps. "Let's eat at the Whitehill café," Rick said. "I don't want to have to go to Loma's first thing and get some of her greenish meat."

Laurel parked on Whitehill's town square, where Rick took Buff for a walk. Old men playing checkers in a store observed her in her miniskirt when she got out of the car. She walked past a laundromat where a discreet sign in the window still read, WHITES ONLY. Inside, the café had a bare look. A lot of old newspapers were piled up in the front window, and she picked up one at random. A black cook stood in the kitchen filling the place with smoke and the smell of frying fish. A blond waitress leaned on a partition laughing with her. "Be right with you, hon," she said, turning to Laurel.

She sat down at a table and found her knees ached and were painful from long, cramped hours with the car's air conditioning blowing directly on them. This was the first year she could remember her knees hurting, and she thought, I'm getting older. Maybe arthritis was in her future. She leaned her chin heavily into her hands and wished the county was not dry.

Locally, there was a small paper once a week; Delton papers were the ones people read daily. Out of an old habit, Laurel turned first to the society page. But her Delton friend Catherine had told her so many new people had moved into the city, they were the ones who were written up; she'd been a bit huffy about the people she and Laurel knew, Delton's real society, having been dropped. Laurel joshed herself: could the newcomers get into the country club? When she flipped on idly through pages, she found this was the edition in which Hal MacDonald's article had been printed. She read it again.

Merely to see his name there as author flooded her with memories of downtown Delton in her girlhood. Along Cotton Row above the Mississippi River there was a huge warehouse with bright gold letters reading MACDONALD BROTHERS. Also, the city's tallest building was owned by that family; way up high the name was minuscule; in a park in the center of town a fountain had a plaque noting it was donated by a certain MacDonald, she could not remember who. It had been a name, a family, that pervaded her growing-up; always, she'd longed to have a name so famous everyone where you lived would know it; to have a large important sense of family; to be known over the whole tristate area as they were, in Arkansas, Mississippi, and Tennessee.

"Mom, did you seriously not know I was sitting here?"

"No."

"Christ on a crutch."

"Where'd you get that expression?"

"From your mother."

"Great."

"The waitress waited and just walked away."

Laurel turned then and looked in her direction. "Sorry," she said when the woman returned again, bringing menus.

"That's all right. I just said to myself, said, That woman's reading something mighty innaresting." Then she looked down at the paper where Laurel's hand rested. "Uh-oh," she said. "When all that happened down in the Delta, I told myself then, said, There was more than one finger on the trigger that night. The MacDonalds aren't the kind of folks that go around shooting folks. It's sad all the way around. What looks good to eat?"

They ordered catfish, as always, eagerly, on their return. Though so late at night, Laurel thought uneasily of the meal in her stomach: fried fish, hush puppies, potatoes. Rick was asking for a substitution, fresh beans instead of hush puppies.

She sat looking at her son, wondering why she could not have done the same thing. She knew why: The waitress might not have liked her. Absurdity, she told herself again.

A country man with a loping walk came in wearing khaki clothes. He greeted the black woman cook boisterously, and they went on laughing with one another. "What you been doing, Mister Ken?"

"What I shouldn't-a been doing. What you been up

to, Lucille?" In a while, he swung round on the counter stool. "That your little dog out yonder? She like to tore me up when I passed the car." And he looked speculatively at Laurel from beneath his billed cap, taking in the points of her breasts beneath a knit top and her knees in a short skirt. "You a long way from home." His eyes twinkled, wondering what she was doing here. She bent to the plate the waitress set down.

"Mush," Rick said presently, about his beans.

"You know they still cook them here the old way, all day long."

"Hicks," he commented.

"OK, Dad."

"How many times are you going to read that article?"

"I just can't stop feeling for this man and trying to imagine his life in a Mississippi prison. He went to prep school in the East, it says here. Choate. And to Chapel Hill. He's from one of Delton's most prominent families."

"Prominent how?"

"You know, important. Like Dad's family. Only his is prominent on a worldwide scale. These people have a big plantation in Mississippi. I think I went to a high school sorority party there once."

"What's a sorority?"

"Oh, you Yankee hick. If you grew up in the South you'd know sororities and fraternities are organizations that are great fun if you get into one and break your heart if you don't."

"What's this guy doing in prison?"

Laurel took a bite of food. "He killed his teenaged stepson." It sounded so awful stated baldly.

"What? Why?"

"I don't know why. He's in prison for manslaughter. That means it was not on purpose."

"Jesus." Rick went on eating. She wondered if Hal had done other writing, his article was so beautiful; she would like to find out. "Let's go," Rick said. "There'll be enough light I can still shoot frogs when we get there."

When they stood at the cash register, the waitress said, "You folks not going to eat some of Lucille's homemade pie?" The man swung round on his counter stool again, to rub his knuckles atop Rick's head. "Boy, you better eat you some of that pie and put some meat on them bones."

" 'Bye, hon. Come back to see us, hear," the waitress said.

Rick went out in the country man's loping stride, sticking a toothpick into his mouth. Laurel followed behind, thinking of the times they left restaurants and her mother would be furious about her father having a toothpick wagging in his mouth, not waiting for privacy to pick his teeth. It seemed there had always been some argument to spoil every outing.

The square was dabbled with red from the sign blinking *Café*. They turned from town over the road that was no longer gravel. Or dust; she remembered how dust once rose up in yellow whorls. They passed cabins dotting the roadside that had been there all her life. Now Rick could say, "I've been waving to people in those same cabins ever since I've been coming down here. They don't recognize us in the new car."

Black people sitting on raggedy porches and little children in bare dirt yards waved back anyway. In bottomland along Gray Wolf River a greater darkness had come, ringing with insects. People stood on its banks fishing with long poles. Trees seemed impenetrable in the growing dark. At this point, they always turned off the air conditioner and rolled down the windows. They wanted to smell the sweet scent of a baked evening beginning to cool, to hear cicadas crying their warnings. "You forgot to say clickety-clack," Rick said.

"Oh." They had crossed a small concrete bridge over Gray Wolf River which in her childhood had been two planks laid over a chasm, the brown slow river below; always, the ends of the planks rose and fell with a clatter beneath the car's weight. "Clickety-clack," Laurel said.

"How come you forgot?" Rick said. She would not tell

him another time she was thinking about the article, and told him she was tired.

Between dips in the road, darkness had come. They crested hills and faced the sun going down, always receding from them. She began to sing, "Down de road. Round de bend. I'm just go-o-o-ing home. Tired and blue. We-e-e-ary too. I'm just go-o-o-ing—"

"Mom."

"Sorry about that. I forget you have musical ability."

"Here's my place."

"OK, pup." Laurel drove off the road into the turnrow of a cotton field and slid over, while Rick came around to the driver's seat. He sat up as tall as he possibly could and began to smile. "I wish my friends could see me."

"Honey, you been driving down here since you were eight years old."

"I know it. How come you let me?"

"You wanted to."

"This year I'm driving to town by myself. Gran says she drove everywhere when she was eleven."

"There weren't any laws back then."

"Can I?"

"I guess so. If you just drive from our place to Loma's store. Nobody much cares here what you do."

Town reared up ahead, four small stores with their gas pumps, the lights murky as if they shone through heavy rain. The road they turned off to their cabin was sparsely settled, with few lights at all. They talked about known places and inhabitants: about Mister Zack's cornfield where he kept beer hidden from his wife; about the curve where Rick spun them off the road and down a bank two years ago and only thick kudzu kept them from turning over. He still talked about the fingernail marks she left in his thigh, clutching him as they went. He'd phoned William excitedly with the details, how they slipped off a rain-slick mud road and went in slow motion down an embankment. William asked to speak to her. "For God's sake, Laurel. The boy's ten years old."

"I know it. You're right. He shouldn't be driving." Then they went away from the pay station beside the road, with Rick at the wheel. She had carried with her the sound of teletypes like castanets in William's office and the muffled and elusive sounds of horns on the avenue below him.

Rick turned up a bumpy driveway now between tangled rambler roses with pastureland stretching invisibly into darkness on either side. Faintly, she saw the white faces of cows.

He said, "Can you unpack alone so I can shoot frogs?"

"OK. Look. Buff's sniffing round her same places."

"Will you sit on the car with me for a minute first?"

"I want to get this stuff unpacked while there's still some light."

"Please. And hold my hand."

"All right. But what's up?" As Laurel sat on a fender and reached across the hood for his hand, she could see his face as a dim spot.

"When we go on trips, I pray we're going to get there safe. And now that we've made it, I want to thank God."

"Sure," she whispered. "But you know I get to cry."

She went out onto a small porch later and was unable to make out Rick's figure in the pasture. The pond had disappeared into night; in the porch light she saw shapes of willows brooding toward the water in curvatures. There was no reason to worry about a boy in this countryside, yet it was dark and Rick was gone. He could hit a bull with his BB gun if he had to. She heard its popping every so often and wanted to laugh, it seemed so ineffectual in comparison to the enormous night, the way everything did. After she called him, he spoke to Buff, and soon two dark shapes moved up a path toward her. Rick stood on the lighted porch laughing at her apprehension.

They stretched out afterward on a double bed in the cabin's main room and watched an old movie on TV: *Birdman of Alcatraz*. Suddenly Rick lit up a cigarillo from a pack. "Where did you get those?"

"At that store when you got the car fixed." He insisted she have one.

"I don't think you ought to be smoking," Laurel said. She knew damn well he shouldn't be smoking; why didn't she make him stop? "I shouldn't either."

"I'll quit when I go out west. Mom, I don't want to go out there."

"I don't want you to go either," she said. She did not want to talk up against what William wanted.

"I read a letter from Dad's friend who owns the ski resort. Usually, he hires kids older than me to work on trails in the summer. He said if Dad was so insistent, he'd take me on."

To learn independence; she thought Rick was being taught it too fast, too soon, and felt deprived of him often. But she told herself William must know what was right for a boy, and she did not like to interfere. She did not want scenes. She had the feeling this year William was jealous of her time here alone with Rick. He had said the boy was too old to spend a month alone with his mother in a place like Mississippi, where there was nothing structured for him to do.

"I just want to be here doing nothing, away from Dad's regime."

Laurel considered smoke curling in front of the TV screen; she had no idea Rick considered William in that light, as she did. When they went to a marriage counselor, she told Dr. Silvers, "Living with William is like living with Hitler." And both men laughed. Laughed! She had not said it to be funny; she wanted some change, but nothing happened. She went on in those sessions for a year feeling a strong sense of male bonding. She thought about Rick's believing all those Thursday evenings that his parents went out to have dinner alone. She thought how William had begun flattering Dr. Silvers on his techniques of marriage counseling; they seemed quite unique to him. Wouldn't the doctor like to write an article which he, William, would edit and place in one of the women's magazines his company published? They'd be quite a team, seemed to be his implication; the doctor would be famous. Dr. Silvers preened, agreeing. Laurel, seeing through this scheme, didn't understand why Dr. Silvers couldn't figure it all out: otherwise, why was she paying him money? They stopped the sessions finally because they were costly; and the marriage seemed on its same keel, which was not particularly a bad one; sexless; but how many women in long marriages were in that same boat? But William gave her the impression he wanted Dr. Silvers to choose sides, as if they were in a courtroom and he must say, Mr. Perry is the good guy; she's the bad one. Why did William wish to be so divisive? From the moment she suggested a marriage counselor, he said, "OK. If you pay half." Laurel supposed she was still just that old Southern female who relied on men and had always been around the Southern kind who took it as an affront for women to pay. When they heard later Dr. Silvers got a divorce, those evenings seemed even more a travesty.

"I don't think I'm too old to spend a month riding cows, shooting frogs and snakes, and roaming around pastures."

"I don't think so either," she said. "I think it's good for your soul."

"I think so too," Rick said. "I feel sorry for Soundport kids. But Mom, you know I'm not going to spend summers like this forever."

"Of course not. Someday you'll get married and your wife won't let you."

"I mean seriously. Maybe not by next summer."

"I know. By next summer."

He sat up in front of the TV and looked at her quickly. "Are you crying?"

"No, it's this crazy smoke."

"I don't mean I won't ever come again."

"I know." But these summers were over. She would not want to come to the cabin alone. Would she not see the South again, or for how long? Rick still stayed up close to her, peering into her face.

"Look at the tube, kid," she told him.

When she was in bed in the second room, falling asleep, she returned to thinking about Hal MacDonald and how difficult it must be for him to be in prison but near his plantation and its different life. She thought back to the time she had had a glimpse of him, once in her life. It had been at one of the enormous dinner dances to which she and her sorority sisters were addicted as teenagers. This one was held on the rooftop of Delton's finest hotel, on a level with the stars. If she and Hal had met then, would he have liked her? There was no sense turning the question around, because already she was enthralled by the society he represented, by the aura of the Mississippi plantation where he lived.

While she remembered, the cool swift scent of gardenias came back from the corsage she had worn that evening, though the cabin smelled of mosquito spray. A girl sitting next to her had whispered, "That's Pris MacDonald's brother," her voice as awed as Laurel felt. He went by like a shy shadow, as if looking for someone. Even then she had wanted to meet him. And now she had to meet him because of the inner voice that spoke to her and because of the extraordinary compassion she had for a contemporary locked up. A man from his background, she thought. She would write and ask if she could see him. And what a chance to visit a prison. That night in high school when she saw him, his army uniform had rendered the high school boys in their white dinner jackets innocuous. She had been so impressed she never forgot that moment. On the bandstand Clyde McCoy had been playing "Sugar Blues," and the saxophone wailed.

4

"I don't want to cook blueberry pancakes," Laurel complained midmorning, though mostly she was testing Rick and hoping he'd change his mind.

"It's almost my last day, Mom."

"You've been using that one ever since you got here."

She was probably ruining him for some poor dear girl in the future, but she got out the griddle. Someday, Laurel thought, he would be grown and gone. Her black portable typewriter from college days sat on a table nearly as dilapidated, and by a window overlooking the pasture, which was fatal, since staring out was much easier than making up stories to set down on paper. "Don't disappear. You've got to think about packing."

"I only have to put some stuff in a sack." Rick sat in the kitchen cleaning his gun; she watched a cloth go in and out of the barrel.

"You're not going out west with your clothes in a grocery sack, you hear?"

"All right, already. Are you on the rag or what?"

"Rick!" What did he know about that? She turned gratefully toward the sound of trace chains coming up the driveway. Mister Zack pulled his wagon to a halt outside the door.

"Let's get more peaches, Mom."

She opened the door, releasing them from the staleness of air-conditioning; even in bright heat, the sky had a tender look, the washed-out blue of babies' blankets. Pine trees gave off a single aroma; their needles shone fiercely, like armor. Her hair was still wet from an early morning jog alongside them, to the road's dead end where the federal dam began, with roiling muddy water that looked too thick to stir. An old man had stopped in a vintage car, saying, "Can I give you a lift?" When she answered, "No, thanks. I'm running for my health," he looked perplexed and said, "Oh. I thought you was out of gas somewhere." Now she stared into equally kind old eyes.

"I found some pretty tomatoes on my doorstep this morning," she said. Along about daylight, Mister Zack snuck up and left whatever was plentiful in his garden, melons and vegetables redolent of warm earth. In return, she bought his peaches. "Rick, will you run get me my purse?" He left off feeding sugar cubes to Mister Zack's horses.

Mister Zack grinned, holding up from the wagon's bed a string of iridescent catfish. "Been to the dam fishing. Pretty peaceful there. No womenfolks chattering. They all gone to Nashtoba because of a price war 'tween the Piggly-Wiggly and the Jitney Jungle. Can that boy clean a mess of fish?"

"Sure. He's learned this summer and he's got a new knife." Where was Rick? At that moment she knew he was reading her unfinished letter to Hal MacDonald. It was on the desk by her purse.

When he came back, Rick's face had a look similar to William's sometimes, angry about a decision made contrary to what he thought. She spoke cheerily, as if to avoid forever any mention of that letter. "Rick's leaving soon so

I can't use many peaches. But I could take Allie some."

"Lord, got'cha. I forgot. Sugar, she bought some. And said tell you and the boy come over this evening, she's turning a freezer of peach cream." Mister Zack seemed petulant as a child, the way men do when something goes against their grain. "Womenfolks don't want to make their own cream no more. They buy it, and that sto'-bought stuff makes me gassy."

"We're filled with gas right now from turnip greens."

"Rick."

He pretended innocence. "Ardella talks about that in the post office," he said.

"It's not exactly what Dad would consider polite conversation."

"Greens'll do it to you too," Mister Zack agreed.

She and Rick smiled as the specter of William passed between them. "See you at Allie's." Raising his reins, Mister Zack set his trace chains jingling. As the sound diminished, Rick said, "What's with writing some joker in prison?"

"He's not a joker."

"What's this bad period you're going through in your life?"

"Oh, you know. The usual. How to write about the South when I live in the East."

"That's not it. Dad's not going to like this."

"Not like my writing to a man locked up behind bars? Don't be silly."

"What's with you and Dad anyhow? What were you on the rag with Gran about him before we left? Saying Will-yum"; again, he aped, "Will-yum."

Had she sounded that bad? "I dont' know what you're talking about."

"Yes, you do." Before she understood what was happening, Rick raised the twenty-two and shot—*spling!*—through the other two rooms of the house. She watched holes splatter the far walls, thinking in the midst of fear and fury that she would have to have those repaired. Her feet seemed to be dancing as if she were keeping them out of the way of the sound as he shot again, and she went on crying, "Stop!"—though he shot first her tennis hat sitting on a table, and she watched it jump, jumping like a frog. "Why did you do that?"

He went out the door not saying anything. She started after him, but stopped. "I hope puberty is not going to be as bad as they tell me it is," she called.

In his raggedy T-shirt, Rick's shoulders shook with laughter; Laurel saw the tall, slim-waisted man he would become. It was frightening to think of things that could happen between them.

She signed her name to the letter.

July 17

Dear Hal:

I was glad to hear from you, and a number of things went through my mind. It was a surprise to receive that printed stationery with instructions on the back. There was nothing on the list of things people can send you I could imagine you lacked—socks, checks, handkerchiefs? I'll have to send you moral support or books to break up the monotony.

Do they really only let you have family as visitors? Today is a third Sunday and I wonder if you are having a picnic under your mimosa. This is a rather bad period in my life too, and I wish I could sit there and talk to you.

My thirteen-year-old son is here with me but is soon going west. He adores Mississippi. But I'm afraid this may be the last summer he's going to come where there is so little to do of a sophisticated nature; he spends time now trying to ride cows, shooting snakes, dissecting frogs, blowing up things with firecrackers, which he can't have in the East, and just roaming around in general with a BB gun which he can't have at home either; he's acquired a twenty-two but can only shoot it at targets in the pasture. I tell him there are places in Mississippi, like the Delta, where more is going on than old men sitting on store porches playing checkers, but he's yet to see anything else. Once he's gone, I'll spend most of my time alone in a somewhat remote rundown cabin. Sometimes I feel a bit scared, though I have a little mutt who's a tough watchdog, and I get a bit lonely. However, I decided this is what I want to do so can't complain. I think solitude's good for a writer's soul.

Is it possible for me to come there? I have a list of books I'd send, but I don't know if you like to read.

I thought, at first, that was a rosebud printed on the stationery and I wondered, How incongruous can they get? But I've decided it's a cotton boll. I'll be here till shortly after Labor Day and hope to hear from you again.

Laurel

Women went on vacations, but housework followed. She complained about the piddling things she had to do. There was a nice feeling, though, when the griddle was clean and the warped floors swept. Even as the toilet bowl came clean, she gave a nod of approval. She took down Rick's clothes from a clothesline outdoors. Their clean scent seemed a compliment. She did not mind crinkled, reddened hands. Maybe she should only have been a housewife; she did not knock the profession. She watched the cabin's owner, Clarence Lee, out in the pasture castrating bulls in his homemade stockade. She hated the single sharp, surprised bellow. Why did he have to do this so often? Maybe Mabel cut off his balls at home. He often made a fire and suggested Laurel join him for "prairie oysters," a delicacy served down at Neiman-Marcus, he said; she declined. She inverted Rick's socks into one another after finding them mates. *I was trained to do nothing in this world after Miss Poindexter's School for Girls and a liberal arts college education,* she thought.

Even so, one thing she could never have done was return to Delton as an unwed mother. She could never have told her parents she was pregnant. What would have happened back in Greenwich Village if William had not stood by her? William did not have his usual humor when he brought up the night he assumed she got pregnant. The night she let the douche bag slip off the shower rod and fall on her head, he said. She might have been amused, but William held grudges. He'd never forget, he had said, with his look later thunderous, how she came crying out of the bathroom with her hair sopping wet.

She did not chastise William for the time back in that same Village apartment when he almost made her electrocute herself. She told him by phone the light in her closet was out and she did not know whether the current was on or off. "Well, stand in a bucket of water," he had said. Later, she told him it had been too much trouble to borrow a bucket and fill it, so she just changed the bulb. "Jesus Christ," William had said.

Before knowing William, she had begun sitting in her Village apartment occasionally cradling an imaginary infant in her arms, completely taken by surprise by her longing for a baby. Married to William, at her first dinner party at his mother's when Laurel was passed a dish, she had asked, "What's this?" A startled look crossed Mrs. Perry's face before she answered, "Chutney." It did not matter much that Mrs. Perry showed obvious surprise at her daughter-in-law's ignorance. When she needed Mrs. Perry, her mother-in-law had proved herself a champion. She wrote to apologize about the embarrassment of the baby coming too soon, and Mrs. Perry replied by special delivery she'd personally punch in the snout anyone who mentioned the date of that child's birth. Her own mother wrote that Laurel always had been selfish and had taken away any joy in her being a grandmother for the first time.

Laurel watched Rick come along with a snake draped over the barrel of his gun. She was grateful for his different past. As a toddler he knew already the fork and spoon at the top of his plate were for dessert, a practice she had learned in Boston. But when she realized her mother had brought herself up out of this countryside, Laurel had more compassion.

She recalled a formal dinner party in Delton when she was of college age, when a white-coated black man presented the entrée on a silver platter. She had served herself and felt him stand behind her rearranging the serving utensils she had replaced incorrectly. But she had felt everyone else at that table was watching. The party had been held at the home of someone kin to Hal MacDonald, one of those wide-ranging tangled Southern relationships, because she remembered the host's first name was MacDonald.

As they drove along the Mississippi roads to Allie's ice cream party, Laurel considered that most of her life she had felt herself heading upstream, alone. Often, she wondered that people she dealt with in publishing did not see down to her true, ignorant, inner depth. So long had she lived, when she was young, in an environment without culture that there was no way she could catch up. She remembered, though, when she and William married and he started his job at Events-Empire, he'd stood with his briefcase, saying, "I'm going somewhere in this world, and you can come along or not." She had looked at him in silence, thinking she'd arrived somewhere already and did not see why he might think she'd lag behind. However, it did not seem a wifely comment.

She and Rick stopped on the way for Miss Mamie's famous mousetrap cheese, but also because a van was parked near the store saying county dogs could be vaccinated there. An elderly gray-haired black man came out, holding a big dog on a rope with a collar saying *King*. "We gone to the dawgs today," he called out. Inside, Miss Mamie was disappointed about cutting her cheese; it kept crumbling. "It hasn't been out of the box long enough. And honey, I wanted it to look so nice for you." Laurel and Rick enjoyed her handmade signs: for sale she had Hair Gromer and Congeled Salad. "A long way from Soundport," he said, coming outside. They drove on eating crumbly cheese Miss Mamie wouldn't take money for, enjoying it, as Buff did. Rabbits made crazy running patterns all down the roads, between ditches laden with kudzu. When they went up to Allie's, widows of Laurel's uncles were sitting under oak trees; they had never seemed anything but blood kin. Sitting on the ground, Laurel suddenly asked what her mother had been like as a girl here.

Her Aunt Letty said, "Kate was the prettiest girl I ever laid my eyes on."

"And couldn't she play the organ. Lord have mercy," said Old Man Agnew, from down the road.

"I thought she only played the piano," Laurel said.

"Honey, she played the organ at both our churches for funerals. When Kate pumped that organ and struck into 'The World is Waiting for the Sunrise,' there was not a dry eye."

"Girl." Her Uncle Tate broke in eventually. "You keep listening to this talk, and that cream's been ready. Come on, you dawgs, and get yours." He set down two bowls full. His dog and Buff came up out of the shade of a crepe myrtle.

"Don't let none of the dogs roaming around get into them peach pits you got out back," A. T. Murray said. "Ain't no sight worse in this world than seeing a dog trying to pass a peach pit."

"Hush your mouth," Allie said, laughing.

"All this mud." Tate continued to talk about farming. "My cotton picker and my combine both are laid up from mud. Their transmissions are strained. Man called and wanted to know if I was coming to grange meeting tomorrow. Said they were going to talk about cotton. I said, Shoot, I don't want to talk about cotton."

"The cost of insurance and the cost of fixing equipment, they're going to eat you up," Sam Upchurch said. He was a black friend who happened along in time for ice cream. "Fields about dried out. I hoped and prayed and watched. And nothing to do but talk about the weather. A man might try not to think about it, but that crop is out there."

"Sometimes," said Tate, "I get in my truck and I start riding. Riding like I could do something about it all, or change things." He laughed. "Only thing that changes is, I end up in a turnrow and having a bill for my truck's transmission too. Always there is next year." He looked off to the road, and Laurel watched all the others look the same direction. "But last year my beans lay in that field *so* long," he said.

"You and me is just outdated, Mister Tate," Sam said.

"Look over there," said Allie. "Loma's out on her store porch trying to see what we're doing. She knows if we're turning cream you won't be buying Smoky his popsicle today. That dog's going to end up with worms and bad teeth both."

"Smoky wants his popsicle, don't you, boy." Tate rubbed the dog's ears.

"Loma going to be giving her produce away if that price war don't end," Agnew's wife said.

"Small storekeepers are just as obsolete as the small farmer," Sam said. A boy in shorts emerged through hedges holding a small melon. "Boy, what you got?" Sam said to his grandchild.

"Found a wallermelon."

"You ain't found nothing. That's Mister Tate's. Carry it on back where you got it."

"We don't need that melon," Tate said. "Tony, carry it on home."

"Sam, I've got cream dished up for Fanny, too," Allie said. "Get home before it melts."

Soon the party broke up. People went away in pickups or cars, and a few ambled off down the roadside.

Mister Zack accepted a ride from Laurel and asked to be let out at his garden. "Going to have a beer?" she said.

"You want one?" He winked.

"No, thanks." She had not thought about a drink since the night they arrived.

"You and the boy always looking around. Come on out the New Africa Road to my tent revival."

Tent, New Africa; the words held magic. She and Rick looked at one another. "We'll be there," Laurel said.

At night, the open-sided tent appeared to be a carousel from a distance; the interior was aglow from a butane light and people swarmed about. A little of that day's broad blue light was still in the sky, and, using it, she parked along the road's shoulder, among a conglomeration of vehicles. Already a wailing kind of singing was going on, and music from strummed instruments. In the short time it took her to park, the early night sky became less silver. In the silence following the cessation of harsh sounds within the tent, they heard the mellifluous lowing of cows watching from behind nearby barbed wire, their nighttime peacefulness shattered. She and Rick laughed. As they approached the tent, Mister Zack lounged outside, talking to another man, and turned, grinning in delight, almost as if he was waiting, waiting there each night to see if she was coming. Laurel resented this; he seemed to feel some claim to her. But maybe this feeling was only obstinacy in her personality: if wanted, she declined; if not wanted, she sought. Something of that in most people, she thought. He introduced them to the preacher, Brother Roundtree, whose diamond stickpin caught the last silvery light and glittered in the early dark. When Mister Zack introduced them as his visitors from up the country—from New York—she decided maybe his attitude was pride, not ownership. She squinted to read a penciled sign tacked to a slit of board outside the tent: FAITH HEALING. ALL INVIDED.

"What kind of religion is this?" she said.

"It's a know-so religion." Brother Roundtree spoke as loudly as if he were already preaching. "Everything about it, the people know is so."

"Pray till you are saved." Mister Zack grinned.

They went on into the stifling heat inside the tent. She and Rick found two folding chairs together in one row. People put out hands kindly to help them crawl past their knees. "Thanks," they each kept saying. They were recognized as strangers.

A simple wooden platform stood at one end of the tent. There musicians sat playing heartily, their shirts already dampened in dark soaked places. Brother Roundtree came inside and leaped to the platform, long-legged and stiff. He rattled a tambourine above his head. In front of Laurel a little girl was asleep with fingers curled into her mouth. She wore a quaint long dress down to her ankles, too young to speak up and complain, I'm made to look strange. Laurel felt for her. She tried to imagine herself in childhood that way, able to sleep amid so much noise. She tried to remember Rick that young.

A blond woman sat next to her, who might not be so old. But her face was deeply lined. Her stomach was pouched, though not from pregnancy, Laurel could tell that. Something amiss about the shape bothered her. Maybe just a country woman old before her time, not knowledgeable about keeping in shape, the way Laurel herself jogged and worked out. The woman handed her her own songbook, though Laurel tried to protest. She had another one to use, the woman indicated, leaning to the man beside her, his book on his knees. Her husband. He was a tall blond giant. She could see his curly hair, his handsome profile. "Last week we got rained out," the woman said. Laurel looked up at the tent top as the woman did; it was full of holes. "One night some niggers come and stood out there." The woman nodded toward the dark. "Brother Roundtree prayed and they didn't come no more." Laurel stared down at the songbook titled *Heavenly High Hymns*. She opened it and saw old-fashioned shaped notes. The musicians ceased when the people began to sing, a dry cacophonous nasal wailing; soon she realized these were people she had always heard referred to as Holy Rollers.

Mister Zack seemed different not wearing his usual khaki work clothes. His attempt to be a town man did not fit him. He was all wrong in a loose shirt with red flowers—hibiscus, maybe—and pants of a shiny material. He had come into the tent and looked sharply about for her. She hid her face, looking at her shoes in the grass and the dust. Yet she knew the look of disappointment on his face when he realized there was no place for him beside her. He stood staring slack-mouthed toward her. "What's with Mister Zack?" Rick said.

"Nothing," she said. She had the sense suddenly of how little Rick knew. He's only a boy, she thought. What had Mister Zack thought could take place with Rick here?

Brother Roundtree spoke closely into a microphone, like a carnival barker. "I'm no high-educated man. I'm a little self."

"So are we all, Brother, so are we all," a man shouted.

Brother Roundtree rattled his tambourine. "Once I was full of denial," he cried. "But, people, I run aground in sin. I stood there then and said, I'm just a little ole widow's boy and I'm lost, God. I'm lost."

"Go, preacher," "Tell us about it." "Praise the Lord!" People cried out from here and there. Now they began to shove themselves forward in their seats. Their feet tapped silently the ground. Brother Roundtree when he shouted rang the tambourine above his head. It seemed it would shed its tinny pieces. "A lot of you are trying to satisfy lust of the flesh," he cried. "You need to be borned again. You need to be submerged in that water. And if one of your hands don't go under, I'll push you down. I believe in submersion, folks. But baptism don't wash away sins. What Amurricuh needs today is more old-fashioned praying Mommas and Daddies. If you don't feel nothing tonight you ain't got nothing. The main thing is Jesus." The tambourine beat the air and the musicians twanged and strummed. In a moment of silence before Roundtree could speak, the cows across the way mooed out loudly. She felt Rick's elbow, smaller than her own, nudge hers and knew a moment of compatibility and sharing.

"Hallelujah!" people cried.

Brother Roundtree said, "Jesus Christ is the same yesterday and today and tomorrow. It's all based on personal revelation. God knows where you live and who you are. He don't get me mixed up with you. Jesus is not to destroy life but to give it. Oh, don't you love him." He leaped into the air three times and then turned around in a circle and stood with one leg extended stiffly before him so that the flat of his foot faced the congregation. "I know I got something in my shoes besides my feet, people. I feel it all over." He wiggled his knees together, as in an old dance. Like the Charleston. They shimmied and shook. She almost wanted to laugh. "I felt that," he said. "If you don't feel that, you're dead. I don't believe in a half-baked cake. Oh, don't you love Jesus. Things I once hated I now love. I know it's great to be here. Come up and confess to Jesus."

The blond woman stood up. Laurel moved her knees for her to pass. She had the blond giant in tow, like a big shaggy dog. Laurel looked again at the grim old-woman face, though her arms were smooth; she had seen that as the woman passed. Her husband looked so much younger, a man who could appeal to women anywhere. She felt again fear of the future, as a woman growing older while William would have the appeal of an older man to a young woman. A successful man, an executive.

The man stood on the platform beside his wife with his same air of obedience. She continued to have her grim look of satisfaction, nodding to him to begin. He held up a bandaged arm. "Last night I was burned so bad the doctor said I wouldn't get out of bed for a week. But my wife sent for Brother Roundtree, and he and my wife and me prayed. In a while I got up and eat supper. Thirty-six years I lived for the devil and four for God. Pray for us while we sing a song."

"Ever' time I do a deed I shouldn't do, I just steal away and I pray," they sang, in their twanging, nasal way.

"Y'all pray for me, and I'll do a lot better than I been doing."

His wife came away ahead of him, her smile fixed, her hands resting on the protrusion of stomach. He wouldn't leave her because she looked like that, Laurel thought. An old man ran forward and knelt on the piece of rug below the platform. "I tithed," he testified. "And I bought some property. I stopped tithing and I lost it. I sold a lot of cows and didn't tithe and I come out owing the gover'ment."

Another old man took his place. "Back yonder when I got married I didn't really mean it. But that was fifty years ago. When I got the Holy Ghost they didn't think it would last. But if I can make fifteen more days, it'll be forty years since I took a dose of medicine or had a habit. You got to take a stand."

People cried and shouted. "Praise the Lord. Hallelujah."

Brother Roundtree sent the tambourine down into the congregation for collection. "Amurricuh has turned into a slipping place," he called. "People are slipping around into cafés and beer joints and into the arms of other people's husbands and wives. Niggers are following anti-Christ. They hate the whites. We got to pray."

"Remember me in this prayer." A fat boy ran forward and knelt on the rug. "I been sick in body." He began to shake and sob. Brother Roundtree started speaking in an unintelligible tongue that sounded like gibberish. People rose in a quiet manner and went forward to lay their hands on the boy's shaking back. "God touched my body," he said, raising his head. "Thank you, Jesus. Thank you, God."

"Oh, if you are with me," Brother Roundtree said, "reach up your hand and wave. Wave to Jesus, people. I love things of this world. I'm a servant of sin, I told him. Don't leave me the way I am, I cried. Oh, don't you love him. Your heart has only one doorknob and it's on the inside. Jesus said, I stand and I knock. Open. And you're borned again. I said, Will you ta-ake me as a potter takes clay?"

People waved their hands in the congregation. She felt the fluttering, a small breeze. It was better than the inadequate cardboard fans that had been going all evening. Sweat ran everywhere all over her. Oh, won't he take me too? Laurel thought. It would be so much easier to be molded, shaped, and formed by someone else, to have decisions taken from her hands. Not to make her own. I surrender, she wanted to say. I believe. She wanted to run forward, too, before the people, and restrained herself. You had to behave properly. You had to go by rules and behave politely according to the society to which you belonged. Yet here she sat with her hand waving high toward the tent top, waving to Jesus. Signaling with all her might, as if to be known one out of so many people. She felt Rick stiffen beside her. She caught from the side of her eye a glimpse of him as he had turned first to laugh, thinking she jested, and realized his mother sat waving to Jesus in some seriousness of her own. She saw his face staring ahead; she saw a white line appear at his mouth.

"Let the Holy Ghost take holt of the reins," Brother Roundtree cried. The tambourine rang. The musicians bent forward to their instruments, between their knees, their heads low. Brother Roundtree flew around again in his spinning circle, ending with one leg stretched out with the flat of his foot toward them. "God don't have any problems. But he's got the solution to yours."

"I'm satis-fied with my Master. But is he satis-fied with me?" people sang.

He cried above them, "If nobody loves you, God does."

"Yes, glory to come," said a cracked voice behind Laurel, which she thought only she heard.

She went out between the crowd, and people put out their hands to greet her. "Come again," they said. "Welcome." She was out by the road then, where the cows had hushed into silence, or slept because it was that late hour of the night. Suddenly she realized Rick was not with her. When she turned to a hand gripping her hard by the elbow, it was not him. She saw the red flowers. "Where your boy gone?" Mister Zack said.

"I don't know," she said.

"You been gone from your husband a long time. You must be about ready." Laurel thought of the summers before when Mister Zack had spoken of William as "the husband you're trying to lose." She had wanted to laugh at that too, thinking herself and William as superior to country people who did not take separate vacations. "You ever do anything out of the family way?" he said.

Laurel felt quite alone on the shoulder of the road, abandoned to the night and the strange setting. She had a premonition about being a woman alone in the world, a woman without a man protectorate. A husband; it gave you identity, attachment, safety. It was something she needed. It was not Mister Zack's audacity that surprised her as much as his acceptance of the fact she'd go to bed with him, that there was no reason for her to object to him personally. She was not able to speak before he said, "I could give you ten dollars."

"No, I'm sorry," she said.

"Twenty-five?"

She shook her head.

"Fifty? Well, I can't go no higher than that," he said sadly when she again shook her head. He went off into the darkness. Fifty dollars? she had considered for a moment. There were actually things she could use that much money for. She was startled that such a thought crossed her mind. You got to take a stand, Laurel told herself abruptly. She turned in the darkness, feeling deserted on the road. Cars and trucks drove away. Only the stars seemed settled.

"Rick, where were you?" She felt dependent on this boy coming along the road toward her.

"I went to see who was out there on a bank toward the end, watching."

"Who?"

"Some black guys."

"What were they doing?"

"Laughing."

"It's their turn," Laurel said.

They drove back toward the cabin, pine trees whispering in the nightside. She said, "Well, people have a right to their own ideas about religion. Last Easter at our church in Soundport we had a trumpet solo and some of the older people objected. They weren't used to that instrument in church." She thought back to that sound and began to sing, "Christ is risen. Is ri-sen toda-a-ay."

"Mom," Rick said.

"Sorry about that. Shucks, I been borned again and I still can't carry a tune."

"Why did you act like that?" he said.

"What," she said, "waving to Jesus? I felt it. I believed."

She turned off the main road, toward their road home. Only it was not home. Home was more than a thousand miles away. She wondered if she had been right to bring him here these summers, to let him see a way people lived that had nothing to do with his life at all. What right had she to change his existence? At what moment could she possibly shatter his world and tell him of her decision? She went up to the cabin with a sense of foreboding about its emptiness. She opened the door without a key, because it had no lock. Out in the country there was not yet fear of strangers, coming to rob you in the night and take away what you possessed.

5

Rick might have been a refugee child shipped off somewhere, he had so few possessions. Maybe a sack would have been all right, Laurel thought. When he threw his sea bag to his shoulder, it half collapsed. At the Delton airport's magazine stand, he inquired how many boxing magazines he could buy. "As many as you want," she told him. While she watched Rick, she thought of a visit they made here when he was five, before it became a regular trip with them. William had insisted she could not research a novel with a child to take care of, and insisted Rick be sent back to him when he had his vacation. She set Rick out at the terminal with his luggage and told him she was parking, a few feet away. But misunderstanding, he said, " 'Bye, Mommy."

"Rick," she had called then, stopping the car. And so long ago, she'd already thought he was taught too much independence. She well imagined the child, at five, going inside and departing. William was admirable in wanting her to succeed, in agreeing to take care of the child by himself. She had worried that other mothers she knew were not making research trips. But when the plane took off, she had a surge of relief about being alone, a startling new sense of freedom about being responsible to no one but herself. That time, when she turned Rick over to the stewardess for safekeeping, she had said, "His father's meeting him in New York," and had been teary at the thought of Rick flying away alone. The young woman with her perfectly painted face gave her a quick look and Laurel read her thought: divorce. She had tried to imagine parents regularly shipping a child back and forth between themselves, like air freight.

"See you in Connecticut, Rick."

"Mom, don't drive so fast the rest of the summer. And I'm sorry about that hat."

"It's OK. If I die of a heat stroke playing tennis today, don't worry about it."

"Some black guys are giving you the once-over. I don't like it."

"I shouldn't have worn my tennis dress to the airport. It's not Delton etiquette. Most women I know here put on heels and stockings when they get up in the morning. Rick, you've got to change your underw—"

"*Basta.*" He put a hand to her mouth.

"Other mothers get to say things like that."

"You don't want to be other mothers."

"Yes, I do. You and Dad are always trying to make me different."

She passed the young black men waiting in a ticket line, who gave her another once-over; she had to smile at their joviality and would like to set straight any Yankee who tried to say the South had not changed. She wondered what it would be like to sleep with a black man. She believed old Southern legends were crap—that black men were more sexually powerful, that white maidens secretly coveted them, and vice versa. She was amused by a small plot of ground outside the terminal, with a few green plants and a sign:

YES, IT'S COTTON. Tired attendants must answer a lot of questions from people like Soundporters, who stepped off planes looking for cotton fields and put-upon bedraggled darkies; but who from Soundport would even come to Delton?

Confronting the maze of parking lots with cars shimmering in the heat, unable to remember where she had parked, Laurel searched until she was ready to cry out to anyone who passed, "Have you seen a car with a Connecticut license plate?" Then she found it by mistake.

This time, too, she had a sense of elation about having no one to see about but herself; Buff was pretty self-sufficient. She would not like freedom as a permanent condition, Laurel thought. She still worried about the time she spent at the typewriter when Rick was a baby, the hours he was told to stay out of her office. Once when he was two, he passed her at her desk and looked at himself in a full-length mirror in an adjoining room. "Get away, Rick. I'm working," she heard him say to himself. Up she flew from the typewriter to ask William whether Rick would some day be complaining to a psychiatrist about her. Calling her a machine, she thought, the way William spoke of his own mother.

It was William who had set her office hours and said nothing must interrupt them. And because of that, the time William broke his own rule her first thought had been annoyance. She remembered his sitting down in her office saying, "Laurel, we need to talk about what's wrong," and she left her fingertips poised on the keys, waiting for him to leave: thinking then, William, you made the rules; you could have talked to me later. Anyway, then she did not see all that much wrong with the marriage; they never argued. What she believed was that William had a disgruntlement in his personality and would have been disgruntled in any marriage. She only waited there to listen; to this day, she couldn't remember anything that was said. She had the idea that William got up finally and walked out. Only in her mind's eye she saw him twirling a brown hat with a darker band in his hands, and she could not recall William's ever owning such a hat. So how much is memory worth?

Laurel pulled into the Delton Country Club, no longer as it was in the past; now the charming old place, wicker rockers on its wide porches, had been replaced by a yellow brick building low to the ground that could be anywhere in the country.

At least today she did not have to worry about older ladies saying, But who are your parents, dear? Where did they come from? as had happened to her in another time. Laurel went toward tennis courts reflecting sunlight as brightly as mirrors; eventually she complimented the other players on their stamina. Along with the ball crossing the net, she saw pink and green stars. Catherine laughed. "You know if we didn't play in heat, we wouldn't have many weeks to play." In Soundport, anyone playing tennis in such weather would have been considered crazy.

The club today made her think about Sallie Mac-Donald, née Parker, who had made a famous debut there when her clothes, flowers, decorations, and food had been pink; she had worn a little silver tiara. What had happened to Sallie and Hal that two people born with everything had their lives come to tragedy? Having known Sallie at Miss Poindexter's, she could imagine she had continued to be a debutante since then. Probably she still wore Vaseline on her eyelids and stuck cotton balls soaked in perfume into her cleavage as girls did in those days. But she had a different concept of Hal after his article and his letter. She thought of him as deep, sincere, smoking a pipe, his hand resting on the head of a trusty hunting dog. At Catherine's house after tennis, she had her first drink since leaving Soundport. "Some refinements of city living are nice." She raised her vodka and tonic. When she left, Catherine's husband insisted on walking her to her car. It was irritating to have him take her elbow as if she could not walk down steps by herself. "I can go alone, Henry," she said.

"I know that, but can't I be a gentleman?" Henry leaned to her car window. "Where exactly is your cabin? I have to see a man in Whitehill about some lumber next Friday."

Was she going to have an affair with her best friend's husband? Laurel did not want to be that kind of person. Yet always she wanted adventure of any kind: After her long, dry years with William, it was nice to be wanted. She gave Henry directions.

On the way to Mississippi, she regretted that date. There was no way to break it; to phone Henry's office, she'd have to give her name to his secretary. There was too much possibility in the intimacy of Delton that the secretary would tell Catherine her Connecticut friend phoned Henry, in an entirely innocent way. Never but once had William exhibited jealousy. But then, she never flirted; she didn't know how. William used her typewriter and found a poem on her desk. "What's this?" She told him it was a poem she wrote because it had occurred to her. "Oh. I thought you were writing it to some guy." It had been a love poem to Edward. William was so unjealous, in fact, that after a month's skiing trip, he looked at her in her slip, her figure slimmed to perfection, and said, "I didn't know you had such a good body. You could make money off a figure like that." She always thought William was suggesting high class prostitution, and that he'd be glad to share in the profits, due to the stringency of a magazine salary and the high cost of living in Fairfield County. William had asked her never to walk around naked; he thought nakedness took away mystery. Laurel could not have been so immodest, but thought they had enough mystery.

Arriving back at the cabin, she wished she had never told Rick the old country belief that hanging a rattlesnake over a fence would cause it to rain; he had left her a legacy of dried ones.

By morning, she could regret freedom; there was an emptiness to waking alone. She talked to Buff and was glad to get to town for the mail. Miss Ardella, the postmistress, said, "You caught one this morning, sugar." She told her Mose Hathaway had been in talking about that woman always running for her health. "She looks healthy to me," he said. Laurel did not stay to talk. She left the post office thinking of important milestones that happened here; here she had received a confirming letter from Mr. Woodsum about her suspicions. Now, this morning, she could hope Ardella did not noise it about that Laurel had received mail from the state penitentiary. She had a little thrill about Hal's name with its number being on the front of the envelope—#78063. The paper was of poor quality. On the back of the envelope, she considered again something smudgy as a fingerprint. What headiness in this correspondence.

July 24

Dear Laurel:

I was so happy to hear from you again. I read your book and loved it. The setting was like reading chapters from my own childhood. Before we moved to Mississippi, I used to spend summers there with my paternal grandparents in a similar place. This was back in the thirties, and on Saturdays there were more wagons and buggies around the square than cars and pickups. It was during the Depression, of course. I lived what I call my Tom Sawyer period and it was one of the happiest I've ever known. It sounds like your boy can still get a bit of it, and that's good.

No, there's nothing on that sheet I need. My sister, Pris, keeps me supplied with food, and we draw $5.00 a week for cigarettes and Cokes. The state even gives us two bags of tobacco a week, but I have never learned to roll a cigarette I could smoke. The prison is quite strict about visitors but there is one way you could come to see me. I have a close friend—a free-world person—who is head of AA. He could bring you in with the idea of your writing something about the prison. We could visit a short while and I'd be able to drive around the farm and see the different camps with you. I've done this with a friend from Delton several times. You can phone Buddy Richards here and make arrangements.

Also, if you want to write to me and not have your letter censored, put it in an envelope, seal it with my name on it, and put it in another envelope to Mr. Richards. To settle your mind about this letter, I'm sending it out by him. I have learned there are ways to do about anything you need to if you are just patient. Most of the convicts have a million small ways to make life a little easier.

Last Sunday I had my second visit from Sallie and our small daughter, Tina. It was agony, but only because I let myself hope for something that is apparently not to be. Both times when she's come I've suffered a fit of depression for several days afterward, but like an illness, I get over it.

Each camp is run separately and it depends on the camp sergeant as to how strict or lenient things are. Here we get all the letters we want, but can't write too many, as he has to read them—and he's a slow reader! About your list of books, I love to read and do so every evening despite the noise.

The stationery does have a rosebud on it—in the name of God, I don't know why. It was a shock to me the first time I saw it when I was being processed in the prison hospital. As part of my job, I've redesigned the paper and from now on it will have the state seal on it. Not as esthetic maybe, but not as ridiculous either.

The penitentiary is extremely patriotic, which translates "ridden by politics." I envy your being able to spend time alone in your remote and rundown cabin. One of the greatest pleasures I ever knew was to spend time by myself, and particularly hunting. I've spent whole days in the woods just watching deer and turkeys and have learned to call them up to within a few feet. I love people, but not by the dozens 24 hours a day. That was what nearly drove me wild when I first came here and was locked up in a cage for the first time. Even in jail I was kept separate from the others and had some privacy. I am more used to things now and we are only locked up at night. And I have more freedom as a trusty. Nearly everybody does something in the way of a hobby. There's a lot of woodworking, and convicts sell their handicrafts. I play bagpipes! Every morning I go out to one of the old buses (they are called red houses and are used by the married prisoners and their wives) and practice for an hour. Can you imagine the nerve it took to do that the first time? I guess I'm thought of as something of a character, and no one wants to be the camp nut. Anyway, everybody's gotten used to it and there's no way to play bagpipes quietly. This letter is long, but it's rare I can write to someone who has an interest in what is happening to me who doesn't already know.

There are many things I could tell you about here, without censorship. It's old-fashioned; the camps are old and the furniture crude. Not at all like an installation of the federal government such as we had in the army. Most of the camp officials are old-time prison employees. They believe a convict is here to be punished and that rehabilitation is a waste of time. The superintendent doesn't think this way.

A lot has been done in the past few years to improve things. The whip is still used, though it is discouraged, and drivers don't use them in the fields anymore. Legally, we can get seven licks, but after three it doesn't matter, so they tell me. The mental torture goes on all the time, and there is no way to describe it. I came here determined to do what was expected of me, and more if possible. I decided no amount of insults, degradation, or unpleasant conditions could make me raise a complaint. I've asked for nothing, and received no bad treatment. Actually, I've known real kindness.

Your friend,
Hal

6

Going to the prison was the farthest she had ever gone into the Delta. She knew little about the region except its reputation for rich land and rich people. The land was rich because of the cyclic flooding of the Mississippi River, long years before its hard-won levee system. She had learned about that from her father and his friends. Wistfully, her father spoke about wanting to live in the Delta, and actually in Swan, the town nearest the MacDonalds' plantation. Like most north Mississippians who had made it to the big time—Delton—her mother never wanted to return to anything approximating country. She saw no charm or beauty to it, having lived so long in fear of never escaping the yellow clay hills she came from. "The Delta," her father had said, "where there's the shanty or the palace but no in-between."

Laurel drove along a narrow highway running straight ahead and so flat it was like a plumb line measuring the distance to the oyster-shaped horizon all around. She tried picturing the countryside with Chinese in coolie hats and flat black slippers and thought of these people as forever alien to where they had come, brought here to build the first railroads. The Irish came later. She tried to picture her own ancestor, who was a lieutenant in the American Revolution and who had married an Irish girl. "Any knives, guns, or cameras?"

In a moment, she said, "No," still confronting the past while in this strange present. A boy who had been sitting in a chair at the prison's entrance—only a stopgap bar across a driveway—got up from the chair. "I have to check your trunk and glove compartment." He reached in for her keys. Instantly, she was apprehensive he would find forbidden things in those two places and never believe her innocent. A welter of objects fell out when he opened the glove compartment; an empty can of de-icer barely missed his toes. He eyed a plastic ice scraper and finally asked what the long-handled brush was she had on the back seat. "A snow brush," Laurel said. "I don't know what it's still doing there." Or in the Delta either, she might have added. The boy consulted a roster confirming her appointment and directed her toward the administration building. Relieved, she drove away from the highway and railroad track she had crossed to a small brick building. A fountain spurted in front, and in its base were the largest, fanciest goldfish she had ever seen. But if this was prison, where were the people?

Beyond her there were frame houses, which must be where prison personnel lived; their yards were full of clotheslines and kids' toys and collared dogs roaming around. Why hadn't she cleaned out that glove compartment? she asked herself, like mourning. Her parents were shaking their heads. So often, it seemed, she waited to be berated. In the largesse of silence, this could be anywhere on a peaceful country summer afternoon. She supposed she had expected a scene from an Edward G. Robinson movie, with him and George Raft leading a prison breakout, and she would be propelled into national prominence by some daring role in saving lives. Hadn't she always wanted that—fame of some kind, however minor—because she believed that fame would cause her to be loved? In downtown Delton's heyday the ornate Loew's Palace was where she had pretended to be Shirley Temple dancing down its stately marble steps accompanied by Bill Robinson, while autograph seekers stood on the sidelines. Last summer she and Rick followed another of their rituals and went to a Clint Eastwood movie. The lights came on to reveal not only the seediness of the Palace but their two white faces in a sea of black ones. Pretending to be undisturbed, they went to their car and quickly locked the doors.

"Mom. Were you scared?"

"No. I just thought I ought to be. I did remember my friends kept telling me no white people go downtown in Delton at night. I thought them bigoted. But you find out: no white people go downtown in Delton at night.

"Rick, in high school, Kevin Shea and another couple and I decided one night to visit a black funeral home. We were snickering white teenagers on a lark and walked in saying we wanted to look around. A courtly black man rushed up and said he'd be glad to show us everything. What else could he do? Can you imagine it? He wouldn't have called the police. He was so nice, we were sorry we had come. He was sweating, and the place was dim and spooky, the lights were in red glass holders. He lived upstairs, and I'm sure we scared him coming in. He showed us a room where blood was drained out of people. Bodies were on slabs and had sheets drawn over them. One body had feet sticking out. They were whitish on the bottoms, like chalk was on them. But bluish, too. When we got in the car, nobody said anything. Then I remember Kevin saying, 'Those feet really looked dead. I mean it's like, dead is dead.'"

"Unreal," Rick said.

Her sense of disappointment changed when around the corner a mule appeared pulling a garbage wagon driven by an old black man in a gray-and-white striped prison suit, and who wore a pillbox hat of the same material, as in old movies. Rapture filled her heart.

A middle-aged man in tan perforated shoes came from the administration building and introduced himself as Buddy, Hal's friend. In doffing his hat and calling her "ma'am," he placed himself in a different society from her own. While they walked inside, Laurel made polite conversation, asking if he had always been a friend of the MacDonalds'. "Oh, no, ma'am. I was goggled-eyed like everybody else when they come down from Delton and built that big plantation home. In the middle of the Depression, too, when the rest of us was wearing clothes made of meal sacks and scratching ground to eat. I reckon Mister Mac would have more money today than Croesus if it wasn't for his doctor bills."

"He's sick?"

"No'm, his missus. Most men couldn't have what he's still got, though, and support her habit."

"Habit?" Laurel said.

"Of being sick. I didn't have truck with planters in my line of work. Mister Mac came to Rotary, though, and talked to you nice as any man."

She liked the word *planter* as she had liked the words *cotton farmer*. Images from *Gone with the Wind* readily came to mind.

Buddy showed her to a yellow plastic couch. "I can't get Hal out yet. And we have to see the superintendent first." What did he mean, get him out? The words had a terrible sound and made her want to rush to save Hal from where he was, a female knight to the rescue. "Mister Mac," Buddy was saying, "is a gentleman of the old school. Not many of them left. I believe Hal's trouble has been, he's always been in his daddy's shadow. Then got in with the wrong crowd, got to drinking, married the wrong woman, and you know the rest.

"Hal's stood up to this place better than most men that come up like he has could have done," Buddy continued.

"When he gets out, I believe Hal's going to be his own man. And not his daddy's son any longer."

She nodded in a satisfied and even proprietary way. But why wasn't Hal already his own man at his age? Despite obstacles in *his* way, William had not let himself be overshadowed. Again, she imagined Hal as kindly and too sensitive for his own good, a man without the heart to usurp his father's position. "I think on the outside Hal will stick with AA, too," Buddy said.

"But he's not a real alcoholic."

"Oh, yes, ma'am."

Laurel felt superior. He was not the kind of alcoholic she meant: not a stomp-down, out-and-out drunk. Obviously Buddy was not of Hal's social set, so what did he know of his life before prison?

Along corridors; the building inside was ordinary too. Odd to Laurel that she was walking with Buddy while Hal was elsewhere, and they were waiting to meet. Secretaries looked up from small offices. In William's giant building, there were so many cubicles on the floors she was reminded of a hornet's nest. When William recently quit his job on the travel magazine and took the new one, she was surprised when one of his Boston cousins said, "We'd wondered how long William was going to do something so childish." She had loved William's job and the trips it took them on, only not his office hours. She had tried seeing things through his family's eyes and failed. Had something William sensed from his family led him to change jobs? Did he hear, when his mother broadly proclaimed what an interesting life they led, some false note, possibly read in her eyes words she once asked Laurel: "Is he going to be an Events-Empire hack?" Laurel had brooded over those words as if criticized herself, and in some ways she had been, for without intention Mrs. Perry pointed up the vast difference in the way they saw things.

Remembering the superintendent was enlightened about prison reform, she was glad to meet him. Mr. Grady shook hands warmly too, saying he was glad to have her look around. "We have nothing to hide." She could tell he wanted to help her with an article because of Hal; Mr. Grady seemed anxious to help Hal out, if only to break up prison routine for him. "All the way down here from New York," he said. But Laurel let the remark go; another one she grew tired of all summer. Even her Delton peers seemed to think Connecticut was only part of that larger city; they never realized she lived in a more rural environment than they did.

"Hal's done a real good job on the paper," Mr. Grady said. "He's the first editor we've ever had in this country prison who could read and write."

They laughed and parted company. She waited on the couch while Buddy went to get Hal out, whatever those darksome words meant.

Sandy-haired, he appeared around a corner like a scared rabbit. His hazel eyes sought her here, there. When he saw her, their eyes met briefly, and his own lost a look of confusion, even fear, and he seemed merely shy. Anyone locked up for a year was at a disadvantage; Laurel felt for once she must be in control of a social situation. She stood up, put out her hand, and looked the man straight in the eye as William taught their son. "Hal," she said.

"Hey."

Her knees felt weak. She heard that old Southern expression so seldom. It made her feel at home, but that was ridiculous in this place. Still, the place was bucolic enough to make it more like her home place in the hills than a prison. When Hal spoke that one word, it was with a kind of chuckle in his voice. It deepened over the word and made her feel shivery. She had never heard a voice like it. He was not so tall as she might have wished; but after she had once broken off with a boy because she did not like the socks he wore, she had taught herself not to make superficial judgments. "Buddy'll be here in a minute. We're supposed to wait at his car."

Hal opened the door and stood back, one arm upflung against the doorframe as he waited for her to pass. She went by. Laurel always had the same feeling in such moments—even with a man who was a stranger, in a restaurant or a store, anywhere—a momentary recognition of his maleness and her femaleness. Of necessity, she had to brush by his sleeve lightly. She was surprised he wore a white Oxford-cloth button-down shirt, a familiar look from her courting days to the present; it seemed odd a prisoner had one on. She had the sense, then, when he held open the door, that she was small and helpless, an impression Southern females grew up to rely on. Admittedly, it was one she cherished. But a friend had said she had that awareness of sex even passing beneath the arm of her stepson. Laurel had been glad to find herself similar to other people, something she worried about.

The white shirt and white jeans Hal wore were dazzling in the sunlight; blue stripes down the sides of his pants snaked and swam. He was dressed like the boy at the entrance, and yet there was a difference she could not pinpoint.

The day was so hot mica in the steps might melt. Leaves lagged on the trees, as still as moss. Hal cupped her elbow as they went down steps. Apparently, good breeding outweighed printed warnings on his prison stationery about contact between prisoners and visitors of the opposite sex. She would like to have told him, also, she could walk by herself. As they stopped in the skeletal shade of a mimosa, Laurel recalled his writing her that a certain mimosa was his favorite tree here. "Laurel, not many women would want to visit this prison. I've worried about your reactions."

"Why wouldn't they want to come? I'll like everything." But that seemed an inappropriate statement for where they were, and she made a mess of trying to explain what she did mean.

"My brother-in-law, Pete Rogers, came down one time. He said he was never coming back. He couldn't take the place or seeing me in it." Hal gave his intimate-sounding little chuckle. "Pete spent the day calling where I live my dorm, instead of my cage."

"I know Pete!" Laurel cried that out a little too gladly. She wanted Hal to understand their whole pasts were not dissimilar. She knew people he knew, though she had come to know them later in life. "I dated him one weekend when I was a junior at a college in Washington and he was at Annapolis. In those days, I had to wear a hat and gloves to leave the campus and had to stay on the college floor at the Biltmore, where no boys could come up. Did you used to meet under the clock there?"

"Sure."

"After that, I went to Bard College. Quite a change."

"Went where?"

"Never mind." Laurel felt a renegade again that she had chosen a college no one in Delton had heard of, and wouldn't have gone to if they had heard of it. "Does Pete know I'm here?"

"I didn't tell anyone except Pris. And asked her not to mention it. I hope you won't either. There's talk about me up in Delton, I hear. People are saying I live in a special house here and have no contact with other prisoners."

"That's so *unfair,*" she said. "How do—"

"I think because some guys from Delton who're my friends can come to see me pretty much when they want to. They got interested in a pre-release center Mr. Grady wants to build, and they and their wives are helping to raise money. Politicians won't allocate funds for it because they think this prison is for two things, punishment and profit. People know these guys have dropped in when they want to and have gotten the wrong idea. That's the only reason I can think of for the rumors."

Surely, he must realize a lot of people might like to say unkind things about him; that was not a topic for conversation. "You sure are tan," Laurel said.

"I take a lot of sunbaths out behind my cage."

"I agree with Pete about that name. But I don't understand his not being able to face it here."

"Pete will be the first to tell you he'll only see a movie where Betty Grable's the poor show girl who ends up with a millionaire."

"Oh, those Depression era movies we grew up on. They gave me false notions." Romantic ones about men and women, Laurel added to herself. "Was it Eliot who said people can't stand too much reality?"

"Eliot?"

"Not some Eliot in Delton." She assumed herself teasing. "T.S.?" she ventured. "I only like realistic movies and books. I don't understand wanting to escape, do you?"

"I never have thought anything about it. I've been using an aluminum reflector Pris brought down. Have you tried one of those?"

"No." Laurel did not reveal she no longer sunbathed, wishing to avoid further sunspots, wrinkles, and freckles. Reality seemed a dead subject; she would like to have pursued it. In the silence, she was aware of the uncomfortable heat. Unexpectedly, a dried mimosa pod drifted down to her hair, and Hal removed it. "Thanks," she said softly.

"It's a different day from when we did grow up," he said. "Movies. Everything. The first time I heard my father mention sex, he was driving me to Delton to take a train for prep school. He said there were girls in the world who were not nice and to watch out for them. That poor man stuttered so bad and turned so red trying to say that much, I had to feel sorry for him. Mama, of course, never told me anything."

She said, "We were made to be secretive. So many rules, you had to break them."

"One of those buildings over there is my cage. They're like army barracks and no more uncomfortable. The main trouble is noise. A TV at the top of the room goes constantly. My cage mates' favorite program is Lawrence Welk."

"My husband and I almost never look at TV. I watch

with my son, though. Our favorite—" Why was she telling Hal about her and Rick's special time? Forced to explain, she ended, "Do you like Judy Garland?"

"I don't know enough about the girl's singing to comment."

In this part of the world you were a girl till you died of old age. She had looked at the barracks when he nodded toward it. "They don't care if you just take sunbaths?"

"Why should they care? I've got plenty of time."

"Oh. Sorry," she said, and looked at her feet in the dust.

Buddy took up more than his fair share of space on the front seat. Laurel in the middle tucked her elbows to herself while he drove them along roads in interstices between fields. Going around curves, she swayed and favored Hal's direction. Buddy was still a stranger. His car was air-conditioned but had little time to cool as they stopped so many places, which she visited with Buddy. Hal, as a prisoner, was forced to wait in the car. They were all sweating, and when she swayed against Hal, damp hairs on their arms brushed together. He smelled of mingled sweet scents. William used no men's toilet articles except shaving cream. She did not recall that William sweated, but then people from Boston perspired. In hers and Hal's summer dating days, there was a sense of intimacy to sweating all over one another while necking or dancing, slimily and slickly, like eels.

"Pete coming to the dove hunt this year?" Buddy said.

"He won't come here anymore. Daddy's coming instead and bringing Jiggs." As Hal put an arm to the back of the seat, Laurel felt nestled and held herself stiffly. Hal explained Mr. Grady had invited him on a dove hunt last fall. He had let him ask his friends from Delton who were interested in the pre-release center. "Pete went by Matagorda and brought my Lab. That dog was so glad to see me he almost had a fit."

She smiled over the picture of dog and master reuniting, though inmates on dove hunts was not exactly her concept of prison. She was glad he saw the irony too. Hal laughed. "Grady even let Pete bring my own gun."

"Do many prisoners go on dove hunts?" she asked.

"I'm the only one. The only one with friends who have money, I guess."

"Mr. Grady cares a lot about your position here, Hal," Buddy said.

"He knows I won't run even with a gun in my hands. I'm a prisoner he can trust." Hal looked out into a cornfield where dark, elephant-eared leaves formed shady funnels. "Why do they keep trying, the poor bastards?"

Laurel liked prison lingo: to run would mean to escape. "But no one is guarding."

"You don't think so?" Hal bent forward, pointing to a tripod of white wooden legs. In observing them, she had thought they led up to watchtowers for fires. Now, looking up, she met the eyes of a guard holding a rifle who stood on a widow's walk outside a tower. He seemed that moment to peer directly into her soul. "There are invisible gun lines," Hal said. "Every prisoner knows where they are; he'd better, by God. Step beyond a line, and those guards have the right to shoot without warning."

She thought about the danger in which he must live. She had been naïve to think country peacefulness was what this prison was about. He'd have a lot of inside information he could give her. Inside info, Laurel thought. She got out to visit First Offenders camp with Buddy. Seeing a lot of tow-headed, redneck kids with pale eyes, she thought it rather nice to be back in country where there were mostly people like herself, of Scots-Irish descent. Hal said he had not been put into First Offenders because of the age difference; those boys' music alone would have driven him nuts. A record had been playing loudly. A record made by the prison's own colored band, Buddy had said. A black man was singing, "I'm settin' here on a prison farm. I ain't done no harm. Umm-umm. Settin' here for the rest of my life. All I done was kilt my wife." *Umm-umm,* Laurel went on singing to herself. Hal talked about First Offenders as the camp where there was the most homosexuality. "When I first came here," he said, "an old con named Purvis told me I was lucky not to be in there. I might have been cornholed. That was my introduction to prison. He scared the bejesus out of me." Laurel envisioned her article printed in *The New York Times* magazine section, stunning people because of a woman's sure knowledge of the vicious inner life of a Southern prison. In accepting a Pulitzer Prize for journalism did you have to make a speech?

There were more than twenty thousand acres to the prison. Was Buddy going to show them all? After viewing Maximum Security from a distance, visiting the one women's camp, the firehouse, the dairy, and the hospital, she wearied. Finding she was hungry, she knew something of a loss of freedom when she could not satisfy a whim. Buddy stopped various places on AA business. She and Hal were left alone, but always within Buddy's eyesight. Prison was as bitchy as any small town, he said. When she tried to answer how she'd ended up in the North, she could understand Hal's thinking her moving away strange when his family had owned the same land for three generations and farmed it long before his parents moved to it and built their house. He talked about his life and frequently mentioned Pete. There were humorous anecdotes of their hunting dove, deer, wild turkey, and duck. She knew Pete's sisters would be the same as relatives to Hal, and the people they married, and so on till there was a whole tribe of people feeling kinship one way or another. Poor Rick, his first summer down here, traveled the hills on his bike enumerating houses where he had blood kin, claiming his grandmother's aunt's daughter the way he would a first cousin, having none, the way he had neither an aunt nor an uncle. "People are better off growing where they are planted," her mother often said. "Here we are up here all by ourselves." Mrs. Wynn spoke about the East as if she and Laurel stood alone atop Mount Everest. "And not a soul in the world to come to my funeral."

"I'll come," Laurel always told her cheerily. Privately,

she shared some of her mother's misgivings and fears. Who in Soundport could she count on to fill pews in a church where even the minister would not know who she was? She wondered if only Southerners were so obsessed with burying. When they stopped for Buddy to visit what he called a "colored camp," a black man stepped from the shade of a chinaberry tree and walked to the car to shake Hal's hand. "How you doing today, Mister Little Hal?"

"All right, Eat-um-up." The man moved away. Hal said, "That old boy used to work for us on Matagorda. I ran into him in the commissary here one day. He said he never had expected to meet up with me in prison. I said I never had expected to be here. As you can tell, he got the name because of eating. On the place, the Negroes called Daddy 'Mister Big Hal,' so I got my name." He laughed. "They say when Eat-um-up went to trial for killing his wife, he claimed he killed her by accident. Then the judge leaned down and said, 'Shot your wife four times in the back by accident?' That boy later tried to drown himself in a rain puddle."

She laughed, wondering if the anecdote was true. "I see prison is no equalizer."

"I don't think I follow you."

"You're both inmates and trusties, but he calls you Mister."

"Isn't that the way it should be?"

Laurel was glad Hal laughed. She teased him back, saying he was no better than his redneck cage mates. "Who are all the people in with you?"

"Middle-aged repeaters mostly. There are twenty men in my cage." Then in a moment he said, "Twelve of us have killed someone." She asked a few questions, and he spoke haltingly, telling her about the people in with him. "One man raped his niece and was paroled and raped her again. Another guy got his daughter pregnant. Daughter-daubers, these men are called. In prison, you never ask why a guy is pulling time. Eventually you find out. There's a real social hierarchy. Child molesters are on the bottom.

Most cons won't speak to them. Those guys are so lonely, sometimes I have to feel sorry for them." He lit a cigarette. "My case was different, Laurel. When I came in, I'd received so much publicity, everybody knew who I was. The night I first walked into a cage, a local newscaster was just going off saying I'd been taken to prison that day. Everyone tried not to look at me."

That must have been terrible for you, she was going to say. But a different look had come over Hal's face. He seemed to be grinning to himself. She had no right to criticize him, Laurel thought. It was human nature to enjoy the limelight, even for the wrong reasons; human nature to want it. Hadn't she been warding off imaginary autographs because of her fictionalized tap dancing since she was six years old, preparing her acceptance speech for the Nobel Prize for Literature since she published her first short story? She had been proud coming here today to know the place's most prestigious prisoner, proud not to be some ordinary housewife at home baking cookies.

"We don't have any big-time criminals here," Hal went on. She took notes. "No Mafia or Chicago racketeers. A lot of the guys have robbed filling stations or small-town banks or churches. In case you're interested, I'm told Baptist churches are the ones to hit. I sit around in my cage now talking about stealing the way my friends and I at home sat around talking about farming. At first, I kept my things in a footlocker with a padlock. Then one day a guy bet me he could open the lock quicker with a straightened-out paper clip than I could using the combination. He won. Since then I've never locked it and never had anything stolen. The funny thing is, I like these men. But they'll kill." Hal leaned an elbow on the open car window. He spoke as if to himself. "It's so damned easy to kill a person."

She looked toward the chinaberry tree where Buddy stood talking. She wanted to grab him by the lapels, crying out, What happened, Buddy? What happened out on that plantation that night? But Buddy wouldn't know; there was the possibility even those involved didn't really understand what had happened. She looked down at Hal's hands resting on his knees, at tapered fingers she would call artistic. Their padded tips looked capable only of gentle touching. Her own hands were blunt and square. William called them honest-looking and said they showed the sturdy, good stock she came from. She bent fingers into her palms to hide her nails, always unsightly.

Sitting so long in the heat and waiting for Buddy, she began to find even the crotch of her pants was wet. She suspected this could be because of her closeness to Hal. She thought back to his describing himself as the terrified man who entered the prison one winter night. He was unloaded out of a van full of men, then left to lie on a cot in a processing camp for days believing that was to be his existence for the next nine years; an enforced idleness. One night his cage mate Purvis said, "MacDonald, when you last slept? You ain't spoke to nobody for days. Every time I wake up, I see your cigarette glowing in the dark. You better ask to get out for some air." Instead, they took Hal to the psychiatric camp; he was lucky there was one in this day and time. In times past, men who didn't seem to adjust were called troublemakers. They were taught to conform by being beaten, purged with water hoses, having milk of magnesia thrust down their throats, and being immersed in cold water. He was kept in the psychiatric camp only a short while. There, a psychiatrist had said, "How do we rehabilitate you? A college graduate. And you're no habitual criminal." Hal had ended his article by saying that the first time he heard a hall boy close a cage door behind him, and a lock snap, it was a sound he never got over. Laurel had another thought: she would never have had to go to a psychiatric camp. She grew tougher in exact proportion to however difficult her situation was.

Shortly, Hal said, "What terrified me most about coming here was being locked up with men I knew had raw nerves. These guys' self-control and ability to reason can leave them at any time. I've seen a lot of fistfights break out. They're over quickly. But the fear is getting caught unintentionally in the middle of one. It's strange, but politeness is a way of life in prison. You knock yourself out not to step on someone's toes. We had two fistfights in my cage last night. The guy who's cage boss called the sergeant. Then the man who had done the beating went totally out of control. He and the cage boss went at it. Others joined in. The cage boss ended that fight by hitting the man on top of the scuffle with a metal chair. The man who started it all gave up finally when the cage boss pulled a knife."

"You live in such constant fear?" She thought of how peacefully asleep she had been in the solitude of her cabin. She thought of Hal with awe that he lived as he did, and that he was able to endure it: a man soft-spoken and of gentle breeding. She yearned to spare him everything.

Hal had said, "I'm scared a lot. But not about being hurt. The idea of being killed scares me. I'm determined to avoid trouble. Though, Jesus, it's bound to catch up with you in this place sooner or later. I've learned to turn blind in seconds. I'll take any kind of insult, any kind. Fortunately, I've only had to accept the generally degrading kind free-world people make about all prisoners."

"I'm sure those aren't personal about you."

"I guess not. Everybody here knows I'm not a habitual criminal. The psychiatrists I've seen called mine a crime of passion. Statistically, then, it seems I'm the least likely person ever to commit another crime."

Laurel was relieved, but that was something she'd somehow known all along. She had to tell him, "I certainly do admire you, Hal," meaning the way he handled the situation he was in.

Buddy drove them back toward the administration building. "I can leave you alone in the library till I'm ready to leave the farm."

Laurel felt the day's whole thrust had been toward the time when she and Hal would be alone. She sensed the others had the same thought, and, uneasy, she broke the silence. "Why don't they have you doing agricultural work here with your expertise?"

"Free-world people rent out these fields," Hal said. "They don't want some con giving them advice."

"Local country boys rent out this land," Buddy said. "They don't want big landowners giving them advice, is what it amounts to."

"How many acres is Matagorda?" she said.

"Five thousand."

Wow. "Have you-all been as worried about rain as in that little town where I'm staying? They had a special church service to pray for rain. Last year they prayed for it to stop."

"Has it been that dry?" Hal bent closer to the window to look out. "The crops are a little stunted for this time of year."

A little! Her head was filled with statistics about how awful things were. Prison would cause his sad lethargy; she wanted to rouse him from it by showing her own interest. "What is that crop there? Soy beans or cotton? I don't think I'm ever going to be able to tell the difference."

He looked out the window again. "Those are field peas." Hal spoke in the intimate, chuckling manner she liked. Laurel knew she fell in love that moment over two words, field peas.

After all, here was the man of the soil she had come to see; a farmer. Those two words contained the whole of her Southern past, bringing to mind summers when she woke in a feather bed to find her grandmother already gone to her garden before the sun was too high. She came back in muddied garden shoes and carrying sacks full of warm vegetables and flowers. Country people talked all summer long in soft cadences about the kinds of peas there were: Black-eyed, Lady, Speckled, Crowder. These names filed past in her memory now, evoking the same magic, until in this strange and contradictory place, Laurel finally felt at home.

7

Buddy in his kindly bearlike manner said, "I'll leave you as long as possible." He opened a door into a large sad room. In its center stood a conference table surrounded by chairs. But what is wrong? Laurel wondered, stepping forward over the doorsill. What was wrong, when the room was brightly ringed with books whose shelves met cordially in all the corners? It was the table itself, she decided, in its varnished emptiness, for there were no ashtrays. No one was coming here to convene; nothing of importance would ever be decided here, no secrets shared.

Feeling she owed the room something, she started around to read titles. Hal remained in the doorway in conversation with Buddy, making arrangements. Since these concerned her, she was annoyed that, malelike, they did not think her important enough to be consulted. She went past the bookshelves, her back to the room, and felt like a virgin bride now that she and Hal were to be alone. What were they to talk about further when conversation was not her forte, and what had they in common besides being born in the same city?

Names, Laurel thought, names would surface, as Pete's had, common ground. Southerners always played who-do-you-know-I-know, forming bonds any unlikely place. Hal would have grown up among people whom she came to know through the fluke of going to private school, which changed her life's direction. The hallowed hallways of Miss Poindexter's School for Girls rose up for review in this prison farm. Entering into a new society, how gingerly she had trod, sensitive to the slightest nuances of behavior. By the time she dined at Mrs. Perry's, she'd come a long way.

A click meant the library door closed but, entering, Hal had made no sound. Laurel turned to see him through a nimbus of sunlight as he sat down, deflated; she looked at the smallish man thinking if he were a child she would hug him, saying, Everything will be all right. He made her have that instinct. He looked back at her with a sad, waiting expression, and she thought, What will happen? She needed to start a conversation.

"You have a lot of good books here. Does anybody ever read them?"

"I've never seen anybody come in or out of here."

"You don't?"

"My friends and family keep me supplied with books and subscriptions to everything but the Sears catalog."

"That's nice." He seemed to have a support network of people who also must think his whole situation was a terrible mistake.

"A cousin sent me *The New York Times*." He smiled in recognizing this would be her paper. "I can't say I see too much in it."

"I suppose not when you're in prison. There's even a Eudora Welty here. An old edition. I wish I had it."

"Tell me why I know I should know that name."

"A Mississippi writer."

"I'm an unlettered cotton farmer, Laurel. I don't know

much about literature. But I'm willing to learn. I'm looking forward to the books you're sending."

"Unlettered." She laughed. "You may have read everything at Choate and Chapel Hill. What was your major in college?"

"Spanish history."

"Why that?"

"I had to major in something. The class wasn't filled. I know now I'd have been better off going to Ole Miss and studying agriculture. People like me didn't go there back then. I've been a snob all my life. If I had mentioned it, Mama would have had a fit."

"All of us were snobs," she said. "Would your father have let you go?"

"He wouldn't do anything Mama didn't want. Being in this place has helped me overcome a lot of old attitudes."

"Living in the East helped me. Nobody knew who your parents or grandparents were, and nobody cared. You made it on your own merits as a person."

"That would be a strange way to live, not knowing each other's families. My oldest daughter, Connie, lives in Canada. She's thinking about colleges and I tried to interest her in Ole Miss. She wants to be closer to her mother."

She heard a sadness in his voice. "If she still lived in Mississippi, would you have wanted her to go to Ole Miss?"

"I'd never have considered it."

There was such a distance in the room between them. To sit down at the table opposite him seemed too formal, but to go around it and sit next to him seemed too forward. She stayed by the bookcases. "Have you ever used your major?"

"Never even remembered a damn thing about it. What was the use? No matter what I did in life, I was always coming home to farm Matagorda. That had long been laid out."

"I wonder if my father was ever there?" In explaining how he dynamited ditches and trees on farmland, she wondered if her father would only have been a workman at Matagorda.

"I don't remember that name. I'll ask Daddy. I used to blow stumps on the place myself, with Negro help."

"You used dynamite. Hal!" She heard herself squeal in a ridiculous way, like a cheerleader, and was embarrassed.

He flicked open his cigarette lighter with a thumb, in a masculine manner she admired. Then he sat as he periodically had, in a subdued, silent slump as if waiting for directions. She thought prison would have wrecked his sense of being a man: achiever, doer, director of things around him.

She stood there watching him smoke and could not rid herself of a desire to steal the Welty edition. In this place, she felt she had a right to take it. She wanted to get back at an authority that had put her in a room with bars on the windows. Suppose Hal saw her and was moved to ask, Just who is it you are? Who are your people?

She could not pass off lightly the information that her paternal grandparents had come from a place no one ever heard of in Tennessee, and that her maternal relatives were right up the road in the clay hills. Remember? Once, she had cheated on an algebra exam in high school and passed for the whole year because she made a hundred on that test, sparing herself summer school and a re-exam. How, she had always wondered since then, did you evaluate right and wrong when she had bettered her life by cheating?

"Hal, this room is suffocating. There's no air-conditioning. I can't open any of these windows. Hal?"

He leaped up alertly as if used to being commanded by some female figure of authority—wife, mother, teacher? Hadn't he spoken of his mother as Mama? Laurel thought about playing with dolls, Betsey-Wetsey, in hers and Hal's common childhood days. He would have played with trains, soldiers, guns. Guns! she thought sharply. She remembered some public figure speaking about Lyndon Johnson, saying it was hard to get used to a President who referred to his father as Daddy. She had trained herself in the East not to refer to her daddy; she had been laughed at. My father, she had learned to say, with the elegance of aristocracy. Mrs. Perry, while being honored at a White House reception, ran into Johnson in an elevator. "Laurel," she had said. "He took out a comb and ran it through his hair. 'Got to spruce up for the ladies,' he said." Mrs. Perry had laughed loudly. She could always see the humor of a situation. But there had been something uncouth to Mrs. Perry in the incident, that a man carried a pocket comb at all. Laurel had laughed, saying, "Well, shades of Andrew Jackson."

Hal tapped expertly at the windows and they shot upward. When she complimented him, he said he had learned to do almost everything living on a plantation, particularly carpentry. Then he told her that his first wife, Carla, would not live out in the country. They had had a little bungalow in town. "I can't imagine her not wanting to live on your plantation," she said. Perhaps that was the beginning of differences between them, the reason he left her for Sallie. That, she momentarily thought, was not exactly in his favor. Still, there was appeal to a man who let sexuality overrule his good sense. A stage he would have gone past, since he had matured in prison, according to Buddy. "Oh," she said at a window. "There's that garbage man again. Why does he have on those clothes?"

Beside her, Hal said, "That old man's been pulling time here most of his life. They changed the uniforms, but he wouldn't give up his old ringarounds. He could be paroled, but he won't go before the board. Says he wouldn't know how to live in the free world. So they told him he can just stay on here till he dies."

She would not have expected a prison to be compassionate. But she was not surprised Hal knew the old man's story. Would any of the other prisoners take that time?

Would William? "His hat's like the one the Philip Morris callboy used to wear. Remember him?"

"Of course."

Simultaneously, they raised cupped hands to their mouths and said, "Call for Phi-lip Morr-is," after the old radio program. Then, laughing, they rounded the table and sat down side by side. Only first, Hal angled his chair so that his back was to the wall. Something you learned in prison, he said, never to leave your back unprotected. Laurel looked at him again with a sense of admiration about the danger he lived in.

As he stuffed his lighter into a pocket of his tight, white jeans, his legs parted and his rounded maleness showed. Laurel looked away.

"I'll tell you a funny story about that old man." When he began, she thought how her father would have liked having a cotton farmer as a son-in-law. She saw them laughing together over anecdotes, the way her father sat at a table full of whiskey bottles, talking to his friends. Men who worked in offices all day did not really work, had been her father's belief.

"One day I was practicing my bagpipes," Hal said, "and heard a racket outside. When I had cut loose with my fine rendition of 'Scotland the Brave,' my friend on the trash wagon was just rounding the building. His mule almost got away from him. The backyard of the camp looked like the city dump. I don't think that old man ever did figure out what the noise was or where it came from."

"It's good you can still laugh, Hal." Her father had not had time to know William; when he died, William said, "I thought at last I'd have a father. People are always leaving me."

"Honey, if I couldn't laugh in here, I couldn't stand the tension."

Honey. She assured herself the word meant nothing; it was common usage down here. However, endearments undid her because she had not known many in her life.

"Funny, Laurel. I've never mentioned the tension to anyone else. But I'll tell you something else. I used to have blinding headaches at home. And I've never had one since leaving there."

"From the tension at home?"

"That's all I can think of."

"You didn't mention the headaches to the psychiatrists?"

"No. The headaches went as soon as I left home, even when I was in jail at first. Then my lawyers had me sent to a psychiatric hospital. It was a lot more comfortable place to wait for trial than jail. I was there for several months. My lawyers wanted to enter a plea of temporary insanity. The doctors gave me every test and said, We're sorry, but Hal is not crazy."

Laurel thought if he'd been in a psychiatric hospital for several months, he must have received a lot of help. It seemed the kind of treatment she'd like to undergo, though just a long rest was what she really wanted.

"My little girl Tina was always talking about the sheriff dropping by the hospital to see her mother or coming out to Matagorda." And Hal had to sit helplessly confined, imagining what could be going on, what his daughter could be seeing whether she knew it or not. If nothing was happening, he was tortured by his thought, and that was the point, Laurel thought, feeling sorry for him. She said, "What hospital?"

"The one in Swan where the boy Greg was. You didn't understand he didn't die that night?" Laurel didn't know why that should make a difference, but it did. "Laurel, that boy was up walking around and ready to go home. He lived for weeks. He died unexpectedly of an infection."

"Died in the hospital? Why in the world did they keep him in a little country one? Delton's one of the finest medical centers in the South. Why didn't they take him up there?"

"Daddy offered to move him. His family was happy with the attention he was getting."

"He might not have died in a Delton hospital," she said.

"Don't think I haven't gone over that in my mind a million times. When I found out that boy had died, my whole world ended. I was no longer arrested for manslaughter, but murder."

"And you must have cared so terribly, the boy was dead."

"When I put down that phone, everything turned black. A little nurse had to help me to bed. And do you know, Laurel, despite giving me a sleeping pill, she said she sat by me all night."

"Really."

"She's even knitted me socks and sent them since I've been here."

"Isn't that sweet," Laurel said. "I gathered from one of your letters, you don't want a divorce from Sallie?"

"I've tried to accept the inevitable. I don't want to go home to nothing, like most of these guys here. I don't want to lose another child. I come from the most conservative people possible. I can't go around being the poor man's Tommy Manville."

"Two divorces does sound awful," she said. "I hardly know anyone who's been divorced even once."

"When I was young, I had to be Pete's partner in a tennis tournament at the Delton Country Club. I was embarrassed because his parents had been divorced. It was a stigma that rubbed off on you, I felt. I'd talked about a divorce. But I guess neither Sallie nor I wanted to admit we'd made a mistake. Also, I think she was hanging on to live in my parents' big home on Matagorda. The night we came out of the J.P.'s, Sallie was already hoping we'd have a girl so she could make her debut from my parents' big house."

"I don't understand how someone like you married Sallie."

"You want it put in its simplest terms? I was hot for her box. I was just so—" He looked away into the distance as if unable to explain exactly how intense his feeling had been. Then he looked at her hesitantly. "When you said you were going through a bad period in your life, I thought you might be getting a divorce."

"I want to, but I'm afraid. And I don't know what to do about my son."

They sat there in what seemed a world of their own, with nothing to do but talk on intimately. Hal said the hardest thing he'd ever done was tell his first wife, Carla, he wanted a divorce. Now he would have enormous guilt about his older child except she'd turned out so beautifully. "Children forget, Laurel. But you and your husband will suffer over your divorce the rest of your lives."

But not if I want a divorce, Laurel thought, her dander up. She said, "I'm sure Sallie must be quite lonely now."

"Sallie's not lonely. She's the type person that when we went on trips, she'd know everybody around the motel pool in five minutes. I could have stayed a year and never known anyone."

"I'm like that too," Laurel said. She could see Sallie prancing around the pool wearing high heels with her bathing suit, but there was something in the image she could envy.

"She's got those breasts, if you remember."

"No. I never paid attention to the breasts of other girls." She remembered only being embarrassed by her own.

"Sallie went to a finishing school. She used to come down to Chapel Hill to see guys from Delton. I'd seen her as a child, but that was when I first knew her. She'd pose around the frat house in a sweater, and the guys would be betting on whether all that was really Sallie."

She remembered back to those days when girls wore foolish pointed things called falsies. "That's when you started dating her?"

"Hell, no. She was too much woman for me. I was a virgin G.I., just back from overseas. I started dating Carla in college. She went to a junior college and majored in horseback riding. She'd come down to see her brother. She was an army brat and had lived all over. She was a little more sophisticated than you Southern girls, in some respects. I got sucked into that marriage in more ways than one. She blew me on the first date. I couldn't have been more surprised—or pleased."

"First date?" Laurel recalled her mother once insinuating there was such a practice, and saying that was why men went to prostitutes. She had been glad to be of a more enlightened generation than her mother's. But first date!

"Carla cried when I was graduating and didn't want us to separate. She wanted to get married. So I said, All right."

Just like that? Laurel thought of the five years she had wandered around after college in terror of being an old maid; it would never have occurred to her to propose. Why hadn't she gone to a finishing school and learned to flaunt her breasts, or to a horseback-riding college and learned fellatio? She had learned nothing at all practical at Bard College, but a great deal about the development of the modern short story. Hal's world had been so safe and secure. "I didn't get married for five years after college," she said.

"That was a long time. But Pris said you ran away after high school and married Kevin Shea."

"Why did Pris say that? It was so long ago, I didn't think anyone in Delton even remembered."

"I guess because she's uptight about you coming here. She's uptight about everything, so afraid something might happen about my parole. But I don't think a thing in the world could interfere with that."

"How much longer do you have?"

"Two years."

Only two years, for a life? She could not help the thought surfacing. "I thought you had nine years." The law, too, seemed then to realize his being here was all a mistake.

"That was my sentence. I'm eligible for parole in three

years and have served one. Actually, there's a chance I'll get out earlier. This prison is all politics. There are men at home the Governor owes favors. They're getting up a petition asking for my earlier release. There's opposition. The boy's grandmother, I'm told, has had her whole garden club write letters to the Governor asking for me not to get out early."

"Letters like that would count?"

"Flower power. We'll have to wait and see what value it has."

Laurel shyly asked directions to a bathroom. When she got up, she had the strange impulse to carry along the wastebasket he had littered with cigarettes and empty it. Hal did not like walking without Buddy in the administration building, despite being a trusty. "I made trusty in six weeks," he said.

She said belatedly, "Congratulations." But wouldn't he assume he'd make trusty right away, being who he was and a college graduate? Had he done anything to merit it? she wondered.

When she came from the bathroom's booth, the room's whole atmosphere changed. Everything grew still, as before a storm. Birds hushed. The sun seemed to shine with brighter intensity. She looked out past the railroad tracks paralleling the prison—the ones she had crossed coming into it—and past the highway she had traveled to get here. Men stood in the yard of a camp over there gripping a wire fence. Then a train came roaring past, a gossamer thread speeding on toward New Orleans and hooting in the distance, *You can't catch me*. . . . Hal mentioned lying awake at night, listening when a train came through and thinking of freedom, and knew other men lay awake listening too, but no one ever mentioned a train.

She stood drying her hands on a soggy, grayed roller towel. Beside its canister someone had written on the wall in pencil:

In Case of Fire
(W)ring This Towel

She laughed over the wit of country people. When she returned to the library, Hal looked at her beyond Buddy's back. "Time to step along, young lady." Buddy recognized from their faces this was no ordinary leave-taking. He walked on ahead.

She went along the corridor beside Hal, longing to touch him. "Does the prison give you these oxford-cloth shirts?"

"No. I have my own shirts from home. I have my own pants, too. I order these jeans from Pettibone's in Delton. The pants the prison issues are too baggy."

Clothes make the man, she supposed, but thinking of fashion here seemed inappropriate. Anyway, she'd have taken whatever the prison handed out. She realized now why the trusty at the entrance looked different from Hal. She wondered if the country boys resented his better clothes or knew enough to know the difference. They went through the foyer. "I wish there was something I could do for you on the outside." In the free world, she thought.

"Well, how are you at turning collars on shirts?"

"Are you kidding? Genies do that."

"You know what I really miss, Laurel? Something so simple as a baked potato and sour cream. Here, all the cooks know to do is fry potatoes or mash them."

"I'll send you some. And sour cream mix. How could you cook?"

"I have a little oven. Pris keeps the cage supplied with food. She has themes. Chinese. Mexican. French. The guys won't eat half what she brings because they don't know what it is. It gets tossed out."

"I'll send baking potatoes for everybody."

Laurel felt very much part of a couple walking along with Hal. Never before had she sat for so long talking to someone, one on one. Hours had passed. Without a key being turned, they had been locked in together. They had sat in the two straight chairs, close together but never touching, the whole outside world a totally remote one as if they were never to see it again. And with no diversions but conversation. Buddy watched them approach and said, "Hal, I was thinking. I can arrange one more visit for Laurel, with some other prisoners for her to interview. But also, the day I take you out to cover the Indian Fair, she could meet us there."

"Meeting a woman on the outside for a whole day would be like getting back to reality. Could you come?"

She certainly could come and took down directions to a town she had never heard of. As Buddy drove away with the trunk of his car lifted, it wobbled as if in goodbye. "I have to be searched again going out?" she said. "I was planning on stowing you away."

"I'd almost try it. Some guys hid in the free-world bread truck but got caught. That's about all that delivery man can't do for you. He's the main supplier of drugs or liquor or anything you want. They make home brew in here, too. I could have a drink any time. But I never have. If I could get one look at Matagorda, I think I could pull time a lot better."

She was glad he had refused to take a drink. "Why doesn't Buddy take you by when you're out?"

"I'm not allowed back into my county until I'm paroled. It's part of the deal I signed when I accepted the nine-year sentence the night before I was supposed to go on trial."

"You didn't have a trial?"

"The District Attorney told my lawyers he'd have to try me for murder because that's what I was charged with. But he knew it was a manslaughter case, and he thought that would be the jury's verdict. My lawyers agreed. It spared everyone, not having a trial. My little daughter Tina would have had to take the stand, even."

"But didn't you take a chance? A jury might have let you off."

"We never claimed I didn't do it. Only that it was

manslaughter. Not murder. I never shot that boy on purpose, Laurel."

"I never thought you did," she said. Did he think she would have come here if she had thought so?

Hal put out a hand to shake goodbye and held to hers. "When I find something good, I hate to let go."

"I know," Laurel said.

8

Laurel drove north with a sense of relief that she had no farther to go than the hills. She felt something enormous had happened between her and Hal, and she sensed he felt the same way. No one had ever seemed to match her capacity for feelings, but she thought he might. She would write him cautiously, protecting herself in case he did not feel as she hoped he did. *Hal, I don't know about you but it seemed to me something extraordinary took place between us. I don't know words to describe exactly what I mean.* His letter crossed hers in the mail:

August 6

Dear Laurel,

Since our visit yesterday I have thought of little else. I hope you got something out of coming here. There is a story; there are many stories. I'm amazed at the speed and depth of our relationship. Ordinarily I'm not so quick to give of myself to a person, and I have a feeling you aren't either. Perhaps if we had known one another longer or lived closer together such a thing could never have happened. You have no idea how good it felt to say what I knew was the truth and to be able to talk, letting my guard down. Some of the things I spoke to you about I have never been willing to admit before, and that was forever frustrating the poor psychiatrists who worked with me so hard before my sentence.

Your visit had one result I didn't foresee and was totally unprepared for. I have tried to put it into this letter but I cannot. Perhaps later. Right now my view on your divorce situation is practically worthless. After being with you for one day I've lost my objectivity. I'm looking forward to our upcoming visit more than to anything for a long time. I've never had a harder time writing a letter.

Hal

Laurel danced cheek to cheek with Buff around the cabin. She wrote out their full names and crossed out all the similar letters, saying Love—Marriage—Friendship—Hate over the letters left, to see how things came out. She worked over the letters various times, using her maiden and her married name and the two in combination, until she got Marriage to come out at the end of both their names.

She knew this was all foolish and childish. But she was seventeen again and the feeling was wonderful. Their letters kept crossing in the mail as they wrote every day, waiting to see one another. Then one night Clarence Lee came from his house, tap-tapping, and announced a phone call.

"Hey."

She choked back Hal's name. Clarence Lee's wife, Mabel, had turned down the television set, either out of consideration or to enable herself to hear. "How is this possible?" Laurel said.

"I've been to an AA meeting with Buddy. We stopped at his office on the way back to the cage. I'm using his WATS line. If anybody comes, I'll have to hang up quickly."

"I'm not—you know—either."

"Alone? Talking cryptically is something we'll have to get used to. I'll be able to call you off and on this way." They went on trying to convey a lot with few words, and their voices shook. Lovers kept apart are bad enough, she wanted to say. But lovers who cannot be lovers? "Exquisite misery." She remembered the words from his letter.

"I finished the books you sent," he said. "We'll talk when I see you."

"Only tell me if you liked *The Death of the Heart*."

"That little girl's loneliness broke my own heart."

"I knew you would like it too."

She heard the creak of a door, and footsteps. It was like listening to an old radio program. The sounds fit into all the incredible excitement. "I've got to go," he said. Did he say Honey or did she imagine that? As Laurel returned through the living room, Mabel said, "Don't sit over yonder pining your young 'un. Come over here any time."

Laurel smiled. Mabel had misinterpreted lovesickness.

Hal came down the steps of the administration building. The most natural thing in the world would have been to rush into his arms; if only she could take his hand. "Hey," she said, smiling to herself. He did not know she made half a joke.

"Hey," he said. "Baby, Buddy's got another con for you to interview in the library. We don't have long. And he's not going to be on the farm long, either. I'm so tired of being at his mercy."

Baby, she thought. She had always longed for a man to call her that.

"Let's go to the rabbit hutches," Hal said. "We can have some privacy. That day at the fair was nice, but having Buddy at our shoulders, I don't feel we said anything."

"I know," she said. "But without him, we'd have had nothing. Whose rabbits are they?"

"They belong to Purvis. He says raising them is all that keeps him sane. I don't know how he got started."

"With two rabbits," she said.

"I wanted to buy you something at the fair. But I'd have had to ask Daddy for the money, and I didn't want to answer questions. I'm going to tell my family something about us soon."

"Don't worry them." She felt such sympathy for his parents. His poor mother, Laurel thought. He said she still cried over her first sight of him, when he was allowed visitors for the first time, after six weeks. His head had been shaved when he came to prison. Laurel went with him toward the rabbits, thinking how demeaning prison was and that at his age he had to ask his father for pocket money.

"I got this for you, though." Hal handed her a spoon shaped into a bracelet. "I give the boy who makes these my state-issued sack of tobacco each month. I'm never going to learn to roll my own cigarettes."

"You didn't have to give me a present."

"What I wanted you to take home is a replica of a Conestoga wagon one of the guys makes out of matchsticks."

"That's just what I've always wanted," Laurel said.

Hal turned and, seeing his face, she quickly apologized.

"Eastern humor," she said. "Sorry." It was out of place.

He said, "Things these guys think up to keep busy and to make money, I find touching."

"I do too, Hal," she said, keeping step. She was thinking how, before him, she had never been the sort of woman who prompted presents; she'd always wanted a man to give her a teddy bear. William brought home unexpected flowers from vendors in Grand Central, and she was touched; they were often a little the worse for wear, but she told him truthfully it was the thought that counted, and she put the flowers in a vase in the kitchen. That was where she would see them the most. Her father never in his life gave either her or her mother any present but cash. She had grown up with a lot fewer expectations than many women.

"We can't stay out here long. I just heard some of the guys complained about me having a woman visitor out of visiting hours last week, even a journalist."

"I didn't know anybody paid attention to us."

"These guys know everything. The closest to a big-time criminal we've got here is a boy named Gus, from Illinois. He told me today I seemed to have had a hard time saying goodbye to that writer. I told him I had, and I hoped something was going to come out of our meeting. These guys all know about my situation with Sallie. That she's waiting to hold me up for everything I've got and wants full child custody. Gus said, 'The best thing that could happen for you, Hal, would be for your wife to die'; then he said, Laurel, 'I know a Mexican boy who'll come up from Monterrey and wipe anybody's ass for five hundred bucks, in case you're interested.'"

"What in the name of God did you say?"

"I said I thought I'd pass."

Laurel went on thinking how little a life could be worth, thinking of Sallie so innocently at home not even knowing her life was being bargained over. And wasn't it incredible she and Hal were involved in this kind of existence?

Hal said, "It was as natural to Gus as arranging a golf game." He nervously lit a cigarette. "I was planning on another visit, but Buddy's started worrying these guys will jackpot me. Get revenge. They've done it to him. Guys who resent AA told others in the program Buddy was establishing a relationship with them to get into their wives' pants. Buddy said when I started in the program, 'I don't care if you like these guys. I just want you to learn to love the sons of bitches.'"

"He won't help us?"

"He thinks what's happening between us is fantasy. He's seen so many boys hurt he doesn't want it to happen to me. He says you'll leave and that will be the end of it."

"Hal, I'm not like that."

"I told him that. That I never trusted a woman the way I do you. I can put you on my list of visitors and tell Mama and Daddy and Pris not to come next visiting Sunday."

There were so many reasons she could give for not arriving at home when she was expected. Loyalty overtook her. "I have to be home on Labor Day," Laurel said. "To get Rick ready for school."

"I understand." They entered the shed.

The old trusty rose up, holding a watering can. "I've got guard duty, Hal. This is the only time I've got to feed and water them."

"It's all right," Hal said.

Laurel moved along with him and stuck her fingers to a wire cage. "Aren't they cute," she said, touching a rabbit's wiggling nose. She knew what it must be like for a man to walk around with a hard-on. Hal had gone to the far end of the shed and stared out back. Something bothered him today, maybe that this was their last meeting. She stood looking out too. "What's all that?" she said, seeing an old Delton City transit bus, an abandoned school bus with the name of a town half painted out, a dilapidated trailer, and shacks of nailed-together boards.

"The red houses I told you about," he said. "For conjugal visiting. It's touching the way these guys take care of those places, painting and cleaning and planting flower gardens around them. One old boy nearly worked himself to death, and when he took his wife up to one on her first visit and explained what it was for, she said, 'You certainly don't expect me to go in one of those.' He said, 'Of course not, honey.' I've never seen a man so crestfallen in my life." Purvis stood chuckling in the background.

"I can't imagine why she wouldn't go in one," Laurel said. Right then, she knew what visiting Sunday could have meant; Hal had a lenient sergeant who looked the other way about "wives" who visited. But no, she had to be home on time.

And she knew who Purvis was; he did look older than his years, as Hal had said. He, too, had killed his stepson but was serving a life sentence. For murder? she wondered. He had befriended Hal in the beginning. Then one day he had received his divorce notice in the mail, the way most men learned the news. "It's pitiful to watch," Hal had said. Purvis pretended not to care, but Hal followed him to a guard shack and found him crying. He talked a long time to Purvis, who suddenly said, "Hal, you're going to make it in here."

"How do you know that?" Hal said. "I don't know it myself."

"By your eyes. When you came in here, I never had seen such suffering in the eyes of another human being."

"Laurel, I was amazed," Hal had said. "That old man's semiliterate. How remarkably wonderful people can be." They had agreed it was strange he could learn to appreciate people in a place like prison. Hal had written: *I used to think Negroes had no feelings except in rare instances. And poor whites affected me the same way. I was so surprised when I came here to learn they did. Also how interesting they can be. I always thought they were niggers with two thoughts, sundown and payday.*

She wrote him back then. *You've been to hell and back and are a better man for it.*

"Buddy'll be waiting." When Hal dropped his cigarette without grinding it out, she stepped on it hard because of the wooden structure. She walked on thinking they would not want their first kiss with someone else present. Hal would make no move toward her in the shed because, as much as he trusted Purvis, in prison you did not totally trust anyone. She tried to comfort herself that in another kind of prison they'd have talked through glass and on an intercom. Then she realized Hal was not behind her, and looked back to see him talking to Purvis. She was surprised by his angry manner. Purvis gave him a gentle shove in her direction. "What's the matter?" she asked. He came up with a tic in one cheek; she remembered noticing it other times.

"I just asked him how he could stand keeping those animals in those goddamned cages."

She needed to be more like Sallie, lighthearted, gay, and capable of chatter. Though possibly Sallie wasn't as much that way anymore. Her mother had always said men did not like serious women. Needing to change his mood, she began to talk off the top of her head. "Rick had a pet rabbit once. We bought it out of a ten-cent-store window the day after Easter because we were worried its feelings were hurt. It was the only rabbit left. We kept it on a screened porch. I found it all stretched out dead one day. I'd kept feeding it lettuce, and apparently it died of diarrhea. I didn't know rabbits couldn't eat as much lettuce as they wanted, did you?

"It was an old ten-cent store like the kind in the South. Soundport has nothing like that anymore. Now it's filled with what my mother calls boutique shops. One time William asked a salesgirl what kind of fur a skirt was made out of. She told him 'Lapin.' He nearly died laughing. 'You mean rabbit?' But the salesgirl didn't know what was funny. In Soundport now I wouldn't know where to go to buy a spool of thread, it's so posh and chic. The kind of cutesy town where at the drive-in bank, they shoot out dog biscuits with your money in that little tray."

"Why would they do that?"

"I mean when you have a dog in the car with you."

"Oh," he said.

She had hated that rabbit's dying. She had felt responsible for its death. A more horrible feeling overtook her walking through this prison. She hurried on. "Well, anyway, pet rabbits have such a boring life. Just locked up in—" and she glanced at him. He did not seem to be paying much attention. What man would?

"Got a match, Hal?" A trusty rose from hunkering on the ground. He was overseeing prisoners under guard, legmen, digging a ditch. They wore blue with yellow stripes down their pants legs. He spoke close, lighting his cigarette. "Grady's right. We ought to have free-world guards. There's too many scores to be settled among prisoners guarding each other." He squinted at Laurel through smoke and went away.

"Do you agree with that?" she said, in interest.

"I don't have to guard prisoners being in my office all day."

"I know, but what do you think about—"

He interrupted gruffly. "I had a wet dream last night, Laurel. Do you know what that's like for a man at my age? This is the first time I've had the desire to fuck a woman since I've been here. I was afraid I'd lost all that feeling. Buddy's offered to take me to a whore in Greenwood, and I've refused. I was afraid he'd begin to think I was one of the gal-boys we've got here."

"I doubt that," she said, smiling.

"I don't want a whore. I never have." He looked at her in the sunlight, his eyes laughing beneath those handsome, dark eyebrows. "I'm saving myself for you, baby."

"You're damaged goods. But I'll take you."

"All night I lie in that cage imagining all kinds of things."

"I do too."

"I've thought about it and told myself I couldn't ask that of a woman like you. To drive alone and meet me somewhere in a motel room for a few hours."

"Why not? If Buddy will take you out to a whore, why not me?"

"If you'll come, Laurel, I'll ask him."

"Haven't you had at least the desire to masturbate?"

"In a cage with twenty other men? I hear some of those guys beating their meat at night. No thanks."

"How about in the old bus where you practice your bagpipes? I think it's mean the guys won't let you learn to play them in the cage."

"What do those hicks know about music? All right, if the impulse comes over me, I'll tell myself Laurel told me to."

Why do I have to tell you? she wondered, sorry again for the glimpses of passivity prison had brought on. Outside the library door, she stopped and said, "Did you have affairs when you were married, other than with Sallie?"

"Once with Carla. Not once with Sallie. Why, hell, if you meet me in Greenwood, you'll be getting practically a virgin. That's more than I've ever gotten."

Laurel laughed, and Buddy opened the door. He introduced her to a hefty middle-aged prisoner. All during her interview with Joe, she thought of Hal. "I got busted the first time when I was seventeen," Joe said. "For robbing a filling station. When I come out, I couldn't get a job because I been in stir. Nobody would hire you back then. So I had to rob again. After that, my family wouldn't have nothing to do with me. I left St. Louis and started roaming."

"That's the usual vicious circle, isn't it?" she said. She thought about Hal being the gentleman he was, yet saying he wanted to fuck her; no man had talked to her that way before.

"Yes'm, it is," he said. "I been busted in more states than I could name you."

"How does this prison stack up?"

"Missus, when I got busted in Mississippi, I told myself I had come to the end of the road. I thought I'd never get out alive. But it's the best place I been. The most humane."

"How is that?"

"In Leavenworth I didn't see the sun for ten years except as a slant of light on a wall at a certain time of day. In wintertime I didn't see it at all. Didn't see a dog all that time. I been paroled here once. First thing I done I bought some whiskey before I got on a bus for St. Louis."

"You were going home again?"

"Missus, I'm forty-five years old and I done run out of places to go. I don't know if my family would have anything to do with me. I didn't find out. I got drunk on the bus. The driver had me arrested for disorderly conduct time I hit Delton. Done broke parole. Hadn't been gone from prison but three hours. They come got me. Nine hours later I was right back where I'd started."

"But why would you do that?"

"Used to the custodial." Joe looked sheepish. "It's been my life. It's what I want and I've faced it. Ever' time I've gone out I've come right back in."

"You ought to just stop getting paroled."

"It'd save the taxpayers some money, now, wouldn't it?"

Buddy returned with Hal. Impatiently, she and Hal waited, like polite children, for the others to stop talking.

"She wants to write about this place, she ought to be here for the rodeo," Joe said. "They tie money to the horns of steers. Turn loose all them old boys to get it how they can."

"That colored boy that got gored up so bad last year is doing better," Buddy said.

Joe laughed. "He'll be out yonder again come fall. I got a new man in my cage. He's talking about winning. Shoot. He ain't got the sense. That boy got busted for robbing a chain store he managed. It was opened with a key. And he had the only one." Laurel could not help enjoying the moments they stood in camaraderie. Part of her lifetime, now, seemed to have been spent in this room. Hal hung back so meekly at the door; she wished he would step forward and join the other men. "Come on back here and cover the rodeo," Joe said. "It's open one day to free-world folks."

"Young lady, I won't be more than an hour or so." Buddy opened the door and shut them at last into privacy.

"Baby, he says it's go." Hal held her by the elbows for a moment, their lips barely met; this place was too heavy with fear for both of them. They ran enough risks.

Sitting in their accustomed chairs, they let their knees touch. He held her hand to one knee. "You've got to realize, Laurel, this trip out could be a carrot dangled before our noses. Something can always happen. If a boy escapes, the prison closes up like a nutshell. All leaves are canceled."

"I understand." They made plans; she would meet Buddy at the prison, to make certain they were going; then she would park down the highway and go the rest of the way with them. He worried about her driving back to her cabin at night alone. Laurel laughed and explained she went about a lot at night, to tent revivals, black churches. . . . He was perturbed by her being with black people, though she said she went with a black woman friend.

"Come on back here in the fall, baby. You can combine the rodeo with a visiting Sunday and maybe one day out with Buddy. It would make your long trip worthwhile."

Any time would be worthwhile. She let her hand rub the inside of his thigh. "I don't know what to say to get away from home," she said.

"If you're getting a divorce, you won't have to say anything. What are your thoughts about that?"

"The same. That I want a divorce and don't want to have to go through what you have to to get one," Laurel said. She could not imagine telling William or Rick.

"Start your divorce as soon as possible. And come on back here. We need something to go on, piece by piece, till I'm out of this place for good."

"Till I've crossed those tracks," the prison expression went. She nodded; but there was so much she didn't want to let go of with William.

"Fall's a sad time for me," Hal said. "A year ago, I was waiting for my trophies to come from Africa; then my world fell apart."

"I didn't know you'd been to Africa." She hated thinking about that night.

"I planned on it for years. Read everything by Robert Ruark. Went to the Delton zoo constantly by myself to study the animals. And do you know, Laurel, I was forty-one years old and afraid to tell my parents I was going. Sallie had to tell them."

"I can understand," she said. She always had some project in mind she was afraid to tell her parents. She moved her hand again along his leg in a kind of commiseration, thinking of their similarities. "Did Sallie go with you?"

"She toured other places with friends. They always travel together."

"That's nice." She'd like that kind of small-town compatibility.

"I met up with them in Scotland. That's when I got my bagpipes. I've always wanted to learn to play them. I wanted to meet the head of my clan, but I was too shy to get in touch with him."

"Why didn't Sallie do that too?" Was the edge in her voice directed toward him or Sallie?

"Sallie had shined her ass enough, I was told. Prancing around trying to make the guards at Buckingham Palace laugh."

"Oh, good God. No wonder you wanted a divorce."

"It's such a waste, Laurel, that I killed that boy. If only I hadn't hung on so long. I think if I hadn't killed him, I'd eventually have killed Sallie." Hal held both of her hands between his. "There's been so much frustration in my life. I should have broken away from Daddy years ago and farmed on my own, like a lot of my friends did. I didn't know how to tell him. He ought to have turned things over to me, and I think he wanted to. But he didn't know how to do it, either. It's just been a sad situation for years. I was doing well, married to Carla and farming. Then I had to give her everything I had. I went on salary and after a while I deteriorated so, married to Sallie and drinking, Daddy couldn't turn anything over to me. I could farm that place, Laurel. I used to make better decisions than Daddy, and he wouldn't listen. One year we lost half a crop because he poisoned at the wrong time, when I'd told him not to."

"Maybe now you can take over. Tell him you want to. You've grown and changed here."

"That's what I plan on."

She said, "Do you have a grape arbor at Matagorda near a swimming pool?"

"We used to. It blew down so often, Daddy left it down."

"Then I've been there," Laurel said. "To a high school sorority party." She told how there were grapes set out in silver bowls that seemed elaborate to be by a pool.

"That sounds like Mama," he said.

She had kept eating grapes, one after another, until a boy spoke to her about it; not hearing him exactly, she had been afraid to ask what he said, something that reflected on there being something wrong with her.

"I never did get to see my trophies," Hal said. "I had to write the taxidermist to hold them for three years. But I brought a few home and had them mounted here. An old Negro on the place named Field looked at the zebra head and said, 'I ain't never seed no striped mule before.'"

"Oh, Hal!" There was that god-awful squeal again. "Matagorda sounds wonderful. I wish I could see it."

"You will. I dreamed the other night about us making love in my bedroom."

"Well, that won't happen at Matagorda," she said.

"It will when we're married," he said.

She laughed. "You haven't even asked me to marry you."

"Will you?"

"Yes," Laurel said.

"Then you belong to me now." He sat with his back to the wall again, holding her hand. She leaned forward and touched her hand to his cheek. They could kiss just once quickly again, but there were footsteps out in the corridor, and a group of prisoners went by the windows.

"Hal," she said, sitting back. "Can we have a baby?" She thought Matagorda needed an heir, and she wanted to provide one: to make up for the son he'd never had. He and Carla had planned on another child, hoping for a son and namesake, but then they'd divorced.

"If it's safe for you," he said. "Maybe this time it will be a child I can keep."

"Suppose Sallie won't get a divorce?" she said. If Sallie had not met someone else in three years, maybe, past forty, she would decide Hal was better than no one. Past forty, a woman was made to feel she was without much chance of finding a man.

"Then I'll get the divorce. I promise."

She felt a tightness in her throat and chest at his words about keeping a child. More than ever, she wanted to take care of him. He seemed to need it so much. Laurel went to the door reminding herself that what self-sufficiency she had had been taught her by William. Without it, she could not have thought of leaving him.

9

She carried a toothbrush along in her pocketbook. A toothbrush, at least, seemed necessary to take along on an affair. Something was wrong. That was apparent as soon as she saw Buddy's face. He gave her a note. *Baby, I could die!*

"They carried them out of here at dawn by the busload," Buddy said. "Took them down to the Gulf Coast to clear up all that debris after Camille." Laurel had read on, and she nodded. "There was nothing he could do about it."

"I know that, Buddy. Thanks a lot for waiting." She drove the round trip back to the cabin.

Early the next morning she burned her final garbage, watching ashes fly away in varying shapes. She and Buff drove out of town, and she had that strange feeling that no one would much care or miss her; lives went on. She felt pain at leaving Hal, fear about when they could possibly meet; and she took their engagement seriously. Yet she could not help wanting to get back into her old routine, her life. She was tired of other people's houses and their supper tables; she wanted her own. Soon winter clothes would have to come down from the attic. Bees would gather around apples fallen to the ground, humming their closed-in sound.

She passed the outskirts of Knoxville with a salutatory, unseen handwave. She expected to stay on the borderline of Tennessee and Virginia, as usual. But had no luck. Hours later, she was still driving through an obscuring rainstorm. And she had investigated every motel, the sleaziest kind. Her jaws clenched in fatigue. She repeated a magical phrase in time to the windshield wipers: If I make it, Hal and I will be married. A voice spoke back in its sardonic manner. Make it? her father said. Hell, you've got to make it. Only he spoke about more than this paved road or the rubbled ones that spent his life. She was nodding at her legacy as she turned into a Holiday Inn knowing she had to stop, finally, and would sleep here in the parking lot if necessary. The clerk was sorry they were full. He looked solicitous as she wavered at the desk. "I've been driving thirteen hours," Laurel said.

"Nothing up the road, either. I've been phoning for people all night."

"Someone should have told me that a long way back."

"There's a woman in town who sometimes takes in a person overnight. I'll phone her."

She found the woman's house somewhere out in a dark, strange town and went inside, too tired to carry in her overnight case. She and Buff slept in a canopied bed, with nothing for dinner but candy bars Laurel had bought in the motel's lobby. Leaving at daylight, she would arrive home earlier than planned, having spent so much time on the road the day before.

Only her mother's car was in the driveway. The smell of chicken frying drifted outdoors, and she saw her mother inside, darkened by the screen door. Mrs. Wynn stood too long staring out a kitchen window, though she would know her daughter had arrived. She came to the door. "You're early." Her cooking fork was poked upright in one hand as she offered her cheek for kissing.

Laurel wanted to tell her about that long, horrible night. She wanted motherly comfort. But she had learned in life to keep back so much information; too often it was turned against her. Her mother would say, Nobody but you would have started out Labor Day weekend without a reservation. "Where's everybody?"

"Rick's gone on his bike." Mrs. Wynn returned to the stove. "William went to the Hamptons. He went yesterday to play golf with some men from work. I stayed with Rick. He said he'd be back today before you got home."

William had given up golf years ago as a boring, time-consuming, old-man's game. His clubs had long sat in the attic. I imagine he did expect to be back before me, Laurel thought, carrying her luggage upstairs.

Mrs. Wynn called after her. "I'll finish cooking and go home."

"You don't have to go." Her mother deserved not to be alone over the holiday when she'd been housekeeping, staying with Rick. "Stay another night."

"I don't want to spend the night," Mrs. Wynn said. "You can catch me up on family news later."

"Well, stay for dinner," Laurel said.

"William says this thing of you going to Mississippi every summer has got to stop."

Why should William tell her what to do? Laurel thought. And never see the South?

Mrs. Wynn said, "There's three New Mexican chipmunks up there in a cage Rick smuggled back on the plane. That's all you need, more animals. This house already smells."

"Hello, Jubal." Laurel turned to greet him as he shuffled toward her. "Hello, Amos." In Rick's room she greeted their errant cat, which sat atop the cage. "Glad you made it through the summer."

She sat down in her bedroom, with chicken frying

below. Every sense of the summer was with her, ponds, roads, faces—the library. She read Hal's letter, written after they were last together.

> My darling:
> You have just driven away. My mind is not here. My heart left with you, and so at least that one small part of me is free. I wonder if society would be chagrined knowing I am cheating it that much. Right now I am so completely wrung out I can bearly move.

(*Barely*, she spelled, smiling to herself.)

> I finally fell into bed a while ago, and because of the utter desolation I felt, the tears simply came. I have cried before, once when Greg died, once in jail just before I pleaded guilty. I thought I was all through crying. In the name of God, get your divorce soon. Our hours together will . . .

Will never be, Laurel finished. She thought his misspelling endearing. In a while she hid the letter where she knew there would be a cache of them, hearing William come in.

"Hello. Hello, Grandmother," he cried. Always, coming into the house, he made his presence known. Laurel liked that. She had grown up in a household where people seldom spoke, passed by one another in silence. She listened to the low murmur of his and her mother's teasing voices as William came upstairs.

She turned away from his trying to kiss her. "Something told me you were going to get home early," he said. "I just suddenly picked up and left."

"You didn't go to the Hamptons to play golf," she said.

"Are you accusing me of something?" His face grew thunderous. She turned from his look of cold and silent fury. And she would make no more comment. She wanted to avoid confrontation, arguing, screaming. Maybe she did not much care what he had been doing. She would not lower herself to demand the names of the other players and call them up if he could give them to her. She wished simply to tell William she was sorry he had had to cut short his stay in the Hamptons. At that moment, she heard Rick on the stairs.

William began unpacking his overnight satchel and arranging things from his toilet kit on their usual bathroom shelf. She unpacked her own cosmetics and suddenly said, "When did you start using baby powder?" eyeing a large can.

William started, then laughed and looked happy; evidently he wanted her to notice his reactions, to know implications; William was strange about that, she thought once again. "I just got on to it," he said. "It's great after the beach. I like the smell. I'd like for you to start using it."

Rick came into the bathroom and received a handful and rubbed it along his bony rib cage. "Yeah," he said. She dabbled some to the noses of Jubal and Buff, and they sneezed.

That night she was glad of the width of the king-sized bed; there was no sense of intimacy lying there. She waited for William's light breathing to settle into his part-time snoring. She thought about Hal in the dark thinking about her; they had agreed the moonlight was the same wherever they were. William turned toward her, and she had a moment of panic. The easiest thing would be to lie there and cross her legs up over his back, the way he liked. But how often had she moved across this bed to touch him and had his back remain stationary. Now, there was Hal.

She felt William's frame against her, and his arm around her. Why was William making this move she had wanted so long, now that she had found someone else? She stared out at a sycamore tree near a window, its branches turned gold and silver in the moonlight, a fairy-tale tree. "I'm too tired from all that driving," she said.

In a moment, William rolled away. That night she dreamed about sunlit waves and beaches, the pleasures of love in the afternoon in a motel, a faceless girl with her hair spread round on a pillow, a nameless girl who had started the whole family using baby powder. Laurel turned over her dusted body.

Buddy kited out letters for Hal and he was able to write more than through normal prison channels. She wrote to Buddy enclosing letters for Hal, though they could not overburden him, and wrote through the prison too. William noticed a change in her. "You're so remote," he said. She kept a catlike purr of satisfaction about her secret love, who was not even her lover. She had to get the divorce but could not make a move. She wrote Hal finally and asked him to do what might hurt; she wanted to know what had happened on Matagorda that night. His reply was painful, but it answered her questions.

> It was Saturday. I went to my deer camp to look for a place to erect a deer stand for the coming season. No one else was there since the hunting season had not opened. That night alone in my cabin, except for my dog, I drank most of a fifth of bourbon while reading and listening to the radio.
> Next morning I began to build the stand in a low tree. I had seen a beautiful buck on this spot the previous day. It was hot, and around ten o'clock I drank a beer. During the morning as I worked I drank several more, and arrived back at Matagorda. We were to leave shortly for an afternoon party. I fixed a drink to take along in the car—"a traveling drink," which is a common custom here where there are such great distances between places.
> Sallie and I arrived feeling no pain; we were in a friendly mood. I had had neither breakfast nor lunch and at some point ate a hamburger one of the girls cooked, at Sallie's insistence. During the course of the

afternoon, I blacked out. That is, I simply ceased to remember anything. This had happened before if I drank early enough and kept on long enough. Apparently, my behavior does not appreciably change when this happens. I have surprised friends sometimes by asking what happened at a certain time when they were not aware I was especially drunk. From what I can learn, at some point Sallie and I had a disagreement and ceased talking. I remember for a while taking a sunbath around the pool's edge. From that point on, all I know is what I've been told. When we arrived back home, the children had come in. Some of what happened I remember from a statement Sallie gave the District Attorney. Some of it I was told by lawyers. Sallie and I continued to argue. I went to the kitchen to fix food, remarking that I had to do it myself, that Sallie wouldn't. I told her son to leave and go to his father's, where he was supposed to be staying anyway. I suppose my wife was going at me all this time. I apparently got one of my rifles and loaded it. I have no idea why. I can only guess I wanted to scare her or impress her with how much I meant what I was trying to get across. I honestly don't know what I was trying to prove. I happened to pick out a rifle that was equipped with a telescope sight, making it useless outdoors at night, or indoors anytime. All this is in retrospect; I do not remember any of it.

As I understand it, I then started toward the door. The rooms are so arranged that I had to round a corner to do this. It seems that as I got to the door, it opened inward, and Greg and I almost ran into each other. I seem to have been carrying the rifle in both hands, with the muzzle pointed toward the front, the only way it could go through the door. It went right into Greg's stomach. There is some speculation as to whether he grabbed the barrel or not, trying to push or pull it out of the way, to one side. The weapon had a set, or hair, trigger. It takes almost no pressure to fire it.

At the sound of the explosion my memory returns somewhat. I recollect the noise, but it seems to have been particularly quiet for that particular gun. Sort of a pop, as though it was a long way away. I remember seeing Greg lying on the porch, screaming that it hurt and not to touch him. I went to him and fell on my knees and tried to hold him in my arms. When I put my arms around him, I felt his intestines all in my hands and I tried to put them back where they belonged, and I thought, This won't really help him, I've got to call a doctor. I don't remember this, or anything else, until later when I was trying to call the police, the hospital, and couldn't find either number in the book. All this had already been done, but I didn't know it. While I was sitting there, the deputy sheriff came in—the ambulance had already come and gone—and he and I walked around and went over everything. Some of it I remember and some of it I don't. He told me to wash my hands, they were bloody to the elbows. Then we went to my parents and told them what had happened.

Later I learned that after I left Greg on the porch, I went to Tina's room where the baby had been sent. She was in her bed, and I sat down and read her fairy stories, just as I did every night. When Sallie was ready to go to the hospital, she came and got her. I did nothing, just sat there and kept right on reading the story. I have no idea how long I did this. I don't remember going to the phone.

The lawyers had an architect reconstruct rooms of the house where things took place, to show that I could not have seen Greg in advance of what happened. This would have been used at the trial. The hardest thing to explain is why I loaded the rifle, why I got it out in the first place, what I was going to do with it. There is no satisfactory answer to this that anyone would understand. That I have done it before to frighten Sallie, to try to get through to her, is not explanation enough. But I have none better.

Please understand I offer no excuse for what happened. Some things have never been explained, such as the fact that the rifle was not where I would have dropped it or put it down when the deputy found it. It was about ten feet behind where I stood, in the living room. There is the question of where Sallie was all this time; she said she was right behind me, I think, and did she do anything—push me, pull me, grab the gun? Greg and I did not have any fight before the shooting, this much I know. Maybe we had words; we probably did.

You must know what it does to me to write all this down. Please please let it be the last time. For weeks afterward I seemed to find flecks of blood on me when I looked at my hands. Under my nails, in the quick, in the winding stem of my Rolex, which I scrubbed and scrubbed in jail with my toothbrush. I will hear that screaming until I die and I suppose as long as there is breath in me I shall see those guts streaming all over the floor when I close my eyes, and remember how it felt, trying to put them back. They wouldn't stay.

I have gone over this a thousand times, usually at night. But not always. Sometimes at work in prison it comes to mind whether I want it to or not, and I lose touch with reality awhile, trying to figure out what happened and why. I have never found a satisfactory explanation.

Before you came here, I had long ago decided I owed something to somebody for what happened, and I was adjusted to the idea of pulling whatever amount of time society required of me. I had no particular desire to get out as soon as possible, once my fear of the place began to subside. It's a peculiar way to repay society for what took place, but if that's what it took to square things, then I was willing to do my part. But what no one will ever understand is that keeping me here is not the real punishment I suffer. I carry that with me, wherever I go, and I have no idea how long it will last, perhaps always. Someday I hope I can think of this without the hurt that wells up in me every time the thing comes to mind. Time has helped a lot. I had to tell the psychiatrist at the hospital under sodium pentathol what happened, but the nurses said I had so little recollection of the whole thing that my sense of guilt was unrealistic; there just wasn't any, except that I knew I was involved somehow.

Sallie said afterward that I had been jealous of Greg. I don't agree. I can see why I should be punished and why I should be made to suffer. But what I cannot see is why anyone else should be made to. Why should you?

I have no bitterness over all this. There is no resentment in my heart toward anyone, and I am looking for no one to blame. If I had been a little older and wiser, I don't believe any of it would have happened. But I did not know what to do to ward it off; I did not know how to stop it.

Laurel, I loved that boy.

10

When there were escapes, the sergeant was too busy to distribute mail. It lay in the hallway, stacking up in a frustrating way: worse than when the sergeant sat there censoring it slowly, his lips moving over each word. Finally Hal had so much mail from Laurel he laid it over his cot, forming what seemed a patchwork quilt.

> The guys have begun to tease me. Once they hid my mail, but I was so morose they produced it quickly. It's hell to wrap your life around one moment of each day.
> Another day guess what I found on my pillow! The tiniest pair of Dr. Denton's nighty-nights you've ever seen—complete with feet. I'd forgotten just how small babies really are. Everything collected for the victims of hurricane Camille and unused has been sent up to the prison. Yesterday a whole truckload of

paper plates arrived. What a place. I hadn't known it would beat Matagorda for nuttiness.

With Laurel on his mind he had begun to fear what others did—Buddy; his new confidant, the chaplain; Pris—that he might run. *Are you crazy?* she responded. But he continued to write about escapes. After a runaway was caught, obnoxious rules were made which did no good. People kept running. The only convict he'd talked to who ran said that an hour after he left he'd have given a thousand dollars to sneak back into his cage, but could only run.

He nearly died of hunger and thurst and mosquito bites and got an added ten years. Last night, the turkey boy on shift at the poultry farm stole Grady's horse and swapped that for a pickup and abandoned that to hit the woods. But those hills and woods were unfamiliar to him and the hounds ran him all over, and he got tired. The sergeant had gone into his locker and found a note from his wife which read simply, *"Baby, I need you."* He had six more months and now has three years. So much time for so little freedom. Once I would have thought such thinking was crazy, but now I understand.

Thirst, Laurel corrected. How could convicts help imagining things their wives and girlfriends were doing? He got out the only picture of her he had, with an interview in an old *Mid-South Review*. There was a picture of him at a party in Delton in evening clothes.

I wish you could have heard the comments about the picture here. "Don't he look dig-nee-fied," and "Where do you keep your wall safe?" After I showed your picture and explained something about you, Gus said, "I knew you'd end up taking one of these little split-tails with you, but I figured it'd be some of this local talent." I wonder if he's ever seen any of the local talent. I love the way most cons put women on pedestals. Split-tail, yet! It makes you sound like a tropical fish.

Laurel, when I first saw that picture I was sitting on my porch at Matagorda and remember thinking your hair made you seem like an angel. I thought how lovely you were and I thought, I bet I could love that girl—but she'd be too intelligent for me. The voice that spoke to you in Connecticut sent you to me, and you did appear like an angel—a gift from heaven. I will always wonder at it.

Images rose to his head. What about her agent, her editor, book reviewers: were they all trying to get into her pants? What about William, even—he was in the house! *Hal*, she wrote him,

I don't need that pressure when I'm contemplating a divorce alone, worrying about what finances will be, and thinking about leaving my child for you if Rick won't come with me. Three fourths of my married life has been totally without sex. And one fourth has consisted of quite brief affairs and a few attempts with William. It is unbelievable to look back on when I realize what it will be like to be married to you. My sap has only begun to flow again, it seems, since the time when I was a teenager.

I feel strongly that what you should be saying to me is, "Why in hell didn't you leave him or have more affairs?" My life consisted of thinking day by day, I can't exist like this. Only I kept at it year by year. Really, I look at all these long marriages around me and think, I did achieve one. It is an all-right marriage. I went on believing I was doomed to a life of loneliness, though by the time I was forty I was despairing, and then all that ended the afternoon I walked into that crazy prison.

There was a period, though, of about seven years

when I had no sex at all, either with William or anyone else. My seven lean years, I call them. To tell you the truth, I resent surprise and criticism from you concerning anything I've done. I feel that with William as a husband, I should have been looking around constantly in hopes of an affair. I wasn't, and I turned down chances because I didn't picture myself running around when I was a mother. I wasn't anybody's wife. I was William's housekeeper and knew every Sunday night for years he was shacked up and I sat there alone those Saturdays and Sundays, and other times too. As a woman who knew herself not to be bad-looking, to feel time passing, to feel in ways I'd never been married, is it a wonder I despaired? I told you about my affair with Edward. The first time he touched me I cried because a male creature had touched me. Because I had some physical contact with another human being, a grown-up. Well, to hell with it all. I'm sick of thinking about the past.

But she returned to his past.

You poor suffering man, you beat the walls of the jail with your hands till they bled? If only I'd known that day in the library, I'd have kissed your fingertips and your palms. You say jealousy helped destroy your marriage with Sallie, that you are your "own worst enemy," and so I hope to hear no more; you know I'm never going to behave as she did. But why, if you never strayed, was she so jealous about you? Was it her own insecurity or because you had left Carla and might then leave her? You are right that when you put your head between my breasts and heave a huge sigh of relief, you will be safe. And I'll be safe when I'm next to you. Today is such a nuzzable day, I wish you were here. If ever with separation, time, and distance, you think that we've been swept away by our emotional natures, you don't have to feel committed.

We can resume again when I come back south. Meanwhile I will not desert you, I promise. But whenever we are finally together, won't we drown in one another?

Apologizing about his jealous nature, Hal recalled to her he was mighty innocent about affairs. Remember, he had told her that was the way he was, strictly monogamous. *What's an all-right marriage? baby,* he asked.

Laurel set a triumphant foot on the stairs of a small office building in Soundport. For years she had frequented a dress shop on the ground floor without realizing law offices were above it. Soundport was becoming a different town to her. She thought of Hal looking at her picture in the magazine several years ago, evidently in loneliness, or he'd not have thought of loving her then. It was strange she had gotten the name of a lawyer through her mother. She had a friend whose daughter was also divorcing. She had her husband followed and found out he was seeing ten women. "That's better than one woman, Mother," Laurel said.

She looked out from a window on the landing; the town had such a sense of normality. The large white Congregational Church opposite seemed to stare back at her. Stores had window boxes full of late-blooming flowers, overflowing impatiens. Laurel hated being the self she was, going upstairs with pink bunny-rabbit tails bobbing at her heels, keeping Peds from slipping into her tennis shoes.

Time-wise, she wrote Hal. *That's the way people here talk. Time-wise, I had to see this lawyer in my tennis dress. Right away, Mr. Cohen told me he could not get Rick for me at his age. A judge would ask him who he wanted to live with.* With me, Laurel thought. Only what about moving south? On their first meeting, she decided not to tell Mr. Cohen her future plans. He asked for a retainer, and she thought again about the expense of running one's life alone.

Things continued to be different from when she was an ordinary housewife in Soundport. Now she had a tiny key to a long slit of mailbox, in a nest of them at the post office. Daily she turned that key with a stealthy air. Suppose an acquaintance appeared asking what she was doing with Box 56 or, worse, suppose someone asked William why his wife had what seemed an unusual possession for a suburban matron? Who were all the other people opening boxes? Secret lovers too? Even business people had an air of suspicion attached to them. Box holders had shady natures. She was stunned by the smut mail that arrived for her box number: solicitations for dirty books and films with explicit pictures of sex acts. She sent them along to Hal through Buddy. *Might as well give all the men in the cage a thrill,* she wrote. She felt herself a traitor to her sturdy aluminum box at home, its faithful red flag ready to go up or down, a traitor to a Grandma Moses scene along her road of apple trees, as if she were a rotten apple hiding among perfect red ones on Grandma's round trees.

When she set out for the beauty parlor, William asked why she was going on a Saturday afternoon. "We ought to do something together then." She wanted to tell him, William, it's fifteen years too late for you to be saying that. Yet there was an implication of future companionship she ought to consider. William used to spend all his leisure time with Rick. Now Rick had his own pursuits. He confided, too, that he left home to avoid his dad's list of chores attached to the refrigerator. She might tell William, but she did not want to get Rick in trouble, or herself for meddling. William's words, however, made her sad for him. "Let's practice my backhand when I come home," she said. Then in the shop she wrote: *I'm in the stupid beauty parlor with heat blowing all around my ears, but since I'm unable to hear anything, I feel a little alone with you.*

When hunting season began, cars and trucks streamed past the prison on their way to the woods. Hal wrote about the scene longingly, but kept his humor. *Huh?* he replied.

You can't understand how a friend was allowed to drive in and deposit two bucks at my camp? They just let him come on in. It was nice to get that close to the woods again. I used to live for fall and winter, when I could spend time in the woods and be with animals. Some of the times I've been least lonely were when I was alone there. Another person might not understand what I mean, Laurel. But I think you do.

The sergeant was a little nonplussed about the deer, until Hal promised him venison. Fortunately, a cage mate knew how to butcher, too, and helped him.

The sergeant wants to know if I'll take his boys rabbit hunting later on. I said sure. Can Jubal learn to track deer? I can't wait to share these things with Rick. You'll be amazed, baby, at how patient I can be in bringing about the sort of relationship I want with him. I can last a long time and take anything in the way of rejection. In the end I'll make him see and feel my love. It's so hard to explain that I did love Greg and wouldn't have deliberately hurt him anymore than I would have if he were my own son. You are pulling me out of a maze I'd never have found my way out of alone.

Having chastised him for his jealousy, it was her turn to feel it.

Guess who came by my office when she was visiting a free-world friend here? The little nurse, Rosalie, who sat up all night with me at the hospital.

The one who knitted him *socks,* Laurel sneered.

She wanted me to kiss her goodbye. I said I couldn't. I didn't mention you. Rosalie said she was just so lonesome. Aren't we lucky all that loneliness is over for us, angel? Yes, I did call Sallie "baby." And, all right, I didn't mean it, if you say so. But "angel" is my own word for you. I've never called another woman that. Or said to another woman before that I adored her.

Last night, Laurel, I lay on my bed loving you hour after hour. I finished at three in the morning and had to cram the sheet in my mouth to keep from crying out in my agony. I feel that prison has reduced me to so much degradation. A grown man has no business behaving like that.

Rosalie was certainly forward, Laurel thought. After all, on her second visit to the prison, she only asked if they could have a baby. With William I never felt we made a baby out of love, or started one either. Aside from thinking of Matagorda, she thought Rick would be wooed there more easily if there was a sibling.

There was a price to pay for Hal's confiding in the chaplain, for enlisting his help in kiting out letters. The chaplain also let him phone sometimes on his WATS line, the way Buddy did. Or let him call from a public phone when they were away from the prison. In return for these favors, Hal had to agree to be on the chaplain's speaking team. He had been asked before and refused. Unlike the time when he was out with Buddy, he had to stand up before strangers and bare his soul about why he was in prison.

I've been once, Laurel—right after we missed our chance in Greenwood. Today in my unhappiness I looked back, trying to figure out why fate would play such a cruel trick. Maybe this is the aspect of prison where society gets paid off. I wondered if God might think I was becoming too complacent because I had you, and that I needed more punishment. But that can't be because you are punished too. I do believe

> in God. I depended on Him when there was absolutely no way out, and I made it. And after all, He must have sent you.
>
> With the speaking team, I stood on a dais before a youth group. No words would come out of my mouth. Such sorrow welled up inside me about our missed chance, and images of you as I'd thought to know you. When I began talking, my voice wavered. Soon there was not a dry eye in the house; even the chaplain had tears. He put his arms around me and said no other prisoner on his team had ever made such an impact. I felt guilty that I suffered, not over transgressions already committed but over one I longed to commit. You won't stop loving me?

She suffered over his demeaning himself to help them, and loved him more.

> The only way I could stop loving you, Hal, is to cut out my heart, my soul, my marrow, the essence of myself. We'll have to forgive God the hurricane that kept us apart.

Always when Hal grew morose, she tried to lighten his mood.

> Who was going to pay the whore in that little town if you'd gone to one? Nobody offered to pay me. Got any baubles, beads, or a little corn to barter?

They went over and over their missed chance.

> Darling, when you wrote about the fight breaking out in the bus on your way back from the Gulf Coast, and how the walls were covered with blood, I went cold. Suppose something does happen to you! How will I know? Now Mr. Grady is talking about buying an airplane to fly in important visitors and wants you

to be the pilot? How much else must I worry about? I wish you didn't know how to fly. But you could keep going and fly to Connecticut. That place is insane. They let a visitor land in his two-seater and take his trusty friend up for a flight over the camp!

Hal, I can imagine what it was like for you that day being driven across those tracks in a bus, looking out and expecting to see me driving in. You are right: If our eyes had met it would have been like some old movie. Also you are right that I've got to let Mr. Cohen actually start this divorce. I must tell William. Then if you get a two-day pass in November, I could certainly come down. I'm sorry I missed the rodeo. No matter what happens, Hal, I've got to come down there soon. I'm dying, as much as you are. What do you mean, you refuse to plant flowers around a red house for me, like the other guys? Don't you love me? I'm glad your turkey and fixings were good last year, even if you had to eat them with a spoon.

". . . birthday," William had said. She stared up from the breakfast table, thinking of Hal. What had William said? He could not afford to buy her a birthday present this year? "That's all right," she said. Not one inexpensive thing after fifteen years? He had been talking about something before that. A new roof. She shrugged away the importance of a present. She was glad not to have lived the way Hal confessed he and Sallie had lived, always in debt. He bought two airplanes he couldn't afford and used to do acrobatics—and yes, he wrote, wearing Snoopy goggles and helmet and scarf—landing in fields near the pools of friends at parties, to their delight. He had been a card. Till the day he suddenly decided he could kill himself, and he quit. She was of two minds about Hal's life. He should have been past all that at his age, industriously working to save money the way she and William had been, always with goals in mind. On the other hand, admittedly she was intrigued by the high-flying Delta social life, by all the partying and drinking, and felt she had missed out on something. There was a recklessness in her nature that longed for Hal's past life. How could William be so short of money?

She put a few peanuts beneath a counter. "I wish I could see the little guy," Rick said, shrugging into a heavy sweater. "You will," she said like a promise. He had turned loose his three chipmunks in the house and they ran about, hiding at will, until they escaped outdoors. One had begun to return, finding its way in from behind the stove. She looked up from reading, quiet afternoons in the house, and the tiny thing sat on its haunches staring at her, sharing moments in a way she would not have thought possible. When she lay still, it climbed all over her. William, in wool, went by in a whiff of mothballs. She should have aired out things better from the attic.

When the house emptied, she sat in her housewife's silence, near tears. Because someday the chipmunk would simply not appear anymore and someday she would not sit in this house again either. It seemed so difficult to think of leaving.

In the houses where they lived, William kindly gave her the extra room for her writing, saying it was only fair since he had an office in New York. He did not keep much business at home. In the top of his closet there was a box with things filed for income tax time. Laurel walked the box off the shelf with her fingertips. It had a folder with numerous receipts for dinners for two at Trader Vic's. She got a chair to replace the box exactly in its dust marks. William could see up that high without help.

> Dearest Hal,
> There are so many kids here in the afternoons, I drove my mother to a nearby cemetery to talk. I told her about new evidence. She said, "Maybe I shouldn't have talked you out of a divorce before. William's a sexual deviate." I told her, "Only in the

sense he needs the excitement of a chase. He's not turned on by sleeping with his housekeeper, which is what a wife is."

"He's a cock-chaser," she said.

I nearly fell over. "Mother, that's not a term I'm familiar with," I said.

"I just know a lot more than you think I do," she said. "I heard your daddy and his friends talk nasty all those years."

"I believe the word you want is cunt," I said. A nice ladies' conversation.

She said, "Listen, I can't stay in this cemetery any longer. I've got to pee."

"You mean piss," I said.

My mother and I are being brought closer together.

Then I had to tell her. "Mother, wait. There's something else. . . ."

"What!" she screamed. "Throw your life away on somebody who's never drawn a sober breath? A mur—" but she couldn't go on with that. I said alcohol was available in prison and you'd never taken a drink in a year. Then she said, "Oh. If he hasn't had a drink in a year, then he can quit."

There you have it from the horse's mouth: she did. "Bah," she said. "Two years. Anything can happen. Period."

Her opinion is Sallie will never let you go, and that Rick will never move south. She would not either, she said. She wasn't going to move in with me when I was a poor divorcée. I wouldn't have thought of asking her; but up here is so expensive. The cleaning lady asked me for a raise. Forty dollars for two days and she leaves at two thirty! I remember your being surprised by that term, but I can't switch now to cleaning woman.

After a glimmer of consolation, she began berating me for my whole life. How embarrassing I had been for her and how unstable. I wanted so much to ask her, didn't she realize how *her* drinking and *her* instability had affected me? But I lack that kind of courage. I like to spare hurt. The truth is only in the eye of each beholder. I see you as someone else from the way a lot of others see you. My mother said, once I was divorced I was nothing but a failure. I told that to my editor and he said quietly, "Most mothers would be very proud of you."

As soon as she sees a place to dig in, she's going to; now she sees a flaw in William. Why had I picked him? I wanted to laugh; always before she's been so proud of my marrying into such a family and someone like William so devoted to his son. Though she simply accepts infidelity as part of the male character; having grown up with that idea, I do too. It's the degree we're talking about, and neglect. If only William had slept with me too we wouldn't be in this mess.

She said I was vindictive, that I always had to get back at people and was getting a divorce to get back at William; that I'd done it to her by making her an alcoholic in my last novel. I muttered under my breath, "You *were* one."

Further, I thought, you told me you never read that book.

The thing about my mother is, she doesn't mean half she says.

Laurel thought of Rick in his nighttime attire, black watch cap and dark clothes, stealing about the cemetery with a friend, an eerie figure turning over gravestones. She thought his behavior boyish pranks; she was brought up to believe little boys were devils. Her mother said they all stank. Her father said he soaped hilly streetcar tracks as a boy, and her uncles blew up rural mailboxes.

Rick had had to atone because they were strict, yet they could not help being a family that laughed. "Old buddy,"

William had said. "No one with real criminal intent would have gone the night before Easter to desecrate a Catholic cemetery: not in a town where the entire police force is Italian. And the family custom is to lay wreaths on graves on Easter." He went on shaking his head. With every policeman in town assembled the next morning, a few overturned gravestones became a *cause célèbre*. No stone was left unturned (pun intended, Laurel said) till the culprits were caught. When the same duo broke out a downtown plate glass window, she cried, "Rick, why the bookstore when I'm a writer?" They'd never exhibit her books; in all her years in the town they never had. "Of course not," said a Jewish friend. "You're a goy." I knew I should have moved to Darien, Laurel said.

Heavily, she and her mother contained their secret talk.

They drove into the yard, and Rick greeted them with kisses in front of his friends, a boy not yet old enough to be embarrassed. "So sweet," Laurel told him. "I was thinking of your nighttime capers. I ask you again, Why?"

"I don't know," he said.

In saying goodbye, her mother whispered, "Sleep in a separate bedroom." Laurel moved into the guest bedroom in the middle of the night. William asked next morning if he had snored. She did not see why William cared if she slept elsewhere, but unfortunately William did care.

> Laurel:
> I'm so glad you've spoken to your mother. I don't understand, though, why she so continually berates you. It's as if she's stopped drinking but has found nothing else to replace it and still has her alcoholic's personality. In a critical pinch I have a habit of holding an informal conversation with God. When we couldn't meet as planned, I questioned whether He was trying to tell us something. I consider that most things we hold dear, very valuable, don't come easily and that's what makes them so precious, for if they

were that easy to obtain, they'd be cheapened, wouldn't they? I don't believe He was trying to tell us our love was not to be, for it is. It exists already.

Missing one another that time has made the sexual tension even worse. I had hoped I was through with this teenaged sexual throb. But damn it, it happened again last night. I hope it stops before the real cold weather sets in here or I'll freeze getting up and changing shorts. Speaking of that, I wonder what the others think about me throwing my underwear in the hamper in the middle of the night. We toss it into a cotton sack in the middle of the cage—no way to be secretive. Oh, Laurel.

You've told me to go ahead and feel every emotion but hate. Older convicts have told me many times I'd experience both hatred and bitterness before I got through. I did not believe them. Now I see so clearly what they meant. But Laurel, who? No person has done anything to me as an individual. Do I hate society, the system, the Establishment youngsters talk so much about? I don't hate anyone or any of it. I am just filled with an overwhelming sadness and sorrow.

Last week was revival week here. A Baptist minister showed up bringing a busload of schoolchildren to sing at various camps—Brother Walker. It turns out, Laurel, you know him. He mentioned previously he'd had a church in Itna Homa and I asked if he knew your uncle and aunt. And then found out he knew you, Rick, and Buff too. I wanted to say, Preacher, we are saying nice things about the girl who belongs to me and with whom I'm going to spend the rest of my life, once the state returns it. I've never even held you as tightly as I've wanted. I've hardly touched you. If we hadn't come so close to having a few hours, perhaps it would have been easier. This evening while those children were singing, I wanted to walk off. The tears just fell down my face, as they have before. And I couldn't tell anybody why. I had to get the pastor to drive the bus back to the administration building, rather than me, while I sat in the dark with those children. A man needs to be alone to cry, and I never am.

As a Presbyterian, I don't understand these Baptist services. Why do they want you to come forward like that? It looks like you'd be saved dozens of times if you did as they ask you to do. Hell, I've already been saved, otherwise I wouldn't be here, would I? I hate prison! In the cage, everybody's in a violent argument because of the revival. Separate discussions are going on and Bibles are fluttering all over the place. One old con said, "This prison is a dressing room for the Kingdom of Heaven." My own opinion is it's a toilet bowl for hell. Every time I get into a conversation they think I'm spying as editor of *Prison World* and want to make sure I know how to spell their names.

Hal, she wrote,

>I don't know which is worse, going to bed longing for you or waking up longing for you. There's an article in *Time* about the loneliness of wives of men in Vietnam, and I feel like one of them. In memory your voice does things to me I can't describe. Now I have you but I don't have you. It's cold here. But I think only of standing in a dusty cotton field with you, kissing.

As a mother, she did not want to be sitting with erotic thoughts outside a school waiting for her child. Rick had to go to town for new shoes. Loaded yellow school buses pulled away, and then he came toward her wearing the special shy smile kids wear when they are being picked up. His shoulders were broader and moved in a more manly way. She remembered her own sense of importance about going from grammar school into junior high. No longer carrying a book satchel but her books stacked to her chest, the way she'd watched older kids carry them so long, and having a locker in the hallway and changing classes rather than staying with a homeroom teacher. She had to tell Rick about the divorce today, away from home. To tell him there would taint that house forever, she felt.

"Mom. Guess what! I was made quarterback."

"Fantastic. Exactly what does one do?"

Rick closed the car door. He patiently explained as he'd known he would have to. She began to cry; she lied and said she cried over wishing her father could have had a kid who made quarterback. Rick understood about her childhood. He'd even asked once in whispered wonder, "When will you ever get over it?" How could she tell him and take the stars out of his eyes when he had been made quarterback?

Black people were in a car ahead, an unusual sight for the town. She could not forget the uproarious town meeting she attended last spring; there was a discussion about bringing a few black students into Soundport from a nearby industrial town. A panel member in favor of the idea said he'd received threatening telephone calls about his wife; someone in the back of the room jumped up crying, Who gives a damn about your wife! What about our kids? She was stunned by the rudeness; in the South people she knew would not have yelled. How preciously false liberals in this town were when confronted with the reality of a minority being put on equal footing. These liberals were filled with compassion only when gazing out a train window at Harlem. They liked being supercilious about the South, seldom knowing anything first-hand. But one of her periodic live-in Southern maids when Rick was small put things straight forever: Down home you know where you stand, she had said. Up here prejudice is hidden. Sara made her pronouncement during an afternoon rest period when she drank beer and wore William's house slippers, and Laurel hadn't had the courage to ask her to stop either practice. She remembered coming home from that meeting filled with fury, saying, What do these Soundport liberals think will happen if three black students infiltrate the school system? She thought the woman driving ahead must be the mother of one of the students finally admitted.

"How's the black student in your school doing?"

"He's dumb as hell," Rick said.

"Rick."

"Whaaa...? He's dumb as hell." He threw out his hands.

"He hasn't had your advantages."

"I'm not into something heavy. You asked me and I told you."

"It's not his fault, and I certainly hope you have compassion."

"Gid outta here," he said. "I don't want to hear that bullshit."

She said automatically, "You shouldn't talk to me like that. It's not bullshit."

He got down onto the back of his neck. "I wish we'd never brought up the subject of the little nigger."

"Rick!" He was kidding, but she was jarred.

"Relax," he said. "I was captain of the basketball team in gym and picked him first."

"Oh. Well, that's good."

"Yeah. He's the tallest boy in the seventh grade."

"Jeez, you're a great guy."

"I ate lunch with him, though. Some of the kids won't."

"That's incredible. If you hadn't had your exposure to the South, maybe you wouldn't either. What'd you talk about?"

"Mostly what his older brother tells him about making out with girls."

"I'm sure that was interesting."

"I'm not sure it's all true."

"I'd imagine it all is."

"I'd ask you, but I can't."

"You can ask me." He slid farther down. She said, "Has it occurred to you I might know?"

"Mom." He sat up. "Shit. This isn't the kind of thing guys want to talk to their mothers about. Anyway, guess what else. I got invited to a Jew-in."

"Rick!"

"I can't help it," he said. "That's what the kid who invited me to his Bar Mitzvah called it."

"Jesus," she said. Her stomach was nervous, and in town she fell back on a Southern remedy and said, "Let's have a Coke." She walked fast toward a luncheonette but Rick stopped outside a drugstore. "I've got to get something."

"What?"

"Pencils and some baby powder."

She jerked his sleeve. "No, you don't," and she went on.

"What the—" He was probably afraid to curse again, thinking his mother about to go over the wall.

"I'm sick of that stuff dusted all over your room. I have to clean it up."

"Dad uses it."

"Yeah. Well, that's his problem."

"I don't even want to go in there and have a drink with you."

"I don't want to have a drink with you either." She heard the childishness of her tone, and they were made to argue when they almost never argued. She had to have the courage to do what she had put off so long, and thought herself ready to fly on her own wings. "Go on to the shoe store. I'll be there in a minute."

"You're weird," he said.

Laurel pushed into the drugstore as if into a headwind. There was the smell of hot roads suddenly pockmarked by a cooler rainstorm, but it was an odor from the prescription counter. She dialed William's number, scarcely thinking of the numerals, she had called it so long. Not to falter, she spoke quickly. "This is Laurel. I've told you before I was going to get a divorce. And now I am. I've got a lawyer, and I advise you to get one too."

She hung up wondering if she was a coward to have done this by phone. As always, seagulls were wheeling and dealing over the river through town. The day was growing dark toward 4 P.M. Many people did not like night so early, but she and Rick liked being at home and cozy, pulling down the shades, being safe where you belonged. She entered the shoe store. Rick's feet looked huge in Keds he was trying on. "You'll grow to your feet." She repeated an expression she always heard, even about puppies. They did not hold grudges, and Rick was no longer mad. "Want some socks?" she said. "New bedroom shoes? How about tasseled loafers?" She spoke out of a generosity he would shortly understand.

"What about Dad?"

"Wear them home and then we can't return them."

"Why are you doing this?"

"You're a good kid, even if you are a juvenile delinquent."

"I'm going to wait. We'd better ask Dad."

She drove them a route home longer than necessary, along the Merritt Parkway. And abruptly she pulled into a commuter's parking area and stopped the car. "Rick, there's something perfectly terrible I have to tell you. I've got to get a divorce from Dad."

Rick's face changed color. Total comprehension crossed over it, the pupils of his eyes darkening. "If you and Dad are getting a divorce, I'm splitting."

"No," she said. "No. You mustn't do that."

They drove home in silence. Rick went to his room carrying his new shoes, and she began dinner. William phoned and said in a terse voice, "I'm taking an earlier train. The five-oh-two." Laurel could not help but wonder if there had not been other times William could have taken that train. She knocked on Rick's door before going in. "Dad's coming home earlier. We can have dinner together around six thirty."

Rick sat on his bed. He had taken down from his closet boxes long abandoned there. They were full of inexpensive plastic soldiers that came originally in cellophane bags. She, or her mother, used to always buy them for him. He collected regiments of them and called the soldiers "little men." He was always playing with them under a huge forsythia bush in the backyard. The soldiers were arrayed around him on the bed and covered his knees. He did not look up at her. Rick went on moving the little toy men, having them fight one another, and making the same childhood sounds he always had. *"Chuk-chuk,"* he was saying as one guy after another one bit the dust. Laurel closed the door. She went downstairs to peel carrots, thinking this would be the last dinner the three of them might sit down to together.

 Darling:
  This situation is insane. I go on and on cooking and serving William's dinners, the old New Haven being late half the time, and apparently we are to go on living here as if nothing had happened. Since William refuses to mention the divorce, I don't think Rick believes one is happening, either. And this is not good for him.
  William is nice about things he never was before. He begged me to stay and said if I'd try another year and still wanted a divorce, he'd give me one instantly—would write that down for the lawyers—and give me everything. I suppose if there weren't you, I'd agree. The next morning after I told Rick, he threw up his cereal back into his bowl (yuck) and stayed home and was close to me all day; we sat on the couch midmorning and watched an old movie on TV, and he played with toy soldiers that date a long way back. The only thing he did say was how did I expect to control him alone as a teenager when I'd never had any authority in this house?
  My mother said, You always have been the underdog here. Stop being it.
  Yesterday William and I jogged around the block

as usual in the morning. It's strange but we are having the most compatible time. He got all worried about a pain I had after running. I have wanted you so badly, I could want him. Jubal even! Buff keeps jumping on him and Jubal seems to think she's trying to bite his fleas. The vet said Jubal doesn't have any street experience. Hal, it is such a relief that I adore a man capable of deep love and therefore fidelity. God! When am I going to be with you?

The other day was a Jewish holiday and Soundport like a morgue. It's a good day to shop. My mother and I always go to a suburban Bloomingdale's. She bought me a gray skirt as my birthday present. When I wore it, William cocked his head and asked if I'd consider having it shortened a few inches. So I will. Rick asked me not to. He said it made me look like a mother. I promised to wear it first to a PTA meeting at his school. One night in the kitchen, William did say it would be so much easier not to get a divorce. I certainly agree with that. He spoke in a lost way that was not at all belligerent. He said we had a better marriage than a lot of people. "Better than most," he said. We seem to frequently be in the kitchen. As he reached up for a glass over my head, I ducked. He looked down and said, "I'm not going to hit you."

Since he has never hit me, I know this is a terror that comes from the past, and not from him. It comes from the times my father hit my mother, and the times he hit me when I was trying to defend her. Once I was quite young, and when he hit me I fell off a chair. My mother said, "Don't hit her." You see, my mother often tried to defend me, and despite other things that have happened, I've always had to be grateful to her. I never would have known Christmas without her. She bought toys, she got up those mornings. My father never joined in; he slept off a hangover. There was horror then, but something tantalizing in memory about those days. I can't analyze it out. I know it is there. Strangely, I've wondered if my ducking from William had something to do with your letter that arrived that day. I had asked you, Why didn't you ever control Sallie?

You wrote back: I laid down the law as best I could. Sometimes, I beat hell out of her. Well, I'm glad you didn't do it regularly. But only now and then. Maybe you are right, that when she sat on the floor and peed in her pants, she shut her mouth because she finally realized she could get hurt. Maybe you are right about her doing all she could to bring it on, knowing what would happen. What is it that I've always feared about William? His displeasure, I suppose. Just as he fears his mother's even when she is not present. The simplest tasks have monumental goals of perfection, his family tribe always sitting in judgment in his mind's eye. Darling baby farmer, you believed so much in your love for Sallie, you got a divorce to marry her. Let's not be dreamy.

All these things happen about a divorce that I never knew happened. I had to take my lawyer a deed to the house for him to put an attachment on it, though I do not understand exactly why. Mr. Cohen says I'm the most naïve client he's ever had about money. I don't want to tell him yet about the certain future I have ahead. William had to be served papers at the train station by a sheriff. I never knew Soundport had a sheriff; I thought they only belonged to little country towns in the South. We had him served there to avoid his being served at home in front of Rick. And I had to go down and point out William's car. I felt strange in that dead place pointing out William's old, broken-down station car to a stranger. He has let Rick and his friends paint graffiti over it, which seemed childish to me; but William lives through Rick a childhood he envisioned and never had; we don't worry about having a better car or keeping up with somebody else. I was mortified before that sheriff. I do not wish anything bad to happen to William.

Then he came home making a big joke about having some man accost him out of the dark, waving papers and telling him he was getting a divorce. Instead, it was I who was left with a kind of hurt that he would laugh.

Last night he cooked my birthday dinner and served everything himself. Only he left the birthday cake on a counter in the kitchen, and when he went out for it, Jubal had eaten half—candles and all. We ate what was left. In the middle of dinner, William said, "This family's got to start making plans for a summer vacation. But what we need to spend money on first is new porch funiture." Rick had a guest and there was nothing I could say till the boys left. Then I looked the length of the table and said, "In light of the reality of things, do you think this is the kind of conversation we ought to be having? In the first place, it's not fair to Rick."

"What is the reality?" he said.

"That we are getting a divorce."

"The reality is you'll never be granted one."

"You're going to get your hole in a crack."

Laurel turned in front of her bedroom mirror, astonished by her mother's crudity. Any other time, she would have laughed. She was leaving in an hour for the airport and would spend two days with Hal, at an AA convention in Vicksburg. Her mother must understand how ecstatic she was. And nothing would have kept her from going. Not her mother's piece of advice. Not even a warning from Mr. Cohen if I'd told him, she thought. She had no idea a divorce could be so hard, that William could stay on in the house. She had never hated William, but a little slow hate crept in the longer he stayed. No one knew her secret life except her mother, though others saw the toll her present life was taking. A friend had said she looked haggard. Frightened, Laurel wondered how she would look to Hal. Her gray skirt was better shorter, the way William suggested. But it was too loose at the waist. Rick had guessed that she now weighed less than Jubal. And Jubal went to the railroad station, another of William's uncommon suggestions. Rick had been right. What were they doing as a family one Saturday morning at the railroad station weighing a dog? "Mother, are these heels all right?" She needed help. "Hal's not so tall."

"You sound just like you did in high school."

Oh, why couldn't she be kind? Laurel thought, walking around in a motel room. There was that little tag end nagging in her mind about her mother's being right. But what is wrong with being in love? She liked all this racing and beating inside herself, and a craving for someone. She hated even now lying to William, but William still spent all the nights he wanted to in New York. When she turned over her prison article in despair to William for his expertise, he said the piece lacked feeling. *Doesn't that kill you?* she wrote to Hal. He knew she was a woman who all her life had been dependent on men, who wanted to be, but she should stop turning to William as if he was gospel, about the length of her skirts and what to write, he said. How did she think he felt, locked up, unable to fight for his woman, with William in the house and the possibility of her weakening? *Darling! Darling!* She had covered pages with scrawls; didn't he understand how she loved him and how wonderful their future was going to be? She told William she was giving the article one more try, one more research trip for two days.

A car door slammed, and she was at the window, peeking out. There were Buddy and Hal in the parking lot. Buddy had a room here too. She let the curtain close. The risk they ran was in seeing someone Hal knew, maybe an agricultural salesman who dropped by Matagorda, he had said. He told her how such men never cursed in front of his father or told a dirty joke, they so admired him as a gentleman. Hal looked up to him, and she went on dreaming about, finally, being part of his family, and cherished already how things were going to be. When he came in the room, they could kiss as wildly as they had so long imagined doing. "Let me catch my breath," Hal said.

He dropped down into a chair by the door. He was a nervous wreck not knowing till the last minute whether they'd make it across those tracks; he had imagined Laurel arriving here for nothing, a fiasco like Greenwood. "I hate being totally dependent on someone else's charity for every goddamned step I take off that fucking farm," he said. She sat in his lap with her arms around his neck. "This hasn't happened to me much in my life," he said more quietly.

"Sallie never sat in your lap?" He shook his head. Laurel thought about a party years ago in Delton when she saw Sallie sitting in Big Greg's lap and swinging, swinging long legs. She had been envious and intrigued that Sallie could be so uninhibited in public, or at all. And she felt a great circle was completed that she was back among people about whom she had so many memories. Though maybe Sallie never sat in Hal's lap because she didn't have to bat an eyelash to get him.

Hal slid a hand under her skirt. "I think you're ready, baby," he said, his voice low. They lay a long while under a tent of covers in bed, his mouth resting on hers without any pressure; quietly, they went on breathing together. "I think you're as desperate for affection as I am," he said. She nodded. But she grew restless and even bored. When was something more to begin? He might be worried about not having been to bed with a woman in a year, but she had not been with anyone either. His fingers fluttered to her private parts, in the obligatory gesture men know they are supposed to do. She made herself breathe hard and fast, remembering some man once told her what made sex exciting was the other partner's being aroused. She rolled on top of him. She always thought it difficult staring face to face that way, eye to eye. She buried her face in his neck. Once, after sex with her, William had said he hated the dumb look women got on their faces. She had to rise up for air, and she moved down to the end of the bed and put her mouth on him.

She liked the way men cupped your head then in a gentle way, holding their hands over your ears till it was like being inside a seashell. She liked the way they lay there mesmerized, with their soft skin, without taste, hardening and rising in your mouth. Her knees were curled near his head, and in a while he obliged her and put his head between her legs. Soon he was on top of her. When Hal lay smoking with his arm around her, he said in the beginning of their marriage, Carla asked for oral sex and he wouldn't think of it. He had not been able to imagine it before.

When Laurel went home, Rick said he missed her at first, and by the second day forgot all about her. *Did that hurt as much as I think it did, angel?* Hal wrote. *Anything that hurts you hurts me now too. Because we are one.*

11

Laurel MacDonald stood inside the big house at Matagorda watching her mother-in-law's hand slide down a curving banister. It was November, but she and Hal stood in tennis shorts waiting for Mama. Their legs were not even cold. Laurel thought back over the two years she had waited to be here, two years of struggling to be together, so much agony and longing. She had thought then that never again could she bear so much aching, and now she felt the same tremulous pain waiting for Rick to come here to visit, missing Rick.

On the landing above her a high arched window with beveled glass looked out over the lawn, the orchards, the Negro shacks, and the railroad. An I.C. train passed, hooting its laughter. Blacks in the orchard were picking up pecans. Tommy Savano rode his tractor back and forth giving whatever orders seemed to be given about anything around here. Soon it would be Christmas and Rick would come again. Rick.

She watched Mama's hand with the heavy coral ring sliding down the banister. She fingered her light tennis sweater, wondering, What is wrong with this sweater? She tugged at its waistline.

If only she could ask William, What kind of sweater do I need? How had she this insecurity when she'd lived so long in the East, with proximity to New York fashion sense and with William's advice? Why was she not more chic than anyone else? Hal stood in his tennis sweater from prep school days aged a golden color and banded with navy and maroon. "Brooks Brothers 1940," he had said, grinning. All that long-ago time you were already way ahead, she had thought. Mama traveling to New York to buy you the right clothes. The right schools. All that long-ago time when I didn't know anything. Once I remember running down a block in Delton in my new Buster Brown oxfords, believing I'd run faster because that was the advertising slogan: KIDS RUN FASTER IN OUR SHOES. I ran no faster, the awkward shoes going *clop-clop-clop* and I learning betrayal.

Every Friday night they had to eat oysters with Mama and Daddy in Swan's only restaurant. Daddy drove at a snail's pace over dark roads the ten miles from Matagorda. Mama turned one night, saying, "A woman moved here from Baltimore once and didn't unpack her trunk for two years. Have you unpacked, Laurel?" In the darkness, she had said nothing. No one noticed, as she had not thought they would. She and Hal were in the backseat like chaperoned children, the way they had been with Buddy those two years she waited. Flower power; it won. He was holding her hand when Mama turned and he hid it from view. In my relationship with my parents we never discussed the possibility of sex, he had said; there had been only the one sad time he went off to prep school. Yet when he told Mama he and Sallie were married, she said right off, "And is a baby coming? I think that's lovely," without a word of criticism. He said, too, his family had never offered a word of criticism about his killing Greg.

At dinner Daddy announced he had finished paying

for painting done on her and Hal's house months before. She remembered holding her oyster fork in astonishment; her father never let a bill languish in the house overnight. Being a Delta planter maybe Daddy had a more relaxed attitude, or was short of cash. Only she recalled Hal's saying once, they were not considered to be Delta people, they'd come down here from Delton.

In looking back over those long months she waited for Hal, when finally her divorce was over and then his, and their relationship known, she visited him in prison and stayed overnight in this house so many times; it was then she began to love it, she thought. She believed she would always see herself a tiny figure traveling those interlocking rural highways alone. The times she was here Mama would be locked away too, having what Daddy called a nervous condition. Back then, Hal had said she would get used to Mama's "oddments" without being very specific, she realized now. She believed, too, that being as sexually aroused as she was by Hal, and alone for long evenings with Daddy as she was, it was inevitable that something would happen. She was glad they never indicated even by eye contact that particular evening.

Lock, stock, and barrel. God! That was just how she had moved a few days before Hal came home, and Daddy helped her set up the household. She had never before shopped in Sears where he took her to buy a stove. Her own was left in the house in Connecticut where William and Rick lived; better not to think about it. Yet she knew a moment never passed that she did not wonder what Rick was doing. He was right that Matagorda was too lonely a place to live, for him. But mostly he was intent on finishing out his boyhood in Soundport and deserved what he wanted. She had sensed in Sears Daddy wanted to be conservative and agreed the wallpaper in the master bedroom was fine. So they lived with Sallie's selection of ivy leaves and cabbage roses; only later had she started to wonder what memories they brought up for Hal. In the same way, did he ever think about sleeping in the bed with her where she had slept with William for fifteen years? In the wide bed, Hal looked so small. Maybe Daddy was strapped for money because of what Hal's defense had cost. Here her husband stood, a dependent still, in his late forties. It was a stunning surprise arriving in the emptiness of this plantation to learn Hal was not going to farm again, that he had never farmed but a fraction of Matagorda's acreage; a token job? In his third year in prison, she had not paid enough attention when he kept writing that Daddy was renting out more land. I'm beginning to feel set adrift, he had said. She looked into the orchard, thinking, Adrift? We are sinking.

Just as Hal was about to be paroled, Daddy rented the last land to Savano. She had wanted ever since to ask if he could not have saved the orchard for Hal. She was afraid to ask. Daddy's thinking of our future. She remembered the letter Mama wrote to Hal at the time, which he sent along to her. In Connecticut, she had not understood the full implication of Mama's words then. Those months they had waited were diabolical. Hal had said: *I feel the way Scarlett did about Tara. Once we get home to Matagorda everything will be all right. Meanwhile we can only bend with the wind like bamboo. I guess that's the only way to survive under conditions of oppression.* Well, she had survived as she had told him she could:

> I stood too much in my childhood and said to myself too long nobody and nothing will ever defeat me, and nobody and nothing ever will. William told me I was the toughest girl he had ever known. Shy with a streak of steel, he said. But in steeling myself, something else closed up inside me. Nothing has dissolved it until you came along.

With all the strength she possessed, she had fought to reach the safety and security of Matagorda, Hal, and Daddy. And here I am, Laurel thought.

Back on one of her visits, Daddy said he did not believe Hal had ever liked farming. She not only thought him wrong but that he had held Hal back. Then he said that evening, "I believe Hal's problem's been, he's afflicted with immaturity." She had looked off, knowing Hal had changed in prison and knowing, too, how much he loved this land. He had told her that as a child, if he saw a boll weevil in the house he'd jump on it in a mad frenzy. And that evening she had looked out across the old grass tennis court which kept sprouting Johnson grass, so Mama simply set a birdbath in its center, and been amused.

That evening, Daddy excused himself to take a shower. She thought he went upstairs. What prompted her, what was in her, that made her sit there sipping continuously from a decanter of creme de menthe—until, sickish, she went to the downstairs bathroom? There Daddy was just stepping from the shower—upstairs, there was only a tub—wet and naked. He drew a towel up to himself. He smiled and said, "Come in," and was not at all his usually extraordinarily shy self. She remembered that most clearly, his blue eyes laughing. Perhaps he was only able to pass off an awkward moment. She moved on forward, in a kind of blind but wanting manner. They only clung together there a moment, his wetness pressing onto her; she could feel the faintest stirring of his organ beneath the towel, like the waggling of a small boy's: two lonely, frustrated people. She reasoned that out later. She hurried upstairs to bed. He said that next morning they'd never mention the incident again. He had said, his eyes again holding the blue light of mischief, "You don't know how many planters I know, about whom it's said, his grandchildren are his children." She understood that now, living on a plantation that was a world of its own and where there was so much proximity to one another.

On those visits Daddy used to tell her maxims he believed in: "A man on land is rootless neither in society nor the universe." "A man not able to work land any longer loses the fundamental basis of his dignity and authority." She then assumed he included his son. She and Hal were secure about having the answer to living—a life of intellect and the land.

In the orchard, Savano's tractor ground away over branches. We don't have either thing, she thought. The fact was as difficult to swallow as both gall and oysters.

When her moving van arrived at her house across the orchard, she was already exhausted from dismantling the house in Connecticut, with only her mother's anguished help. Wordlessly, day after day, they packed up. William had asked for mercy in what she took. She had said Hal had no money to buy furniture either. She ransacked the house, her loyalty with her new husband. Rick pleaded, "Not my bureau, Mom! I'll pay you for it. How much does one cost?" Her mother said, "You can't take his TV." And she could wonder now how she had done all she had.

Daddy silently watched her moving van being unloaded. Then she heard his quiet voice. "You certainly took everything on trust, Laurel." Seeing everything she owned being carried into that old farmhouse, her family left behind, not knowing a single person herself in the entire Delta, seeing herself through Daddy's eyes, she nevertheless wanted to say, But, Daddy, you are the MacDonalds. Who was it he didn't trust? she wondered later.

Once she and Hal settled into their own house, he said one night, "If it hadn't been for you, I'd have joined the Foreign Legion." Along with Gary Cooper? she had wanted to laugh. What did he mean? That she had drawn him into a female spider's web and prevented him from going, to his secret regret? Or was it a compliment: if it had not been for her rescuing him, he'd have had no life but to cop out? She still did not know.

She thought back to prison, when he suggested their living in Delton. His friend Preston up there would give him a job in his hardware company. If he was going to live in Delton and sell hardware, she needed to rethink the whole goddamned thing! she told him. Didn't he realize that was the kind of life she left Delton in the first place to escape? Then he considered going there to work in the fine men's store where he ordered his jeans, Pettibone's. He liked clothes, he said. *That's all your ambition?* she cried out in another letter. Sheepishly, he reported he thought a job selling might lead to something in retailing. She was to let William and his family know she married a hardware or clothing salesman? *Jesus God,* she said. *What about farming?* He wrote he agreed, the answer to living would be "a life of intillect and the land." *How did you get through Chapel Hill without knowing how to spell?* she finally asked.

That night in their farmhouse, he also said an uncle offered to get him a job on the Alaskan highway, where he had influence. Wanted to get you as far away as possible, she had thought, jolted. Why hadn't he told her? She'd have gone to Alaska. Hal had already begun to drink several weeks after coming home, and said in a half-tight sneer which infuriated her, "You wouldn't have left Rick-kk."

"I did leave Rick," she reminded him. She believed Rick had enough adventuresome spirit he'd have gone to Alaska with her. Women's lives could be formed so willy-nilly according to whom they married. "I'd have gone to the Peace Corps," she said. Hal had not received the pardon he hoped for. Even his lawyer wouldn't go out on a limb for him, he had said, because Ben Wray wanted to run for Governor. She thought how many times she had checked *no* on applications to the question, Have you ever been convicted of a felony? without expecting ever to know someone who could answer differently. Now she was married to such a person.

With the land all rented, Hal came home to no job and had an idea. He would start a game preserve on Matagorda, a hunter's paradise, where people shot the kind of exotic animals he'd hunted in Africa, the way vast acreage in Texas was being used. She imagined now giraffes craning long necks up out of cotton and soybean fields. Mama and Daddy did not want hunters, eland, and elephants roaming the place. He decided then merely to start up a small zoo. But they did not want Matagorda opened up, either, to any Negro or redneck with a quarter. Who would put up the money for these projects? she had asked. And she remembered Hal's silence.

In prison, he had begun sending her correspondence

from other people, without seeming to understand how revealing some of those letters were. She should have thought harder about his older daughter's letter, which said on her last visit to Matagorda, just before the tragedy, she had found her father to be a self-indulgent, self-pitying drunk and she hoped prison had made a man out of him. Pretty heavy stuff to write her father, she had thought. She tried to imagine Rick's having to write such a letter. After worrying about why Hal would show her that letter, she decided it was an act of penitence. You can make me into a whole and complete man, Laurel, he said. I've needed you for years. If we'd been married in the beginning, I'd be rich and settled and filled with self-satisfaction instead of poor and at sea and frustrated. No one but Sallie could have made me deteriorate that way.

Was it fair to blame another person? She stood worrying about her own deterioration, about Hal's drinking patterns. Her efforts to intervene had been perhaps too feeble. Wasn't this the truth? She did not want him to stop drinking completely because then she ought to. She had been such a different person, back in Connecticut, when he wrote her he phoned his older child early in the evening before he had a drink, and she had thought what a sad way to live: now it was her way. Only sometimes Rick phoned and caught her. She would hear the telephone ringing: Oh, don't let that be Rick. Don't let me answer. Then, propelled forward, she would hear him say, "Have you been drinking again, Mom?" Again? Again? She could not help but have pity for Hal. They lived free at Matagorda because the plantation was incorporated, but Daddy had to give him an allowance. They lived frugally but could run short. She had paid for all the groceries the months she had been here; that had begun to irk her. Now she had different expenses, like Rick's plane tickets. Oh, the hassles that came from divorce, she thought in irritation, were not worth it. She already longed to live again as innocently as she once had—as one family unit, no choice about which holiday your child spent with you.

When they ran short of money, Hal had to trudge

across the orchard to ask Daddy for just ten dollars to get them to the end of the month. Daddy lived in the past about the cost of living; yet how could they complain when ordinarily his son would have been on his own by now? She had one unsettling memory: another letter of Mama's she wished she had not seen. *I'm sure, darling,* she wrote him, *you're not thinking of remarrying till you are settled and able to support a family. Daddy and I can't keep on and on supporting wives and children.* But couldn't Daddy see what he was doing to a man already filled with humiliation? Laurel wondered.

And a man who had no confidence in himself, she thought. Once she was free, she could not help but write him frantically about getting his own divorce. She had hated putting pressure on him, but Hal had understood:

> If it's insecurity, angel, just let that be us because that's the way we are. I don't know what caused my insecurity. I've just always accepted it for what it was. I forced myself to fly, married to Sallie. It's why I have so many pilot ratings, because I was determined to do it without fear. I've never admitted this to a living soul and don't you tell anybody either. Just as I've never told anybody but you things we said in the library.

Laurel could be astonished by what Daddy, this gentle man, had weathered so late in life; by what a man so fine had come to know. Hal's trouble took everything out of my Hal, Mama had told her. Laurel had said about Sallie's divorce, it seemed unfair Hal was being unfaithful while locked up in prison, before Sallie was caught doing the same thing. Frankly, she thought under the circumstances Sallie had a right to do anything she goddamn pleased. She had had the thought then: When people's lives touched Hal's, they often ended up hurt. Sallie was reported at the Ramada Inn's bar late at night while Tina slept on a banquette, her schoolbooks at her side. The principal of her school wrote Hal she understood from others how he had grown in prison. She hated seeing Tina turn from a sunny, open child into a bewildered one. Sallie caused scenes at the school, and Tina tried to soothe things over. She was too young to understand the nature of her mother's behavior and why no children were allowed to come to her house to play. Laurel's heart went out to Tina, as she thought back to her own youthful traumas. The principal asked if Tina couldn't be sent to summer camp, if different living arrangements couldn't be made for her. She remembered being so glad his townspeople knew of Hal's change and proud the principal wrote to him. But what single thing had ever been done for Tina? It seemed to her she worried more about the effects of all that happened on the child than Hal did.

Back then, nothing released her from her compassion for Hal. Mama wrote him she was selling family silver to send money to Connie for college. And despite her own monetary situation as a divorcée, she offered to dip into her inherited stocks and send Hal money, to give him money for Tina's camp, too. After all, soon he would be taking care of her forever, she had said. *When I think of you as a contemporary locked up there, I find it hard to swallow. I feel so much for you I don't know what to do. How in the name of God you got there is the damn thing. It makes me want to run amok sometimes, trying to save you from what has already happened to you.*

What single thing here had turned out to match her dreams for it? Laurel listened to the silence of the fields and had one answer: nothing.

And she had worried about money once she was alone; when she and Rick went to a movie, she was outraged when one cost three dollars apiece: *Easy Rider;* Rick was furious the South was portrayed in a bad light. He insisted he saw familiar sights along the highway. She had to tell him the movie was not even supposed to be set in Mississippi. He loved the South so, surely he was going to move with her, she had believed. Her mother cried all the time, more worried than Laurel about the situation. One weekend when Rick and William were gone, she went to the movies alone, but the line was too long to wait. Then she had written Hal about the strange sensation of wandering about Soundport by herself on a Saturday night. She wondered what women did who were by themselves all the time. The only low-down mean thing she could think to do was to buy a package of cigarettes. She had gone home to write Hal of her longings for him, and these were made worse by his constant anguishing over her:

> I feel so strapped down in this place, Laurel. I want to be way deep inside you, and never come out. To put my mouth in your mouth, my tongue with yours, Oh, God, baby, I am torturing myself and can't stop. I love you, Laurel. I want to kiss your eyes, taste your breasts, love them with my fingers, my lips, my tongue, I want to be drowning in you all the time. I'm loving all the rest of you. I want to entwine my legs with yours, baby, to stroke them, to wrap you round with my arms. I want to put my face on your stomach. This is senseless writing but I'll be damned if I'm not being helped, sharing these longings with you. I may bathe you, soap you all over. My muscles are in knots. Jesus Christ, I need to get in bed somewhere, Laurel. Well, baby, if I can get that wound up sober, think how I'd be with a snootful of bourbon.

That letter sent her to Vicksburg. A turning point. Coming home from there, she had felt sorry for William, an emotion she had never expected to feel in her life. He called on their friends explaining he was staying in the house to hold the fort for Rick. William wrote people to make sure they were still friends, even her Uncle Tate and Aunt Allie. Don't be embarrassed if you see me in the lift line, he wrote mutual skiing buddies; we can still take a run together. At that time, the wife of one of his friends at work said her husband had been telling her for years about William and she wondered why Laurel had stayed married to him. And then she regretted having been a fool for putting up with what she knew was going on behind her back.

Rick's escapades had gone on, landing him in Juvenile Court. It was required he have his behavior assessed by a psychologist. She and William saw him also. The doctor reported Rick was impotent with rage because of the divorce. Privately, she told him her reasons for it. And he said William had stripped her of all confidence in herself as a woman. He thought the divorce was a good thing, that Rick could use distancing from his father. He was taken aback about her future. "Is this man kinder to you?" he asked. She had said, "Infinitely. And I love him." "It's a good thing he likes women," the doctor said. "Or he'd have shot his wife."

For the first time, she handled situations. She went to see Rick's main teacher and counselor. In case he noticed any difference in Rick, he ought to know his parents were getting a divorce. She would never forget that man's absolutely startled look. "I've always thought of Rick as a boy always laughing," he had said. "Suddenly, Rick has stopped laughing. And I wondered why." That was a time, she thought, looking back, she wished she had not been able to steel her nerves as she had.

She considered then that Rick would go to college, grow up; she'd be left with William, who already had in mind leaving her for a younger woman, someday. Even if that was not true, she thought, she'd never have with him the sexual excitement she had with Hal. At that point, she had thought she did not want to look back on a life without it.

Booze! While living in the house during the divorce, William stuck notes to the refrigerator, and she went on taking care of him. Rick had said if she did not fix his dad's dinner, he would have to. She recalled the evening she left a potato out on a counter for William to bake himself, and she heard his roar as soon as he entered the house. Rick asked, even after so long a time, when she was going to stop sleeping in a separate bedroom. She had told him that was required by law when you were getting a divorce. "Then you ought to drop the divorce," he had said. "Dad's trying to hold the family together."

"Oh. Dad's making me the bad guy," she had said.

"You are the bad guy," Rick said.

Those months, instead of playing tennis, William began spending weekends alone in the den, watching sporting events: she could not help but sometimes want to go down and watch with him companionably, the way they had been in the marriage. She felt sorry then for what seemed suddenly William's misery, his solitude. But she stuck to her guns. She remained in her bedroom, where she remained at night when he came home. I'm caged, too, she had written Hal.

He had hated her feeling sorry for William. He's been too cruel to you in the past for you to be taken in now. I used to feel sorry for Sallie, but no more. The ones I feel sorry for are the souls they will continue to drag down and abuse, the way they did us.

William never dragged me down, Laurel thought.

Back on that dimly lit road to Swan, she wanted to say, Mama, I know just how much you hated unpacking your own trunk here. Barely had they moved to Matagorda when Daddy told Hal they were going back to Delton. "Mama couldn't adjust," he said. "I almost hated her." He was still in his Tom Sawyer period. "But you stayed?" Laurel said. "Mama realized she'd never have a house anywhere else like the one she had at Matagorda." Laurel thought her mother-in-law should have returned to the Junior League, the Delton Art Academy, people like herself, and saved her soul.

Pris got herself out of the country by the time she was twelve: foxier than Mama. She told Laurel Pris came home from school all the time crying about how mean the teachers were to her; they were jealous of the MacDonalds back in those Depression years. They had sent Pris back to Delton to Miss Poindexter's to board. Afterward, she went away to camps, a distant boarding school, college, and then married. She had scarcely lived in the country again and yet was filled with criticisms about how Hal's wives had ignored Mama. "Well, she never shows her face up around here," Laurel said. She had had to give up too quickly her dreams about being family with Pris. Pris had never been warm to any of Hal's wives and now was perhaps just tired of changing sisters-in-law. Laurel had turned to her once and knew to expect nothing from now on, still to her regret.

As soon as Hal came home, they went up to his parents' attic to retrieve his stored guns. Legally, he was not supposed to have them any longer, but typical Southern lawmen here told him to go on hunting, just not to make no show about it. Up in the attic here, she saw things Mama had discarded—a kiln, palettes and easels, antiques from when she'd tried to run a shop, little desks from when she'd tried to hold art classes for black children on Matagorda, her heart always in the right place—and a woman's whole life seemed stored away in the attic. Laurel feared for her own life in this place.

After William had been in the house for months, Hal started ranting about that, when supposedly he and Laurel were getting a divorce. He told her it was damned embarrassing for him in front of his family, and they could not understand what was going on. Instantly, she went to Mr. Cohen saying to stop his gentlemanly, leisurely divorce or she was getting the most disreputable lawyer in Fairfield County to have a messy one, using evidence Mr. Cohen so far had held back. Soon William moved to the city; she felt a kind of lonesomeness about his absence, after all her complaints. The night before the divorce, William stayed in the house again, not to have to commute out. She came downstairs in the morning to fix coffee. She looked at William sitting on the side of the bed in a bedroom off the kitchen. He looked out the window with his hands in his lap. He had the air of a small, wondering boy; she thought of his mother, who had never quite wanted to bother with him. And what were they doing that morning getting a divorce? She had thought, This is crazy. "William," she had said, "I don't want to think I'm never going to see you again." She embraced him and could recall now the familiarity of the tall, hard frame. William had said nothing. In this year and a half since, she had continued to wonder what William was thinking and why she did not ask him.

At the lawyer's bargaining table, she was told William wanted first refusal when she sold the house. Everyone knew her plan; Mr. Cohen had said it sounded like a bad novel. She agreed to the request and, glancing at William, saw his eyes filled with tears; they pleaded. She looked off miserably, thinking, It's too late. We should have shed our tears before now. She knew it was easier for her getting the divorce because she was going on to someone else. Her mother was waiting to be her witness. At the moment Laurel came up to her, the lawyers pushed open double doors into the courtroom, and she faced it. "Why do you have on that shade of lipstick?" her mother said, squinting up close. She wanted to scream at her. Didn't she understand what was happening in her life? She had stepped forward, her mother's voice close to her ear. "You could wear a shade so much more becoming," she said. Laurel had never felt so alone in the universe.

Out on the courthouse steps again, she had blinked in sunlight: I'm divorced, she had thought. It's a very strange feeling. She was something of a pariah, and had felt odd about going home to Rick no longer married to his father. After they got into her car her mother closed the door. "Well, now you've ruined your life," she said.

Laurel had wanted to hit her. She told her to get out of the car. Her mother refused. Not knowing anything else to do, she drove them on to Bloomingdale's as planned. *Hal, I shake all the time but I've gone ahead and done what I said I'd do, and knowing it means belonging to you eventually is what has made me able to do it at last.*

November sunlight in the orchard was like a silver cloth, without shine or luster. Daddy with his usual attendant expression waited for Mama: frail, aged beyond their years by what they could never have imagined, much less been expected to endure. She could not further burden them and cross the orchard tattling on Hal's return to his old patterns. Just then, with Mama's shadowy approach and Daddy's quiet, waiting manner, Laurel knew, with certainty, they had never said one thing to Hal about William living in the house.

Who was she to emulate here, Mama? Mama even tried Catholicism and, attending a Sodality of Mary meeting, viewing what were supposedly dried tears of the Virgin Mary, not understanding, she thought what was passed beneath her nose were mints, and she ate one. The stalwart, devout ladies screamed! The incident was retold these years later with laughter, but Mama had never lived it down. Back then, the rural South was considered missionary country; a bishop was sent down from the East to speak. Mama invited him to hold a service for the blacks on Matagorda in their own church. The farmhands were not at all impressed by the solemn mute ceremony, mumbo-jumbo and lighting of candles, or even by what seemed the costume the man wore. However, when the bishop showed them wood from the Holy Land that came from Christ's cross, there was a stir in the congregation that became a commotion. An elderly black man jumped up, crying, "You say that's wood from the cross my Savior died on? Hallelujah!' and that shout was taken up. Soon there was foot patting, hand clapping, a rollicking hymn from the pianist who'd only sat in boredom waiting, and they had a good Baptist service going shortly. The bishop lost his miter on the way down the aisle and never went back for it. So the story went. People looked around often for it on the head of some darky in the fields, but no one ever saw it. Mama kept trying to help the blacks. She was either an innovator or a damn fool, Laurel was told. When she sent round toilet seats for all the hands' outhouses, these ended up on the walls of their cabins as picture frames. Laurel supposed that one day Mama just gave up. When might that day come for her? Would she go on here measuring time by Rick's next appearance?

She had started going to doctors like Mama. A rash, a sinus headache. "Have you been around any pecan trees?' the sinus doctor asked. "I live in an orchard of five hundred of them." Then he told her, "I believe you're allergic to pecan trees bearing."

"Great," Laurel said.

She casually met women at first when she and Hal might be shopping. "Do you play bridge?" they asked right off. She felt handicapped when she answered, "No." Later she knew invitations might not have been forthcoming if she'd answered in the affirmative.

In an old portrait in the hallway, Hal peered down with a look of petulance or resentment, possibly a boy's at being captured in a green velveteen suit; but an old look by now, she thought. A lock of hair fell over his forehead in the picture, as one fell forward now in person. He wore his hair longer since prison. Often he blew the lock upward and smiled into the eyes of whatever women were present. The act made her heart jerk, it caused movement in her crotch. In her tennis shorts, she had what she considered to be a perpetual hard-on for Hal; it had been there from the beginning. He himself had written, *In the foyer of the administration building when I saw you, that was the moment it all started. Almost as if I had willed falling in love.* They had both been ripe for that happening. Often she had seen similar expensive portraits in fine houses in Delton she came latterly to know. She compared this one to the childhood picture of herself over her mother's bed in Connecticut, a tinted photographer's studio portrait.

She thought that Hal's neediness and his dependency on her was heavy stuff. They gave her a sense of pride and worth as a woman. Her bosoms had even swelled with

TLC. There were moments, as now, waiting for Mama, when Hal hovered, touching elbows, being near, that she never had with William and which made darker times with Hal more able to be endured.

Mama passed the beveled window and came around the curvature in the stairs. Her eyes were vanilla. Today they were neither crazed, dazed, nor glazed. She had been talking on the phone to her brother in Delton and gave the news. "Betsey's getting married," she said about her niece. "At last! We're all so happy." She took another step down. "And nobody cares he's a Jew," she bawled.

"Now, now," said Daddy.

Hal and Laurel smiled.

By day, Mama wore crepe dresses, smart pumps, and jewelry from matching sets according to some plan of her own. Soon after moving here, Laurel was invited to a party to meet Mama's friends. "Hal," she reported back, "she scared the fire out of me. She drove straight through a four-way intersection without stopping while telling me how dangerous that corner was. When she couldn't maneuver into a parking space in front of the woman's house, she parked up on the sidewalk!"

Hal said one of the Negroes still left on the place was always supposed to drive her, Pepper. "Then why doesn't Daddy do something?" Laurel said. "He's never been able to control Mama," Hal said. His own friends had told him while he was married to Sallie, he should have kept her pregnant all the time. What outrageous male thinking, Laurel thought, wondering if it was confined to the South. A man needed to be able to control something and preferably his wife, she knew that much. But Daddy had his son. Without even a job, living in a house his father owned, Hal had nothing in the world to control now but her, and helping him out, Laurel was quiet, dutiful and obedient, but these things naturally fit her nature.

She was still guilty about the day she drove to the party with Mama. She had looked over at her jewelry, and particularly at her necklace, saying, "That's beautiful. Is it jade?" Being bombed, and having a generous nature, maybe

Mama would take it off and say, Yes, and you have it. But Mama only forded the curb, leaving her guilty about her ploy but peeved that it had failed. Already Mama had given her a string of polished pearls, just as Mrs. Perry gave her two strings from her family when she became her daughter-in-law. She wore the three strings together these days, asking her bedroom mirror, "How many strings of pearls from the families of other people will I have?"

Her parents individually had said they inherited not a damn thing. But her mother owned now an exquisite diamond ring and a fine diamond watch. "I never expected to have anything like these," she had said humbly. Had she ever told that to the roughneck salesman who got them for her? In being the first to inherit these things, Laurel would start a new family line, and that seemed wondrous.

Out through the screen door stepped Hal and Daddy. Father and son, they went out. What a family group they seemed on this old and dreaming land. No matter that every decade or so Hal brought a different partner into the picture. When he confessed he could never go to a prostitute even with his buddies on hunting trips, she had said, "You don't stay married to anybody long enough to get bored." Though she had thought, too, his refusal had something to do with his sincere, sweet nature.

In Connecticut, when Rick finally realized what was taking place in his household—that his mother was divorcing his father and marrying a prisoner who'd shot a boy to death and was moving to Mississippi—he had suddenly understood that Hal had been married twice. "Suppose he leaves you, Mom?" he had said. She had replied confidently Hal would never do that. If nothing else, he would have to have loyalty after her loyalty to him. Hal and Rick began finally to correspond: *I may have a difficult time, Hal, adapting to my new situation next fall, with my mother moving off. I often wonder why my family situation can't be a normal one, but maybe it makes me a more complete person.*

Living alone with Rick, she one day found a strange

substance when she was straightening his drawers. She sent a mite to Hal wrapped in aluminum foil. *Be careful opening this,* she wrote. *Is it what I think it is?*

Great God, Laurel, he replied through Buddy. *Yes. It's marijuana. Don't mail any more to me in this prison! About smoking pot, though, I don't know a damn thing. It was considered so terrible when I was coming along, I never saw any. Now marijuana seems as common as—well—as grass.* She was struck then by his humor, and her own naïveté. Divorced from William, she depended on Hal, locked up. She had not thought through a lot of things back then, and people had tried to tell her so.

Jubal in those days knocked a bottle of Beefeater's out of his doghouse. Rick's progress reports showed him to have a bad attitude in class. She had told him he had no right to act up because his parents were divorced. "Dad and I both had more screwed-up backgrounds than you've had," she said. But there then stood the question between them: Is that why you're both so screwed up? After Rick skipped school one day, he charmed her out of punishment. He got up and sang and acted out all the Ray Bolger, Judy Garland, and Toto parts from *The Wizard of Oz. He affects me like you do, Hal,* she had said. *I can't get mad at him.*

Savano got down off his tractor and started toward Daddy and Hal. Thinking about Rick, there was not a moment's cessation to the pain she felt about leaving him. Nothing here turned out to be worth it. Days were long. She could hardly bear the yellow school bus dropping off black children on the highway fronting Matagorda, or being at a new friend's house when her children came home. She thought back to that psychologist's advice: "Think of *numero uno,*" he had said. And he had been wrong.

Mama said softly beside her, "Laurel, the sky seems more blue when you and Hal are about." How could she not love Mama? When her novel came out, Mama said it was the most touching love story she had ever read. Her own mother wanted to know why they had such a large, glaring picture of her on the back. Mama went on. "I hardly saw my son when he was married to Sallie. I hope out of all that's happened, Tina can know right from wrong and grow into a fine woman."

"She's a sweet girl," Laurel said. How could she have known it would be Tina who would tell her the truth: out of the mouths of babes? Hal had always written about her as his "toy child." She had been in love back then with his use of diminutives. He wrote how he saved the "tiny plants" on Matagorda once, on a Saturday when there was no Negro help available and a storm was coming up. How could Daddy have said Hal didn't like farming? she thought back then. She started toward the porch too. On a hallway table sat a silver bowl brimming with Halloween candy. Mama had known no children would come out to Matagorda. She used to embarrass Tina, she had so much candy for just her and her friends, Hal said.

Laurel looked into the sunlight. Did the leaves here never change colors? Her last Halloween with Rick, a policeman brought him home merely because Rick was walking along a road alone. The young policeman said, "I recognize this house. It's where you've got a table made from a ONE WAY DON'T ENTER sign."

"I bought that at the Fantasy Shop downtown," Rick said.

"Not with SOUNDPORT POLICE DEPARTMENT on it, you didn't," the young man said.

A man from Juvenile Court came and said Rick was in danger of being sent away to a detention home. She had jumped up, not afraid to be defensive for once. "Are you crazy? A boy like him doesn't go such places. You'd ruin him for life." She said to Rick afterward, If they take you, there might be nothing Dad or I can do about it. She had been driving him to counseling sessions at Juvenile Court for years. "All those trips to South Norwalk. Aren't you getting anything out of them?" They drove there another day and stopped to buy a male mouse. "If you won't listen to me, listen to Dad."

"Dad doesn't make decisions about me anymore."
"Oh. Who does?"
"You do. I live with you now. Mom, sometimes will you talk baby talk to me so I will know I'm loved?"

She had been able only to nod her head. And to accept the task of being responsible for Rick, more than William was, for the first time. They had lived with other revealing moments. By her last fall in Connecticut an ordinance was passed against burning leaves. Rick stared at the piles they had raked and at the large green plastic bags. "What do we do now?" he said. "Get a teaspoon?"

"You're funny," she had said. She bent her head toward the rake's end. "As funny as Dad," she finished in a muffled voice.

"You hardly ever talk," Rick said. "The house is so quiet. It's so quiet without Dad."

"I never did talk," she said. "You just never realized."

Mama spoke in her gentle way. "I think Hal was an instrument of God's peace used for the good of his fellow men—through *Prison World*—to glue those broken lives together."

She might have laughed, but she could not.

Mama said, "I had begun to look forward to those visiting Sundays as the highlights of my life."

Laurel opened the screen door. What's it going to be like, Hal once asked, when we don't talk anymore about escapes and chases and people hurting one another, of fear and frustration and longing and despair? How could she have told him then, It will be boring. She missed the excitement they had lived through too; she had further dread of becoming like Mama in this place. She agreed. "Those were heady days."

She had longed so always to be at that prison. She sat so wearily by herself in Connecticut. Hal had covered a Halloween party in First Offenders—costumes and all, he said. *I think there are so many queers in that camp they use any excuse to impersonate females, even witches.* He had more fun than she did, she complained. William was dating someone his own age, she had said.

> He says he can't make it with the twenty-year-old set. He says something called singles bars have sprung up in New York; two of his married friends went and got VD. Sad they would go, I thought. Or was William speaking of himself? Living your prison experience vicariously, I find myself becoming streetwise, the way you say, against your will, you're learning in prison how to scheme.

She wondered if reality ever matched dreams. It was not a question to turn and ask Mama. They were here on this place serving their own sentences. She could hear Savano's pants legs go *whiff* against each other. Daddy had spoken admiringly about him: "Once he didn't own anything but forty acres from one bayou to another one." Now Savano owned a chunk of the Delta and rented out most of Matagorda. His own father was first-generation Italian here, a string bean farmer. He came to Matagorda bringing Mama young fig trees and planted them. He took off his hat and said, "Thank you for the opportunity you give my son." Laurel had whistled "God Bless America" beneath her breath.

This is not good countryside for women. Where had she heard, There is a reality beneath the appearance of the world? The only way life here could be better was not to have known other places as she and Mama had, or had different husbands.

Hal had moved away from the men's conversation to the edge of the porch. His knees were too rounded and cute-looking in his tennis shorts. He looked like the Gingerbread Man in her old storybook; Run, run as fast as you. "Mister Mac." Savano was talking. "That's dog-bog land. Rains and it's so slimy a dog can't walk on it."

"I was waiting—" Daddy said.

"These trees should have—" and Savano was out of

earshot after more conversation. He glanced toward the porch's far edge, where Hal escaped menfolks' talk, and muttered what was not supposed to be heard: "No more ambition than a lap puppy."

Daddy looked toward the porch, smiling. "When I lift up my foot, I take my time about setting it down."

Mama was tired and would go upstairs to play her Confederate records. The music often wandered out over the orchard, a thin lonesome sound like that of a penny whistle. *The spirit of the South reminds me of the spirit of the prison,* Mama had written.

> Men who saw night coming down on them could somehow act as if they stood at the edge of dawn. Out of defeat they could still win something if nothing more—and it was everything—than a victory over the age-old impersonal foes of the human spirit. They were never quite licked because there can be something about human beings which in the last analysis is unconquerable. We all fight battles all our lives within ourselves, and to fight them as beautifully as our Confederate soldiers is a wonderful inheritance. So many men at the prison are like the Southern soldier the way they are fighting the battle.

She had never known whether these were Mama's own words or someone else's, but in Connecticut she had been driven more toward the family she would adopt.

She married not only heady days and this land but the South's whole history.

"Are you still going to your AA meetings, son?" Daddy said.

"I hate going there and standing up, saying, I'm an alcoholic."

"Of course you can't do that, darling," Mama cried. "You're not an alcoholic."

12

In the old farmhouse, she felt cozy with the late winter storm outside, slashing against the windows, falling on the roof, springing up from tin rain gutters, falling down the bedroom chimney and into ashes, sending up their acrid scent, as if from all the fires that had ever been there. She stood at a window reaching from the floor almost to the ceiling. " 'That the small rain down may rain.' "

"Huh?"

"I was quoting something. Don't you like 'that the small rain down may—' "

"You're crazy," Hal said.

"Crazy?"

He had gone out. "Christ, that my love were in my arms and I in my bed again," she said. Soon she wondered where he went and followed him to the breakfast area. "Don't you like to be all cozy inside when it's raining?"

Hal continually brought things back from his parents'

attic. Now he bent over looking inside a green tackle box at fishing flies. Yellow furry things were scattered around him, which looked like rags. "What are these?" Laurel asked, poking her foot at a bundle.

He held still above the tray of flies too long. "Deerskin," he said.

"Deerskins? What are you going to do with them?"

"What do you want?"

"I don't want anything. I was wondering what the reason is for keeping them. What does one do with old deerskin or deerskins?"

"Are you going to keep on standing over me?"

"I'm not standing over you. I was only looking."

He shoved in the rickety tray of the tackle box. "These are my things. Do you want me to give them to Rick?"

"Why should you give them to Rick?"

"The same way you made me lend him the Holland and Holland."

She cast her mind back months before. "How could I make you? I asked if he could use a gun. I didn't know that one was so valuable. You gave it to him. You've said you wanted to teach him to shoot." Did it rankle him that his own children had not been here for Christmas? That was not her fault. "How did we get off onto the subject of Rick? We were talking about deerskins."

"You were running your mouth about them."

"Hal."

"*Hal*," he said. "Apparently I'm not going to be able to look through my things."

"Go ahead. I didn't realize it would bother you to have me look too."

"He didn't clean it when he finished shooting."

"Oh, dear." She switched back to the gun incident, feeling mired in the twists and turns of conversation. "If you told him to clean it afterward, I'm sure he will from now on."

"Didn't his daddy teach him anything about guns?"

"You know William doesn't have a gun, or hunt. He

couldn't have taught Rick about one. In Soundport, he couldn't even shoot his BB or his twenty-two."

"I thought William's family had everything."

"Jesus. How do conversations get so confused, or turn into not being conversations? I'll never know what one does with old deerskin or skins."

She went back to the love seat in the bedroom. Here she was sitting the day Rick came in and set the gun in its rack. She listened to him go to his room. She looked in and he was lying down with his eyes closed.

"Meditating?"

He looked at the ceiling. "I'm thinking. Seeing, I guess."

"What?"

"The buck I just killed. My first deer. I thought I wanted to."

"You didn't?"

"No. I was in the stand. I kept telling myself, I'm a boy in Mississippi. The woods. Rite of passage. I kept praying no deer would come. Then four! Four came out of the woods and started by. I told myself to shoot. But I was so far away, I didn't think I could possibly hit one. By the time I thought all this, they were almost gone. I thought they were safe, and then I said, 'Oh, no!' The one at the end, the big buck, slowly crumpled. I started to cry. I said, 'Forgive me.' He was alive when I got there."

"Deer have to be culled; there has to be a hunting season."

"It's OK, Mom." He closed his eyes. "It's my vacation. I just want to rest now."

In the bedroom then, too, she wished she had realized you could not change your own life without changing the lives of those involved with you. In a while, Field, the old Negro helper, came singing unmelodiously from the direction of the orchard. He came from his cabin beyond Mama and Daddy's for his evening chores. Passing the windows, he wore a green poncho, Hal's old Wallabees, and an old hat of Daddy's. Field was senile, but half-witted also. He swung plastic milk bottles tied together by rope;

these were for carrying home a water supply from their house to his. She thought it wrong in this day and time Daddy did not supply water for those left living on the place. Pepper had complained.

She wanted Field to stay at home more, but he had nothing to do there, and at her house he felt necessary. All day he regaled her with religious sermons, which at first were quaint and by now were tiresome. She picked up a magazine. He came in saying, "Evening, Miss Laurel," shedding rain and tracking mud across the light-colored carpet. The kind of thing you let go. "How you this evening?"

They had only parted at lunchtime. "Fine. How're you?"

They made small talk about the weather. "I heard from Rick today. He's done well on exams at school."

"I say."

"Only thirty-two more days, and he'll be back."

"I'll sho' be glad to see him."

"He said tell you he has that picture of Jesus you gave him up on his wall."

He looked up from laying a fire. "Say he do. Carried that picture all the way?"

"Oh, yes. He loved your giving it to him."

"You want me to light this now?"

"Sure," she said.

Flames splayed up against the walls, lighting up the cabbage roses. Field held his hand out to them and then rose stiffly. She wanted him to stay. "We going to see his sweet face in the by-and-by then," he said.

"Just about a month more."

"Ma'am?"

"Are you talking about Rick?"

"Talking 'bout Jesus."

"Oh."

"Everybody be the same in heaven."

"You mean there won't be blacks and white?"

"No'm. Everybody be good and everybody be happy."

"Where are the bad?"

"Bad folks go to hell. H-e-double-l, hell."

"Who are the bad? People who kill people?"

"Oh, yes, ma'am. Peoples who kills peoples, they sho' be bad." He made his slow way out enumerating. "Peoples who takes po' folks' money...." She looked into the fire. It was five o'clock. Ice cubes fell singly into a glass in the kitchen. She would wait and see if Hal asked if she wanted a drink. How long would he remain there in his accumulative world, with possessions no one else must look at? What went on in Hal's head?

What difference did it make if he quit AA? She knew he would after Mama's remark. But attending a meeting one night a week had done nothing but put off the hour he had his first drink. Not to drink seemed impossible here, evenings were so long. She had well understood the lonely drinking he did in his hunting cabin the night before he killed Greg. She drank that way herself when William was not at home, she had confessed. She fought the pattern as a divorcée, not wanting Rick to be ashamed or to jeopardize her custody of him. Unfortunately, she had read an article in *Vogue* at the time about letting lemon peel remain in a bottle of vodka till it turned yellow; delicious, the article had said. *And it is!* she wrote Hal. She had said, *"The world is no longer as lonely a place as it was. Even if you died, it still wouldn't be, for after so long, I've finally touched another human being. I could never again believe there could be no one, that forever I was abandoned to wander about lonely.*" During that long waiting period, her mother took her for drives, to get her out of the house. She still wondered what other suburban divorcées did; there had been no reason for her to get a job since she was leaving Soundport. What did she know how to do, anyway, but write novels that never made money?

Now at least, she thought, Hal has a job. Her mother said over the phone, "Thank God and little fishes." She had been sympathetic all along about having a man at home all day. "You marry for better or for worse but not for lunch," she had quoted, and went on in her characteristic manner, "And that's that. Period."

However, Hal came home for lunch, like most men in these parts. She ought to explain her former life to women here when they complained about long hours their farming husbands kept. It was a simpler life, to her. Why say your husbands are nearby in fields, pop in and out during the day, and are home for supper by sundown? Wintertimes, they had a long laying-off period. Hal had written her that while his friends were playing poker at the Swan Country Club, he used to spend days in Miss Jimmie June's grocery, drinking beer and eating the best corn pone he'd ever tasted.

She had looked forward to such times; they did not exist, like much she had expected. The woman had died and her store fallen into disrepair like little cabins left on Matagorda, which once housed a hundred families. Today a plantation is a factory under the sky, just business, Savano had said. And Hal had no head for business. She had come too late. Nothing but dregs of a real plantation life remained, a commissary across the highway going to ruin; the last shells of cabins had been burned, not enough left of them to claim arson and collect insurance, as was customary around the countryside. Cabins left where the few blacks on Matagorda lived were not much better.

The day they played tennis, she had waited in the car and thought Hal looked cornered. Daddy talked to him urgently, waving one arm up and down like a maestro, as was necessary when he tried hard to get thoughts across. Each word had its own accent. Hal's slowness had come from Daddy and another side from Mama.

Listening that day, Hal shuffled his feet about on a walkway that had been built by German prisoners of war housed nearby during World War II, who were given jobs by local people. She had not known the war came that close to home. Mostly, it meant shortages to her, no White Shoulders cologne or Spalding saddle oxfords. Then on VJ night, she had danced with friends in a fish pond in the lobby of a Delton hotel. ". . . love and laughter and peace ever after," someone had begun to sing. A bluebird flying over the white cliffs of Dover could render the world right. They daringly splashed in the hotel's pond believing they celebrated the end of wars forever, so naïve had the times been.

Too late, she had thought that day waiting in the car, for close contact with German prisoners to have effect on her. She had had to learn secondhand also about the hundred families and about the plantation bell that had been at Matagorda's entranceway and called them to the fields. It had had an especially sweet sound because it had silver dollars embedded inside when commissioned by a MacDonald in the past. Belonging to Daddy's family, nevertheless Mama donated the bell to the scrap iron drive during that Second World War; the family were outraged, but Daddy made no protest. This much later, Laurel thought, What a futile gesture. The entranceway now had a great gap in an iron fixture where the bell once hung. Hal got into the car, his tic beating. He couldn't tell Daddy they had a fixed time for a tennis court. What was all that about? she had asked.

"A proposition from Savano. I can work for him."

Benefits from a job flew to her mind. "That's great," she said.

Hal spun wheelies on the long gravel driveway. "Yeah. I can work for somebody who rents land from me. I'll be Robert Ruark's little pigeon-breasted clerk."

She was the sweetest a wife could be. "It could lead to something else." She seriously imagined Savano and Hal building up a little empire. "You could go into truck farming together. Invest in irrigation and plant rice." She talked about other ideas she had heard kicked around, talked further about her own. "Reading about the population explosion and the difficulty of feeding people, I don't see why it's said farming's on the decline."

"Eight hundred a month," he said. "That's not bad for around here. Daddy will match that. We can still live free on Matagorda."

That was the only real reason for living here, she had thought, looking out the car window. They had passed the brick pillar and the iron arch where the bell no longer sounded. Mama's maid Carrie had told her, "Hands be all over this place when that bell rang." Then Carrie told her sadly, Miss 'Cilla had brought her in from the fields to work in the house. "She said, 'Carrie, you don't want to be doing that hard work in the sun.'"

"I said, 'Yes'm, I do.' Then Miss 'Cilla said, 'Aw, Carrie.' Then I said, 'Miss 'Cilla, I wants to ketch air with my own color sometimes.' She let me go on back to the fields one day a week then."

"You liked picking cotton?" she had asked Carrie.

"I sho' did. Be in the field and everybody laughing and carrying on. Be shady and cool under them plants."

She had laughed. "Don't tell anybody else, Carrie. You're not supposed to like picking cotton."

"All the folks I knowed liked picking it." Carrie gave an elfin grin. "I never did like to do no cooking."

Sisters under the skin, she thought. She had moved heaven and earth to win her way here, changed her existence, but one steadfast thing remained: shopping for food and cooking it. Hal did not like Almond Mocha ice cream, and these days she was on the lookout for his favorite food, canned white asparagus, a rarity here. Twilights were long, and often she stared out her kitchen window, thinking of her Connecticut kitchen, and Rick being there; the enormity of what she had done pressed in on her. Why when she so feared loneliness had she brought herself to this devastating kind?

When Hal came home shortly after five from his work at the nearby cotton gin, she tried to be expectant about his arrival. He leaned with his back to a wall of the kitchen and waited apparently for her to begin to chatter as Sallie must have, waited in silence. She tried to extract interesting information about his office, the price of cotton, to make him rail against legislation passed in Washington concerning farmers—anything. "What happened today?"

"Kathleen, that woman who's Savano's secretary, brought in a carrot cake."

"A carrot cake?"

"It had real carrots in it. It was delicious."

"My goodness, a cake with real carrots in it. Why don't you go on and watch television while I cook."

"Sallie always liked for me to be in the kitchen while she was fixing dinner."

Sallie had a different personality and mentality. "Well, it gets on my nerves," she told him, ending those moments.

Heading on toward the tennis court, she thought how Hal would never again farm, and looked back toward the big house, which had dwarfed them all standing there, with its great columns, screened porches, wide verandas, and the dark orchard overshadowing everything; Daddy looked so small going inside; Savano rode the shiny tractor that was like a Tootsie Toy. They had faced then their own house a stone's throw away through pecan trees, and it was nearly hidden by privet hedges flattened against the screened porch that ran across its front; because in the old farmhouse the windows were nearly as tall as the high ceilings, there was light. A tall privet hedge divided their house from a cabin next door where three blacks lived: Annie Mae cleaned for her; there was her sister Marcie, and Willie, who was Annie Mae's husband but father of the baby Marcie was soon to have. Nearly hidden by nondescript bushes, Pepper's cabin was in front of Annie Mae's. Along the highway, other blacks lived, not connected to the place. On down the highway, with a railroad paralleling it, lived her closest white neighbor, eight miles away. Just then, Hal had put his foot on the brake, crying, "What the hell is Field doing?" He had been cutting their grass for the last time of the season. Hal got out to explain. "You've got the belt on wrong. You're cutting the grass backwards."

"I say."

"Whoa!" he had been crying when they stopped. "I'm telling Mister Little Hal on you," talking to the stubborn mower as once he talked to mules when he was a hostler.

I wanted the old South, and I got part of it, she thought. Try not to let things she was not used to irk her. Daddy had promised any blacks who remained on Matagorda free houses as long as they wanted. Otherwise, they can go to town, Hal said, when she mentioned their living conditions. All Field required of her was a bottle of Dr. Tischnor's on the kitchen windowsill; he took a tablespoon a day for his dizzy spells. She begrudged him nothing. She used to be fearful finding him stretched out on a floor in the house, but found him so often she stepped over him now and stopped worrying about his being dead. In the kitchen, he endlessly wiped out an ashtray, reporting what happened beyond the kitchen window. "There go the sick wagon carrying Miss 'Cilla to the horsepital again," he might remark; then she joined him. She needed diversion too. She again saw the sliver of white heading in and out among the old pecan trees. When Mama breathed strangely and could not wake up from her pills, they rushed her to the hospital. Then she would be contrite; no one ever spoke the truth about why she was there. A flu shot perhaps had not worked out with prescription medicine she was taking. When she arrived here, she so innocently had asked, "How many flu shots does Mama get?" It was too bad, she thought, there were doctors always to give a person like Mama what she wanted.

From this bedroom Laurel had looked out in amazement to see Mama running through the orchard and crossing the railroad track, flagging down Savano in his truck in front of the old commissary, where he stored seed. Daddy discovered her missing and was soon there. She had wanted Savano to take her to town for a flu shot. Another time, she came over to "borrow" Hal's truck to get to town herself but bogged down in mud outside Annie Mae's, and Willie escorted her home. Laurel had to think in amusement of Rick, longing for the grandparental relationship he read about in youthful books, the kindly old couple on their farm, spending the night at Daddy and Mama's. He woke to doors opening and closing, to Daddy whispering, "I knew you had some hidden. Where did you get them?"

and to his warning her not to wake Rick. She was doing her best as a daughter-in-law. She had started down her own driveway to catch Mama that day and was soothing her by Savano's truck when Daddy arrived; he thanked her. Hal said Pris hoped Laurel would treat Mama better than his other wives had.

Every Friday Mama had her hair done. It was painful thinking of that last time she phoned about going out for oysters. There had been no reason for her to tell Mama she'd have to ask Hal, except her own ingrained Southern habit of being subservient to men. And she did try to be different from the way Hal described Sallie, and to build Hal up into being the man of the house, running the show. But my God, he was so passive. Her role model was William, and the comparison was not fair, she knew. She declined the invitation to that thin voice coming from across the orchard, heard for the last time the voice as faint as a star that never learned to shine.

    Hal, too, was still haunted by his refusal. The night of the funeral he made hard love twice. She could not forget when the phone rang later that Friday, Daddy's own voice that sounded as if he was under the sea. "I couldn't save Priscilla this time," he had said.

    Mama died under the dryer; she would have hated dying with her hair in rollers. I would have, Laurel thought. Daddy as usual was waiting for her outside the shop. His parents' lives filled her again with a dreaded sense of future boredom with Hal; things were bad enough now. The beauty shop's owner said she and the girls had seen Miz MacDonald asleep under the dryer so many times; this time they knew something was different. Miss Millie put the bottoms of small match boxes over her customer's ears to protect them under the dryer. She called from her Golden Peacock Shop wanting to comb out Mama's hair. Laurel had to tell her, "That's been done by the funeral parlor." Miss Millie began to cry. "It won't be right," she had said. The funeral director had left a card with his slogan: *The Difficult We Do Right Away. The Impossible Takes a Little Longer.*

The card had no longer seemed humorous, and she remembered shredding it. When she stood over Mama's gravesite in Delton, she told her silently, Mama, you lost the battle.

"People just don't understand. Priscilla and I were together so long," Daddy had whispered. Comments must reach him, the kind his children made, who each said, "Daddy is a saint." But she went on with her private feeling that Mama had something to suffer in her life's lot, too.

"One thing you can say about Priscilla," Daddy had said. "She certainly knew how to run a house."

Mama's ultimate compliment; Laurel cringed for her and for her epitaph. She sat at the funeral wondering what in the world Hal might say about her some day, fearing it would be something as far removed from what her life was really about.

When it was known Mrs. MacDonald had died, people flocked to the house bringing food. For weeks, notices came in the mail of monetary gifts to charities in her name. She and Pris set up a filing system and divided the work of answering four hundred letters of condolence, having to cross-index what else these people had offered, memorials, flowers, food. She still felt dizzy. The cortege in Delton had filled several city blocks. As she sat writing the letters, remembering the funeral, she wondered where all those people had been when Mama was alive, dying of loneliness. She wrote to names so important to her in the past, when she had been awed by country club members, and looked back to the night she first saw Hal MacDonald, and Clyde McCoy had been playing on a hotel's rooftop, and wondered who, back then, could have imagined she would end up as mistress of the legendary Matagorda, so lonely in its fading splendor.

When the house cleared of visitors after Mama died, a nephew of Daddy's was left. He was wearing a long overcoat from World War II down to his shoes. Camellias had been blooming at the back door. He said he was setting up a company to sell a detergent of his own invention, X-Cell. "It removes surface tension from water," he said.

"You can float a pin on it." He asked Hal to be vice-president, and she sat with her blood running cold, she remembered. It was the first time she admitted the kind of faith she had in her husband. "Boogey," she said behind Martin's departing back, relieved by Hal's refusal and complimenting him on how sweet he had been. Field had been emptying ashtrays. He spoke aloud to himself. "Freaks don't bring forth no fruit. God hates that."

She could go on laughing. Streak of fat, streak of lean, she thought. The kind of salt pork her mother told her to cook with turnip greens. She thought that way about Hal's family; the members seemed made up of two streaks, sanity and insanity. She thought with a great deal more pride about the solid country folks who were her people, up in the hills: my stock, she told herself.

That day when Field was settled with the lawn mower, she said, "What is Annie Mae doing?" The girl had come out of her dim, raggedy house next door and run a few steps toward the highway.

Hal had laughed. "Jogging. Copying you. I saw her the other day." Annie Mae had already gone home.

"She'll be playing tennis next," she had said, her racquet between her knees. She was sorry about changing her own jogging route. She had liked running through the orchard and ending up coming past Annie Mae's. But early on a man's voice inside there cried, "Who does she think she is, a man?" And another voice she thought was Pepper's went, "Sssh." She hadn't met Willie yet, since he worked in town. He did not come to her welcome-home party for Hal; she hadn't known anybody else to invite, so she asked all the blacks on the place. She had liked Carrie's throwing her apron to her face and crying, "This is a happy day!" Annie Mae had been sipping punch and said, "Willie say he sorry he can't come." Laurel had thought, I'll bet, eyeing the privet hedge. She was much more aware of him in that house beyond it than if he had been in the room with her.

Jogging was not in vogue here for women, or not for women her age. There had never been a YWCA for sports, because blacks would have to be admitted. They outnumbered whites in the region. When she asked Hal his reactions to Africa, he'd said, I just felt at home. She went on laughing about dropping into a grocery on the highway one Friday evening when she first came. She suddenly realized she was the only white person in the store. God, she had thought, I'm in a black grocery and they're too polite to ask me to leave. Then suddenly she realized she was only in the Mississippi Delta and it was payday. A black woman customer had said, "I like that coat you're wearing." She had thanked her and been about to say, I got it in Bloomingdale's, then remembered she had nobody black or white to talk to her about her former existence.

The threesome next door was inherited. Previously the girls' mother worked for Sallie. But Gertrude and her husband were members of the NAACP and moved to Chicago. Gertrude reported also her grandmother up there was dying, and the grandmother said she could not die till Gertrude got there. The couple were the kind of blacks she wanted to know. Gertrude came by obviously to give Hal's new wife the once-over before letting Annie Mae work for her. If she had known what was ahead, she would not have passed muster. She served Gertrude cucumber sandwiches and iced tea in the living room, and Carrie reported back, "Gertrude say you a nice white lady." She inherited Gertrude's cretin daughters. How could they belong to those parents! She worried that her liberal's heart bled less. "Why don't you and Marcie go to Chicago?" she suggested, implying they ought to be with their mother. "Us don't like it up there," Annie Mae said. Carrie was no help. "Up there you be a town mouse hiding from the cat. I rather stay home and be a country mouse eating cheese in peace," she said.

Maybe Annie Mae wasn't supposed to know better than to polish a leather table with ammonia. "That's for the bathroom," Laurel told her between clenched teeth; however, her old insecurities rose up, and she let her know if Annie Mae did not clean bathrooms, she would do it.

Often she was remorseful, looking around at furniture

here, which she and William struggled so hard to buy, making Hal comfortable. He seemed to have been given most of what he had by Mama; now his furniture had departed with his wives. She did not take the pleasure she expected in her new pieces. She remembered hoping the MacDonalds would think what she had was nice enough. Her new things were bought with money William gave her in buying back the house he gave her in the divorce, which he'd been paying the mortgage on all along. That the down payment on their first house came from her money was not so much comfort. "I'm up to my ass in debt," William said on one of their last encounters. She'd had the feeling he meant forever.

When Annie Mae came to clean, bringing large bundles of laundry from her own household, she felt she ought to be grateful she did her laundry and Hal's too. Marcie wouldn't stay alone in her old house, and she came along. Most of the day she slept across the kitchen table. Ought she offer the pregnant girl a bed? Field might be stretched out on the floor somewhere. Marcie had begun to watch TV, and she hadn't had the nerve to ask her to turn down the sound because she could hear it where she was writing. Typing, at least. What was she doing, except keeping to her old schedule? Her mind was fractured; too much had happened to her. Anyway, people had told her the South she had in mind was gone. But she had to come on and find out for herself. The sixties had ended while she waited for Hal in Connecticut. No longer was she comfortable going to the hills, poking about and listening, because everyone there knew who she'd married.

Hal had a coterie of friends who remained loyal. They gave a dinner party, which was her introduction to them. She looked back at that night, thinking of all she learned, so quickly. There had been the clean slate and Hal refused a drink. His farming and hunting buddies chided him as being ridiculous. A man asked her, "Why didn't Hal sleep with Sallie like everybody else? Why would he marry her?"

And she realized Hal thought Sallie's sexiness enhanced him, and that he had looked like a fool to his friends.

One guest was a widely respected planter who was known as a patron of the arts; she could already wish she'd met a Delta man like him. He was the only person who had ever spoken to her about her own work, or Mrs. Perry's: the only person who seemed to understand she'd had another life. She never saw him again; he refused an invitation to a dove hunt, saying he'd like to have talked to her further. Then she knew, too, the divisiveness that was here about Hal. Walter Harold Sills sat down and asked, "What's Hal going to do now that he's back?" She repeated things she was told. "His equipment was sold. It's too expensive to buy more and start over at his age. Do you think so?"

"It is for Hal. Because he's never known anything about farming." Then Walter stood up. "But I guess he never had anybody to teach him. Mr. MacDonald's never known anything about it either."

How instantly all her ideals about the MacDonalds had been shattered. At dinner Hal was persuaded to take wine. He held her hand. But on his other side a woman said how cute he looked with crinkly lines he'd developed around his eyes. The host said during dinner, "There's a silent majority in the United States deprived of a hearing, because the big communications media are in the hands of a lunatic fringe of leftist liberals. Most of them in New York."

She silently toasted her old friends back at Events-Empire, William's co-workers. A guest used his starched place mat to wipe his greasy chin; the napkin was too damned little, he said. He'd also said at her house, "Hell, no," he didn't want a cup of tea when she offered one. He and Hal had come in from hunting. Nobody cared he wadded the place mat and wiped his hands. This difference was what she had come for, she thought. The time Hal wrote he had been chairman of the local Republican party, she had said, *You probably voted for Ike!* He replied, *Of course, and for Strom Thurmond, Dewey, and Herbert Hoover.* So much seemed funny then, he seemed more astute. She assumed she didn't seem the same as in her letters either. She wrote about the day Kennedy was shot, saying she had rushed to the school bus to tell Rick in a gentle way. He said, "I know. The bus driver announced it. All the kids clapped." Hal wrote that Soundport sounded like the kind of town he'd like.

She rode home from that dinner party, beneath the canopy of Delta sky, feeling so soon tricked and cheated that her husband and his father were not respected planters and, worse, friends of her husband's thought him stupid.

Hal had not played tennis since the summer his older daughter started beating the shit out of him. Laurel cried out "Good!" about his shots, wishing there was not a reversal of roles and that he was the coach as William had been. She remembered how a young tennis instructor once told her she was stupid. She stayed rooted to one spot, never thinking to trick or outwit him, to place a shot beyond his reach. She went on steadily returning balls to him in a direct, honest manner. Her stepdaughters had come to visit and she found it difficult being stepmother to two girls with different mothers. There was naturally animosity on Connie, the older girl's, part. Tina was entirely unaware of it. At dinner, on one visit, Connie talked of being a child in Swan, and Tina said, "Oh, you used to live here?"

"Yes, Tina," said Connie. "I used to live here."

What she did not understand was Hal's being entirely unconscious of the nuances in the conversation. He had never realized Connie did not like Sallie, he said. "She wouldn't mend my clothes when I was a kid and tore them," Connie said. Now Laurel used up all her energy seeing Tina had a good time when she was here. Girls were different. They were always washing long flowing hair and drying it just when it was time to go somewhere. Hal made a disparaging remark about Sallie's drinking one night, and Tina was in tears. "Momma doesn't drink. She might just have one on the board when she's ironing in the morning." She thought it remarkable the child had any innocence left. She thought of Carla and Sallie, put out into the world alone by Hal and unprepared; like most girls she grew up knowing, they went directly into marriage from living with their parents and had never even held a job. When Tina said, "Momma says you'll be good for Daddy, but he won't be good for you," she had felt a compassion Sallie had for her. "Promise me, Laurel," Tina said. "You'll never leave me overnight in the house with my father. I'm not supposed to be here if he's drinking."

"I promise." She would not report the truth to Sallie if Tina wanted that much to see her father, and she did not wish to cause a rift in her marriage.

Rick came every vacation. She would never stop being grateful. What would she do without those times? William had married a woman with several teenagers, and she went on trying to be brave about that. "Now you have siblings," she had said. Dad married for companionship, Rick said, when she commented on his marrying someone his age. They were all there together in the Connecticut house. Well, it was not her fault there was nō baby. In prison, when Hal suffered pain, he was loathe to go to prison doctors until his suffering became too great. Finally he was treated for an infection of his seminal vesicles. He'd had no idea this would affect his and Laurel's life. A Delton gynecologist told her there was no reason she could not get pregnant. She had felt foolish at her age keeping a temperature chart; she'd gotten pregnant with William too easily. Then the doctor said Hal must be checked, and he proved to be hopelessly sterile. He didn't know why he had waited so long in prison before speaking to a doctor about his problem, he said.

When she stared at him across the tennis court, it occured to her to say, Hal, why has not one single thing here worked out? Of course, she could not ask.

After he told her Sallie had no imagination in bed,

and since she couldn't compete with Sallie's bosoms, she decided to be more sexy. She had not forgotten the night she asked him if he liked her new shortie trousseau nightgown, and he looked away. Then staring at the blouse, she realized other women would have filled it out. She had not enjoyed trying to nurse Rick, and she became "dry as a buckshot field in August." Her mother provided the description. Anyway, she had thought being confined to a nursing schedule was a bore, and she had not found the whole experience a galvanizing one at all. But she wanted to nurse Hal, and liked lying atop pillows or turning backward, trying every position that came to mind. She liked his wanting her twice in one night; everything was a new experience. She had learned to suck his balls because he liked that. One night she suggested the wheelbarrow position; though once she explained, he did not feel up to it. She was relieved. She did not have the energy, either, to walk about on her hands while he held her thighs and inserted himself. Yet she would have tried.

Now that Laurel was here in this quiet country farmhouse without the active household she had left behind, she had more compassion for her mother's difficult role as a widow. She wondered if she was right in having refused to move down here when she did. She would wait and see what happened, her mother said, on a foreboding note. Here, she had counted on a family situation. She and Hal had written for months about Christmas in their own house. She had thought about there being grandparents, Mama and Daddy and her mother, and Uncle Pete and Aunt Pris and their children as cousins for Rick. She cooked the first Christmas dinner for everyone herself. Hal shot a wild turkey. By then she wished Natty Bumppo had never existed. And that she had not longed to be the first woman to write intimately about the sacred initiations of the woods belonging formerly to male writers. Sometimes, actively skiing, she and William would quit because it seemed a mindless sport. But hunting! You had to be mindless to sit for hours in silence in a field, or on a log, or in a tree stand in the woods, waiting for a bird to fly or a deer to walk past. She hated the lethal *zing* that brought lives to an end. But she kept up pretext. After Easter, Rick said over the phone his stepmother had dyed eggs and the teenagers waged war with them; what an ache she had felt, thinking of that household. "We went turkey hunting," she had said. "Wow," Rick said. Why tell him the day's reality, how after Bloody Marys at lunch Hal slept that afternoon in a field, flies on his face, snoring so loudly any turkey would have flown out of the county. She lay watching soft spring clouds, wondering if the day was as pretty in Connecticut, wondering what Rick was doing. Thinking how back there they had had jelly bean trails around the house on Easter morning.

Hal's family came late to Christmas dinner. He started the cocktail hour alone. Seeing his condition, she threw his last drink into the sink. She knew she would pay for that later. But she spared them all the horror of having him drunk at Christmas dinner. Conversation lagged despite ten people being present. She missed the way dinners had been with William and his mother; having removed herself from the middle-class boredom she grew up in, she had returned herself to it. Pete did remark he believed this thing of working for money was for the birds. People ought to do something they liked. She remembered thinking, If only she could have looked toward Hal with the sense of superiority about life they'd once counted on.

Hal had nightcaps after everyone left, and her mother and Rick were asleep. She followed his stumbling path to bed thinking, This is our first Christmas in our own house.

The Christmas they were apart, they had agreed to look at the stars at a certain hour and think about one another. She remembered his writing when he put his face to the bars a certain way, he could even see the stars whole, without stripes across them.

By the next Christmas, she left her mother and Rick to have Christmas with Hal. He had a ten-day leave, but not being paroled was still not allowed into his county. They went to a motel in Delton called the Ditty-Wah-Ditty. *It ain't no town, it ain't no city!* the old song went. That motel had been the butt of jokes back in her and Hal's teenage years. She and William were divorced. He knew she went South to see Hal and on her return said, "Your prison friend's a lucky guy."

"I don't think he's so lucky," she said. "Why?"

"He got out of prison and is getting out permanently."

"He got out on a legal pass because he's been a trusty for two years."

"Still, he's lucky. He killed someone."

"It was manslaughter. Teddy Kennedy killed someone and didn't go to prison at all."

"I'm not making points," William had said.

During those ten days, they drove into the Delta, away from Matagorda. When she went home, she was prompted to send him a postcard from Kennedy Airport. *The Delta was the loneliest looking place on a lowering Sunday afternoon—all that flat brown emptiness filled me with a sort of fear.*

Then he sent her a card:

> It is my conviction
>   That loneliness is never
> Where one is, but
>   Who one is with.
> The Delta, though cold
>   And flat and brown
> And full of winter emptiness,
>   Is not lonely.
> Even on a lowering
>   Sunday afternoon.
>
> Or better to say it won't be
>   Anymore.

She was more in love with him because of his placement of the words on paper. She had written, *I feel absolutely wild with love. And desperate about the times I can't crawl inside your skin and be totally one with you. It's why I want to learn to swallow what I could not when I tried.*

For a long time I will feel you, angel, he answered. *My hands, my mouth, all feel you this morning. I remember kissing in all the delicious places. I think men with no ties pull easier time than those of us whose hearts and minds live on the outside with people we love.*

Isn't it amazing, she would say, that last year I was afraid to tell people I wanted a divorce and this year I'm afraid to tell anyone I'm married—and to a prisoner? Those ten days were the most fantastic of my life. They taught me what I've already learned, that to live one must be willing to run risks.

All along a cautionary saying her father liked worried itself out of the back of her mind: If chance is present at the beginning, a dice throw will never abolish it.

Only in extreme circumstances were prisoners allowed to marry. As editor of the paper, Hal had been to one such service. A con had remarked, "The groom was tight as hell, but the bride was anything but."

She had not been certain she would go through with that marriage, even though she arrived with her blood test. Out one day with Buddy, Hal had gotten his. Then again she found herself on a Mississippi highway heading toward marriage, and with uncertainty in her heart. He went into a phone booth on a highway and called the minister they both knew, Brother Walker, who brought the children to sing at the prison. She had wondered at the strangeness of things, that the man had come back into her life. "Preacher, will you marry us?" she could hear Hal saying over the roar of passing trucks. She went into the rest room of a filling station and changed into a soft dress and high heels, thinking, What a strange place to get ready to be a bride.

On their wedding night, Hal said, "This is what I was made for, to lie around and make love. All I've ever wanted to be was a playboy. I just never had enough money."

Those words could rankle this much later. At the time she thought how she and William had struggled and about their aims and goals and the future they wanted for Rick.

But they were in love; while all people thought their love was special, she and Hal knew theirs really was.

They intended keeping the marriage secret till Hal was out—till he crossed those tracks for the last time. Unexpectedly, he told his family after a while; she had had to tell her own, and that included William. Waiting a year for Hal, secretly married except for her family knowing, she began to panic.

Hal, I've struggled long and hard to bring myself up out of what I came from. I can't let my life come to tragedy, or go down the drain. Now I have nothing and no one but you. I wonder if you see the enormity of what you've taken on, that you really are responsible for my life. We got married on money Daddy gave you for your ten-day leave, but we are middle-aged and can't be dependent on him. I wonder if you know how hard you must struggle to stay as you seem to be, and that life won't be all making love. Reality will loom as I'm facing it now about leaving Rick. I've married someone most people think killed a boy on purpose. I can't be left someday, Hal. I am helpless without you and totally dependent. I need to be taken care of emotionally and financially.

If I were not giving up my child for you, it would be one thing. But to have done so and made some horrible mistake is another thing. I've wondered about our drinking together when you've been out, and how easily you seem to fall back into an old pattern. Having an abrupt quarrel on our honeymoon and patching it up making love is fun, but when the great rush of first love is over, are you going to stay changed, as you've said you have changed? I have controlled drinking and been as strong as I am because William was strong, and I need the same strength from you.

It's about to kill me absolutely to give up Rick. Sometimes I wonder if it will mar our marriage, if I can stand it. I wonder if you realize what is happening inside of me because of it. You are charming and handsome and romantic and I'm afraid I fell head over heels in love with you because of that, and you may want someone younger in time. You know, I think that could drive me to suicide. I'm scared.

Then the third Christmas, they were in their own house, so long planned for. She told him afterward, "You almost ruined Christmas. It's not my fault your own children weren't here."

Her nose caught the blow. The moment before his hand flew out, she wondered if she had expected it, wanted it, enticed it, but believed it would never happen. Thank God, her mother had already left. She had turned to Pris: hadn't her sister-in-law any feeling for her that she had married Hal, given him back a life, a place for his children to come, was good to her parents, and her brother was hardly out of prison and back to dangerous drinking? She only asked, "Pris, will you help with Hal's drinking? He's broken my nose."

"Put some ice on your nose," Pris said.

Family? Do they love him that they'll never offer a word of criticism? Laurel wondered.

When she drove Rick to the Delton airport after Christmas, her black eye was covered by sunglasses. "I tried to talk to him, Mom," he said. "But Hal has me boxed in, and knows it. One wrong word and he'll tell me not to come here again, and separate us."

"God in heaven, try not to think about it. There are the good times."

"I know," he said quietly. "I have them with Hal too."

Life without children was so difficult when you were used to them. There was only her and Hal's dependence on one another, a multitude of small conversations, no one to intervene, only the dogs to turn to occasionally. She left Rick at the airport, dreading her return to the silent house. He was taller than she. He looked more like William and his family. "Why does Rick lift his lip and show his gums when he laughs?" Hal had asked.

"It's upper-class New England to look like a horse," she said.

She worried at the airport why Rick had gained so much weight; wasn't William watching him dependably as he always had? He needed a bra, she told him. He had eaten so much at dinner, he excused himself suddenly from the table. "Did you throw up?" she had asked. He said not to worry; he was keeping up his weight for boxing and the swimming team. Rick thought himself too old to hug and kiss, and walked away. Then he came bounding back; they embraced. "See you in February," they said bravely. He said, "Mom, at home I start counting the days. I wake up in the morning and say, Only thirty more days, only twenty-nine more days. . . ." She could only nod. She watched him go along the corridor. She had had two husbands, and one husband was damaged by too much mother love and the other one suffered its lack. How hard the road, she had thought.

She returned to inane evening conversations after Hal had a few drinks. Once when he reminded her she had come from nothing, she found herself crying back, "I could belong to the DAR. An aunt traced it." Overvalue the past and you can't take hold of the reins of the future. Where had she heard that? He told her Sallie was descended from Thomas Jefferson. "From his black relatives or his white ones?" she asked. "Thomas Jefferson never had a black mistress!" he cried out. "Who cares," she said. "I'd like to sleep with a black man." Hal had turned ashen. "In Boston, the Cabots and the Lowells speak to the Perrys," she had said. The remark went over Hal's head.

Now she went to graduate school, which Hal thought

was stupid. "What else am I to do?" she had said. "Nothing to *dew*, nothing to *dew;* don't start that again," he said. What was there for her to do? She asked Rick if he would not ask William, since he had always programmed her life. "Mom," Rick had said, "are you crazy?"

No one would know what it cost her going to that small college farther south in the Delta, the only one within feasible driving distance. Crossing the campus among small-town kids, hugging schoolbooks to her chest, she had wanted instead to be seeing about Rick's going to school. "Well, I guess I'd be going through something like this with Sallie by now," Hal conceded. Sallie? Didn't the man see the difference between them? Not even two dollars' worth, she thought. That was the old story about Pepper. He'd asked Daddy to get him a marriage license in town, but Daddy forgot for a while. When he brought the license, Pepper said he had decided to marry a different girl and needed a new license. "Well, it'll cost you another two dollars for a license with another name," Daddy said. Pepper said, Never mind then. He'd marry the first girl. There wasn't two dollars' worth of difference between them.

One time Hal had laughed, saying every time he got rid of one woman, another one was waiting. Was that what she was to him—a convenience? Once they settled in here, he heard from the little nurse, Rosalie. As he spoke about her letter, a light of reminiscence came into his eyes, the certain light men get thinking back on a woman they have slept with. "Did you sleep with Rosalie in the hospital?" she said.

"Why not? It was available."

She only thought he should have been suffering as fully as everyone else in the case.

The refrigerator door slammed. Ice cubes fell again into a glass. He never would ask if she would like a drink. She got up to fix dinner.

She thought again about the day at the tennis court and another blow to her nose, this one unintentional. She believed Hal was watching a woman walk away from the courts, whose bosoms were jiggling. She turned to watch. He sent a ball her direction, and as she looked back, it caught her face sharply. Hal was horrified. He ran around the net crying "Baby!" She tasted blood. As her eyes closed, she had another flash of memory. They were all in the backyard shortly after Hal had come home. She was so pleased he was teaching Rick to shoot clay pigeons. "Pull," she heard Rick cry. And then he shot.

When she looked around, Tina was hovering in the carport. She went inside. She found her curled up in a chair in this bedroom and took the girl on her lap. "Tina," she said, "you mustn't be frightened by the sound of guns. What happened with your father was an accident."

Tina sat bolt upright in her lap. "It certainly was not an accident. My father said, 'I'm going to kill your brother.' He got the gun and loaded it. I wrestled him for it. I was eight years old. Then he shot him."

She opened her eyes at the tennis court, saying, "It doesn't hurt." People were playing golf on a bright green course beyond them. Black waiters in cropped jackets carried trays loaded with drinks above their heads. Words carved in stone in a building directly ahead of her swam into focus: SWAN COUNTRY CLUB.

I'm a member, she had thought.

13

They gave a funeral but no one came. While she could speak humorously, Daddy's dying, of course, was not funny. He lay comatose for weeks for a reason no doctor could figure out, since when Daddy was cut open and sewn up, his cancer past hope, he was given the least anesthesia. Lying in the Delton hospital, he said one word occasionally, "Mitzi," until a doctor arched an eyebrow and asked her, "Another woman? Everyone has skeletons." She told him, "No. That was a little dog of his wife's that died soon after she did." Why the substitution of names, anyone could guess about. But she and Hal agreed Daddy had had a nervous breakdown in his coma, the only place he dared to, at last.

Another woman? Laurel had stood at his hospital window those months back thinking about the words. What happened between her and Daddy in his bathroom became not even a memory once she came to Matagorda to live as Hal's wife, two years ago. If there had been another woman, though, late in Daddy's life, that woman was herself. Always, the look he gave her out of pale, kind eyes said he knew what she had come to Matagorda to offer—love, trust, obedience, intelligence, and respect: things her husband never seemed to realize. Here I am in Soundport again, Laurel thought, staring out a window and contemplating a world that was one sheet of ice. She tried to imagine the warm weather Hal was having in Africa.

The rented cottage where she stood was like a cocoon; its windows covered by plastic sheeting against the cold closed her in. From an upstairs window, Laurel looked out toward Long Island Sound, a gem of flashing water in the distance. When a school bus shifted gears nearby, she assumed a mother's satisfied smile. Old habits die hard. Yesterday, driving too fast, stopping abruptly, she threw out an arm to protect Rick from the dashboard. They laughed. He was twice as big as she was now. She wondered why she and William had never thought to walk at the beach in winter; it was lovely, and Buff's hair feathered out along her spine.

Neither she nor Rick mentioned her going south again when Hal came back from Africa, in two months. These two months he had been gone were more precious than she had anticipated. But she had not expected the night Rick appeared on her rented doorstep with boxes of his possessions. "I told you you didn't have to move in with me while Hal's gone. I'm fine. You've had enough uprootedness."

He pushed on in, arms loaded. "Dad's getting a divorce. I don't want to live in a house without a woman in it." Then he put down all those things in a room upstairs. "Where you are, Mom, is really where home is."

Those words brought the sharpest pain. Only now did she let herself think about the woman she had been who left him. What had she seemed like to the neighbors, what had his friends said, what had he gone through that she would never know anything about? she wondered.

This time going south, she would not be looking for

something that did not exist—the past. Too long, she had tried to return to her first memories knowing what she learned later. She had wanted to bring the past into the present, to say what she should have said at some time gone past when she had been too afraid to speak her mind, to jeopardize being loved and liked. William had always complimented her about not talking as much as most women; Hal, too, liked that she did not "run her mouth." However, he preferred dogs to people; they did not talk back at all, he said.

These mornings encountering Rick first thing, he threw his hands over himself. He slept in boxer shorts but must hide what she guessed was an erection. She wondered if he was a virgin, and what her son was like in bed, and whether this was a question you could ever ask a daughter-in-law. In the long months before her divorce, when William stayed in the house, she walked into the bathroom once while he was taking a bath. William threw a washcloth over his private parts. She had thought that silly after fifteen years of marriage. Hal was so jealous of William back then, she wondered what he would think, now, with her in Soundport alone, if he knew William was getting a divorce. "William doesn't want your name mentioned in front of him," her mother had said.

The unexpected night Rick showed up with his possessions saying his dad was getting a divorce, she saw something in his face that made her fearful; yet she wanted him to be a man able to go out into the world better than Daddy and Hal, and maybe that took grimness. She had no right to ask about William's divorce and only said lightly, "Without step brothers and sisters, you won't have to go through all that quibbling I watched with Hal and Pris about dividing things up after Daddy died."

Once Daddy died, she and Hal had moved into the big house. They moved everything on flatbed trucks provided by Savano. She told Rick about the morning Hal let the dogs out, so early Carrie's roosters had not even started crowing. He was back in the bedroom and shortly said,

"Laurel. Somebody's in this house." They always had been slightly afraid someone from the prison might show up, even two years later. They went apprehensively down a hallway, hearing noises in the living room. Pris looked up at them. She was sitting on the floor swathing in tissue paper objets d'art from every table and shelf. Hal quietly asked if she'd return the few he had brought Mama from Japan when he was there in wartime. With a look of hatred, she complied. She and Hal could not stop talking about how Pris simply walked into the house, not knocking, not having called. She'd had to leave Delton before daylight to get there at that hour. She knew then, Laurel said, Pris was never going to accept her and Hal as the MacDonalds of Matagorda, never graciously accept that they lived in that house.

For weeks, Pris scavenged the place, bringing her own lunch and six-packs of sodas for everyone. She only said, Pris, we have lunch every day anyway. You're welcome to eat our food. She did not say they always had baloney sandwiches and she'd change the menu for her. She was then writing in Daddy's old office, which looked over the orchard. She used to sit there hating the sight of Hal's black pickup turning down the driveway between the trees at exactly twelve minutes past noon every day. He got out of the truck and seemed dwarfed by the house. Daddy had been slight, but there was a difference. Finally she realized the difference was dignity: something Hal lacked. She longed for it for herself sitting at the typewriter. But every morning Carrie interrupted to ask, "What us having for lunch, Miss Laurel?" She finally told Carrie to have baloney every day, and Hal never seemed to notice. He ate his sandwich carefully pinched between his hands, reminding her of a raccoon. Drinking iced tea, he gave her a sweet gaze over the rim of the glass. His expression was like that of a grateful child whose thirst has been quenched when the child's too young to quench it himself. She sat at the table looking off into the magnitude of silence in the orchard, hating the tininess of her life, wondering that she had brought herself to it. All she could do was make each day pass, and then another day, and not look back. Where was the man who had written her those letters?

One day in the orchard, she and Savano reminisced. She talked about missing the noise she heard when she and Hal lived in the farmhouse: the intermittent crack of Daddy's rifle. He used to sit on the front porch in striped pajamas picking squirrels out of the pecan trees. It took Daddy till his final years to accept what he'd always been told, how great the financial damage was squirrels did to the pecan crop. He became fanatical. Savano had laughed. "A man don't speak no louder than his guns," he said. They went on talking about Daddy's fighting his declining years. She wondered if Savano had not included, too, Hal's obsession with hunting all his life. In the orchard was the only place left Daddy had to affect anybody, she and Savano agreed. "Hal's never had much ambition," she had said.

"A man blessed without aspirations," Savano said. "Or they were youthful ones and never realized. It's the dark crossroads of a man's life to realize you'll never live up to what you visualized for yourself."

"A woman's too," she had said. "But Hal was blessed."

After Daddy died, even things left over in the attic had to be divided. She and Pris were up there, and she had said, "We ought to have a tag sale."

"Don't you get rid of anything till Hal's paid for half this house."

Paid? Paid? The word echoed off the rafters till she could ask him about it that night. "The will says you are to live in this house free for the rest of your life," she said. "It doesn't say anything about paying Pris for her half."

"She and Pete want to be paid."

She went on reiterating what the will said; Hal agreed. He shrugged. "I didn't know what to say, so I said, 'All right.' If I can afford to pay them."

Tina had been in the attic that day with Pris. She kept

opening boxes and taking things out. "Look," she had said. "A Halloween costume." She held up a long white robe, a hood with eyes. Pris blanched; she went home without saying goodbye. Laurel went on laughing. Hal did not think it so funny. She didn't think it was Daddy's robe, she said, but it was some MacDonald's.

He could not buy out Pris and Pete; surely they knew that. She went on begging Hal to stand up to them, but the house went on the market. They would move to Delton. Really, they had no life at Matagorda; Hal—she by association—was always going to be a pariah in Swan. They were cut out of things; she was told that frankly. A man from the North was looking for a location for an umbrella factory, to make use of the Delta's cheap labor. Talk of a factory was the biggest news in Swan in years; it sounded as if the owner was going to hire every black in the county, white people too. The Chamber of Commerce wined and dined him; at one of these dinners, his wife was overheard saying, "Get me out of this burg." Local wives were furious. "Her social life here is already ruined," one said. But if she had to move down here, the wife said, she wanted a showplace: Matagorda was the only one. The eagerness they encountered from everyone about Hal's selling the place became embarrassing. "Mama and Daddy would turn over in their graves if they knew we sold this house. And worse, sold it to Yankees," he said. A painter began taking down Mama's fine imported handpainted wallpaper in the hallway on instructions from the Yankee wife. He looked at Laurel. "Mrs. MacDonald would kill me. I put this paper up for her." Their furniture went into storage. Hal's old Lab Jiggs had died, and there was the new black Lab puppy, Bud. Tenants in their old farmhouse would keep him and Jubal for a while. As plans for the umbrella factory materialized, it would employ a total of thirty people, blacks and whites; it was a factory only to assemble some part.

But they were driving away from Matagorda, their car loaded and a niche on the backseat for Buff. Carrie was the only person there at that moment to say goodbye; she honored them by wearing her wig. Laurel remembered how perturbed she felt about leaving. A light rain fell. The steadfast silence had seen worse times and better ones. The rain fell in the woods, on ponds, lakes, and fields, binding all together the way it had done long before she came to this place and the way it would be doing long after she left there. What must Hal be feeling? "Do you feel sad leaving?" she said.

"Why? What's Matagorda done for me?"

Laurel wished to say "Everything," but she said nothing. What was the point of wasting breath on a fool?

After Daddy's death even Savano said it was ridiculous for Hal to go on being his bookkeeper. He quit work and took her on safari. They stayed six weeks in Africa while he collected trophies. "Ye gods, more heads." Mrs. Wynn had rolled her eyes to heaven. Hal was with the same white hunter he'd hunted with before, a German named Hauser. They were in remote camps. Every day Hauser shouted to contact Nairobi by shortwave radio; it was cackly and filled with voices trying to break in. One morning when he was busy, he asked Hal to call. "Hello, Nairobi." He spoke in his ordinary telephone voice. "Shout, man," Hauser cried. He grew more livid according to the number of times Hal humbly said, "Hello, Nairobi." Afterward, the Germanic Hauser began to humiliate him. "Tell the wogs to bring more hot water," Hauser would say, poking his head from the makeshift shower tent. "Yell, man. They're used to it." Hal trotted the distance to the kitchen tent to deliver the order; Hauser and his wife exchanged contemptuous smiles. Laurel watched Hal's bent shoulders thinking, My husband. She built him up, talking about wonderful things he made from deerskins: moccasins, belts, gloves. "Maybe that's what you should do," Hauser said. "Be an artisan. Open a little shop."

"I probably should."

"Well, man. You've got to find something."

"I'm doing what I was made to do." Hal smiled. "Spend

money and have a good time. I've always known how to spend money, I've just never known how to make any."

"What do you have in mind?"

"I don't know. I haven't thought. I've lived in that small town most of my life. I'm formed, and nothing can change what I am."

She understood why Hal did not understand her difficulties in the Delta. He was unable to perceive the different life she had led before. Having lived in one spot most of his life, with his impressions coming from his daily environment, he had little to compare things to.

One day Hauser said to her, "You've got a real problem." They were walking along on a path and jumping over safari ants. "All you can do is try to keep yourself from going mad."

"That is all I've done," she said. "I go back to Connecticut a lot to visit my mother and son."

"That's not the answer."

"I know. But what is?"

"Ten years ago I could have told you. I'd have said get a dee-vorce."

"And not now?"

He gave her a stare out of hard blue eyes. "Time makes a difference. It's unfortunate but true."

She was forty-four years old. He meant her ability to catch a man was over, which was maddening. She faced for the first time what, really, she had done to her life. She had better be practical and stick with what she had. Hauser was not an unkind man. Having spent his lifetime with animals, he believed they knew the moments of their own deaths. He saw a certain look come into their eyes. Laurel wondered if she was to face that look in glass eyes the rest of her life when she walked into Hal's trophy room. In a rain forest in Africa, she looked at her husband through another man's eyes and saw him wanting. She had known the truth herself; she had only tried to hide it. All the embarrassing moments they had lived through on Matagorda, suffered through, she thought. Connie had said,

"My mom says I don't have to come here and put myself through this, but he is my dad." Also, in her heart, Laurel thought about his children's loyalty; they knew there was money to come: TK.

Hauser was being forced by the Kenyan government to turn over 51 percent of his business to "wogs." He was selling out and moving to the States. First, he wanted to make a documentary and hoped to distribute it worldwide. Hal went back for four months to be his cameraman. She wondered if he would have been selected if he had not had ten thousand dollars to invest in the homemade project. She prayed the venture would widen their horizons and lead to something interesting and worthwhile.

This morning as she made Rick's bed and shook out his pillow, she thought of the shock she had at Matagorda when she found he slept with a pistol under his head. "I told myself I was going to sleep with a gun any time Hal was crocked. That's every night," he had said. Now there was peacefulness; they agreed being in the rented cottage was like being back at the cabin in Mississippi. Soundport was changed in two years. Most of her friends were divorced or were in the process. She'd only been a step ahead, Laurel thought. The look of the town went on changing from being a New England village of old frame buildings to being a modern town of smart brick shops and small office buildings, which lined the river through town and obscured it from view. The gulls remained swooping up and down and intent on their business. Back at the YMCA, she could stand on her head taking yoga.

She and Buff had seen Hal off to Atlanta, and from there he flew to Africa; Southerners didn't need New York any longer for anything. Pris called in her sick cat voice to say goodbye; Pete came to the airport and then by Laurel's motel room nearby. She and Buff would start the long drive to Connecticut the following morning; she had not expected to make it again. She asked what Pete thought of the African venture. "It's worth risking the money at this point," he said. "Hauser's a good man. Hal's not equipped for business. God knows, Laurel. I waited and waited for him to settle his father's estate, until I began to hate him. I prayed about that. One morning I got up and said, He doesn't do anything because he doesn't know how. I'll have to do it. Let's order champagne and oysters."

"What are we celebrating?" But she knew, a night out. And why not? She owed nothing to this family any longer.

Later she could say, "*Salud.* Oysters go down better with champagne." She told Pete about the night Hal threw her out of their car, on the way back from a party; he had done the same thing to Sallie a week before he killed Greg. "You never know what happens to set him off," she said. "I was there in the middle of nowhere, nothing but fields. A man who had been at the party happened along and brought me home. Hal came out and said, "Well, did you fuck her like everybody else?" The man told him no matter what, no man would throw his wife out into the Delta in the middle of the night, at the mercy of any Negro who came along. She laughed. "That's the last thing I'd have been afraid would happen. Pete, is no one going to help me with his drinking?"

"No one," he said. "You're all alone."

When Rick moved into the cottage with her, he had said, "Mom, you know I thought a lot about your and Dad's divorce. Don't worry, it was all in your favor. I began to see reasons for it." She tried to think of William as twice divorced. She knew that did not fit his image of himself. A chain of events had been started and they were not only no longer the people they had been, but not people they wanted to be, either. Rick said he was glad she had not taken him away from his father when he was a baby. "Yes, I'm glad you never had to invent a father," she said. "It's hard enough living with people and still not knowing them."

What about her nights here, were they too mellowed by Scotch, a habit begun at Matagorda when she would think she was going crazy too? The blacks there grew to accept odd behavior as normal. She broke out all the windows in the study one night when Hal locked himself inside and would not hand her out her reading glasses which she'd left there; Pepper replaced windowpanes in silence. He and Field toted Mama's oil portrait off the wall after the night Hal got up and slashed it from one corner to another one with a knife. Carrie spoke matter-of-factly about the nights Daddy half carried Mama from the dinner table when she fell asleep there. "Did you ever say anything to him?" Laurel asked.

"No'm." Carrie gave her elfin grin. "Miss 'Cilla told me one time I was so quiet I ought to jine the Caf'lic church. She didn't even know that man had piles like I knowed it."

"How did you know?"

"I washed his bloody underdrawers in the laundry," Carrie said. "Work in a house and you knows things."

"Marry into a family and you know them too," Laurel said.

Was it mellowed evenings then that had made her overlook what was right beneath her nose in this cottage? In the bottom of Rick's closet there was a television set half covered by a blanket. When she returned to Soundport, she'd expected Rick to have a new set of friends in high school. But boys came so often to this house, hurrying inside and going past her without speaking, not waiting for introductions. Always they had something in their arms, wrapped up in blankets or in boxes. They hurried up the stairs to Rick's room; she asked once why they went up to the attic. When he said, "To smoke marijuana," she'd told him to smoke openly rather than to burn the house down. Rick was a fence. She told herself she was not going to phone William.

Time had to pass before she could speak to him: "Why are you still doing these things?" The television set disappeared, and the strange boys stopped coming to the house. When finally she confronted him one night, Rick said that phase of his life was over. "Maybe I was acting out against Dad's second divorce." Poor William. His second wife had made large additions to the house and now he had to return her that money. William went on buying the same house. "You promise, Rick?"

"I promise. One thing I want you to know is that what has gotten me through all that has happened to me is that you and Dad have always been behind me." Rick talked about his old Juvenile Court sessions; he had looked around at black kids in there with him and realized how much more in life he had been given. "I think," Rick said slowly, "I want to find a profession where I help other people."

Laurel knew if she did not believe her son then she would never believe him again. "I'm glad," she said. They sat talking about Matagorda, its good times and bad. She told him about Daddy's dying. He died in Delton, and people assumed she and Hal had gone up there directly, to Pris's. Pris thought they ought to stay on the plantation. Carrie wore her best uniform, Pepper had on a white starched jacket. The big house was lit up and ready for the company they expected, bringing platters of food as people did when Mama died. No one arrived. The corridor of driveway through the orchard seemed more than ever empty. They got up from the living room finally and took off their best clothes. Hal wore a fine English-tailored suit, which made him look like a small boy in his daddy's clothes, or somehow a rube. "And that," Laurel finished telling, "is how we gave a funeral and no one came."

Then it was snowing; the cottage was locked in tightly around them. The back door opened, and they stood up. Buff ran toward it on clicking toenails, not even barking. Hal came around a corner, looking sheepish and with two months' growth of beard, the length of time he had been gone. As soon as she saw him returned early, she knew that whatever expectations she had had about him taking hold of anything were over. But what could she do but run toward him, crying out a warm and wifely welcome?

14

It must be eight o'clock because Hal's routine never varied. If only something different would happen. If only he would die, Laurel thought. She opened her eyes astonished by morning; only a moment ago she went to bed thinking, I'm sleeping, and watching her own dark descent. She heard him in his bedroom across the hall. Fir trees stood at the windows. Who would have imagined she would end up back in Soundport, Connecticut, with Hal MacDonald or at all?

In her mirrored bathroom door, blue morning glories reflected from caramel-colored wallpaper. Serene. She remembered thinking that word when she bought the wallpaper six years ago. To think back over ten years with Hal, she wondered what truly serene, happy moment she had had. At least they had been stationary for six years: after the rented cottage and then another rental till they bought this house, the move at Matagorda, the move there. Why look back to that now?

Laurel liked this house, though it was run-down. More and more, Hal was reluctant about spending money. That was why now she waited. She waited! Listening to what her husband was doing across the hall. At the right moment every morning, she darted across it to rifle his wallet. Hal had refused for the past six years to raise her grocery allowance.

Laurel threw back the sheet, anticipatory, fearful about her journey across the hall. Nothing would happen at the moment if she was caught, not in the morning when Hal was sober. He waited too; things mulled. Some evening in his drunken nighttime behavior, he would retaliate; she thought, glancing toward the bathroom, of the night not so long ago when he had held her, hard, to the toilet bowl. Something was happening, increasingly so, that she could not see, feel, or touch. But Hal seemed in the ascendancy, to be going past, while she was slipping.

Across the hallway, Bud's dog tags rattled. Hal opened his closet. She paid little attention anymore to his drunken, derogatory remarks; sometimes they were funny. "Laurel, the reason you have an inferiority complex is because you are inferior." She flew to the telephone that night, repeating his words to Rick cross-country, in Colorado. Though the time she reported what he said about her work, Rick was incredulous: "All you do is mess up paper."

"Hal said that? What the hell does he do except blow up a pig's bladder all day or take sunbaths in the yard, turning himself over like a hot dog?"

"You're funny," she had said. "As funny as Dad." She remembered those words on a blue autumn day eleven years ago when she and Rick were raking leaves.

Across town now William would be leaving for the station, and she imagined him calling goodbye to the other members of his household, his young wife and their baby. Since Rick's half-brother was twenty-five years his junior, how could she not but think of William's baby as if it were her grandchild? Who'd want to start over raising a child in their fifties? she had sniffed. Goddamn it.

She wondered when she would have a grandchild, ever? She was afraid by the time Rick finished his Ph.D. he might not come back east to live. He spent so much time roaming about, seeing the world, working in oil fields, with groups of youthful delinquents, here, there, that she worried about his inheriting his mother's wanderlust, her curiosity about the lives of people unlike herself. Though when he becomes a psychologist, he will help other people the way he said he wanted to do eight years ago in the rented cottage. Always, they thought of that time as if they were together again in the cabin in Mississippi. She wondered if Rick would have gotten his degree closer to home if all that had happened had not happened.

Suddenly she could laugh. Long ago, too, in the prison library, Hal said, "Honey, if I couldn't laugh, I couldn't stand the tension." But they seldom used endearing words once he was home, and seldom talked. She blamed this on herself. Her thoughts often remained inward. Their letters; the letters were filled with outcryings they could not have cried to a thousand psychiatrists. In Hal's case, if she thought her husband was dumb, how could she tell him? And if he was dumb, then what could he do about it? Against stupidity the gods themselves contend helplessly. She remembered the thought from one of her graduate classes. Schiller, Laurel believed. She remembered what she was going to laugh about. For years she had believed she did not understand plotting, and that her novels lacked it. The King dies and the Queen dies of grief. But what else happened? By now, she understood perfectly: steps in their lives that have occurred because she made one move and married Hal MacDonald. Into the world, a new life has come because of it: a baby across town eating curds and whey or whatever babies in this different age ate.

Why be surprised to find Hal, last evening, wandering around in the basement crocked at midnight when she came in so late. She was mainly surprised because he was home that early on a Monday night from blowing up his pig's bladder—playing his bagpipes—with the bagpiping band of the Ancient Order of the Scarabees. Usually, he was never home before 2 A.M. The old white house where the Scarabees met was near her mother's, a clubhouse also for other organizations, and whatever B.P.O.E. stood for; there was an emblematic sign out front. The kinds of meetings and people William used to sneer about when they passed, and that Hal sneered about when he was a snob in Mississippi. Back there, Daddy had wanted him to join Rotary, and Hal refused. "Daddy always wanted me to make a mark on the community," he said.

"You did," she told him.

Hal went to practice earlier and earlier on Monday nights and stayed later and later. When she asked where he stayed so long, he said, "In the bar." That figured. Other Scarabees were not commuters, either, and not having to get up as early, they could stay in the bar with him, she supposed. But how were these men able to get to practice by five thirty on Monday evenings? Unlike Hal, they had jobs. Blue-collar workers: a janitor at a school, a carpenter, a groundskeeper for a cemetery.... It might be funny that his bosom bagpiping buddy thought when she mentioned the *Atlantic Monthly* she was talking about a fishing magazine. But in the long run it was wearisome. She had nothing in common with these people, and once Hal did not either. She did respect them, however, more than she did her husband, these men who had come from nothing and had worked themselves up into the world. She did speak up one time when he derided her background. "I'd rather have been like my father and started with nothing and made it, than to have started with everything and not have known what to do with it, like you and your father."

Tremulously, Laurel now dreaded some moment when William or other people she formerly knew saw her going into or out of the tacky places she went with Hal, above stores and restaurants, where the Scarabees held their gatherings. Yes, she had stood on curbs in large towns like Bridgeport and Stamford where the band played in celebratory parades on holidays, waiting for him to come along, piping: to cry out, My husband! when he hove into view, cheeks extended. She could be moved; the skirling sound of the pipers and the deep beat of the drum were stirring. She envied Hal what he had, something like a small family with his band members, their ability to join in a circle, instruments to their mouths, and come out with one wedded sound. That was the trouble, Laurel thought, she had no life to offer as an alternative, no devoted friends, only her solitary profession. At the parades in those large towns, blacks swarmed out terrifyingly from the sidewalks and surrounded the band; often, members found afterward their little daggers, the skean dhus, were missing from the tops of their long socks. Oh, well, after the night he might have drowned her in the toilet, she planned on killing him. There had seemed one solution to her life. Hal had to die, and she would have the rental money for Matagorda from Savano for the rest of her life or until she remarried. Fat chance of that, she thought, according to statistics about women her age.

Laurel knew precisely what she was and made no bones about it: a woman of her age and her generation and her Southern past whose life revolved around a man; who was, because of one. That night of the toilet bowl incident, she acknowledged for the first time the slow, true disdain she had felt for Hal for so long. She knew the quality of the life she would be living if she were still living across town. Oh, pull yourself up; but I have. She had no idea how to recapture alone the kind of life she had with William. To think now, she could have slow tears and would not allow them. Sometimes there was a calm sense of despair. There was her feeling, too, she was required to stay married to Hal. Deserted by God, she believed He would find her if she believed, not particularly in religion but in hope. And hope she had.

Laurel in her bathroom thought about the night bagpiping began in such earnest; it had become an obsession the way hunting once was for Hal. In order to play with the Scarabees' bagpiping band, he had to join the organization. There she was in a room above a funeral parlor in Soundport smiling broadly as his wife, accommodating herself so he would be admitted. Only after that initial looking-over, the membership chairman came to their house, the great stone house they rented before buying this one, and asked Hal to step outside. She could still see them standing in the driveway talking. Hal came indoors. "He wanted to know what the felony was I checked yes to on the application."

He was refused admission to the Soundport branch of the Scarabees when she had not known the organization existed in the town. People she knew would never have joined it. Snobs in Fairfield County! cried the blue-collar workers, who did not live in exclusive commuting towns but in inland ones, formerly vague names to her. They would take him into their branch, they said, and so it began, Laurel thought, sitting on the potty.

She pursued a life of her own. Politely, she refused to join the Female Order of the Scarabees, no matter what the members and their wives thought of her. Her Master's had dragged along because she changed divisions, to Communications, but soon she knew that was a world too progressive for her at her age, and she crept quietly back to Literature. She was teaching a black man to read through Literacy Volunteers. She took Latin one night a week at the local high school. "Of all pointless things," Hal had said. I like to use my brain; she had spoken silently but wondered if Hal would have understood the implication if she had spoken aloud. She was working on her novel.

She wondered what would have happened had they moved back to Delton. Hal would not be a piper. She would not be a piper's wife. Drunken evenings, he said she made him sell the house at Matagorda, she made them move to Soundport. Laurel had lost interest in correcting him. The next day he never remembered, anyway, what he said the previous evening. When Hal came back from Africa, he went to Delton house-hunting, and had she gone with him she would have found a suitable house. But she had wanted those last days alone with Rick in the rented place. Chance played its part. Hal returned saying Pris drove him everywhere and there was not a house around Delton they'd like. "We might as well stay here," he had said. She remembered being disappointed and thinking that after what she had been through, she was not supposed to return east. She had made no protest. It was easier for Rick not to have to shuffle back and forth between states to visit her and William. She would always wonder if Pris had convinced Hal it was his idea to move out of her sight.

They did not have a lot of money by Soundport's standards, which was another reason to stay married. To think of mischance, Laurel asked herself this morning, would I need to have a nine-year-old now? God had known what He was doing. In his cups Hal said she wanted to have a baby to hold onto him. "How?" she said. "Tina didn't keep you married to Sallie." She had not told him she wanted to have a baby because she loved him so much.

What she could not overlook were Hal's indignities to Rick, a boy who remained so loyal. Though Hal did not seem to understand anything about loyalty. When Laurel had that thought, she felt a little fearful. It was unbelievable that Hal told Rick what she and William never meant their child to know. She supposed people in the first flush of love would go on and on telling each other everything, and living to regret it. Telling everything about a former spouse. She even knew so much about Carla's and Sallie's bathroom habits, they'd be astonished. She could not remember the exact conversation that prompted Hal to end it. "What the hell, your mother killed a baby."

Rick had looked at her, wanting a denial she could

not give him. She had to tell, instead, the story about her getting pregnant when he was a few months old. There hadn't been enough room in the brownstone apartment or enough money for another baby. William's announcement was put in a different way. "You can't have a writing career and babies that close together." She had never in her life applied the word "career" to herself, she had only "tried to write." Those were naïve days and innocent years all around. She did not know why, since they paid the doctor in cash, they gave him their real names. He was not some seedy abortionist on a back street the way she would have imagined, but a fashionable doctor on the Upper East Side in New York. Their GP had given them the name and she had wished since then he had refused. Now she could see herself weeks later on a subway barreling along to lower Manhattan to a cavernous courthouse where the grand jury convened. Waiting in jail to be sentenced, the doctor hanged himself. She had always felt partly responsible for his death. She had talked to another young woman also subpoenaed, from New Jersey. This woman heard about the doctor's arrest on a TV newsbreak while watching cartoons with her other kids. For all these years, Laurel had pictured herself and that woman riding back uptown on a subway, in roaring dimness, their faces solemn, their thought indrawn: yet known to one another. She would remember forever a young woman watching cartoons with her kids in New Jersey and remember those days for herself. When she wrote the experience to Hal, she had said, *Best not to think or talk about that, because I have waked up in the night all these years and cried sometimes thinking about it. I had to keep thoughts buried, as if nothing had happened.*

    She was meant to know childbirth again, Laurel thought. Childbirth was like standing in shallow water waiting for a calm wave which comes and thunders and carries you on its crest and you know you are riding it and you are going under and under, never to surface just as the pain ends. God, don't let it come again. Women novelists wrote about abortions in a way they did not happen. There was no physical pain. Yet in novels women usually took to their beds and needed pills and friends around to tend them. She had come home and done a load of laundry down in the dark, scary basement of the brownstone where they lived, in bothersome coin machines. And that was a time she thought back to Delton and an easier life. Maybe that was when she began to yearn and to dream backward. It was years later before William told her the nightmares he had over that abortion, and she had wanted to ask then why he had suggested one, because she had been too unsophisticated for an abortion to have occurred to her, and he had been through one, whether or not it was his baby.

Last night when she turned into this house, it was fearsome. There was no illumination but the streetlight, and the house was set back from the road among fir trees. In calling out to Hal, she had longed to have someone to tell about her evening but had known it was useless. Hal didn't even know what the New School was, way downtown in Manhattan, and could not perceive that her making a long trip at night to take a course in fiction writing might be odd when she had published three novels. She had not been able to tell him she was desperate to have someone to talk to about something and desperate to be with people who shared her interests. Her editor had died and she no longer knew anyone in publishing anymore than anyone in publishing knew her after a ten years' silence, in which she had gone on "messing up paper."

Having come inside the house last night, she turned its various dark corners expecting to meet burglars. Then she saw a crack of light beneath the basement door and opened it and watched Hal wandering around down in the basement. "What are you doing?" she called finally.

"Looking for something."

"What?"

"I can't remember."

She had said, "Boogey," closing the door. There was no one to tell when she turned in a short story and the professor had laughed, looking at her top sheet. "Would you consider using another name?" he said.

"Why? That's my name."

"I know. But there is another Laurel Wynn writing."

"That's me."

"Good Lord. Jackie Collins will be turning up next."

"Hardly," she had said. She was surprised he knew of her.

Hal was in his bathroom and the shower had started. Laurel rushed across to the bedroom where he had moved his clothes, which enraged her. As Bud looked up from the single bed where he slept with Hal, she mouthed toward him, Traitor. She took him jogging but he would not put a paw into bed with her. Things from Hal's pockets were ranged along his dresser, and she took twenty dollars from his wallet. Most men knew precisely how much money they carried, but Hal never missed anything. Some mornings he had so few bills she couldn't take anything, and then she was furious. She felt owed. Why is this my life? Laurel wondered as she fled back to her room to stash the money in her purse.

Hal came from the bathroom and said, "Morning," toward where she sat at her dressing table, and she replied with reluctance, "Morning." They were like strangers meeting in a boardinghouse. Too many mornings she put on her baggy-kneed jogging suit and stayed in it all day; she was past "looking pretty for her husband": why bother, when they would go on and on as they were? When Hal came out of his bedroom, he was dressed crisply and cleanly. He did a lot of ironing in the garage, where the board stayed up permanently; in winter, the garage was heated. If she left a blouse in the dryer, he ironed that for her. Laurel saw no reason to do his ironing when he had nothing to do all day.

In the kitchen, he was sitting at the table drinking coffee and working the *Times* crossword puzzle. She was often annoyed that he worked the puzzle first every day and also on Sundays. Soon he would practice the chanter to his bagpipes, a thin and threadlike sound like a flute. This was a concession to her morning working hours, her need for silence. Afterward he would blow up the pipes full blast and march about his trophy room to some different drummer in his own head.

There, glass eyes stared down; not one but three buffalo heads from the American West, a Tennessee bear, a Mississippi wild turkey; game from Africa that included a fully mounted bongo, the size of a grown cow. "Decadent." "Something out of Teddy Roosevelt days." These were the comments they heard in Soundport, where this room did not go over as in Mississippi, a world of hunting men. "Mom," Rick said one day, "do you realize this room is Hal's monument to himself?" They were drinking tea and picked up their cups and walked out. The least likely man in the world to deserve honor, she had thought. Along the mantelpiece Hal had ranged a regiment of lead soldiers, brightly colored and wearing Scottish raiment, kilts, blowing pipes, charging on steeds, marching into the Battle of Culloden. "Does he ever go *chuk-chuk* with them?" Rick asked.

"Not yet," she said. "He hasn't played with them in the backyard under a forsythia bush yet, either."

Bud, in his soft mouth, brought in the *Times* in its waxy blue wrapper each day. Hal said continually, "The poor bastard." He meant his trained retriever had nothing else to retrieve in suburbia, this place she had brought him to. Aside from the puzzle, Hal never turned to another page of the paper. She needled him because she could not help it. "What's the news?"

"I don't know."

"You didn't happen to glance at the headlines when you opened the paper?"

"No. There's a notice the price has gone up. Fifty lousy bucks a month. We ought to drop the paper."

"I like to read it. What'll you do today?"

"Work on my suntan."

Work! Hal would lie in the backyard naked from nine till five, oiled with that old mixture, baby oil and iodine. She had not heard the expression "work on a suntan" since high school, anymore than she had seen anyone quirk one eyebrow since then, still thinking it was sexy. But she was not indifferent to the dark eyebrow and to that lock of hair falling over his forehead. Laurel leaned over Hal's back, wanting to feel his nearness since they were to go on living together. "That's b-ê-t-e." She pointed to blanks he had left. Hal did not move.

"It is?" he said. He filled in the letters with a tentative pencil point. "Black beast," she said to Bud. "You shall die like a dog."

They started out to jog and Hal headed for the ironing board; they went along a sylvan road shaded by trees like a forest and along a stream where Bud pranced in, tiptoeing highly, and sent skyward a lot of ducks. Laurel lagged and stood against a tree; she wondered about Hal's bent back and how he resisted when she leaned over him, tightening his elbows to the kitchen table. Well, she did not beg, though she asked him to sleep in the same bed with her. Then often she was driven into a frenzy by his drunken snoring. She rose up in bed like a banshee and stood in its middle, kicking at him with one foot till he rolled out.

She could not help it that other nights she lay awake, her fury accumulating that after all their desperate longing while he was in prison, he had chosen a separate bedroom. She got up and went to the kitchen those nights and filled a large pot with water and tossed it over him, asleep. She could not believe the bizarre behavior Hal had driven her to, or how much feeling she could have. Rick liked to ape Hal. When he was in the trophy room before TV, Rick nodded his head, back and forth and back and forth, and finally snapped it to the back of the chair, dropped his mouth open, and was in Hal's nighttime position, where he stayed till the wee hours. Hal called himself "sleeping." She told him, "I call it being passed out." Finally, it was actually amusing that she had sat for years watching his head nod back and forth, her heart leaping in excitement when finally his head snapped to the chair's back, his mouth opened, and he was "sleeping." Blessed quiet. She would turn off the television set, which Hal kept on at a high pitch, claiming himself to be half deaf after all the years guns had gone off close to his ears. Then she could read in solitude. Only how long do you read and how much do you retain, Laurel? Hasn't Rick said to you, "I don't think you ever go to bed with a clear head."

Why had Hal never thought to commit suicide? Rick once wondered. Because he would leave no absence in the world, she said. Laurel sat on the sylvan road thinking how her husband had become a paid piper, an entertainer. He was in demand for birthdays, weddings, funerals. She tried to overcome her sense of disparagement and to be wifely. She told him, "You're so popular, you ought to up your price from twenty-five dollars an hour to thirty-five"—this man who owned thousands of acres of prime farmland. "Maybe you're right," Hal said. "I saw William and his wife at that garden party where I played." Laurel grew tired of staying home so many nights and holidays, and she had accompanied him on engagements but gave up. She was relegated to a corner and no one spoke. She was the entertainer's wife. When Hal played for a men's group at the Waldorf-Astoria, he was asked to wait in the kitchen till his appearance; one of the kitchen help offered him a cup of coffee. They were all Puerto Ricans and Hal could not even spend time joking around with them as he could have with blacks.

Hal went up and up on the social scale in the Scarabees band. He had earned a tall hat with a feathery plume. "I've been made captain of the color guard," he said. She told him that was wonderful, eyeing the feather and thinking of William's picture recently in *Business Week*. That Monday night the Scarabees' band practice began at five-thirty. Hal said he wouldn't have dinner till later. He must! She had it cooked. Laurel went on accommodating herself to his fluctuating hours for practice because she was conditioned by her past. Her husband was owed being fed. And she had spent a long while on gravy for his pork chops that night. She had driven herself to tears of frustration in the afternoon, trying to hide the fact she had melted a bottle's worth of aspirin in it. She believed this dose was enough to kill Hal. First she emptied in the whole bottle and the aspirin bubbled up like a witch's brew and left a filmy yellow scum. Twice she rushed to town to buy more aspirin. Her last batch of gravy was the best: thyme, garlic, rosemary; she worried about having overdone the condiments. Hal must take his tray and go ahead to TV. But once he took a bite, he threw down his fork and rushed to the downstairs powder room, where he spit and spit and rinsed his mouth. "That gravy tastes like vinegar. Or aspirin," he said. God damn! How did he know the exact right mystery ingredient? "Mine's fine," Laurel had said, glued to TV.

Hal worked his way up to Sublime Prince in the Scarabees. "Golly, cat's whiskers," she said. They had to celebrate. He would never complain about how strong she made his drinks. When he was asleep, she would dash him with lighter fluid and drop a match, as if he had gone to sleep smoking. She worried about burning the great Oriental rug from Matagorda. When he ran amok in flames, she would open the door and shoo him outside and run after him with a blanket. She would show the firemen, the police, and medics how she tried to save him, and they would see her singed hands. Did she have that much courage? And could she cry on cue? Maybe it would be easier to put a plastic bag over his head when he was "sleeping." Instead, she would press her thumbs to that bulged-out Adam's apple she had looked at for years when he had passed out. She thought of all the times he had peed on the walls, missing the toilet bowl. She thought about a lot. Laurel bent lightly over him. Hal opened his eyes and looked up with a sweet expression. What maddening deity took care of him, and why? "What are you doing?"

I'm a murderess. I'm trying to kill you.

Instead, she kissed him on the forehead. "Darling, you were choking in your sleep. I was trying to wake you up. Come upstairs now and put on your jommies and go to bed. It's late."

Willingly, he let himself be led; so often he had a submissive, childlike demeanor. She had thought he liked being told what to do, being commanded by women, and she should have been more like Sallie, rather than making her opposite nature even more opposite. When he let himself be led, when he looked up at her smiling so sweetly, she believed what attracted her in Hal's letters was buried somewhere in him. Her heart turned over, her groin ached, although she was aware the aching was over what she had expected, rather than over Hal in actuality. One afternoon, when she was sewing a button, he did come up to her, trembling and ready. Just as she was about to lie back, she said, "Oh, never mind." It seemed too much trouble to take her clothes off in the afternoon. He looked surprised and said that was the first time she had ever turned him down and it hurt his feelings.

She pleaded with band members to talk to him about his drinking. The drummer Boomer tried to help. Otherwise, she noted, band members did not meet her eyes at parties, embarrassed by their nonparticipation. Hal promised Boomer he would do better; he gave an oath. Then there was the gathering one night in a roadhouse in some hinterland of Connecticut. Hal got so drunk the hatcheck girl laughed when he came stumbling toward her, one foot weaving before the other like an inept tightrope walker. Laurel could not bear the sight of him.

There was another time in Bridgeport when he tried to shut her out of the car, intending to leave her stranded on a dark street, far worse than being abandoned to the Delta. She fought him like a wildcat to get into the car, and with a strength she did not know she possessed. She knew better than to argue about doing the driving. When he lost directions, another time, and could not find a parkway exit, he stopped suddenly and put his hands around her throat then, his thumbs holding her again without pressure. But to sit those moments with the thought he could lose reason or shut off her air by accident was to look into hell, like the night by the toilet.

That night, coming from the roadhouse, he made no protest about her driving. He was asleep before they left the parking lot. She hated his appearance and his failure to keep his promise to Boomer, in effect to the band, to do something about his drinking. She had stopped depending on soft promises to her. "I won't do it again." Tina said, too, "I'm so tired of promises." Tina, who grew up to be what she was destined to become.

Hal woke up in the garage. He was like a bug on its back trying to turn over, his legs flailing out the open door till he could figure out where to put them. She had never known such loathing and disgust. She whacked him across the face. Her bracelet caught him above one eye and opened a cut; blood began to spurt. She had locked the kitchen door, not knowing there was a key. But she had feared future retaliation. She feared ever being hit across the head again, as her father had hit her twice and as Hal had, once breaking her nose. There was a humiliation to it that sank deep; there was a sense of fury at not being able to do anything that moment. And what she had, by now, was a terrible fear about her brains ever again being rattled in the way they had been, about their never again being the same.

She had thought herself safe, but Hal came up the stairs. Rounding the bed, he had said, "Laurel, I'm going to drown you in the toilet. It's what you deserve."

There was a long time she lay there in the moonlight before she dared to say, "Hal, you can't make this look like manslaughter."

In a while, she whispered, "Not this time. You'll go to

prison forever. Think how horrible it's already been for your children."

She was there a long while, feeling the beating of her heart near his and wondering in the pale light what he was thinking, what he was looking at inside himself, or if he was even capable of thought then. Whatever possessed him went away. He suddenly sat back. With her neck aching, she had gotten up and turned on the light. She could not believe the amount of blood everywhere; even the walls and the rug had smears. "I'm not going to clean all this up," she said. "You do it."

Hal went away with his obedient air and came back with a pail of soapy water and a steel-bristled brush. He worked silently and well. She said once, "Don't soak the rug with water."

That night she slept with scissors under her pillow because it was the only weapon handy. Hal had stayed in the kitchen awhile where the knives were. She fell into a half sleep, thinking how unbelievable it was to live as she did. She thought about the time when Hal blackened her eye in Soundport and she could not hide the truth from her mother. "Why," her mother said, "why did you have to marry someone just like your father? It happens all the time."

Laurel wended her way homeward with Bud. She had been gone so long, by now William would have come looking for her. It would not occur to Hal something could have happened. Bud stuck by her when she sat by the stream with her head to her knees, refusing to cry. Like many dogs, Bud understood sorrow and trouble in others. He sat quietly, not knowing what to do, only to wag his behind if she looked his direction, expressing sympathy in his muteness.

She felt heavily then the burden of Jubal's death, the way she bore a lot, thinking everything was her fault. In childhood she figured out the reason for her existence was to carry about pain in her heart. She always believed God had happiness ahead for her. She thought He paid her off with William, who gave her backbone and spine and taught her direction, to set her sights high. No divorce she knew about had been mourned as she and William and Rick had mourned. She and Rick never stopped discussing it, as apparently he and his dad did not either. Sex seemed in the long run so much the least part of marriage. They had to go through what they had gone through, she supposed. And rue it. Laurel jogged along home, reminding Bud about Jubal and Buff. "Remember?" Jubal went to prison Hal's last year. Rick assured her they could not have continued keeping him in the suburbs, and they recalled Jubal's swimming in the neighbors' pools and how he ate the homemade soup and then brought home the kettle in his mouth when a woman put it out on her doorstep to cool. He frequented local restaurants. How delighted Hal's sergeant had been to have Jubal, the only full-blooded bloodhound they had. The dog boys taught him "street experience"; she laughed. He populated the camp with puppies. In that way, he lived. Jubal became famous. "And," Rick said, "he was a true working dog, doing what he was born for. Not just a suburban slob." Not only was Jubal a natural at tracking prisoners, but so good he was borrowed by the state police to find a lost child, a hunter lost in the woods. But when Hal came back from house-hunting in Delton, he said Jubal had died of hookworm, and she felt responsible. "Prison was his finest hour," Rick said.

 She looked at him that day and said quietly, "So was it Hal's."

When Laurel came in through the garage, Hal was ironing. "Didn't you miss me? Didn't you worry?"
 He smiled slightly. "I was wondering where you were." He looked strange. On Tuesdays he was always pale and puffy about the eyes after his late Monday night in the bar. This afternoon, as always, he would nap. His hands

would be crossed on his stomach, his Wallabees turned upward; he never removed his shoes.

"I have a meeting of Literacy Volunteers this morning. You can practice your pipes." He went on ironing, his head bent.

Laurel sat down drinking coffee and attempted to work the rest of the crossword puzzle. Hal came inside with his arms loaded with ironing. He stopped by the kitchen table with a pained expression. "Laurel, we need to talk about our marriage."

"What is wrong with this marriage is you are a drunk. You do absolutely nothing. And I have no respect for you in any area of your life."

"Oh," he said, passing on. "No respect for me."

What the hell respect did he think anybody had for him? she wondered.

She was surprised by her outburst and somewhat frightened. What could it mean? She did not want to take back her words but ought to soothe them over. Or else they would remain between them forever like a deadly little silence. She remembered this same kind of thing happening with William. Then she had not feared his leaving her, as she'd had the leverage of Hal. Now she had nothing. And she was terrified of abandonment.

Hal was sunbathing in the backyard when she left. She wanted to speak to him but did not know how to break down her barricade of silence. However she did not plan to mollify him too much because the words she spoke were the truth.

After her meeting, she did not want to return home to either Hal or the house's quiet while he slept. She stayed downtown. She passed the drugstore where once she had phoned William, and had lunch in the luncheonette where she and Rick almost had a Coke; the shoe store was replaced by a fancy foods shop for pets, Lick Your Chops. She groaned. In Gristede's she bought lamb chops and steak as treats with the twenty bucks she stole from Hal.

Ahead was her summer's stint at cooking when Tina came for her now laborious summer visit, bringing a friend; another interruption to her writing. Tina stayed longer each year. Soundport was more exciting than the inland small town in Florida where she lived. Laurel went on thinking Sallie got the short end of the stick, and scarcely any alimony. Laurel had reasoned out long ago that lives that came into contact with Hal were harmed, even Jubal and Buff. Something Fate had not called for happened. Tina dated Rick's friends or met boys on her own. Hal snored away the night, but she heard the long silences in Tina's room and cars going away at dawn. She faced wine bottles under the bed, layers of wet towels on the hardwood floors, and dirty dishes stacked around her room. For years she had tried to get Tina to help out, feeling the girl needed to be taught direction. Tina objected. When Laurel asked her to cook frozen peas for dinner, Tina said, "I can't cook." "You can read directions on the box," she told her, but Hal ended up cooking while Tina watched TV, her summer's activity. Then Tina phoned Sallie to say she didn't feel welcome. Laurel wanted her to work. Sallie phoned Hal. A lot going on behind my back, Laurel observed. "Laurel, I'm ready to get rid of you," Hal had muttered, one of his nasty mutterings. It bothered her. At least Tina had the decency to look embarrassed, the little bitch. Daddy's girl. Hal plucked at a bow in her hair when he passed by to make sure Tina was looking at him. Finally the moment came when she said, "Tina, please help me with your father's drinking."

"Oh, no, Laurel. I want money for college."

So much for the promise I've kept you all these years, she had thought.

Laurel continued down the main street of town, thinking of the behavior of Hal's people, their complete refusal to offer any criticism to help him. Shortly after he got out of prison she stopped expecting to hear from them, stopped even wanting to hear the telephone ring with best wishes, a kind word, an invitation. While he was in prison, they behaved properly; they sent him things. But none of them would have their social positions jeopardized afterward by inviting him to their houses. Her mother was right when she said, "You did them a great favor. If it weren't for you, he wouldn't be in Connecticut." She had tried to be a good stepmother, she had tried to be a good wife. For God's sake, she gave a party for his friends in the Scarabees' band and their spouses. A dinner with card tables so everyone had a place to sit down and eat. She thought about that night and the pitiful creature, Doreen.

"Dough-reen," Hal called her in his Southern accent. What was wrong with the woman? She had long wondered that. Doreen was fat and hefty and wore a stationary, incurious smile on a big white face. The night of her party she figured out one thing wrong with the woman. She has a crush on my husband, Laurel observed to herself. It was such a pitiful situation, she wanted to tell Hal. But men were so susceptible to flattery, she thought it best not to bring it to his attention.

But imagine, Laurel said to herself, how she walked into my house. When she opened the door, Doreen had barged in with her gaze averted. She didn't know enough to speak to the hostess? she had wondered, even if she was a manicurist and obviously from the wrong side of the tracks. But Doreen knew little. She stayed in a corner of the dining room hulked up while others served themselves, uncertain about her behavior. She looked about all night with that smile, never speaking to anyone, though now she was one of four women who played in the band. Once passing between rooms, they met in a doorway. Doreen lifted up her chin and stared off. Laurel felt actually a little fear, Doreen was so much like a big-bosomed hen, and masculine in an aggressive, silent manner. She had thought again, The pitiful creature has a crush on my husband. But what odd behavior. She did not want to be uncomplimentary because she had looked down on his activities enough, so she did not remark on Doreen to Hal. He had started her on the bagpipes. Doreen came to the rented stone house one evening, six years ago now, with an old set of pipes she found in her attic. Hal tried them out, he made suggestions. That night Doreen never said a word either. She sat listening to Hal with her skirt hiked up, exposing huge white knees and thighs. Laurel showed her out in her silence. She watched Doreen with her big behind walk off into the dark, toward a rattletrap car, and could not imagine a life more terrible than to be ugly, alone, and have no money. That first night, she had turned back and said, "She's certainly pitiful," and Hal agreed. "Yes, she is."

Now Laurel thought about Hal's sweet side, how he dropped by her mother's some Monday evenings to break up her mother's loneliness, and how he helped Doreen with bagpiping. She had come a long way in six years. Whenever she went to a Scarabees function with Hal, she found him in endless conversation with Doreen, a monologue. Doreen stood above him with her queer, remote smile, as if not quite taking everything in. Laurel had never seen Hal "run his mouth" so much, an action of which he'd have accused her. She saw Hal as happy he had someone to impress, at last.

She decided to go home from downtown because she could not think of anything else to do. In the house, she could feel Hal upstairs sleeping. The telephone rang and she knew it was not for her; she had hardly anyone to call her; calls were always about bagpiping and Scarabees activities. A woman said, "Mrs. MacDonald? This is lawyer James Moody's secretary. Would you please give me the date of your marriage to Mr. MacDonald."

"Just a minute." Laurel put down the receiver and went upstairs in an obedient manner to rummage in a drawer till she found the Mississippi license in its blue folder. Then she went downstairs and told the woman the date, thinking as soon as she hung up, Why the hell didn't I say I didn't know, and let Hal find out?

She went back upstairs to the room where he was asleep, with a sense of unreality and a pounding heart. She told herself, Not like this. No human being does this. How could he, after all I have done? She sat down in his bedroom on a settee from Matagorda, her hands folded in her lap, her ankles crossed, like a proper scared girl at dancing school hoping for a partner.

"Hal, are we getting a divorce?"

He opened his eyes without looking at her and shrugged his shoulders.

"You can't just—get a divorce."

"There's no-fault divorce in Connecticut."

She saw there was nothing to be said. His mind was made up. She had no choice. Everything was to be stripped right away. Who had brought about no-fault divorce, the Women's Movement? Signs had pointed toward his leaving, but she had refused to believe them. She had foolishly believed in idealism, in justice, and in loyalty.

She could not imagine that Hal had scurried around behind her back and filed for a divorce without her even knowing it. He would have to have been thinking about one for a long time, secretly planning and secretly plotting. She had lived with such a person for ten years? Laurel, when she went into her bedroom, saw ahead inevitable years of middle-aged loneliness, of bravery in the face of despair. She turned around and marched right back to his doorway.

"Thank you very much for waiting until I'm nearly fifty-three years old to do this," she said.

"Oh, are you that old?"

The damn little bastard knew exactly how old she was, or ought to. She returned to her room and closed the door. She might as well now tell her mother this trouble. "Even I," Mrs. Wynn said, "never thought Hal would do something like this."

Before going out, he came into the kitchen wearing his navy blue Balmoral and carrying the case with his bagpipes.

Hal outlined his plan. He would stay in the house until the divorce was over and then he would buy out Laurel's half. She said, "In other words, you plan to exactly copy William. Don't you remember saying when William stayed in the house during our divorce, it was the most unmasculine thing you'd ever heard of?"

"The difference now is, Laurel, there's no one who cares anything about you," Hal said.

15

After the night he held her in the bathroom, Laurel decided she would live with Hal knowing he might kill her. She would only be more wary, she would only be more prepared. No man was ever going to rattle her brains again, striking her across the head. Not unless she stuck a knife through him afterward, or killed him somehow.

After that night, a different silence had existed between them. Not only had she known Hal might kill her, he knew it too. She was a living daily reminder of his past. When she said, "This time you'll go to prison forever," it was as if she had screamed, "This time." Up here in the East, while a few people knew about his prison record, it was not like living where things had happened, it was not like living where people who were involved, one way or the other, were around: people who chose sides, people who condemned. While she attempted to bury his past inside herself, she could not bury the present, that he might kill her. Hal knew that, and it was partly why he left.

Laurel believed this for the three years she had been alone. She who was always so attuned to silence was being driven stark raving mad by it sometimes. Never for a moment had she adjusted to living alone, to a house where no one else was coming, where no one else lived. Today she received a package from Frederick's of Hollywood and watched UPS drive away, thinking of the absurdity of having sent for a bra, one which cost twenty-five dollars and which, as a divorcée, she could not afford.

In the silence of this house, yet another rented house in Soundport, she walked about in the mornings talking to inanimate objects, in order to hear a voice. She would not succumb to morning television, even the news, not wanting to grow dependent on those cheery faces as companions. She was afraid of continuing to sit there and end up looking at shouting, mindless people on game shows. Going about these days, she wore indoors a paper cigar band on the appropriate finger, like a wedding ring. It was her talisman, she decided, the day she found it on a sidewalk. To wear it would mean she would find someone again. She took it off at home only to bathe.

To the house's silence she had said, "You are dark now, but you won't be when the leaves are off the trees, will you?" To a woodpecker busy at the shingles, she said, "Shoo. What are you doing up there?" And she asked her jade plants, "Have I watered you too much?" In a diary she had begun keeping she wrote:

> Hal has stripped me of everything I had, was used to, was entitled to expect—my whole life-style: a large house, married couples as friends, animals, a sense of continuity, progressing on toward old age with a sense of peace, companionship. If anything, I know I am going to die this way of loneliness. The eternalness of getting up and going to bed alone. Solitude! So much. I don't think I can bear it much longer. I'm not such a bleeding heart anymore. I gave everything

of myself I had to give and got in return a roof over my head, three squares a day, and shit. The only consolation I can find is, Sallie got a lot worse.

Feeling her life was in order, she looked over into it as from the edge of hell. She had done all she knew to do; she had tried. She made an error that indeed might be a fatal one: she sold the house she got in the divorce, and with a second mortgage. She was so innocent as not to know a house was something you took off on an income tax, and now she had nothing to declare. Then she moved to Delton. Delton!

Was the past never to be repaired? She fled from there in a year. She would have fled sooner had she not had a year's lease on a condominium. Coming back to Soundport, she liked the first little house she rented. Then unexpectedly the landlord wanted it back for himself. Even her sudden tears did not get him to change his mind. She cried more easily than she used to. She would never forget the torrent of tears that Hal unleashed. It shocked her still, because they seemed to be over something deeper even than his treachery. Deeper than over the future she knew she would have. She was still shaken to her roots by it.

Laurel liked her house by the beach now, overlooking the Sound. But she could not afford to go on paying over a thousand dollars a month, with an increase yearly. Plus utilities, she reminded herself. She had dealt with so much alone since Hal left, she was more astute than she once was. She was less idealistic than before, too, about the human race. Too long she had believed in good in people. God knows, she had learned there was no one to depend on but oneself, certainly not real estate brokers, lawyers, bankers, people she turned to selling her house. I'm screwed. Her mother cried out about that house, "It was falling down around you." It was mine, Laurel thought. Because of the second mortgage, she had no money to put down on a small house. Prices kept rising. No, from now on she could only be a renter, money thrown out the window. And soon she could not afford Soundport; what then?

For so long, it seemed her breasts were like apples, like a young girl's. Since they had fallen, they were rounder and softer and seemed larger. But who was she to capture with this bra, or who did she want to capture among the kind of men she met?

When the telephone rang, she was glad; the voice of a solicitor, even, was a welcome one from the outside world, even if she was writing. She kept on writing. When that stint was over, there was the silence of no one coming home, there was the night ahead. The only solution was to get a full-time job, but what could she do—be a saleswoman? Her friend Chris was calling. Her mother was always asking where she met the strange men she met. But she did not want to make her life among women. If that was an unpopular idea with feminists, she was sorry. But she was doing feminist things when she didn't know what a feminist was, when she had never meant to be any kind of leader. She had struck out from home, she had traveled around alone, had an abortion when it was not acceptable or easy, been one of the first women to publish a story in *Esquire*, gone off and left her husband and child. She had rather go out to dinner with a man and was grateful for each invitation. At sixty, Chris was an unpublished writer and was happy about that. He would go on suffering and writing in a shabby room without water. He took showers about town, at tennis clubs, or at the Y, insinuating himself in. Last night he had taken a shower at her house before their usual Dutch treat date. He always wanted to see porno movies in Bridgeport, and they had a sandwich afterward.

"How'd you like the movie last night?"

"Boring," she said. "I'm tired of looking between legs into vaginas and at engorged, purple cocks."

"I know, but this morning it turns me on. If I came over, would you blow me?"

"Hell, no."

"Have you got time to hear a fantasy?" This, too, was part of their palship, and she picked up a magazine and said, "Yes." She propped onto her knees a copy of *Hers*. It was ridiculous she tried so late in time to hop into the world as a fast-paced journalist, hailing cabs and having a lot of appointments. Her agent got her an assignment at her request. "Living Alone at Thirty and Liking It." She found young women she interviewed beginning to worry about their "biological clocks running out." None of them had seriously interesting or important careers. She told them giving up being a wife and mother was not worth it. They had begun in their hearts to agree. However, they couldn't find anybody to marry and blamed the Women's Movement. It had messed things up quite a bit. They couldn't subjugate themselves to men. Then they would have a hard time marrying, she had thought. Couldn't they pretend awhile? Past their own generation of men, the young women believed things would be better. They had grown up with mothers being at home. Laurel's generation, they meant. No sense telling them she had "done something." She'd just always been around to dispense lemonade also. Maybe Rick had not fallen in love seriously because he could not connect to a woman not content with house, kids, dog.

Laurel turned a glossy page of *Hers*. She had failed at the article she tried because she could not write glib, racy copy. Rick had said, "If you were a girl, would you consider me a hot marriage prospect? Both my parents have been divorced twice. My mother married a convict." She looked back to the couple she and William once were and doubted William understood anymore than she did how their images had changed. Rick had said he would make it because of the first twelve years of stability he'd had—that part of his childhood had been, to him, nearly perfect.

"Hell, you've got to make it, boy," she had told him.

"Are you still there, pal?" Chris's voice was hurried.

She doubted Chris could get it up in person and was

never going to find out. "And you take my cock in your mouth. It's big and throbbing. You stick it up your pussy. I'm getting really turned on. My pants are open. In and out. My cock is shoved inside you. You're hot and ready. Now, we've come. Did you come?"

Laurel read the headline of a paragraph in the magazine. "Breasts Are Out in the 80s. Bouncy Beautiful Bottoms Are In." So much for Frederick's. "Yeah."

"You hang in there, pal," Chris said, signing off.

She tried on the bra; under a sweater it looked as if she were wearing two inverted ice cream cones. Laurel stashed it back in the box. "I'm not going to any more new singles groups," she told the house's silence.

Hal had been married for three years, and here she was still seeking, floundering and searching. Her novel came out, which changed nothing in her life. She thought back to Hal's moving and how his movers kicked about the manuscript, scattering pages. She had worked on a desk that belonged to him, and it was carted off. She had thought her pages safely set away, but they had not been. She did not know how she finished the book, being hit by a divorce in the middle of it, everything in her life scattered and fractured. Last Christmas Rick worried and said, "How much longer does your alimony last?"

"I got it for seven years and three are gone." She thought of Hal's lawyer saying, "Rehabilitative alimony," and remembered how Hal mumbled, "If she's getting the house, I'm not giving her anything else." His lawyer had said, "She has to have it, Hal." The lawyer would have known then what she found out later. As soon as the divorce was over, Hal sold his half of Matagorda and became an instantly rich man. He seemed to go on creating harm without anything touching him. Never once did he seem to understand he had done anything to her life.

When she thought about the circularity of things, Laurel was haunted. One day Hal had asked if she would be home that afternoon? Leery, she had said, "Why?" The sheriff was coming by to deliver divorce papers. She fled to downtown Soundport like a hunted animal—but when she came home, the papers were on the newel post. Afterward, notice of the divorce having been filed appeared in the local paper in Court Reports. There for all to see was the fact Hal was suing her for divorce, embarrassing for her and Rick in the town where they had lived so long. She'd have filed for divorce if he'd told her he wanted one. That day the sheriff came to see her, she thought about William's having been accosted at the railroad station, in the dark, and about William coming home laughing. She believed, this late, William laughed when he was hurt the most. No matter the circumstances, rejection hurt. She knew that hurt with Hal. The day they left the lawyer's, having discussed alimony, he curled his lip. "You took me to the cleaners," Hal said. She had that curious sense again that he was oblivious to anything he had done to her, and she thought how she and William had never stopped suffering.

The day she told William she was married, he had come by her house to pick up clothes still stored in the attic, and he dropped an armload. He said, "Congratulations. You sure are a creature of impulse." She had begun to cry and told him she was terrified about money since Hal had a year left in prison. "Don't let anything terrible happen to me," she said. William had put an arm around her and promised. Then he said he would be up to his ass in debt buying the house back and asked her not to take much furniture, but her loyalty had been with her new husband. She had said, "I have to be cruel. Hal doesn't have money to buy any more, either."

"Was it this guy's idea about the private detective?" William asked.

"I didn't even know Hal when I did that," she said. She saw William realized how uncharacteristic of her the action had been, but William had not realized how desperate she had become.

"I'd have fought you tooth and nail about that divorce," William said. "But I figured you had another guy, and in the long run I'd save myself some money. When I get married again, I don't care if my wife turns to stone, I'm staying at home. Middle-aged dating is for the birds."

They were teary, saying they didn't know why they couldn't have worked things out. If they had been the people they had become, they could have. "There was nothing I could do about whatever it was that kept me from being able to make love to you," William said. "As you know, I had a fantastic sex life and was a shit and screwed everything in New York while we were married. I look back and blame myself for the fatal error. I broke the promise and went right back to that girl within a week after we agreed to no more affairs. If I hadn't, I believe we could have made it. I blame myself entirely."

The fatal error was she had married Hal MacDonald, Laurel thought. That day when she and William were still teary, they decided to have a drink. She had said, "Could you keep paying me alimony and take it off the purchase price of the house when I sell it to you?"

"Let me get this straight," and William had put down his glass. He didn't believe his lawyer would go along with that proposition, he had said. When he left the house that night, it was as if they were still crying. Before the year was over, she had to take money from Daddy till Hal got out of prison.

When Rick asked about her alimony, she had gone on explaining it to him. "Seven years was decided on, based on the supposition that in seven years my mother will be dead. Isn't that nice? I'll have inherited her money." I'm an unashamed alimony drag, Laurel thought. What otherwise could she have done? "The marriage was only for ten years," Hal's lawyer had said, bargaining. Only! she could scream that now. "And no children," he ended. That wasn't my fault, she had said to herself.

Rick said, "What are you going to do if Gran hasn't died?"

"It's quite simple. I have to kill my mother. I've done everything else I know to do. Gotten what jobs I could. Sold my collection of first editions. That broke my heart."

"I know. I always wanted to inherit those."

"Forget it. Your inheritance keeps shrinking all the time."

"Yeah. Thanks for getting a divorce. Now I've got Dad's new family to share it with." But he was smiling.

"Maybe Paul Newman will make a movie out of my novel we dropped off at his house in Westport."

"I can't believe we did that."

"I can't either. But I'm tired of being what someone called 'Soundport's best unknown writer.' Maybe we should have said more in the letter to him. This well-received novel is filled with potential for violence, sex—"

"Mom, the book's fifteen years old."

"I know. Maybe we should have written the letter to Joanne Woodward, too. Maybe I should drop off for her my other novel that—"

"Mom. Seriously. Suppose Gran lives a long time in a nursing home and all that."

"She can't. Or at least, she can't die in a nice place, with dignity. Maybe a state institution. Or maybe we could put her in Grand Central Station. They take care of people there. I've read about it in the *Times*. They give them a nice sandwich, an apple, a carton of milk. She wouldn't be lonely. Maybe I'll find a nice eighty-year-old who'll think I'm young. Only men that age marry twenty-year-olds too."

"You've been married for a quarter of a century," Rick said. "Let's find out who Laurel Perry is. I mean MacDonald."

"Wynn," she said. "I changed my name back legally. I wasn't dragging that MacDonald name around with me." She had said, "Besides, I know who I am. A middle-aged divorcée in the suburbs without enough money. The last role I ever imagined for myself. One I always dreaded. I'm too stupid to sell real estate like the rest of the women like me. I've never made any money off writing. I look forward to grandchildren. That's a hint."

"Dad's strapped for money too. I've got to make it all on my own. I don't know when I can afford to get married."

She would not wear the bra anyway tonight. She was going to a seminar she read about in the local paper: Adult Children of Alcoholics. Well, I'm one, she had thought. Any men there would be more interesting than the kind who went to singles groups. Her mother told her to give up. She couldn't, Laurel thought. She dreaded meeting her mother at Bloomingdale's, dreaded the accusatory look in her eyes: Look what you have done to your life. Only what her mother meant was, My life. Without a marital situation, Laurel did not offer the haven she once did. Now that she was older, Mrs. Wynn grew more lonely. Best of all would be if Laurel had never left William.

Why didn't her mother give her credit for what she had done since Hal left? Forget publishing a novel; that never meant much to her. But right away, she had gotten a job. And now, she was teaching Freshman English at the community college. Her heart was in her throat at every teaching job. At least this was the literature semester. She was slightly more familiar with the subject than when, back in Delton, she taught grammar to freshmen. Things had grown easier this semester since a student asked if they couldn't use audiovisual aids. "What are those?" she had to ask. Finding out, she had had students constantly listening to records of writers reading their work, reading Shakespeare, looking at movies that took up two class times. As a teacher she had hardly had to say a word in class since discovering this other method of teaching.

It was not easy getting Hal out of the house. She kept telling her lawyer everything was on her side, Hal's past, his arsenal of guns in the attic, proof of his beating her. The law moved slowly and curiously. Hal went out every night. Newly alone, who was she supposed to know to go out with? Married couples never thought to invite you over for a simple supper, a sandwich, not to eat alone always.

The day after Hal announced the divorce, she went to play tennis. A friend said, "I saw Hal Sunday in Stamford. He was there to play in a parade, but it was rained out. He was in a pet shop waiting for it to stop."

Something in the friend's glance made her say, "We're getting a divorce." Though she had not thought she could tell anyone: *divorced twice.*

"That's good," the friend said. "He was with a woman. They were all huddled up next to each other. That's why I noticed them. When he saw me looking, the woman went out a back door."

She raced home in disbelief, because she believed in him. She threatened him with her tennis racquet. She threw his clothes out windows and threw a suitcase he kept in his room down at him. Dodging and running around, he kept crying, "You're trying to kill me."

In her madness, she stopped and said, "With a suitcase? You damn sissy." He ran out to his lawyer's and came back and put away his clothes and said they'd be carting her off if she did anything else, the law on his side.

Mr. Woodsum was no longer in the phone book. The new private detective was out of a dime novel. He brushed her breasts when he helped her off with her coat. She explained about the women in the band. "Forget one," she had said. "Doreen. She's too pitiful for Hal to fool with." He would have to find out about other female members because she did not know them.

Later the detective discussed them with her. "One is sixteen. Would your husband—?" But she said confidently, "No." He followed Hal away from the house one evening while she watched him start out to tail him, and she felt more than ever curious about her life and the circles in it. She was summoned to the detective's office and kept on her coat. "It's Doreen," he said.

"Dough-reen," she cried out, amazed. What a fool she

had been when the woman stomped on her heavy haunches into her house, taking her husband away before her eyes, making no bones about it. But who behaved in such a manner? What a mouse she was in comparison. But, "Doughreen," she could only say again. And she felt quite sorry for Hal.

16

Before Hal was put out of the house, he began asking if she did not realize he came home sober, that he was cutting down on his drinking. Yes, she had noticed he came home sober and began to drink afterward, no matter the hour. But he wasn't drinking as much because of Doreen. "She doesn't drink," he said. Then one evening he told her, "Before I started seeing Sallie, she offered me some soup on a duck hunt one time. It was eleven o'clock in the morning and it was so laced with vodka I couldn't drink it." She stared at him, thinking, That was nearly thirty years ago, and you're still trying to absolve yourself of guilt and blame things on Sallie. The way his family went on absolving him so that he went on destroying lives. "You caught me at a vulnerable time, my family says," he told her. *You* were vulnerable! she wanted to scream. She pictured Doreen clucking over the story about Sallie, drawing out other tales so she could smooth and comfort and mother, the way he wanted. A big-bosomed woman like a pouter pigeon, one who had to be grateful to Hal because she had had nothing else in her life and never was going to. Laurel thought she would give her eyeteeth to know if Hal was still drinking. He had said, "I can't put another woman through what I've put you through," then left. A forty-year-old manicurist would get the best of him. He had found a level of superiority way below the one he was born to.

When Hal was put out of the house, he rented a place near Doreen's. It turned out Doreen lived across the street from her mother. "Streets I was driving over long before I ever thought I'd meet Hal MacDonald," Laurel said to herself. The house was not far from the Scarabees' old white house where they practiced the band. Those nights Hal dropped by to see her mother, when she thought sweetness prompted him, it had not been at all out of his way, as she had thought. The band had always practiced at seven thirty. She laughed about those nights Hal ate two dinners, hers, and then Doreen's, when he was supposed to be at band practice early.

Once the divorce was over, Hal moved his furniture, his furnishings from Matagorda. And he took Bud. Then the house was stripped nearly bare, and she rattled about with her heels echoing hollowly through rooms, and over stairs, that no longer had carpets. All the time, she longed for even the rattling of Bud's dog tags; she longed to encounter him when she came home. Instead, always, there were the four walls and silence. To make up her bed, even though Hal had not slept in it for a long while, gave her a terrible, empty feeling. A sense of her solitariness. It seemed the saddest thing in the world to sleep by herself, to think that she always would. Laurel looked back to that same sense of emptiness and shock when William had started to sleep in a separate bedroom, a circumstance she had instigated. Rooms in her house were without lighting fixtures because the ones they used had been brought from Matagorda. Hal had promised to replace these and never had. When she went through echoing rooms, wires hung from the walls where the fixtures had been removed. There seemed to be no extra money for such expenditures. She worried on about the future and her monetary prospects. As soon as Hal moved, she rented out Rick's room and bath. Then when Hal returned the day his moving van came, he snickered, "Renting out rooms." How else can I make it! she wanted to cry out. Yet she did not wish to sound as if she was pleading for sympathy. His moving van broke off tree branches all along the driveway. She stood looking out into the silence and darkness when the movers had gone, and Hal and Bud. Then, indeed, her loneliness seemed so final. She thought staring into the yard and the dimly lit road beyond the house that never had she thought she would be living in Soundport alone, in a half-empty house, and taking in boarders to make ends meet. That night she had been particularly glad when her renter's car turned into the driveway and soon she heard his footsteps going up the back stairs.

Laurel hung up from Chris and dressed in her baggy-kneed old jogging suit. She ran along the beach, shadowy dogs from the past running at her heels, Buff, Jubal, and Bud. She thought again of the mystery of Hal, and how he harmed lives. The night they moved from the great stone house they rented to the one they bought, Buff disappeared. She had thought the old dog must have crept into woods near the house and died. In the morning, she phoned the humane shelter. Buff had been picked up in the road the night before, hit by a car. Buff, who had never gone into a road in fifteen years. That day when they moved, she had had no room for Buff. She had taken in her car, instead, a cat Tina left with them one summer. Hal took Buff and parked along the roadside and let her out. The old dog must have been confused by the moving. Had she taken Buff, Laurel knew, the dog would have been safely in the house. She never knew what happened to that cat, and she never asked Rick.

 They had had to go to the vet's where Buff was taken

and give permission for her to be put to sleep. She was too old for the necessary operation. Rick made a huge casket and painted a white cross on top. "I thought you didn't believe in God," she had said. "I don't," he said. "But Buff might."

He drove them a long way home to bury her and she finally asked what he was doing. "I'm taking her past every place in Soundport she used to go," he said: past Little League fields, past William's, the beach, his old ice hockey pond. Laurel had decided to take courage from Buff. As an old woman she would be as courageous as Buff had been. Arthritic, Buff plunged herself downstairs and slid on her belly when her legs wouldn't work. Jogging along the beach, Laurel began to sing a simplistic song, "Walk on, walk on, with hope in your heart and you'll never walk alone. . . ."

As instantly as Hal left her, she got up courage and went to Columbia University thinking she would enroll in their M.F.A. program. She might learn to write a novel that would sell, and with such a degree she might get a job teaching. The woman who interviewed her thought Laurel might be a little advanced for the other students. Teaching? Laurel suggested timorously. "I'm sorry," the woman said. "But this is really a tight, closed community. If our teachers have to leave, they recommend a friend." The woman suggested the undergraduate department.

She trudged across the large campus feeling another rejection, and quite alone. The undergraduate chairman said, "*The* Laurel Wynn? Why do you want to teach now?"

"I'm getting a divorce." Quick understanding crossed his face, and she thought what a familiar story hers must be. He flipped through folders in a filing cabinet, showing her how many applicants he had. "Do you have a vita?"

Aveetah? She didn't know what he meant and shook her head. He showed her an applicant's letter out of one of the folders. She read about books published, awards, *teaching positions held.* "When you've had some experience, come back to see me," he said.

She did not dare ask him, If I can't get a job teaching because I have no experience, how can I get a job teaching to get some experience?

She decided to be like other people. She would be organized. She sat for days in Soundport's library reading catalogs and copying down addresses of any feasible college within driving distance, mostly with adult education departments. Rick gave her advice from out west, what kind of paper to have her résumé typed on, what headings to use. He'd never heard of a vita either. She mailed out a bunch of envelopes feeling like a kid mailing valentines. She received a phone call one evening from the very college where she was working on her Master's. It seemed late at night to her. She put down her after-dinner brandy and soda and hoped she sounded all right. Her application had been handed on from the adult education division. The freshmen writing class had so many students, they had to form a second class. "Teach freshmen? Sure, I guess so," she said. Hearing about the class, she had said, "No textbook. What am I going to say?"

"You're a writer. You'll know. You can teach twice a week for one hour. Or once a week for two hours. I believe twice a week gives more continuity."

"Absolutely," she said, based on no authority. For her, twice a week meant two days with somewhere to go.

Gladly she told her class the only instruction she was given. They had to turn in fifty pages in the semester to be considered for an A. Then she dawdled over roll call and talked about learning their names. She looked at two girls she had overheard talking in the hallway about a class one was not prepared for. "Open the top button of your blouse and lean way over him. He likes that," the other girl had said.

Much in the world would never change. She studied

the high heels girls wore with blue jeans, and their eye makeup. She wondered if she could be like them. She wondered if young men in the class could look at her with interest. "Who is your favorite writer?" she asked a girl in the first row.

"Stephen King. To write like him would be my idea of heaven."

Laurel had never heard of Stephen King and would have assumed him to be a rock star. This was a Catholic university and she read them a story of Flannery O'Connor's, glancing always at the clock. How long could an hour be? She had no idea how to make general small talk. Once they turned in work, time could go faster. She finished reading "A Good Man Is Hard to Find" and asked what religious symbolism the students saw. No one said anything. She did not know any religious symbolism either. She read O'Connor because of her Southernness. She would let them go early—a practice that ought to ensure the students' liking her. She lifted her hands and cried out to them, "You're all my children," the way the grandmother in the story cried it out. They left laughing, at least.

She sat at the desk and looked at the book with the remainder of the afternoon to go home in, with the night to come. She would eat at a diner on the way home and hear the click of other people's silverware. In hiring her, the professor said since she was a part-time teacher she was not required to attend meetings or take part in anything beyond her class. He spoke with envy. She had only been sorry.

It was hard to think that after Hal moved she was overcome with worry about him. He wouldn't know how to take care of himself, he didn't know how to cook. Living alone, he would drink himself into oblivion. She had overheard him tell the driver where to deliver his furniture. The second night after he moved, she phoned his house. She would cry out, Oh, let me come and see about you! Doreen had answered.

To know what had been going on behind her back for so long, the plotting and the planning, was humiliating. While she was doing this, that, the other, Doreen was packing her belongings. While her life fell apart, Doreen's began in an unimaginably better fashion. As she miserably watched Hal's van depart, leaving her to darkness and solitude, Doreen's van left too. The vans met to unload in the night, the lovers united at last. The witch was smart; they soon married. Hal had not sense enough to keep the upper hand. Married for the fourth time, he had gone directly from one marriage to another one and never been alone a moment in his life. Yet three women were out in the world by themselves because of him.

Her alimony checks arrived from a small rural town farther north. Not the chic part where writers lived, she consoled herself. In loneliness amounting to rage, she phoned him at night sometimes to see if *he* was sitting at home, if *he* had somewhere to go. If she phoned so late as ten at night, Doreen answered and said, "Hello, Laurel."

What kind of witch was it who walked into her house in huffiness and took her husband away before her eyes? What life did they lead that no one phoned so late, and was Hal drunk?

When she went home from the university and ate in the diner, she stayed as long as possible, but no single man came in she might engage in a hopeful conversation.

For six years in the house she and Hal bought, she was aware that somewhere around a bend in the road there was a Unitarian church where the most famous singles group in the Northeast met. On Sundays, she had heard the church's booming bell. She had never thought she'd be going there. But she had to take some step into the world when Hal left. There was the inner hall of the church with several hundred people milling about, as many men as women. It would turn out, of course, that some of these men were married. She bought a ticket, she made a name tag. She stared about at people in groups; how did you go up and start talking to them? She stood about drinking weak coffee and keeping back tears. She had been given a number, and at a certain time, people filed down to appointed Sunday school rooms. Children's drawings were on the walls. Discussions were advertised as being part of the singles' nights. She had come thinking at least that was a way to spend the evening—talking of foreign affairs or whatever. In a semicircle they sat. The evening's discussion topic was: Should We Kiss on the First Date? She thought back to being in the tenth grade and wondering the same thing.

Afterward, they went upstairs for wine and cheese. Eventually, as weeks passed, faces became familiar. A man asked her out to a nice dinner. She offered to pay half, but he refused. From then on, he expected her to cook. He had worked for a shipping company for twenty years and made twenty thousand dollars a year. She told him he ought to ask for a raise. He had been thinking about it. He thought finally it would be a good idea if they bought a house together out of Fairfield County and moved their mothers in with them. They drifted apart.

All around the county, churches held similar groups. She went from one to another one, through dark roads and towns, never expecting to find her way. Finding it. All events were the same. They began by standing around for a get-acquainted hour. *Hi*, name tags read. *My name is* _____; fill in the blank. She was fearful of ever catching a man's eye; he would think her too eager. Never say you are a writer; men don't like women with brains. Don't drink too much cheap wine, or you'll be sick. Eat. Cheddar cheese on a cracker; but then her mouth was too dry to speak. Men never started conversations first. She had to do it. "Hi! What town do you live in?" She wanted to cry out, I had a life once. I only don't have one anymore.

Always after the first hour, there were round table discussions. "Tonight's topic is, What Kind of Movies Should We Singles See?" a moderator said. When it was her turn, Laurel said, "Movies like anybody else, I guess."

She would have to go on and on pushing herself outward, adopting a personality that did not fit. She made phone calls. "Hi. I met you at International Singles last week. We were talking about skiing. A friend is sick, and I have an extra ticket to—" Maybe the double standard would always exist. It seemed better to wait for a man to call her. Too often, she heard the same reply: "Sorry, but I've just connected to someone." At least no one saw her face burn at refusals. Men spent the night. Sometimes she scarcely remembered their names.

She read every issue of *The New York Review of Books*, not for the erudite literary commentary but because of the singles listings in the back. She ran her finger down the listings looking at numbers. Numbers were what counted. *Would like to meet female not over 40. . . . Gentleman in 60s looking for woman between 25–35. . . . Younger than Reagan*, began a man's ad. How much younger? It didn't matter. She had a couple of desultory lunches this way. She put in her own little ad: *Writer would like to meet. . . .* There were letters, usually strange. A man analyzed her through all her books. *I wish I could have read them in manuscript*, he wrote. *I could have helped you make them so much better.*

She read flyers and went to meetings. A nonsmoking clinic. BRING YOUR CIGARETTES, the announcement said. She bought a package, hoping she did not take up smoking. No one to connect to. She sent her name to a correspondence list. LET US HELP YOU MEET THAT SPECIAL SOMEONE. Letters followed:

> Dear Laurel:
> I got your name from a list one of my friends who locks across the hall from me has. I hope you're not mad at me for writing. Not too much happens here at Attica. . . .
> #81c858

> Hello, Laurel,
> I hope these few words reach you at your best; as for myself, my situation leaves a lot to be desired.

> I got your name from a list. I'm presently incarcerated and I hope this fact alone will not turn you off against embracing my offer of friendship. Here in Indiana—
> #18692
>
> Saw your advertisement. I'm a man in prison who receives little mail and have been in Dannemora for—
> #28695
>
> I'd like to be the man in your life. I'll be getting out of Parchman in—
> #45050

She was foolish enough to accept a collect telephone call one night. A prisoner would like to make her rich. He could put her on his visiting list and gradually she could bring in cocaine in a little sack stuffed up her vagina. It was done all the time. She went to a dating service in Soundport and filled out a long questionnaire. Her name would be sent to compatible men, and she would receive a list of names. "Don't wait for the man to call. Take the initiative," the dating counselor advised. She met a man at a dockside restaurant who lived on a small boat in South Norwalk harbor. He rowed her out through the night to see it. "No, don't worry about my high heels," she had said. They climbed aboard. He had nothing else in mind. He rowed her back to shore. She sang through the trip under her breath, "Row, row, row your boat." She had dinner with a man who moved furniture, and several other "compatible" people. She fell away from being able to cook for herself. She ate Lean Cuisine dinners. In the mornings, she sometimes found those little self-contained aluminum pans sitting in her kitchen without remembering having eaten the contents. In the middle of nights, she woke up sweating and restless with the worry, Is this my life forever? She might get up and cook a whole can of popcorn and eat it drowned in butter. She didn't know whether she ought to be getting fat or thin from what she ate.

Men somehow surfaced; there were adventures. When a younger man picked her up on the train when she was coming out from New York, she had to be flattered. He worked in the city but she was never certain doing what. He spent a lot of time fishing and brought lobsters to her house to cook. She always thought of him as "the lobster man"; he called her "doll." In her living room, the first time he visited, he suddenly stripped to show her what he liked to use, a cock ring. It was black and ugly and made her think he might pull out a black whip. He explained the cock ring stopped blood flowing to his veins. "Women like it," he said. She got up and drew the living room blinds. He told her where she might buy a "little leather outfit." He wanted her to try another favorite of women, cutting a condom off and rolling it and fitting it snugly around the base of his cock. She told him their relationship was going to be to eat lobsters. She was tired of going to bed with men in whom she had no interest, though his ideas were intriguing.

During her middle-aged singles years, she fulfilled what was supposedly her hidden Southern desire. She went to bed with a black man. He taught a Black History course she took during her Master's. In bed one afternoon, he wanted to know if she thought about his being black. Her only different reaction to him had been surprise at how dark his organ was. She could tell him truthfully, "No." However, she said, "Just don't tell my daddy." The professor thought about her whiteness, he said. He was from the South, and they had a rapport. He went away on business and called her from Chicago.

"You in nigger heaven," she said.
"Have you been thinking of me?"
To flatter his male ego, she must say, "Yes."
"What did you think?"
She sought something to say. "That I like to kiss you."
"That's all? What else?"

She was not cut out for this kind of thing, Laurel realized. "That I like your penis." This would be what a man wanted to hear.

"Penis. That's what you call it?"

"When I call it anything," she said. She had trouble saying that word; she had wanted to call it "your thing." "What do you call it?"

"My dick."

"I've heard that."

"What do you like about it?"

"It's big." She went on giving required answers.

"It's nine inches. Six inches is average."

"I wasn't aware of that statistic."

"I've got a surprise for you when I see you next."

She was sorry never to have experienced the girl he was going to bring along. Before that time could take place, she had moved to Delton.

By the time she returned home from jogging on the beach, she decided her life would come down to Chris and a few other men who took her out to dinner or whom she cooked for. She would continue with the singles group that went to the Hartford Symphony, despite the dreary cheese and wine gatherings afterward. She had joined PEN: Poets, Essayists, and Novelists. She did not know why she hadn't joined years before. She could volunteer for a committee. Despite their gatherings being downtown in Manhattan at night, she would keep going. No matter that she had gone in to readings and turned around and come directly back to Connecticut never having said a word to anyone, because she did not know how to start up conversations at such a gathering where she knew no one. She would never recover from all that had happened to her. She went off with a singles cross-country skiing group and got frostbitten. Her toes were never going to be the same. She rubbed them, taking off her jogging shoes. The day, while exhilarating, had been frightening. She had never been cross-country skiing in her life and took off with the group on a five-mile tour. When she went back to her car, she could not open the door, her fingers were so stiff. Her toes were frozen in her boots. She stood helplessly off in New York State. Suppose something devastating happened requiring medical attention. Family to call? There was no one but her mother. She was no one to any of the other people, already in their cars and driving away through a frozen afternoon. A long while she stood trying to unlock her car, finding herself in a parking lot alone, until she could move her fingers.

Driving alone again through nighttime suburban streets, Laurel told herself this was the last new event. She had found out about Adult Children of Alcoholics by running a finger down the alphabetical list of clubs in the biweekly Soundport paper. Not only singles seemed to be looking for companionship. Beekeepers. Computer lovers. Gravestone lovers. Whatever got you through the night, she supposed. Jim Beam bottle collectors. Rabbits. Whales. And she went back to point A.

She supposed she was going to be late because she really did not want to go. She went around through Soundport's dark but familiar streets and on to a neighboring town, to a Catholic church. There was always something so hushed and holy about them, she dreaded entering. But the church itself was dark. There were lights in a basement room, and she could see people sitting in rows of chairs. Another entrance; another room full of strangers. She might have been less conspicuous had she arrived on time; at the door, she wavered and finally went in.

"Come in."

A priest stopped speaking and nodded.

A woman patted an empty seat in a circle of chairs, and she sat down. She thought of an old child's game in kindergarten where she skipped around a circle of chairs to the teacher's playing of a yellowed piano. A chair was removed, and when the music stopped, there was a scramble for the chairs remaining. Someone had to be left out.

She remembered standing there with nowhere to sit, feeling personally rejected. She was never able to scramble for a seat, being an only child and not used to fighting for something. She remembered how in her own house she had shrunk from Doreen.

"A child in an alcoholic environment grows up with a sense of rescuing," the priest had continued. "Technical rescuing, it's called. In such homes children take responsibility for the drinking. They grow up with a poor self-image. I am not worth love, a child thinks. I must merit it. In such families, the children take on varying roles. There is the lost child. There is the rescuer who is the hero. There is the wit, the entertaining one. There is the nurturer." The priest stopped and smiled. "That's why you find among Irish Catholic families so many children become nuns and priests."

"Suppose you were an only child?"

Laurel was surprised by her daring. But in three years as a single, she had come out of herself. She had to, facing classrooms of students, facing strangers.

"Then you played all the roles," the priest said.

Among other people in the room, there were sighs or soft muttered comments. "I always tried to make my parents happy," a woman said.

"Tried," the priest said. "But we can't make anyone happy but ourselves."

Yes, she had been silent trying never to be trouble, Laurel thought; wouldn't she then be loved? Often she did assume blame for her parents' bitterness and their quarreling. All along their lives had been their own. Never to share feelings meant looking elsewhere for things to be better. She had gone about seeking love, escaping even to Mama, who wrote lovely letters before Hal was out of prison, and who she thought would be a mother unlike her own. I went over the rainbow, Laurel thought, but never got back home like Dorothy, though I tried and tried.

"There is a wall of isolation in alcoholic families," the priest was saying. "It's difficult to break the conspiracy of silence that goes on. No one must know what is happening inside the walls of the house. The inhabitants don't talk about it to one another."

A woman spoke in tears. "I was always so afraid to bring friends home. I never knew when my mother would be lying out on the floor drunk."

"I was always trying to figure out what normal was." A man looked inward. "It led to a lot of erratic behavior in my life, to a lot of moving."

"All of this sounds as if you have lifted off the roof to the house where I grew up," another man said, "and looked down at my own life."

There was relief to finding people like herself. As the priest talked, as other people told their experiences and feelings, as she could share them, she found guilt began to erase itself, a burden lifted; layers of the past began to peel away. All around the church there were exclusive towns, with well-tended lawns, big houses, and so much pain inside people they did not create for themselves.

In a circle, they stood with their arms around one another. People unashamedly had wet faces. "Our father who art in heaven," they began.

"Keep coming," the priest said. "Remember, don't let the past dominate your thoughts."

Tonight she would not stand about and chat. She felt like being alone another time with a silence that would begin to break. She would never know what might have happened differently with William and Hal if she had talked more, but Laurel understood reasons that drove her to save Hal. Her impetus needed to be put to more productive use. She had never spoken up to William, Hal, or her mother out of fear of rejection. Always she had expected to be an abandoned child. Hal had made this a reality. Once he left, she had cried as never before in her life, out of the marrow of her bones, out of the deepest recess of her soul. But for more than him. She had cried not only over the past but longing for it to come back, no matter its pain. The priest's last words took hold. But she could never forget. Always she would be a person with scenes of the past overlaying themselves in her mind's eye, colorfully in the present. Yes, she had been willing to be a victim because she had grown up as one. It was the only role she knew, and fit comfortably. She would not be one again, but she felt the role slipping away as if she had lost a companion.

She reached the door as someone behind her whispered, "He's a recovering alcoholic," about the priest. She shook his hand. "I'll be back," she said. "If I'd known these things before, my whole life would have been different."

"So would mine have been." The priest smiled wryly.

She drove back over suburban roads wondering if under different circumstances he would have been a man who gave himself to God.

17

She was meeting her mother for lunch at Bloomingdale's. Seeing her across the room's subdued light, Laurel straightened up and walked to where her mother waited at a table. She could see her diamond ring flashing as she held a cigarette. In her other hand, her mother held a small rubber child's ball. What was she doing?

"Are you limping?" Mrs. Wynn asked when Laurel sat down.

"No." In her chair, she felt pains shooting up her buttocks. "What are you doing?"

Mrs. Wynn gave a small smile. Her long nails enclosed the ball with its swirled colors. They reminded Laurel of pastels, sherbets. "The cancer society women brought it by this morning." She went on squeezing and squeezing to demonstrate. "I'm supposed to do this to strengthen my arm since the operation."

"Oh." Laurel was relieved her mother had not regressed to some form of childhood. She had sympathy about the mastectomy. Still, there was a familiar core of resentment about her mother saying the operation was Laurel's fault. If Laurel had not moved back to Delton when she did, Mrs. Wynn said, she'd have gone for a biopsy earlier. "I couldn't have an operation by myself. No one to look after me." Having been alone in the world now for five years, Laurel had a tougher spirit. And she understood the past much better now after Children of Alcoholics sessions, and the need she had had to be a willing victim. But no more. A competitive spirit had begun to rise. She stared directly at her mother saying, "No one but you, Mother, would have had seepage around a nipple for so long without going to a doctor. He said if you'd come sooner, you wouldn't have had to have a breast removed. I could have come back from Delton. You could have come there for the operation." Because no matter what had happened, no matter that she had returned, there was a feeling, still, of being on Mount Everest by themselves: a feeling that the truest friends were back where they came from, doctors they could have depended on better. She had accepted a sense of being displaced about living in the Northeast.

Her mother kept demonstrating how she flexed her arm by squeezing the ball. Patrons at another table were watching, their munching temporarily suspended. Laurel wanted to laugh. She watched the network of old skin on her mother's arm like fish scales and knew someday she would have them herself. But her mother didn't look eighty. She had more fashion sense than Laurel felt she had and was never dependent on someone to help her. How had she acquired it, being the country girl she once was? Her mother looked into the distance as if thinking about her operation. And suddenly Laurel thought that she stared into an abyss, into the grave and beyond. What must it be like to have so little time left to live? she wondered. She had herself a diluted sense of so much of life being over as she neared sixty. She could see her mother alone in her apartment talking to a stranger from the cancer society.

She was more acutely aware of the silence of her mother's apartment, now that she was herself alone, and more acutely aware of her mother's making some kind of life on her own as a widow. She emptied a glass of water in nervous apprehension over their time together.

"Don't drink all that water. You won't be able to eat."

Laurel stared at the glass. "It is drunk," she said.

"It's all that jogging that makes your hip hurt."

"Maybe it's sitting over the typewriter."

"Doctors now say jogging is bad for women. You'd know that if you'd read."

"I read, Mother. I just reread *Madame Bovary*."

"Or watch television. There was a talk show the other morning about jogging. You need to keep TV on for company now that you're alone."

"I don't want it on for company." Laurel put the rim of the glass between her teeth.

"What did you say?"

She repeated and then she said, "You need a hearing aid, Mother."

"I can hear everybody but you. You mumble. Everybody says so."

"Who is everybody?"

"And Rick," Mrs. Wynn said. "He mumbles too. Rick thinks he is just so-o-o—" and she made an airy gesture with her hand, not knowing what she wanted to say.

So intellectual? Laurel said to herself. This was still a stigma to her mother.

"I don't think Rick will ever get out of school."

"It takes a long time to get a Ph.D."

She looked up in relief when the waitress appeared, a big-bosomed woman in a tight pink uniform. On an eye level with those bosoms, Laurel tried not to stare or to think about the pouter pigeon who took her husband away. While her mother and Rick constantly assured her she was better off without Hal, and while she felt a great sense of relief about no longer being caught in her life with him, she was still so lonesome. Since starting sessions with Adult

Children of Alcoholics, unlocking a silence she had lived with so long, she could not help wondering how things would have been with William or Hal if she had spoken up more. But she did not dwell on the past any longer.

The waitress presented them with large pink menus. "Ladies. The special soup today is gazpacho."

"What did she say?" Mrs. Wynn hissed across her menu.

"The special soup is gazpacho."

"Ugh. Green peppers give me indigestion." She stared up at the waitress with a little smile as if to say, What did she think about that?

The waitress said, "The special entrée is chicken with piquant sauce. And for dessert Bloomie's pink peppermint ice cream."

Laurel winced over the word "Bloomie's" as she had winced at "ladies." The words made her feel she was a matron with time to kill, though she had spent a lifetime trying not to be like her mother. However, her mother was right about one thing. It was a common occurrence for people to return to the source of their pain; in marrying Hal, she did marry someone like her father, as if to acquire once more what she remembered from childhood. Her tendency toward alcohol was common for the children of alcoholics too; it came down through the genes.

As Laurel said, "I'll have tuna on pita bread," she remembered learning from William's family not to be redundant and say tuna fish.

"Why do you want tuna fish? You can have tuna fish at home." Her mother removed her reading glasses and waited for an answer.

"Mother, just let me order. What do you want?"

"I don't want anything." She told the waitress conversationally, "It's a waste of time eating out. I feel like I'm just throwing away money, they give you so much food."

"I'll get more water."

Laurel watched the waitress walk away. "Mother, decide before she comes back." She dreaded drinking another full glass of water. Her mother, as if she heard command, read the menu.

Long trickles of water were poured into her glass. The waitress had freckle-spotted and brown-spotted hands. Like my own, Laurel thought. But she wouldn't hide them in her lap and put them on the table. She had tried to squelch the squirming in her stomach. "Have you decided?"

"What do you want?"

"I've ordered."

"I'll give you ladies more time." Again, the woman went away on her softly clad feet.

"Think of something, Mother." Laurel drank water.

"Why? What's your hurry? You don't have anything to go home for. Nobody to cook for tonight."

She didn't understand why this woman wanted to inflict pain; Laurel looked into her lap and knew there was nothing she was going to do about it this late in time. An old woman sat opposite her, and it was too late to tell her what she thought. Too late to express the rage she felt. She tried not to look at herself walking into her house with the sense of emptiness and betrayal she always felt, and she tried not to wonder what quality of emptiness her mother's death would leave. In the end, she might mourn only a mother she never had.

It was strange sitting across the table from death; it was written on her mother's face—something she longed for, she said. If she had cyanide, she would kill herself. There are ways if you wanted to do it, Laurel longed to say. Her mother worried all the time about her future. Who was going to take care of her business when she died; what was Laurel going to do with all the junk in her apartment? If only she could have died during her operation, Mrs. Wynn mourned. And Laurel had no comfort to give her. She would like to tell her mother to stop thinking about herself, but what was she to think about instead?— she had never prepared herself for anything except bridge. She could only wonder if she loved her mother, or if she even liked her. She did not feel obliged to do either thing because this woman was her mother. She did not feel that her reactions had anything to do with geriatrics; they had to do with her mother as herself, with the personality she had always had, with the person she had always been. Only now, with the sessions Laurel had been going to, she had learned not to blame herself for the past, not to accept guilt, not to be shoved around. Understanding reasons for past behavior, Laurel could forgive herself a passive role among other things. Not only did she feel herself well, she felt herself more well than a lot of people she knew who'd never thought anything was wrong with themselves.

"Decide, Mother," Laurel said with an airy gesture of her hand. Then to her astonishment and amazement, she realized this was an exact copy of the way her mother often raised hers. She had even heard in her voice an inflection that sounded like her mother's. She would grow on and on to be more like her as she grew older. She heard her talking about her own mother as she walked about her apartment, Laurel's grandmother. "I'm getting to be just like Momma," Mrs. Wynn kept saying, meaning her nervousness and a way she had of flicking the side of her skirt. It is inevitable, Laurel thought, that I shall keep getting like her. Therefore, I must fight harder against it; she swore to herelf.

The remaining water in her glass ran over her nose and tickled it. She let her nose remain buried. She thought of the things her mother's desperate loneliness had driven her to. She knew a change had to take place and that she was the one who would have to take charge of it. Her mother talked about cleaning her apartment and yet dust lay everywhere. Mrs. Wynn was "too nervous" to have help come in. She wore greasy or dirty clothes, saying she "didn't give a damn." A way of thumbing her nose at life, Laurel supposed. She tried to pay her mother a compliment; maybe her crustiness was a way of making herself know she was alive. It was a pain in the neck to other people.

Her mother had fallen into the habit of dropping by

her doctor's office and sitting in his waiting room. She managed to look chagrined, saying this was a way of being with other people. As pitiful as that was, Laurel thought. How could she solve her mother's life, her problems? The doctor told her to wash her clothes, to comb her hair, and that she was "crazy." He had been supplying her with Valium for years. He sent her to a psychiatrist, and now the psychiatrist was supplying her mother with antidepressant pills. Drugs to a drug-dependent person, Laurel thought. What could she do about doctors who prescribed pills and walked off and left other people to cope with the patient they had created? Why didn't doctors think? She thought of being moved to pity by a homeless woman asleep in a subway station in New York in a puddle of her urine and how she'd tucked money into her hand. When she came home, one of her mother's friends called to ask, "What is wrong with your mother? I saw her at the grocery and she used to be always so well-groomed. She didn't have any makeup on, her hair wasn't combed. Her dress had spots." She hadn't known how to transfer her pity for the woman in New York to her own mother.

"If you're not hungry, Mother, why don't you have a frozen fruit salad?"

"Ugh. That's nothing but ice. It gives me a headache to eat it."

"How about cottage cheese and fruit platter? That's light." She was not going to let her mother rile her, she had decided.

"Don't tell me how to order. I know how to order." Mrs. Wynn plopped down her menu. "And stop squinting. Wear your dark glasses."

"I don't want to wear them. They're prescription and I'll get dependent on them."

"Then stop squinting. It's not going to do any good to get your eyes fixed if you keep squinting. If you want to have the operation, I'll give you the money."

Laurel was afraid to take money from her mother, she was afraid of repercussions. All the time her mother worried about not having enough money for her old age; suppose she turned out to be nine hundred dollars short because of my operation? Laurel thought. When would I hear the last of that? Anyway, she went to a surgeon in a panic as soon as Hal left; while there, she said, "My husband thinks my breasts are too small," and inquired about enlargement. Imagine that she would do that, she thought now. She had considered back then there was no sense telling the doctor her husband had already left her. "Your husband's crazy," he had said. "You have beautiful breasts for a woman your age. Why don't you have your face lifted instead?" Well, thanks for nothing, she had thought, walking out, and decided she'd keep for now whatever God had given her. Why were women always being made conscious of their ages? She thought of rebuffs that had slapped her over and over since she had gone about trying to meet men. In Delton, an old friend had said, "You were so beautiful, you could have had anybody in Delton." Then realizing his meaning, his words, he had looked embarrassed and had whipped out a folder and showed her pictures of his two young children by his second, young, wife. She had cooed over them.

The waitress said, "Ladies, have you decided?"
"Mother. Order."
Mrs. Wynn sighed hugely. "Just bring me the clam chowder."
"Large or small?"
Her mother rolled her eyes toward the waitress. "You decide."
"Mother," Laurel said.
"Well, bring me the large." Mrs. Wynn leaned confidingly over the table behind the waitress's back. "It won't be anything but hot milk and potatoes. There's never any clams in it."
Laurel curled her toes to the soles of her shoes and watched the blue smoke ring her mother blew toward the ceiling.

"Maybe I'm not hungry because I smoke so much. I think my ulcer is back. From worrying about you."

"Don't worry."

"I can't help it." Her eyes swam about behind her cigarette smoke. "I feel like all I'm doing is waiting to die."

"That *is* all you're doing," Laurel said. But she softened the words. "That's all anybody is doing."

"I guess I'm never going to live to see any great-grandchildren."

"Probably not. And don't put any pressure on Rick about that."

"Well, you just don't know what it's like living with depression."

"I wish the psychiatrist hadn't given you that word. You've latched on to it too conveniently. And I don't think you should take those antidepressant pills. He should be treating your head, not your body. He says they're not addictive, but it seems to me they are. I can always tell when you've had one; you're different."

Mrs. Wynn stubbed out her cigarette. "I think they are too," she said. "I went to see him yesterday and told him I had to get off them. I told him I can't stay in that apartment by myself any longer either. I've got to go somewhere. He wants me to go to the hospital to the psychiatric ward for several weeks."

"Mother, that's great. I wish I could go too."

"You want to go? Why?"

"I'd like to have somebody take care of me."

"Not many people are there my age, he said. Mostly, young people are there. They're the ones who can't take stress these days. A forty-year-old woman in town jumped out of her apartment window the other day."

My eighty-year-old mother in the psycho ward, Laurel was thinking. How did everything come about? "If they keep you on medication there, nothing will be gained. Tell them you want to get off pills. What's the answer after that? You still have to come back to your same apartment, to your same life. Your friends who have died will still be dead. The ones who have gone to nursing homes will still be in them." Laurel realized the loneliness of old age but thought she'd never live in an apartment. She'd always have a little house and a yard to putter in and a dog fenced in. Would she still be a pain to Rick? Probably so, she concluded. "What day are you going? I'll take you. I've got to get my hair done. I want to look my best taking my mother to the nut house."

Mrs. Wynn smiled. "I'm going Thursday. I've got to wash my clothes."

For that moment, Laurel thought about their long association. She thought about the past they shared that no other human being alive knew about. She did not want her mother to die, she thought. In looking back, she supposed she had moved to Delton searching a haven one more time. After so many months alone in Soundport, her teaching stint ended, nothing else available, after so many months of singles groups, Southport seemed a dead end. Her mother had told her not to go back, that she would not be happy there, but she had sold her house and moved. Her mother once again stayed put, adopting her wait-and-see attitude, and then Laurel came back.

I would have come back sooner, she told herself, if I could have found a sublease for that condominium. It had brown walls, and to live in it was like being buried; the walls closed in gigantic with shadows. People she had known thirty years ago were as remote as if she were in Connecticut; she was cut off from some people because of her past association with Hal and should have realized that would be the case. Anyway, it was all too late for her to have come back. She was not used to a city, and driving about a sprawling one with endless wide, flat streets was like being in a terrible maze. She longed for water of any kind, a pond, a brook, a stream. She had little in common with people she had long known and needed to find a whole different group of friends in the place she had come from, an arduous and long process and one that seemed too difficult. She went to the dog pound and got a puppy. While she paid for him, a black man came from the cages holding the dog gently in his arms. He spoke to it. "Now you don't have to be lonely anymore," he said.

Her throat had filled with tears. It is I who am lonely, she had wanted to say. The dog was impossible to keep confined; it yapped all the time at night. She put it into her bed and could not keep it on the other side of a pillow barricade. The puppy had to sleep against her. She had to return it. But, too, this dog taught her about life. She liked its determination in climbing over anything she erected to get out of the kitchen and find her. The fact that it would not sleep except next to her taught her more than anything else that people were not meant to be alone. At Christmas, she returned to her mother's. It was not fair to ask Rick to come where he knew no one. Delton would never work out. And really, she had expected her old high school days, girls going about in groups to sorority meetings and going by carloads to drive-ins to see boys.

Her old friend Catherine gave her a party in Delton and invited all the single men she knew. Laurel had felt she was making her debut late in life or as if she were on an auction block. When none of these men asked her out ever, she felt she had failed Catherine. And Henry, Catherine's husband, had followed her about at the party, and said, "Who's been eating you lately?"

A waiter had been nearby moving glasses. "Hush," she had cried out. "Are you drunk or crazy? The waiter can hear you."

"Let him. The nigger probably does it too," Henry said.

Laurel was appalled and tried to escape him. "Well, who has been?" Henry said, blocking her way and laughing. "You're blushing."

"No one," she hissed at him.

"Remember when I did?" Pushing past him at last, she said coldly, "No," because the one time they met, they had not been that intimate. Had this memory really failed him, or did his male ego make it necessary to brag, now that he was in his sixties and sexual escapades could not quite match the past? Growing older herself, she was no longer so interested in adventures, just when, being alone, it was necessary for her to have them or go crazy staring at her walls in solitude every night.

She wandered away into a room with women she had known a long time. She sat down gratefully on a sofa and listened to their discussion and wanted to join in. She wanted to belong and not to be the different person who had left home and come back again. It was difficult enough being a single woman in a society of couples, having attached to her the aura that her husband had left her, and for someone younger. People would assume that. The word was about in Delton that Hal was remarried; it made everything so obvious.

The women were talking about estrogen. Her acquaintance Rosemary said, "Pills don't help me. I have shots. I know when it's time for one. I find myself driving down the street gripping the steering wheel and gritting my teeth. Gnashing them. Like this." She made a snarling, animal-like look.

"I have to use estrogen cream for dryness now," another woman said. "Poor Larry. What he's been through. Sometimes I just screamed."

"Having that dryness and sleeping with someone is worse than childbirth," Laurel said. Then she was embarrassed, for who was she supposed to have to sleep with now that she was single? She thought of the men there had been from singles groups and chance encounters, young, old, and middle-aged.

"I ground my teeth so at night, my dentist gave me a plastic mold to sleep in to see how I was wearing them down. When I went back, he asked where it was and I told him, 'I chewed it up,'" Rosemary said.

Laurel nodded to mean she did belong. And yet she was apart and separate from them, no longer being a securely married, middle-aged matron. She had her secret singles life, one they could not have conceived of. It went on in Delton. A ménage à trois took place with a professor at the university where she taught and a female student who was his friend. By tacit agreement, she and the girl did not touch one another, except in a brief strange instant. Making love with the professor, she reached past him to the girl on his other side. The girl clutched her hand just as hard. "Reach for it, baby," she told Laurel. She asked to stay on in Laurel's apartment and drank beer and ate food Laurel cooked. After three days, Laurel had to phone the professor to come and get her. She supposed the girl was looking for a mother too.

There were others at Catherine's with whom she had a long association. There was the gynecologist she had gone to, trying to get pregnant with Hal. "Do you know," she said, "for all those years when Hal was drunk he'd tell me you and I cooked up the whole scheme about proving him sterile to embarrass him." The doctor said, "Laurel, I've always thought Hal was dumb." And present was one of Hal's lawyers who had come up from Mississippi. It took courage, but she brought up the subject, saying, "I don't understand still why they left the boy down in a small-town hospital." Ben Wray said, "That boy was not going to live from the moment the shot was fired. It was a steel-headed bullet which didn't expand. It went on a downward path to his lower stomach." In a moment, he said, "You know, Hal was always kind of pretty-looking to me, with those small bones. Why did you marry him?"

She tried to explain how it all had been, about growing up in Delton society and not feeling part of it. He broke out in loud laughter. "There's never been any society in Delton. It's made up of horse traders, gamblers, murderers, and country people from Arkansas, Mississippi, and Tennessee. There's never going to be any real society here."

She smiled then. "I've learned that, but too late. I was in the mainstream all along."

She had wandered on through the various groups at the party thinking of her Master's requirements and how she was required to take a foreign language. While many of these middle-aged housewives were setting out on their orderly days, she was sitting at 8 A.M. with people half her age saying, "*Hasta luego.*" She had been asked to be a teaching assistant and teach Freshman English: a T.A. in my mid-fifties, she kept thinking to herself. There was a woman present whom she knew to be a widow of a few months, wearing a cherry-red dress like a badge of courage. She had drawn her aside to say, "You've lived here all your life. Never moved away. Are things any different for *you*? Do old friends call now that you're alone? Can you tell them about your loneliness?"

"My friends don't want to hear my troubles."

"Why can't you cry out to people, I'm in pain? Why can't you say, I'm devastated by what has happened to me? Why can't you say to people, I suffer?"

"I don't know," the woman said. "But you can't."

When she was driving back to Connecticut, she told herself it would be the last time she would make that trip. She supposed now she would go back to Delton to bury her mother some day. She did not want to be buried there herself, despite there being a family plot. She might be buried by her grandmother, Laurel thought, beneath cedars and in a graveyard in Mississippi, which was different from a cemetery.

She had driven back to Connecticut alone with her jade plants wobbling on the backseat. She went past the WELCOME TO CONNECTICUT sign and held out her money to the attendant at the Greenwich toll. A young man leaned out of the booth and waved her on. "It's free today, miss."

"Why, thank you," she called out. And breezed on. She had been glad to be called "miss." She found out the Mianus Bridge on the Thruway at Greenwich had collapsed and that the tolls were waived to encourage people to use the Merritt Parkway instead. But she chose to go on believing that the free toll had been her welcome home.

As the waitress set down her chowder, Mrs. Wynn reared away from the bowl. "I couldn't eat all that in a million years."

"Eat what you want," Laurel said sharply. "You need to eat, Mother." Mrs. Wynn was more frail and thin since her operation. She couldn't let her mother die of loneliness before her eyes; she would find an answer. And Laurel reminded herself to have patience. A reversal of roles was taking place. Her mother was becoming the child, and she the parent. No longer afraid of her mother, she told herself not to feel fury again. Instead, Laurel leaned forward over the table and spoke to her mother gently. "I see a clam."

"Ugh. I don't even want one."

18

She walked from Grand Central Station, saving cab fare. She was determined not to be afraid of New York's early evening streets. If she was afraid all the time, she wouldn't go anywhere. Here goes nothing again, Laurel thought. Attending Poets Essayists Novelists gatherings was becoming ridiculous since she continued not to know anyone there, or how to start up a conversation, and after standing around awhile, smiling a frozen smile, standing hopefully at the edges of other people's conversations, never being included, she would have one more glass of wine, get her coat, go out back into the evening hollowness, take a cab and the train, and go back to the suburbs. She never told anyone that was her evening. She made her outings sound like fun: "I went to New York—"

Several poets were reading tonight, ones she would like to hear. She gave her coat over to an attendant and went downstairs to the powder room, as she needed that place to tell herself, Don't be afraid. Try to meet someone. People here are interesting. She breathed in deeply in front of a mirror and adjusted her bra straps, pulling up what she had to look a little more interesting—not like Frederick's. She told herself again, This is ridiculous at your age. Her turtleneck sweater already felt too hot in the overheated building; in a sweater, she had thought she might look her best. She needed air going back upstairs; her cheeks were flushed. She felt how hot they were with both hands. Droplets of perspiration went down her spine. She must remember never to wear tight wool sweaters to places where she could not control the heat—where she could not rip off the sweater when she wanted. She thought back to the conversation in Delton about estrogen. Complicated, like everything else, she said to herself, stepping smartly along the dark oak stairwell. Smile, my dear, whether or not you look like an idiot. And don't let anybody see that wadded-up toilet paper you are dabbing yourself with. Why do you always forget Kleenex?

She bought a ticket for a drink—well, maybe two tickets; waiting in line had been so long. Don't drink much, you're alone. You're responsible for getting yourself home. Remember the little escapade when you slept all the way to New Haven and had to take a taxi back to Soundport.

She walked around, smiling, sweating. If she stood by someone, they looked around as if she might be a waitress hovering there; or as if she were strange. She smiled. "Oh, I was looking for someone." A blond woman in one little group gave a dubious smile toward a man in the group, her lip curled. Drunk? she wondered. A mental case? There were going to be odd types at a place like this, hangers-on. And if you were not in, you were *out*. Why the hell didn't they open a window? Then a man bent, fiddling at the casement. "Thank goodness," she said, standing behind him. "Hasn't it been hot in here?" Are you by any chance single? she wanted to say. Are you the janitor? I don't care. He gave her a weak smile and walked away.

Maybe she wouldn't stay for the reading; it must be scheduled late in the evening. She might as well spend her drink tickets and then go.

Who was that? A tall man who looked familiar stood laughing in a group of other men. She wore a name tag which no one had read, because no one cared who she was. If they didn't already know her, they didn't want to. Look a little lost and lonely and you're dead.

Laurel circled the group of men again. The tall man went on laughing. If it was he, then he was heavier and his hair now was gray. His cheeks were much fuller. She went as close as she dared, knocking accidentally into a man's elbow, who gave her an annoyed glance. Squinting as hard as possible, her eyes like a mole's, she read enough of his name tag, without her reading glasses, to clasp her hand to her own name tag, to stand further forward and say, "Edward, do you know who I am?"

"Laurel," he said. "Of course I know who you are."

"It's been about twenty years. I wasn't sure it was you. I'm divorced from William."

"I believe I heard that somewhere along the line."

"Did you come over from Princeton for this?"

"I live in New York now. I'm divorced too."

"I didn't know that. I mean, I didn't know either thing. I wouldn't have assumed you'd get a divorce. You seemed happy back then."

"Can you excuse me? The bar's closing before the reading. I've got to use up these tickets."

"Oh, of course. It was nice to see you." She wondered how she looked to Edward, knowing he would not be interested in someone her age now. She headed for the window, to some escape from the heat of the sweater and her body's heat. There she paused and let cold from the street chill her; it was worth getting flu to end her perspiring and dripping. A man was sitting alone on a small sofa. What are you doing there, man, lost in thought in the middle of all these people? How do you ask, Are you married? "Those are the most wonderful-looking boots," Laurel said, sitting down. He explained they were very practical for where he lived in upstate New York; she told him she had gone to Bard College. "Not recently," she said, smiling. What do you and your wife do there? she was going to say.

Edward stood above her, saying, "Well, there you are."

"Edward," she said, because she couldn't think of what else to say; she was glad not to have made one of her numerous forays to the powder room, which she visited continually in order not to be observed simply standing around. He might have missed her. Having to crane up at him, she stood. "Do you come here often?"

"No. I've never been before. I only came because a friend is reading. However, I didn't realize if you stayed for one reading, you'd have to stay for all three. I don't really like them. Are you interested in staying? Or would you like to go out to dinner?"

"Dinner," Laurel said quickly. "I mean, that would be nice. It's going to be too late for me to stay for all three."

When she went to the hat-check woman, Laurel remembered the long-ago period when, on one of the few times she saw Edward, he held her coat, saying, "Here you are in your little white coat." It had been made of pony skin and was left over from Delton days. Her mother had wanted it for her and saved for it out of her grocery allowance, as it was a luxury her father would have raised Cain about. Her mother had her first fur when she became a widow and bought herself a mink jacket.

It had begun to rain when they went outdoors, a light mist that could end up as sleet. Edward turned up his coat collar, and she lifted her face to the mist and gladly breathed in. Dampness against her skin felt wonderful. It was always the case, they agreed, that you could never get a cab in New York when it rained. They began to walk, and Edward lifted his hand when cabs passed, and they watched them speed by with the white faces of passengers inside like little demons. "We're almost at the restaurant. We might as well just keep walking." But Edward that moment caught himself up and sagged on one leg.

"What is the matter?" Laurel asked quickly. "Is something wrong?"

"This is a long walk for me." He had injured a knee that would have to be operated on.

She didn't want anything bad to have happened to Edward; she was sympathetic and took his arm as if to help him. She looked along the street herself for a cab, but only the slickness of streetlights reflecting on dark pavement came back.

When they were in the restaurant, at a table in a window recess, Laurel said, "How did you happen to ask me to dinner? You were with friends." She cupped hands beneath her chin and then rested them in her lap, not quite knowing what to do with them, or almost how to behave. It had been so long since she was out with someone compatible. She thought of going rowing through the night singing, "Row row row your boat," and of the three hundred dollars wasted on the dating service.

"You seemed lonely there," Edward answered.

"I was lonely there."

"I don't know what I was doing there either. I wasn't really interested in my friends."

"I was using it as a singles club," she said.

They agreed they would not talk about their divorces; then, as always happened to divorced people, they began to talk about them. They gave what reasons they could, as vague as some of them sounded. Maybe she shouldn't tell him Hal flat out left her: "An abandoned woman," her mother called her. But, she thought, Edward wasn't going to invite someone her age out again. She looked down to the city street and around the restaurant and thought, Enjoy.

After she started her story about Hal, Edward interrupted. "Why did you marry him in prison?"

"That's too long to tell now."

"You rolled the dice."

"I never thought of it like that. I suppose so."

"I've been doing that all my life." Edward lifted a finger and signaled for more drinks. She reminded herself not to drink too much; she had been cutting down, but this was a celebration.

"Maybe Hal's inevitable end is, he'll end up with a woman more evil than he is."

"That's exactly what happened." She finished her story.

"He sounds like a sociopath. Someone who doesn't think or feel the way ordinary people do. Someone incapable of guilt. There's a book about them."

"I think I'll read it."

Edward ordered wine. "So you didn't enjoy your sojourn in mid-America."

"I never thought of Delton as that. I suppose now it is. Condos, shopping malls, fast-food chains. Every place is becoming the same. Only the heat makes you know it's the South."

Then, while they were eating, he said, "I don't plan to get married again. I don't see any reason to at our ages, do you?"

"Not at all," she lied.

"How were the sales of your last novel?" Edward eventually turned the wine bottle upside down in its bucket.

"What sales? Publishers publish my books because they feel sorry for me."

"How many copies did you sell?"

"I don't know."

"You don't read your royalty statements?"

"I open them. But I don't know what they're talking about. There are just a lot of red numbers."

"Authors I know, today, are vitally interested in how many copies of their books are printed."

"What difference does it make? They're not going to print more or less copies because I know how many they print."

"Most writers are pretty business-minded now. They

know all about their contract, reprint rights, translations."

"I'm lucky. I don't have to worry about those things. My agent's never made enough money off me to pay for postage for sending my things out. Maybe I'll write a best-seller."

"You're never going to write a best-seller."

"I think you're right. I've just always expected to have a man to take care of me. Now I'm wandering around on alimony."

"You should try to become independent."

"I don't want to be independent. I hate it. I've never wanted anything in life but to be married, have children, and lean on some nice man. And I still want to lean on one. Life would have been simpler if nobody had published what I wrote. Why have I messed things up so much?"

"Oh, Laurel, nobody could feel sorry for you."

"Rats," Laurel said.

"The women I know don't take alimony."

"Well, damn you," she said. Tears sprang up. "What else could I do? I'm going to graduate school."

"Why are you doing that?"

"I think it's going to help me get a better teaching job. I've gone beyond the number of years you're supposed to finish a Master's in. They gave me a special extension. I get what jobs I can. In Delton, I taught the grammar section of Freshman English. That was terrible. Gerunds, Edward. How was I supposed to remember what they were? Next semester, I'm teaching writing in the adult education division of the local high school."

They waved away the dessert cart. Edward looked at his watch. "What train are you taking?"

"There's only one more now. At midnight. The last train to Soundport. How does that grab you as a title?"

They collected their coats and headed to the door, while she told Edward she was ready to at least live with someone, even with a man who was only a platonic friend, that she did not much think she'd like living with a woman this late in life.

They came up steps from the restaurant onto the street and Laurel thought, Well, here I am again in Greenwich Village. A gray cat was huddled on the fender of a car, fluffing itself against the weather. She touched its ears, and the cat twittered and bounded away. "Sorry, cat," she said. She went on through the rain, making an indrawn, soft, sucking sound.

"What am I with, the whistler?" Edward said.

"Oh, sorry. I didn't even realize I was whistling." As they walked across Washington Square park and along Fifth Avenue, she looked about for a cab. She would take a bus if she had to. Edward was then laughing, and she said, "What are you laughing at?"

"Now you're singing to yourself."

"I was? I never sing in front of people. I can't carry a tune."

"I know what that's a sign of. Someone who's lived alone too long."

She was glad Edward could have this perception, but she must be careful around people. They passed by two young girls who had their arms wound about one another and were kissing deeply. The rain was harder. They stood at a corner and looked hopefully up and down each way for a taxi. Then suddenly Edward put his arms around her and kissed her, his hat brim shading her from the rain. "You don't have to take the last train to Soundport, do you?"

"No. As a matter of fact, my mother worries about me coming home late at night, getting off the train alone."

"I don't want your mama to worry. I'd be worried about you too, this late. You can stay at my place."

"All right. Any port in a storm." She linked her arm into Edward's, hoping to spare his aching knee.

"Sleep in your makeup. You'll look better in the morning." Laurel spoke to herself in Edward's apartment. She stood with one of his pajama tops over her like a tent, slipping off her bra beneath it.

"Take off your goddamned clothes and let me see you naked," Edward said.

"I can't. I haven't worked my way up yet to walking around without any clothes on. Anyway, this is like a first date again."

Edward was leaning against a bureau and singing a rhyming ditty, a ribald song. He stood with no clothes on and had forgotten to take off his hat. Laurel suddenly heard a faint and strange sound. She almost began to look around for it. Then she realized it was the sound of her own laughter, a sound she had not heard in so long. My God, I'm laughing! she said to herself. She thought she was laughing, not only because of Edward but because the time had come. She liked Edward with gray hair. He was cute. But something had passed from her that was never going to come again. She would never again have the ability to fall wildly in love, completely and trustfully and with all her heart. Maybe that was a good thing.

"We had a lot to drink tonight," Edward said.

"I know. But I refuse to feel guilty."

When he got into bed, she reminded him about his hat, and he was nearly asleep before she got in beside him. "How late can you stay tomorrow?" He took her hand.

"Late enough." She covered his hand with her own. She could stay till time to teach her class next week, but she must play this cool, Laurel thought. "I have a busy schedule."

He began to breathe in a different way, and she knew he was asleep. She turned over into her best sleeping position, her back to him, putting herself close enough to know someone was in bed with her, someone she wanted to be there.